WALKING
AFTER
MIDNIGHT

WALKING
AFTER
MIDNIGHT

KAREN ROBARDS

Delacorte  Press

Published by
Delacorte Press
Bantam Doubleday Dell Publishing Group, Inc.
1540 Broadway
New York, New York 10036

Library of Congress Cataloging in Publication Data

Robards, Karen.
    Walking after midnight / by Karen Robards.
        p.   cm.
    ISBN 0-385-31034-X
    I. Title.
    PS3568.0196W35   1995
    813'.54—dc20   94-26178
                                                CIP

Manufactured in the United States of America
Published simultaneously in Canada

February 1995

10 9 8 7 6 5 4 3 2 1

BVG

This book is dedicated, as always, with much love to the men in my life: Doug, Peter, and Christopher.

It also commemorates two family weddings: my sister Lee Ann Johnson to Sammy Spicer on February 8, 1993, and my brother Bruce Hodges Johnson to Susan Wearren on June 12, 1993.

WALKING

AFTER

MIDNIGHT

CHAPTER ONE

"Why can't the dead die!"

—Eugene O'Neill

She hanged herself from a plant hook.

One of those white, *faux* wrought-iron things that screw into the ceiling. It was guaranteed to support up to one hundred pounds. If she had weighed more than ninety-eighty pounds soaking wet, the darned thing never would have held and she would be alive today.

That was almost funny, considering that she had had a phobia about getting fat—she was only five feet tall—and had spent her entire adult life on a rigorous diet to keep her weight under a hundred pounds.

But then, such is life.

Life. The spirit—for she was a spirit—dreamily contemplated it. As she did, she felt a tingling within, like the slow awakening of a blood-starved limb.

Did she want to be alive again? The spirit pondered.

How it had felt to be alive was hard for her to remember. It was as though she were viewing life from the perspective of an underwater swimmer, as though life were a bright day seen through a distorting veil of water.

The underwater world was so much more real to her now that she was part of it. She was content here, in this floating, dreaming, distorting netherland that had been her abode for—how long?

She didn't know. Time had no meaning for her now. Simply, she had been here since she died.

Since the night when her stockinged feet had rested on a cool metal desktop and a length of nylon rope had been looped around her neck. Since the night when she had choked and kicked and fought, fought, fought to breathe. . . .

Memory was swamped by the emotions she had felt at that moment, which burst through now with dazzling clarity: terror, disbelief, despair.

The water-veil cleared, and briefly she was back in the room where she had died, floating up near the ceiling, near the self-same plant hook that had done her in. Despite its grisly history, no one had bothered to take it down. It still curled like a beckoning finger against the dingy plaster, forgotten.

Why was she here? What pull was so strong that it had sucked her back from her lazy swim through eternity?

A face flashed into her consciousness: a man, blond and handsome. Followed by another, swarthy and rough-skinned.

With the faces came a name. Her name, from the life that had ended: Deedee.

Deedee. She'd been dead, but now she was back. Not alive, but conscious.

For a purpose. One thing she had learned was that everything had a purpose.

While the purpose remained to be revealed to her, she drifted out across the ceiling into the endless night, content to wait.

CHAPTER TWO

Toilets were the pits. Especially men's toilets. Nasty creatures, men: didn't they ever hit what they were aiming at?

Summer McAfee wrinkled her nose in disgust, tried not to think about just exactly what it was she was down on her hands and knees scrubbing off the floor, and plied her brush to the tile with a vengeance. The sooner she got the job done, the sooner she would be out of there.

"*I can't get nooo SATISFACTION . . .*" Summer crooned the Rolling Stones' thirty-year-old megahit in a throaty undertone as she worked. So she sang off-key. So what? There was no one in the vicinity to hear. Bringing her Walkman was a no-no on this job, so she had no choice but to rely on her own less than musical voice for distraction. Not that it was working. Despite the imaginary presence of the mythical Mick, she was as twitchy as a tied horse in a barn full of flies.

"*I can't get nooo . . .*"

Another lingering creak from somewhere beyond the closed door of the men's rest room almost made Summer choke on the rest of the line. Her gaze shot over her shoulder for what must have been the tenth time in a quarter of an hour. Not that glancing around did much good. The rising Lysol vapors were so thick in the small rest room that she could scarcely breathe, let alone see through the tears that filmed her eyes. Maybe she'd gotten a little carried away with the Lysol, but the men's room had been so darn filthy.

Summer had enough vision left to assure herself that the rest room door was still solidly closed. As for what lay beyond the door —well, she just wouldn't think about that. Whatever the creak was, it was certainly harmless. The building was over a hundred years old; of course it was going to creak. Harmon Brothers, a chain of funeral homes, was her struggling cleaning service's biggest client. She was not about to blow the account over an idiotic case of the willies. Her worthless Saturday night work crew had failed to show up for the second time this month (she should have fired them the first time!). There had been no one else available to clean the flagship mortuary of the Harmon Brothers chain on such short notice. The bottom line was, the buck stopped with her. It wouldn't be the first time she'd had to do an entire job by herself. In fact, when she'd started out, despite her bold claims to the contrary, she'd been Daisy Fresh's sole employee: chief executive officer, chief financial officer, head of marketing, and cleaning lady, all rolled into one.

That the place she was cleaning tonight was a funeral home shouldn't matter, not to a professional such as she prided herself on being—but it did. It was two a.m., she was beyond tired, and her imagination was starting to go into overdrive.

There were dead bodies in the other room. Rooms, rather. Three corpses, nicely laid out in coffins, ready for their funerals on the morrow. And one more, under a sheet in the embalming room.

Maybe it was just her, but Summer was discovering that she had kind of a thing about being locked in a dark, deserted building in the small hours of the morning with a bunch of dead bodies.

The key was not to dwell on it. Summer suppressed a shiver as she forced her errant mind to focus on the job at hand. The place between the base of a toilet and the wall was always the worst.

"*. . . good reaction. / And I've tried / and I've tried / and I've tried / and I've . . .*"

Creak. Creak.

Summer almost swallowed her tongue along with the last *tried.* What *were* those sounds? Shooting an uneasy glance at the door again, she knew she was being ridiculous even as she did it. All right, so it was the dead—no, not a good word—the *middle* of the night, she was all alone in a restored Victorian mansion cum funeral parlor in the midst of a six-hundred-acre cemetery with four dead bodies, and she was letting the knowledge spook her. As long as she recognized that fact, and the sheer absurdity of it, she would be just fine. Corpses could not harm her, and there was no one else around.

"I'm the only person alive in the whole damn place," Summer said aloud, then made a face as she discovered that the knowledge did not make her feel appreciably better. At this point, the presence of another living, breathing human would be more than welcome.

Finishing the third and final toilet at last, she sank back on her haunches with a thankful sigh and tossed her scrub brush into the plastic bucket nearby. It landed with a clatter that sounded abnormally loud in the echoing silence.

Summer winced, but of course there was no one to hear and be disturbed by the noise. As it died away, silence once again reigned.

It was probably the silence that was getting to her, she decided, giving her the feeling that a thousand unseen ears were listening and a thousand unseen eyes were watching everything she did.

"*I can't get nooo . . .*" This time the song was hardly more than a breath of sound, pure bravado really, and quickly abandoned. Unable to shake the uneasiness that gripped her, Summer gave up on the Stones. Perhaps such unreverent music in a funeral home was stirring up the spirit world. . . .

How ridiculous! She was a thirty-six-year-old grown woman who had proven, time and again, that she could more than handle whatever life threw at her. Having survived the death of a parent, a failed first career, and a hideous five-year marriage, there was little left that could scare her. One thing was sure: She was *not* afraid of no ghosts.

Or was she?

"If there's something strange / in your neighborhood . . ."

The theme from *Ghostbusters* brought a flickering smile to Summer's face as it popped into her mind. Maybe she should sing it for courage. But she didn't think it would help—and besides, her contract with Harmon Brothers specified that Daisy Fresh employees were required to behave with dignity on the premises at all times. Her cleaning crew was not even allowed to bring a radio to this job, and she would not have invoked the Stones if she hadn't been so thoroughly demoralized by various stray sounds that in bright daylight would have seemed like less than nothing.

Summer's smile twisted into a wry grin as her mind painted an almost irresistible picture of herself: There she was, five feet eight inches of well-padded, slightly-over-the-hill woman, looking mousy as heck in the neat black polyester pants and tucked-in white nylon shirt that was Daisy Fresh's uniform. Hazel eyes flashing, sweat-dampened strands of dark brown hair straggling loose from an off-center, precarious bun, yellow scrub bucket in hand, she was prancing through the funeral home toward the exit, punching the air with her fist and bellowing *"Who ya gonna call . . . ?"* at the top of her lungs.

Not a very dignified finale even in her imagination, she had to admit. But cheering. Very cheering.

Grimacing—scrubbing a tile floor on all fours was hard on the knees—Summer got to her feet, placed a hand in the small of her back, and stretched. Peeling the rubber gloves from her hands, she dropped them into the bucket and frowned down at her stubby nails in disgust. She had once had the most beautiful hands. . . . But that was long ago, and her life was much better now even if her hands were not. How important were manicured nails in the whole scheme of life, anyway?

Reaching for her supplies, she forgot about her hands. She had only to drape the paper Daisy Fresh banners over the toilet lids, gather up her belongings, and go.

Her obligation to Harmon Brothers would be fulfilled, and the knowledge made her feel good. Not that she would have settled for anything less. Reliability was the company byword. Daisy Fresh always cleaned, and cleaned well, exactly where, when, and how the contract specified. That was why she was still in business after six years, when so many small janitorial services failed to last as many months.

Securing the last banner, Summer picked up her bucket of supplies and headed toward the door. Pausing with her hand on the knob, she gave the rest room one final, satisfied glance. Two-tone gray tile sparkled. Silver fittings gleamed. The mirror was spotless. On the shelf over the sink, a small glass vase held the single fresh daisy that was the company's signature note. By morning, the Lysol fumes would have died away to a pleasantly fresh scent, and the bathroom, like the rest of the building, would look and smell pristine.

And Daisy Fresh could chalk up another satisfied client.

Genuinely smiling this time, Summer pulled open the door, flicked on the light switch on the wall outside, turned off the bathroom light, and stepped out into the solemn hush of the hall.

Thick gray carpet muffled her footsteps as she walked the length of the narrow hall that ran along the back of the building, perpendicular to the larger center hall off which the viewing rooms opened. The rest rooms were along the back hall to the left, the embalming room along the same hall to the right. A rear door affording easy access to the overflow parking lot bisected the long back wall. A single glance assured Summer that it was still securely locked. Of course.

It was her policy—*company* policy—to require employees to make a last, walk-through inspection of all jobs, to insure against faux pas such as forgotten dustcloths or lights left on. Harmon Brothers in particular was very strict about lights. The building was always dark when Daisy Fresh entered, and Mike Chaney, the general manager, had stressed that lights were to be turned on strictly as needed, to save on costs.

Tonight Summer had followed standard procedure, though she'd been sorely tempted not to. Beyond the hall in which she stood the building was as dark and quiet as a vast, echoing cave. The silence was broken only by the low hum of the air-conditioning. Knowing Harmon Brothers' penchant for cutting costs, she was vaguely surprised that the unit was kept running overnight. Nighttime July temperatures in Murfreesboro, Tennessee, which was nestled into the base of the Smoky Mountains, averaged around seventy-two degrees—not typical air-conditioner weather. But then, given the nature of Harmon Brothers' business . . .

Summer considered the effect of heat on dead bodies, shuddered, and quickly switched her mental focus to the few things that remained to be done before she could leave. Far be it from her to question Harmon Brothers' decision to run the air-conditioning twenty-four hours a day.

The light in the back hall was the only illumination in the building. She would turn on the huge chandelier in the center hall (fortunately, the switch was by the front door), then return to douse the back hall light. Retracing her steps might take just a little longer, but the alternative—just flicking off one switch and hurrying to turn on the next—was clearly unworkable.

Call her a coward, but not for anything on earth did she intend to plunge herself into pitch-darkness in the bowels of that funeral home.

Who ya gonna call . . . ? Summer mentally shooed the ridiculous song away as she headed toward the front door.

The intermittent creaking that had been preying on her nerves since she had arrived had stopped, Summer noted as she flicked on the chandelier's switch and set her bucket down beside her purse and the vacuum cleaner that already waited by the front door. Maybe that was why the air-conditioning seemed abnormally loud. The unit's previous gentle hum now had more the quality of a menacing growl. In her mind's eye, she envisioned the unit's metal casing taking on the form of a fanged gray beast, and the ominous sound it emitted building to a full-throated roar as the beast grew. . . .

Too many Stephen King movies, she decided with a grimace as she hurried to turn off the back hall light. To comply with Daisy Fresh's final inspection policy, she forced herself to glance in each

open doorway as she passed it. No forgotten dustcloths, no squee-
gees, no wads of paper towels. Just immaculately cleaned viewing
rooms redolent with the scent of the floral tributes that surrounded the earthly remains of departed loved ones, who were
dressed in their best and displayed in elegant satin-lined caskets.

*What if they were to rise up out of their coffins and converge on
her? What if they hadn't been ready to die, or were displeased with
the prospect of being buried on the morrow, and decided to take a
grisly vengeance on the one living mortal within their reach? What
if she had somehow stepped into a nineties version of* Night of the
Living Dead, *and was about to become a featured player?*

Really too many Stephen King movies, Summer scolded herself.
She was going to have to put a lid on her imagination before she
conjured up an ax-wielding maniac out of thin air. Or a slobber-
ing, rabid St. Bernard, or . . .

Ghostbusters!

Summer was almost running as she reached the light switch in
the back hall and turned it off. That done, she had only to unlock
the front door, turn off the chandelier, dart outside, lock the door
again, and the job was finished.

Whew.

She hadn't realized she was so easily unnerved, but the atmo-
sphere of the place was really getting to her. The air-conditioning
was sounding louder than ever, almost as if it *were* building to
some kind of deadly climax. If she listened hard—or even if she
didn't—she could almost make out a rythmic *redrum,
redrum.* . . .

No more Stephen King movies as long as she lived, she vowed,
moving back toward the center hall. Reaching the intersection of
the halls, she glanced to the right—and felt her stomach sink clear
down to the soles of her neatly tied canvas Keds.

Though the metal door was closed, she could see, through the
narrow frosted-glass panel at its top, that she had accidentally left
the light on in the embalming room.

Every nerve ending she possessed cried out for her to leave it. If
Mike Chaney complained, she could apologize for the oversight
and promise it would never happen again. The repercussions

would be minimal. Harmon Brothers would not cancel her contract over such a tiny misdemeanor.

But Daisy Fresh was her baby, painstakingly rebuilt on the ashes of her former life. Daisy Fresh would never leave a light burning all night, when they had been specifically requested not to do so. For the honor of Daisy Fresh—and for the sake of the substantial monthly check that arrived as regularly as clockwork from Harmon Brothers—she was going to turn off that damned light.

Damn it.

Gritting her teeth, Summer headed toward the embalming room, impartially showering curses on her unreliable cleaning crew and Stephen King and light switches in general as she went.

At least the body in the embalming room was under a sheet. She wouldn't actually have to see it. Fortifying herself with that thought, Summer swung open the metal door and glanced around for the light switch. Common sense dictated that it should be right beside the door.

Her peripheral vision registered the sheet-covered corpse reposing on a wheeled metal table pushed against the wall, then skittered away to focus desperately on the gleaming steel of the twin sinks, the spotless countertops, the freshly mopped floor. If she could do nothing else well in life, she thought with a spurt of satisfaction, she could clean.

How was that for a talent?

The switch was a good two feet farther to the left than any consideration of logic dictated it should be. Stepping inside the room as the door swung shut behind her, Summer reached for it.

Her gaze, free to roam now that the switch was located, lighted on the metal table's twin. It was pushed up against the wall opposite the first table, the wall through which she had just entered via the door.

There was a naked man sprawled face-up on the table.

A naked *dead* man.

Shock widened her eyes. Her mouth gaped. This particular corpse hadn't been in here when she had cleaned. Had it? Could she possibly have overlooked such a thing?

Not possibly. No way. There was not even the remotest chance that she could have. The unadorned corpse, almost obscene in its grim testimony to death's indignities, filled her vision, her mind, her senses, with horror.

Even from where she stood, some six feet away, she could see the bruises, the awful trauma to the body's face and chest. An accident victim, no doubt. Had he been brought in while she cleaned?

It was the only explanation. The creaks she had heard must have been real. Someone—an ambulance crew, a team of morticians working for Harmon Brothers, she didn't really know how these things were handled—had brought in a freshly deceased body while she had scrubbed on, all unknowing.

Summer's knees shook. Her stomach churned. Coming face-to-face with death in its rawest, crudest form ripped away the last of her courage. She couldn't even pretend not to be scared out of her wits.

But she could go home. And fire her worthless Saturday night work crew. And make sure she had a backup work crew on call at all times just to prevent such a situation from arising in the future.

Never again was she going to put herself in the position of having to clean a funeral home alone in the middle of the night.

Rationally she knew that there really wasn't anything to be afraid of. When all was said and done, the battered body was *dead.* Except for in her overwrought imagination, it couldn't harm her.

Doing her best to compose her shattered nerves, Summer flicked off the switch. Light, softened and muted from the frosting on the glass panel, still filtered in from the hall as she had known it would. She was already at the door, one hand on the knob, when she heard it: a slight slithering sound, as if something in the room behind her had moved.

For the space of a couple of heartbeats, Summer literally froze with fear. Visions of the Undead rose to dance in her brain, only to be sternly battled back by common sense. She had imagined the sound, of course. When she really listened, silence, echoing, stretching silence, was all that met her straining ears.

In any case, it was time to go home. Thank God.

Pulling the door open, she could not resist casting a last, scared glance at the battered corpse. The light spilling in from the hall was uncertain, but what she thought she saw in that one quick look was this: The dead man's right leg moved.

Her eyes were already darting away when her brain registered what she had seen. Her head snapped around in a classic double take. Transfixed, she watched as the dead man's knee lifted a good three inches off the embalming table before dropping back into its original position with a soft thud.

The hair rose on the back of Summer's neck.

CHAPTER THREE

*W*ho ya gonna call? The refrain, with its endless punchline, pounded hysterically through her brain as she fled. Summer had almost reached the front door and safety when it occurred to her that she could not just abandon a corpse that did not seem to be quite dead. Tales of the Undead aside (and every sane thought she still possessed assured her that such stories were pure hokum), there were two possible explanations for what she had seen: some sort of bizarre after-death reaction—a muscle spasm, perhaps?—or the man was really not dead. Someone—an ambulance attendant, an ER physician, who knew?—had been too quick to write him off.

Her first impulse was to say tough luck and good-bye.

Her second was to dial 911.

Her third, and most rational, was to call Mike Chaney at home and tell him to come take a look at his newest corpse for himself.

But even as she headed toward Chaney's private office—the first door to the right of the main entrance—to use the phone, Summer hesitated. To call her biggest client at two on a Sunday morning was not a thing to be done lightly. Likewise, summoning police and ambulance attendants to said client's poshest funeral home was an action she would be wise to think over first. In the latter case, the publicity that almost certainly would be generated was not the kind that Harmon Brothers would welcome. In the former case, Mike Chaney would probably think she was a nut.

The honor and reputation of Daisy Fresh—to say nothing of Harmon Brothers' monthly check—were once again on the line.

She *needed* that money.

Of course, if the man was really not dead, preserving what was left of his life had to be her primary concern. Harmon Brothers would certainly thank her for calling such a slip-up to their attention.

But how likely was it that someone had made such a mistake?

Not very, Summer conceded gloomily, and dropped her hand in the act of reaching for the knob to Mike Chaney's office door. For just an instant, she gazed longingly at the imposing double doors of the front entrance. Her vacuum cleaner waited beside it; her bucket of supplies was there, along with her purse. How easy it would be to tell herself that what she had seen was strictly her imagination, or even a normal after-death reaction, and just go out that door and drive home and forget this night had ever happened! So easy—and with every atom of her being she longed to take the easy way out.

But what if the man really was alive? She had read of cases where victims are pronounced dead and all but buried before their vitality is discovered. Suppose he died alone in there on that table during what was left of the night, or (hideous thought) was killed in the morning via premature embalming, all because she was too much of a coward to follow up on what she had seen?

One way or another, without her intervention his eventual fate was all but certain. If he wasn't already, by this time tomorrow he was going to be just one more corpse.

Unless she did something. She had eliminated all the possibilities. All except one. Shuddering, Summer realized what she had to do.

Check out that thrice-damned corpse for herself before taking any further action.

Shit.

She would rather—far rather—be headed to another Bruce Lee retrospective than do what she was about to do. The comparison wasn't one she made lightly; the previous weekend had been spent in precisely that way. The man she was seeing, knowing she was something of a movie buff and being a big fan of karate movies himself, had treated her to a day and a night at a Nashville art cinema featuring Bruce Lee in all his various incarnations. By the end of the eight hours she had spent listening to Lee scream "Aiiee-yaw!" every five seconds, she'd had the headache to end all headaches—and the sneaking suspicion that her romance with the well-off dentist was doomed. *He* had enjoyed every excruciating minute, clenching his fist and grunting "yes!" whenever Bruce Lee kicked bad-guy ass—again. Her friend's plan for this weekend had included a Chuck Norris festival. Summer had pleaded work.

As usual, her sins had caught up with her. Having lied and said she had to work Saturday, she had ended up doing just that.

Whatever heavenly Being was in charge of these things was up there laughing at her now, no doubt. Standing outside the closed embalming room door trying to calm her thudding heart, Summer could almost hear the otherworldly snickers as the Being proclaimed that her current dilemma served her right.

Aside from the muted roar of the air-conditioning, the funeral home was deathly—no, bad choice of a word—*utterly* still.

She would rather sit through ten Bruce Lee festivals than go back in there again.

May you be doomed to spend eternity with your ghoulies, she cursed a mental image of a maniacally grinning Stephen King, and swung open the door. Light from the hall in which she remained firmly planted—she had made sure to turn on the light again, and to hell with Harmon Brothers' restrictions—illuminated a narrow walkway into the dark room.

Redrum, redrum . . .

Stop that, Summer ordered herself. Ignoring her speeding pulse, hand firmly holding open the self-closing door, she took

two steps forward and forced her eyes to focus on the now motionless corpse. The light did not quite touch where he lay on the
table, pushed close against the wall. The body was shrouded—bad
word again—*cloaked* in shadow. But she could make out the pertinent details: short black hair; battered, swollen face, eyelids
closed, liberally streaked with what looked like blood; bruised left
shoulder, with a thick wedge of black hair perhaps concealing
more bruising on his chest; in any case, said chest exhibited none
of the rising and falling that signals life; strong-looking, muscular
torso; pale, limp genitals nestled in more black hair; immobile—
immobile—limbs. Of course the man was dead. Of course he was.

One thing he was not was one of the Undead. He was not going
to rise up from that table and come after her, soulless eyes staring,
arms outstretched to grab . . .

Ghostbusters!

If this turned out to be some kind of *Candid Camera*-ish setup,
she would be very, very thankful, Summer thought. She would
even be ready to laugh at the joke herself. Ha, ha.

Please, God. Please.

But no Allen Funt clone appeared, and she could detect no
camera hidden behind a potted palm. In fact, there was no potted
palm. There was only herself and—the dead man.

Summer shuddered.

She was going to have to step farther inside that room, turn on
the overhead light, and actually touch the corpse before she was
one hundred percent positive he was dead. However much she
hated facing the knowledge, she knew herself well enough to recognize the truth.

Overkill—no, another badly chosen word—*obsessive thorough-
ness* was one of her major faults.

If this was a bad dream, she was ready to wake up. If it was a
practical joke, she was ready for the punch line.

If it was her real life, she was putting God on notice right now
that she was tired of being the butt of heavenly humor.

After thirty-six years, enough was enough.

The corpse still hadn't moved. Except for the hum of the air-conditioning, the silence stretched endlessly. She could almost hear her vacuum cleaner calling to her from beside the front door.

If there's something strange . . .

Gritting her teeth, Summer took firm hold both of her by now almost nonexistent courage and her wildly burgeoning imagination. Slimer was not going to come barreling out of the ductwork; Cujo was not going to bound through the hall. All she had to do was check the guy's pulse. Three minutes, max, and she would be out the front door.

Sliding her left foot out of her sneaker, she wedged its rubber-soled toe under the corner of the door. If she stepped toward the light switch and the door swung shut, she might only be left in the near-dark for a couple of seconds—but that was all it would take for her body to dissolve into Jell-O. In the morning, Harmon Brothers' employees would find a quivering mass of human flesh in a puddle on the floor. *Whatever do you suppose happened that night to send Summer McAfee to the looney bin?* would become one of the hot questions of Murfreesboro's summer.

Door wedged, Summer stepped away, turned on the light, and took a deep breath as the bright fluorescent fixture banished all atmosphere-producing shadows. There, that wasn't so bad. Was it?

Glancing at the corpse, Summer answered her own question. Yes, it was. But there was no help for it, so she might as well get it over with. Grimly she headed toward the dead man.

It helped if she didn't quite look at him.

There were drawers beneath the metal table on which he lay, she discovered as she approached. Long, narrow drawers built into the table, which would be easy to overlook if they were closed. One of the drawers was ajar. Inside, Summer saw the gleam of instruments aligned on a green cloth napkin. Embalming tools, of course. She tried not to think of the use to which they were routinely put as she stopped a good two feet away from her target.

Oh, God. She couldn't do this. She simply could not bring herself to touch the thing that lay there. The very idea made her want to wet her pants.

One touch. If his flesh was cold, that would be good enough. If he was cold, he would have to be dead. Wouldn't he? Of course he would.

Screwing up her nerve, Summer reached out to gingerly place a forefinger on his arm. His flesh *was* cold . . .

His hand closed around her wrist in a move so fast that Summer didn't even see it coming. One second she was touching him, and the next she was staggering off balance, jerked forward by a cold, dead hand. She gasped as the battered, bloody corpse came up off the embalming table at her like a vision out of Stephen King's worst nightmare.

Then she shrieked. The hand locked around her wrist tightened cruelly as he spun her around and twisted her arm behind her back. A chilled, hairy forearm clamped around her neck. He was immensely strong, and his body was cold, cold. The smell of death —rotting flesh? formaldehyde?—enveloped her as he did.

Another shriek ripped out of her lungs. The arm around her neck tightened with vicious purpose, cutting off sound and air in one swift clench.

"Scream again and I'll break your goddamned neck," the dead man growled in her ear. It was only then that Summer fully realized that the erstwhile corpse was not dead at all. He was very much alive, with homicidal intent.

The Undead could not have been worse.

She was on tiptoe, bent so far backward that her spine threatened to crack, dangling from the V of his elbow that entrapped her throat. The arm that he held twisted behind her back ached. Lack of air was making her light-headed. She was conscious of two sounds: her own terrified heart pounding in her ears, and the harsh rasp of his breathing.

"Don't hurt me. Please." The plea forced its way out of her crushed throat. The words were hoarse, barely audible even to herself. If he heard, it made no appreciable difference in the cruelty of his grip.

"How many others?" The arm around her throat tightened, strangling her. Instinctively her free hand rose to claw at it.

"You're choking me!" It was a desperate little gasp.

"Scratch me and I'll break your damned fingers."

Her clutching fingers stilled and flattened on his cold flesh. Funny, he still felt dead.

Terror washed over Summer in waves. She couldn't decide which was worse, a dead attacker or a live one.

"How many others?" Urgency roughened his voice, underlined the little shake he gave her.

"Please—I can't breathe." Summer tugged on the arm around her neck. To her relief, the chokehold eased. She took a deep, shuddering breath.

"Answer me."

"Wh-what?"

"How many others are there?"

Dear God, what was he talking about? Was he deranged? Impossible to believe that this was really happening to *her.*

"I—I don't know what you're talking about. Please, you've obviously been in an accident, or—or something. You need medical attention . . ."

"Don't play stupid with me. How many others are there?"

The chokehold tightened again. Forced to an *en pointe* position the likes of which she had not attempted since fourth-grade ballet, Summer clung to his forearm with her free hand to keep from being hanged, and despaired.

"Six?" she guessed.

The chokehold eased. She was allowed to balance on the balls of her feet. Clearly her answer had been acceptable.

"Where are they?"

Was he a homicidal maniac, or simply a nice, normal middle-American male who was suffering delusions as a result of the truama that had brought him to the funeral home in the first place? In the milliseconds she was allowed to ponder that question, Summer came to a conclusion: It didn't matter. For whatever reason, he was seriously dangerous. Her best course of action was to humor him for as long as she could, then escape.

Whoever had opined that it was best to let sleeping dogs lie had certainly known what he was talking about. The same could be applied to sleeping corpses. And would be, if she had the last ten minutes to live over again. Why, oh why, had she not simply gone out the front door when she had the chance?

"Damn it, where are they?" He tightened his grip.

Summer almost yelped. "Out—outside."

His arm loosened. "Where outside?"

"Uh—in the back."

He was silent for a moment, as if thinking over what she had said. Summer licked her lips and took a deep, shaken breath. Her answers were appeasing him, for the time being. The key was not to panic.

The pungent smell that enveloped him filled her nose and mouth and was drawn into her lungs. Summer suddenly identified it as kerosene.

"If you want to live, you'll tell me that you know a way out of here."

The menace in his voice made her stomach knot. The chokehold tightened, and Summer found herself *en pointe* once more. She nodded feebly.

His arm relaxed, and she was again able to breathe.

"You know a way out?"

"Y-yes."

"Without being seen?"

Summer nodded.

"Screw me over, bitch, and I swear you'll be dead before I am."

Her arm was suddenly released. Moving it sent sharp tingles of pain shooting all the way up to her shoulder. Wincing, Summer flexed the fingers of her right hand, barely aware of a metallic scrabbling noise behind her.

"See this?" A shining silver scalpel was held before her eyes, and suddenly Summer forgot about her throbbing arm.

She nodded.

The overhead light glanced brightly off the razor-sharp edge as he brought the blade to her neck. The cold metal pricked the vulnerable flesh just beneath her left ear. Summer stopped breathing.

CHAPTER FOUR

"One swipe—*here*—and you're dead in just a few minutes. Hear me?"

Afraid to nod—the feel of the blade poised just above her racing pulse was terrifying—Summer moaned instead. Apparently he took the despairing sound for the assent it was.

"Don't give me a reason to do it."

The scalpel moved away from her neck to glitter in front of her eyes once more.

"Do we understand each other?"

This time Summer nodded. Vigorously.

"For your sake, you better hope so."

With the scalpel gleaming just inches from her nose, Summer didn't dare move as his imprisoning arm slid away from her neck. She stared at the deadly instrument with the horror a mouse might feel for a python as sheer black waves of terror threatened to engulf her. Beating them back, she also did battle with her nervous system, which was sending a tidal wave of adrenaline coursing through her veins. Her body's fight-or-flight response had been triggered in spades, but she could do neither. Instinct warned that for the moment, docility was her best defense.

When Summer felt his hand dig deep into the knot of hair on top of her head, she did no more than utter a single surprised "Ouch!"

Ignoring that, he raked his fingers painfully through the untidy bun, freeing the fine coffee-colored strands with ruthless disregard for whether or not he hurt her. Half a dozen bobby pins went flying to land with tiny *pings* on the linoleum floor. Summer's roots shrieked a protest as they were all but yanked out of her scalp, but she forced herself to endure the assault without resisting in any way. Every bit of instinct for self-preservation she possessed shrieked that she was just one wrong move away from a hideous death.

Her mother's oft-repeated advice to her three daughters had been, "If a man tries something out of line with you, knee him in the nuts."

The nuts were there, bare and vulnerable, and her knee was ready, too. The only problem was, she was facing the wrong way around, and likely to stay that way.

What now, Mother? she wailed silently.

"Now show me the way out of here." His growling voice was the most frightening thing Summer had ever heard. In an instant her mother's smiling image vanished. In one hand he clutched the scalpel; the other was imbedded in her hair. Even if she had been foolhardy enough to brave, by struggling, the threat of having her throat cut, she couldn't have broken away from him. Her hair was wrapped around his fist so tightly that it hurt.

If she'd gotten the boyish haircut that common sense—and her mother—had urged her to adopt for the summer, he wouldn't have been able to tether her so effectively, she reflected bitterly. But no, she hadn't been able to bring herself to part with her one remaining vanity—her shoulderblade-length hair. What price vanity now?

"Move," he ordered. Swallowing, Summer moved.

Mindful that his delusionary "they," whoever they were, were supposedly out back, she led him toward the front door. He stayed right on her heels as she moved out of the embalming room and down the back corridor. At that hall's junction with the main hall, he jerked her to a stop, pulling her against his body with a yank on her hair so unexpected that it made her bite her tongue. Heart thudding, eyes watering from the pain, Summer nevertheless stood meekly in his hold. The knowledge of his nakedness was, in its own way, as intimidating as the scalpel. Being held so close against him made her skin crawl. Though she could see nothing of him beyond the occasional glimpse of broad, bruised shoulders and blood-streaked, hard-muscled bare arms, she could feel him, everywhere. He wasn't a lot taller than she was—maybe a hair under six feet—but, God, he was broad. And he felt strong.

He was tense, seeming to test the air almost like a dog.

What kind of creature was he? Was he even human? Visions of vampires and werewolves and zombies careened lightning-fast through Summer's mind. Which was stupid, she told herself fiercely. Of course he was human. He was just a man. A violent, cruel man clutching a scalpel with which he had threatened to cut her throat. The stark truth made her mouth go dry. It was a toss-up, but on the whole she thought she would prefer a vampire or his brethren.

Panic threatened to swamp her again. Summer squeezed her eyes shut. Oh, God, was she going to die tonight? She wasn't ready to die.

"Move."

Opening her eyes, Summer obeyed. With every step she took along the plush center hallway, her fear increased. What would happen when she led him outside? Foolish to hope he would simply let her go.

"Please . . ." she whispered as they reached the front door. He loomed close behind her, his harsh breathing swooshing past her cheek, stirring the few strands of her hair that had eluded his hold. His breath smelled stale.

Daring to glance over her shoulder, Summer immediately wished she had not. In the bright light of the overhead chandelier, the apparition that met her gaze was as frightful as anything Stephen King could have conjured up: Frankenstein's monster in shades of purple instead of green, the face so hideously distorted by bruising and swelling that the humanity of his features was almost obscured. His mouth was twice the size of a normal mouth, skewed down and to the left, with a line of dried blood snaking down from the left corner. His nose was huge and misshapen, the nostrils ringed with dried blood. More blood, black and crusty, was smeared across his cheeks and chin. The left side of his forehead down to the bridge of his nose was so purple, it was almost black, and the area around his left eye had swelled into a big puffy mask of discolored flesh that reduced that eye to little more than a slit. His right eye wasn't a lot better; it wasn't as discolored as the left, but it seemed to be swollen completely shut. She was surprised that he could even see.

He could. He was glaring at her, and the menace in that one viable eye was the most terrifying thing she had ever encountered. If she had ever had any doubts that he could, and would, kill her without a second thought, they vanished when she met his gaze.

"If you screw me over . . ." He didn't finish the almost whispered threat. He didn't have to. The scalpel pressed against her pulse again, harder than before, and for an instant, a hideous instant, she thought he would slice her throat there and then and be done with it.

"I won't. I promise."

Her shaky answer was met with a grunt and the shifting of the scalpel so that it no longer touched her skin. The large, blunt-fingered hand holding it moved to rest on her right shoulder. From the corner of her eye, she could still see its gleaming silver threat.

"Open the door," he said, and she did, because there didn't seem to be anything else to do. For a moment they stood poised together in the doorway. His naked body pressed against her back, her buttocks. She could feel the bulge of his genitals against her hip, and barely managed to repress a shudder. His grip on her hair tightened as he seemed to listen.

Outside, the night was alive with the hum of cicadas. This was the year for them, of course. They crawled out of the ground every seventeen years, and this was the summer that Murfreesboro got lucky. After the soft hush inside, to be greeted by the endless low chirring sound they made was oddly comforting. It was good to know that there were other normal living creatures in the dark.

"That your car?"

Her car, a used Celica hatchback, was parked to the right of the entrance. As it was the only car in the vast parking lot, it hadn't required a feat of genius for him to figure out that it belonged to her. Apparently he realized that, too, because he didn't even wait for her weak nod before pushing her toward it.

The door clicked shut behind them, snuffing out the last sliver of artificial light. The only illumination now was provided by the moon, which was hidden from her sight by the ring of tall pines around the mortuary. A scattering of stars twinkled with incongruous cheeriness against the inky black of the predawn sky. A soft wind, warm and redolent with the scent of the pines, caressed her face. From underfoot, a low crunching sound marked their progress. The thousands of cicadas celebrated their rite of passage by shedding their skins, and the dried, brittle shells littered the ground like leaves in autumn. The feel of them shattering beneath her bare foot was unpleasant.

Briefly, uselessly, Summer mourned the shoe left behind in the embalming room. Would its absence slow her down should she get a chance to run? She dismissed that thought with the contempt it deserved. If necessary, she would sprint barefoot over broken glass to escape the monster who held her hostage.

"Get in."

They had reached her car, and with those words he thrust her against the passenger-side door, which was closed. Her hip made painful contact with the jutting handle before her fingers could grab hold and lift.

Nothing happened.

For an awful second that seemed to stretch as long as all eternity, Summer measured the size and scope of the acute danger in which she now found herself.

"Are you deaf? I said *get in*."

"It's locked."

"What?"

"It's locked."

"Unlock it, then."

"I—I don't have the keys." Her voice quavered.

"You don't have the keys? Where the hell are they?"

"Inside. In m-my purse. By the door."

He swore, filthy and threatening strings of oaths that were no less chilling because their low volume made them largely unintelligible. Summer didn't even try to decipher most of the abuse he hissed at her as he dragged her back toward the mortuary. Stumbling in his wake, bent almost double by his grip on her hair, Summer tasted terror. It was sour on her tongue, like vinegar.

She heard, rather than saw, the click as he tried and failed to turn the front-door knob. Click, click, click, click . . .

"This door's locked too."

Summer cringed.

"Tell me you don't have a key. Tell me the goddamned door's locked and you don't have a key. Tell me that the key to this door, and the keys to your car, are locked inside this goddamned building. Tell me. I dare you."

He had the situation summed up in a nutshell, but not for all the world would Summer have admitted it. She didn't need to. He took her silence for the assent it was and let loose with a sound that was a cross between a growl and a snarl and put the fear of God into her.

"I'm sorry! Please . . ." she babbled as he jerked her upright so that they were suddenly eyeball to fearsome eyeball. Murder was written on his distorted face.

The bright glare of headlights sliced through the darkness. A vehicle was turning into the private lane that led to the mortuary's parking lot. Summer felt a wave of thankfulness so intense that it weakened her knees. Saved, she was saved.

"Shit."

Not so fast. Deliverance was snatched from her grasp even as she embraced it. He ran, with a heavy, lumbering, almost crablike lope indicating, she hoped, that his left leg might be severely injured, around the corner of the building and dragged her with him by her accursed hair.

As she stumbled in his wake, the two of them barely ahead of the pursuing headlights, a scream died in her throat without ever making it past her lips. His grip on her hair was unbreakable—and he still clutched the scalpel in his right fist.

"Make a sound and die." Having reached safety, he flung himself against the building's brick wall and jerked Summer with him, her back to his chest. His right arm locked around her waist. She imagined that the scalpel nestled somewhere beneath her left breast. Close to her heart.

His body heaved with each breath he drew. She was panting too, from terror. Sweat poured off him. His skin was damp with it. The odor he gave off was not pleasant.

"Do you have on a bra?"

"What?" The guttural question so surprised Summer that she answered in a near-normal voice.

"Do you have on a bra?"

Summer nodded faintly. From the front of the building came the swoosh of tires on pavement, and then the faint squeal of brakes. Thank God, someone was there.

"Take it off. Take off your shirt and take off your bra and do it *now.*"

The fierceness of the command, accompanied by the shifting of the scalpel from beneath her breast to the pulse below her ear, spurred Summer into complying without question. He meant it. There was no doubt whatsoever in her mind that he would kill her that exact second if she did not do as he ordered, or if she impeded him in any way. Hands shaking, she fumbled at the buttons at the front of her blouse, afraid to even speculate on what he meant to do when it was off. Surely, surely, he did not intend rape. She didn't think he intended rape. Despite his overpowering nakedness, sexual assault seemed to be the last thing on his mind.

"Hurry."

Summer tried, but dread made her fingers clumsy. She still had two buttons to go when he grew tired of waiting. Untangling his hand from her hair with an impatient jerk that made her grit her teeth against the pain, he grabbed hold of her blouse by the back of the collar and yanked it off her. The thin nylon gave with a soft ripping sound, and the remaining buttons shot into space.

The sheer unexpectedness of it made Summer gasp. Instinctively she crossed her arms over her chest. His hands were already at her back, clawing for the fastenings of her bra. When he could not find it, muttered curses intermingled with threats singed her ears.

Feeling as if she were trapped in a nightmare, Summer lifted her unsteady hands to undo the hook-and-eye closure between her breasts. At this point, she was willing to do anything necessary to appease him.

From somewhere out of sight came the slam of a car door. Whoever was driving the vehicle had gotten out.

Let them find me, she prayed as the bra was stripped from her and her arms were dragged ruthlessly behind her back. Please, please let them find me.

Glancing down, Summer was made ill by the sight of her bare breasts gleaming palely in the moonlight. It brought home the reality of her danger as nothing else had. This man could strip her, rape her, kill her, at will. She was at his mercy—unless she did something. But what? What could she do that would not hasten her own grisly end?

The distant crunch of footsteps told her that her potential savior was on foot now, presumably walking through the parking lot. Toward them? But he didn't know they were there. In all likelihood, he was headed toward the mortuary's front door. Who could it be? Mike Chaney? An ambulance crew with another corpse? A cop making a routine check on the building? Who knew?

Please . . . she prayed again, so shaken that she could not even put the rest of her request into words. But God knew what she meant. Please save me. Please.

Her captor was tying her wrists together with her bra. He was using both hands, which meant that wherever the scalpel was, he wasn't holding it just at that instant. If she was ever going to do it, now was the moment to scream, while the scalpel was not at the ready and there was someone nearby to hear.

But suppose the someone could not, or would not, help? Suppose it was a woman, or worse, a woman with kids in the car, who by her screaming would be exposed to the madman's menace too? Or a rank coward who would hear her scream but cut and run instead of coming to her aid?

Summer hesitated. He finished securing her wrists with a brutal yank that tested the efficacy of his handiwork. Her wrists ached already, and her hands tingled from the beginning effects of lack of circulation. Experimentally, she wriggled her fingers, tried to move her hands. The bra—why, oh why had she opted for the indestructability of an eighteen-hour garment instead of the flimsy nylon lingerie she had once preferred?—dug deep into her flesh. The sturdy elastic bound her as securely as a pair of handcuffs.

His hands were on her shoulders, forcing her to her knees.

On the other hand, suppose she didn't scream. What then?

That prospect was the clincher.

Even as she sank to the grassy verge that framed the building, her mouth opened. The die was cast: she had no real choice. Drawing in a lungful of air, she prepared to shatter his eardrums and her own. Her very life might well hang on this one scream.

Before she could get out so much as a peep, her own blouse was thrust between her teeth. Stunned, Summer choked, gagged, and tried to spit it out, to no avail. The wadded nylon reached so far down her throat that she thought she might vomit.

She couldn't vomit. She would choke to death for sure if she did. What she had to do was breathe through her nose. Breathe. Breathe.

He did something more to her wrists, then tilted her chin up so that she was forced to look at him. The scalpel was clenched pirate-like between his teeth, she saw. The slit that was his eye glittered ferally. His distorted mouth was twisted into a hideous grimace that might, on a normal person, have been a jeering smile. As if he found her terror funny.

It occurred to Summer then that there was a strong possibility he was not even sane. Suddenly she was very, very glad she hadn't screamed.

CHAPTER FIVE

"I'll be back," he said, holding her gaze. The Terminator himself couldn't have made the threat sound more terrifying. In fact, Summer decided that she would rather by far be facing Arnold Schwarzenegger at his most menacing than the man who loomed over her in real life.

He released her jaw, stepped away, and vanished around the corner of the building.

Summer wasted no more than a pair of heartbeats staring after him. Then she tried to get to her feet.

Her wrists were tied to something—she glanced around to be certain: a faucet. A plain old faucet jutting out of the side of the building. He had somehow twisted her bra so that it not only bound her wrists but tethered her tightly to the faucet, too.

Damn him. Damn him. She was not going to be able to get away.

Frantically she pulled and yanked and twisted, fighting to be free. This was her chance to escape. All she had to do was get free of the faucet, and run, and run, and run.

The nylon in her mouth impeded her breathing. She was struggling so hard that her overworked lungs screamed for more oxygen. Saliva poured into her mouth in a useless effort to combat the cloying dryness from having a mouth crammed full of cloth. Some ran down her throat. Trying not to cough, or gag, sucking in great rushes of air through her nose, Summer deliberately slowed her desperate efforts. She was trying too hard. That had to be it. How difficult could it be to break free of a bra and a faucet, for goodness' sake?

Summer scooted on her rump as far away from the faucet as she could and used all her strength to try to yank her hands after her. Her hope was that the bra would break. She yanked again. And again. And again. The bra didn't break, but her wrists felt like they might. What was the damned bra made out of, she wondered semihysterically, some kind of industrial strength space elastic?

Just her luck.

Silently she cursed the space age.

Wriggling her fingers, twisting her wrists, she forced her hands into impossible contortions as she fought to be free. Using the faucet as a tool, she sawed the bra back and forth over it, disregarding the rough edges that scraped her wrists. Nothing worked. Despairing, beyond caring if she hurt herself, she yanked once more with all her strength. And, miracle of miracles, she finally felt something give. Something—a strap, a knot—had slipped or broken. The bonds were definitely looser. A few more yanks and she might be free.

Sweating, praying, Summer gave a mighty heave—and glanced up to find the madman coming around the side of the building toward her. There was no mistaking his identity. Even through the darkness, she recognized him instantly. Part of it was his distinctive gait, and part of it was pure instinct.

As his presence registered on her consciousness, she froze, then gave up the fight. Oh, God, she had only needed a few minutes more. Just a few minutes more, and she would have been free.

In the brief time he'd been gone, he seemed to have acquired clothes. Flip-flops, cutoff jeans, and a tight black T-shirt with some kind of writing on the front that she couldn't quite read through the darkness. Something about a dog?

Not that it mattered. He was back, and she was still tethered. She'd blown what was probably her best chance to escape. She was at his mercy again.

Defeated, Summer slumped, letting her head loll forward until her chin brushed her chest. A lamb for his slaughter, that was what she was. The worst part of it was, at that instant she didn't even particularly care.

The distinctive smell of him—kerosene and body odor—made her stomach heave as he moved around behind her. He did something to the bindings on her wrists, and suddenly they were free. Whatever he did was so quick, so easy, that it didn't seem possible she could have struggled as hard as she had without achieving the same results, Summer thought resentfully as she brought her bruised and tingling hands forward to rub them. He reached down to pull the blouse from her mouth. The moist membranes seemed to have adhered to the nylon, and she could almost feel them rip as the wadded cloth was abruptly removed.

Her jaws ached in the aftermath of its going. Her tongue felt dry and swollen. As she moved her mouth, testing to be sure it still worked, she discovered that her lips were numb. She swallowed once, twice. It didn't seem to help. Nothing seemed to help.

Behind her, she heard a squeak and then the rush of water. At the sound, saliva flooded her mouth. She glanced back to discover that he was sluicing his face with water from the faucet. She craved the taste of it like an alcoholic might liquor. Partially turning, reaching out an unsteady hand, she caught some in her palm, raised it to her mouth, and swallowed. The icy liquid felt wonderful to her dry throat and tongue. She reached for more, only to have him turn the water off.

How could she have forgotten? She was helpless, defenseless, at his mercy. He could even decide how much and when she would drink. Her chin sank to her chest again in an attitude of total despair. Dully she watched her mangled bra and blouse land in a bundled heap on her knees, then roll to the grass, where they spilled apart.

"Get dressed. Hurry."

Summer, still wallowing in the psychic quagmire of defeat, didn't move. When she didn't instantly respond, he grabbed her hair, jerked her head back, and waved the scalpel in front of her face.

"Did you hear me? I said *hurry*."

The sight of the scalpel frightened her, and fright reawakened her survival instinct. The will to live pumped with renewed force through her veins. She reached out, fumbling for her clothes, and he let go of her hair. Still he loomed over her threateningly. She could feel him watching her as she pulled on her bra—one shoulder strap was broken—and clipped it together between her breasts after several abortive tries. Sliding her arms into the damp, wrinkled mess of her blouse, she managed to fasten three of its buttons despite fingers that shook. As she tried to fit the fourth into its hole he cursed suddenly and grabbed her upper arm in a viselike grip. Summer gasped as with ruthless strength she was hauled to her feet.

When she was standing, he shoved his face into hers. His one visible eye glittered. His breath stank. She cringed.

"You are about one minute away from having your throat slit. Don't think you can pull some kind of delaying crap on me. *If you slow me down, I'll kill you.* I swear I will. Now get your ass moving. Go."

Acute terror can last only so long, Summer discovered as he pushed her in front of him back around the corner of the building toward where a white paneled van now waited beside her car. Despite her growing certainty that it wasn't a matter of if but of when he would cut her throat, the edge of her fear had dulled to the point where it was more a like a chronic, manageable ache than an immediate, stabbing pain. *Numb* best described how she felt as she was forced toward the van's passenger-side door—until she saw the body.

A man lay on the pavement not far from the mortuary's front door. He was sprawled on his stomach, one arm stretched in a kind of pathetic appeal above his head. He was naked, motionless

—and his head rested in a dark, sticky pool of liquid that Summer had no trouble guessing was blood.

"You killed him!" she gasped before she thought.

"And if you don't mind your p's and q's, you'll be next," growled the voice in her ear. Head swiveling to stare at the body even as she was forced up and into the passenger side of the van, Summer shivered as her terror reawakened with all its earlier force. The icy frisson that exploded along her nerve endings felt almost familiar. Had there ever been a time when she was not afraid for her life?

"Scoot over."

He was sliding in behind her, crowding her out of the seat nearest the door and into the driver's seat. The van's interior was black vinyl, and it had only the two bucket seats. The space in the back was given over to cargo. By the small overhead light that came on automatically as they entered, it was possible to see that quilted gray furniture blankets lay over whatever the van carried.

The passenger-side door clicked shut, and the light went off. Summer was left alone in the smelly darkness with her captor, who casually draped his left arm along the back of her seat. The scalpel was in the fist that rested just below her left ear.

"Behave yourself, you hear?" The tip of the scalpel toyed with her earlobe while Summer stopped breathing. "Hear?"

"Yes."

The arm around her shoulders was removed, and the scalpel went with it. Her breath escaped in an audible hiss as he settled back in his seat, the scalpel now held in his right fist, which rested negligently on his bare right knee. The threat had been withdrawn —for the moment. But his gaze never left her as he massaged his left thigh, seemingly trying to dig his fingers deep into muscles that pained him.

Summer wondered how long it would be before she ended up like the man on the pavement. Bile rose in her throat.

"Drive," her captor said, and handed her a set of keys.

Summer took them without a word. Fortunately there were only four keys on the simple metal ring, and from the GM logo on the longest it was pretty obvious which one fit the ignition. Gripping the steering wheel with one hand, she bent, squinted, and tried to insert the key into the lock.

Her hands were trembling so badly that she couldn't quite do it. Casting fearful little sidelong glances at the man beside her, she jabbed at the ignition a second time, then a third, in vain. Panic assailed her as he quit massaging his leg. He leaned toward her; she could not prevent herself from looking at him. Just inches away, menace gleamed at her from the bloodshot slit that was his eye.

"Get us the hell out of here *now.*"

His tone galvanized her. Summer willed her hands to steadiness and thrust the key at the ignition again. Thank God, this time it slid home. He sank back in his seat. Taking a great swallow of air, she started the van, shifted the automatic transmission into reverse, and stepped on the gas.

The van squealed backward with such force that she was almost unseated. Her instinctive reaction was to slam on the brake, which she did, throwing both of them forward. Her chest crashed into the steering wheel. Grimacing, rubbing her breastbone, she eased away from the hard plastic ring. That hurt. She reached for her seat belt, then thought better of it. Her seat belt would only slow her down should a chance of escape present itself.

"Damn it, don't do that again." Recovering his own balance, his right hand pressed against the dashboard for support, her captor glared at her. The scalpel winked at her from his left fist. If luck had been smiling on her, the jolt should have caused him to inflict a mortal wound on himself with the weapon he used to threaten her. But then luck, at least her luck, was never that good.

"I didn't mean to do it," she said, and took another deep breath to steady her nerves before shifting into drive.

As her fingers curled around the handle that operated the automatic transmission Summer just happened to glance out the passenger-side window beyond him. She was shocked to see the mortuary's front door burst open and three men spill out into the spreading fan of light cast by the front hall's chandelier. For an instant she gaped. There were no other cars in sight. Where had the men come from? They had not been inside the mortuary when she was taken hostage and forced outside, she was sure of that, so there remained only one possibility: Even while she thought she was lying through her teeth to her captor, there must really have been men out back.

Who were they? Would they help her? Should she try a scream now?

Alerted by something in her expression, her captor's head swung around. Like hers, his gaze fixed on the tableau being enacted before their eyes. The men spotted the shape on the pavement and ran toward it. Even as they reached it, it was clear from their body language that this was not the corpse they sought. They stopped, almost bumping into each other, for a moment of milling confusion. One of them glanced up and caught sight of the van, which, thanks to Summer's rocket-speed reverse and frantic braking, was now idling motionless some two hundred feet away. He elbowed his pals, who also glanced up. Their faces were pale, featureless ovals in the moonlight.

"There he is!"

"He's getting away!"

"Sangor's gonna shit!"

"Get him!"

The almost simultaneous jumble of shouts came as the trio glimpsed her captor through the window. Openmouthed at the incongruousness of it, Summer witnessed the headlong charge of clean-cut, respectable-looking middle-aged white men in suits—pulling pistols from holsters beneath their jackets as they ran.

"Hightail it!" her captor yelled. Not waiting for her response, he kicked his left leg across the intervening space and tromped down hard on her foot—and the gas.

Losing her grip on the wheel, Summer was thrown back in her seat as the van shot across the parking lot like a missile.

Firecrackers applauded. Something slapped into the side of the van. Once, twice, three times, with the sound of a hand smacking into flesh. What on earth . . . ? A bullet. A hail of bullets, to be precise. Of course. The sharp pops belonged not to firecrackers but to gunfire. Her mind might be functioning a little slowly just at present, but it still functioned.

Having finally deduced that she faced a new source of mortal danger, Summer ducked, throwing her arms up to protect her head.

"Goddamn it, woman! Get your damned hands on the wheel! I can't bleeping see!" He straddled the space between the seats, balancing on the edges of both, his left foot still smashing her foot and the gas pedal beneath it to the floor. His hands were on the wheel, and his head was cocked to one side as he peered desperately through the darkness at the road.

Too stunned to respond even to her captor's tooth-rattling roar, Summer continued to cower. Seconds later she was thrown hard against the door as, cursing like a juvenile delinquent on a bad night, he yanked the wheel hard to the left. As her shoulder slammed into the door, her single coherent thought was, Please God, let it be locked!

Apparently it was, because it held.

Grabbing for the far edge of her seat and encountering his leg instead, Summer grabbed hold and clung like a two-year-old confronted with a strange day-care center as the van took the turn on what felt like two wheels. Then they were streaking along the narrow black-topped lane that led away from the mortuary through the cemetery and up to the main highway.

"Get your hands *off* my leg, get 'em *on* the wheel and *steer*!"

This time the command got through to her, either because she feared for her life if he continued to drive, or because his bellow was right in her ear. Her bruised and terrorized body sprang into action independent of her mind and she straightened, releasing his leg. He didn't move, though he relinquished the wheel as she grabbed it. His left arm moved to hug the back of her seat. Her shoulder butted into his side as she drove.

The van weaved wildly all over the road. His foot still crushed hers, forcing the accelerator to the floor. The speedometer needle jumped past sixty and kept on going to seventy, eighty, and beyond. Tall pines, treacherous curves, and black ragged ditches of unknown depths along both sides of the lane flashed past, menacing them. Running without lights as they were, visibility was limited to perhaps twenty feet. Everything beyond that distance was a blur of darkness.

Somehow the van managed to stay on the road, kept from crashing only by Summer's heroic efforts. As she wrestled the wheel—if the van had power steering it was the worst power steering with which she had ever come into contact—it occurred to her with chilling force that having her throat slit was one of only many ways she might die that night.

"Get your foot off the gas! You're going to kill us both!" she gasped, terrified anew by the sudden pinpoint of glowing bright red that she glimpsed through the darkness. She knew this road well. The lane ended in a traffic signal at Route 231, a busy highway favored by eighteen-wheelers and locals alike—and the light was red. Without lights, the van would be practically invisible to an approaching vehicle.

"Stop!" she shrieked when it became clear he had no intention of complying. She kicked him, shoving her bare left foot hard into the muscle of his calf. If only she hadn't taken off her shoe! Not that a rubber-soled sneaker would have had much effect. His calf was so hard, it hurt her toe.

The weight of his foot on hers didn't ease by so much as a fraction of an ounce. She might as well have kicked a tree trunk for all the good it did. At the speed they were going—Summer couldn't even bring herself to glance at the speedometer again— there was no way they were going to make the perpendicular turn. Trying would probably only worsen the inevitable crash; the van would tip onto two wheels, then flip over—and over—and over.

Hands frozen on the wheel, Summer stared appalled at the intersection toward which they raced. In what she was convinced were the last few seconds of her life, she spared a longing thought for the seat belt she had decided against wearing. One more thing she would do over again if permitted the chance. With her track record, they would probably chisel *If only* on her gravestone. It would be a fitting epitaph.

"Hang a left," he yelled.

Summer barely had time to thank God that it was the middle of the night and 231 appeared to be deserted before the T-shaped intersection was upon them. Her eyes grew huge in anticipation of disaster as she accepted that he wasn't even going to permit them to slow down. Dread rendered her totally unable to move. All she could do was cling to the wheel, staring through the windshield in horror at a ditch, a fence, and a gently sloping field full of sleeping cows that suddenly materialized directly in front of them. A few more seconds, and those huddled bovines would be tomorrow's ground beef.

"I said hang a left!"

Summer still couldn't move. Cursing, he grabbed the wheel again, jerking it forcefully to the left. Tires squealed, the van skittered toward the unsuspecting cows—and miraculously righted itself, clinging to the blacktop with barely an inch to spare.

Elsie and her pals were safe.

Which was more than she could say for herself. Another mile or so, and they would be nearing the city limits. Even at this hour, there would be traffic in town. Given the speed at which they were traveling, a crash sooner or later was all but inevitable.

Headlights appeared in the rearview mirror. The twin pinpoints of light were perhaps a mile or so behind them, at the mortuary lane's intersection with 231. As there was no reason for any other vehicle to be on the private road to the mortuary at that time of night, the logical explanation was that the three men and their guns had located a car in which to give chase.

Summer didn't know whether to feel glad or scared. The optimistic part of her nature focused on a possible rescue from the monster beside her, but instinct warned her that the men behind them were not necessarily the good guys.

One very telling sign was that they had shot at the van with her in it. Her shock-benumbed brain grappled with that thought for a second before reaching the obvious conclusion: Good guys or bad, they seemed perfectly prepared to harm her to get to him. A fourth route to her imminent death was identified: If the posse behind them caught up, they just might kill her captor *and* her as well.

Who was he? Who were they? What in the name of heaven had she stumbled into? Oh, God, she didn't want to die. She wanted the man beside her, and the ones in the car behind, just to disappear. Zap!

Where was the Terminator when she needed him?

Again something in her expression must have alerted him. He glanced in the rearview mirror and cursed. Easing up on her foot just long enough to shove her leg aside, he stomped on the accelerator again without her foot to run interference. While she fought to keep it on the road, the van hurtled around a curve, out of sight of the chasing car. Without warning he jerked the wheel—and the vehicle was suddenly airborne.

Summer screamed as the van jumped a ditch, broke through a plank fence, bucked across a just sprouting soybean patch, and plowed into a towering thicket of slender cornstalks. She had just an instant to register a looming, bus-size contraption of yellow-painted steel before they were upon it. She didn't even have time to close her eyes as the van crashed into the side of a combine that some hurrying-in-to-supper farmer had very thoughtlessly left smack in the middle of his field.

CHAPTER SIX

The good news was, she wasn't dead. The bad news was, she might soon be.

For a few seconds after the impact, the only thing Summer was aware of was the pounding of her own badly stressed heart. A moment or two passed before she realized she had been in a car accident. It occurred to her that she must have been briefly knocked unconscious. She still felt just a little dizzy and disoriented. Apparently her head had crashed into the windshield.

Grimacing, she opened her eyes. A cautious glance told her that the windshield had survived unscathed even if her head had not. It ached. Her body was slumped over the steering wheel; her fingers were locked around it. She wanted to probe her forehead to determine the extent of her injury—was she bleeding?—but she could not seem to summon the will to open her fingers. Shock seemed to have paralyzed her.

The vehicle's motor was still running. The transmission was in drive, but they weren't going anywhere. Of course, the vehicle was a van, and the van had hit a combine. The combine was what had stopped it, and what kept it from moving now.

The monster beside her: with a terrifying rush of memory Summer recalled him, recalled just how she had come to be in such a fix, and that's when she had her good-news, bad-news brain wave.

Glancing sideways, she saw that he was sprawled in his seat, eyes closed, lips slack. His left arm hung limply beside him. The fingers of his left hand were open, brushing the black-carpeted floor. His right hand, when she peered over him to check, was equally empty. The scalpel was nowhere in sight. Obviously he had lost it in the crash.

As soon as the implications of that registered, Summer regained the use of her body. Hallelujah! She was going to be free at last! Scrabbling for the lock and the door handle at the same time, she wasn't even aware that he had moved.

"Oh no you don't," he growled just as the door swung open, and put a stop to her would-be freedom leap by grabbing a fistful of hair.

"Ow!"

Dragged painfully backward, Summer couldn't take it anymore. A red fog of rage clouded her senses, leaving just one thought perfectly clear: If she was going to die tonight, at least she was going to die fighting.

"Aiiee-yaw!" She whirled with a roar that would have done Bruce Lee proud—it should have, because it was an offshoot of an overdose of his movies—and dove at her captor. Every fiber of her being was intent on doing him serious bodily harm.

"Bitch!" he yelped as the unexpected force of her full-body slam rammed him against the passenger-side door. He had only one hand with which to try to ward her off. His other was tangled in her hair, its length and baby-fine texture suddenly an asset as it kept his fingers trapped. At the moment of impact her nails raked his neck, her teeth sank into his shoulder, her knees sought his genitals—and the door popped open, spewing them both out into the cornfield.

"Shit!" he yelled as they fell. He landed on his back, his legs in the air, his feet still in the van. She landed with a thud atop him.

At the moment of impact she jerked her right knee upward, hard, and thought, hoped, that it went home.

That one's for you, Mother! she thought exultantly.

He gasped, jacknifed his knees to his chest, and rolled to his side, bringing down cornstalks as he went.

Summer was thrown clear, but he still had her by the hair.

"Aiiee-yaw!" Launching herself toward him, screeching her intimidating *Fists of Fury* battle cry, she never even saw the blow to her chin that knocked her cold.

When she came to, she was lying on her back on the ground gazing up at a skyful of stars. Closer to earth but still far above her own head, tasseled corn stalks swayed in the breeze. The hum of the cicadas was punctuated with the less than melodic rhapsodizing of what sounded like a convention of amorous bullfrogs. An owl hooted in the distance.

Her head hurt. Her jaw hurt. Beneath her back, sharp little spears of snapped-off cornstalks stabbed her spine. The left cheek of her buttocks was being slowly pierced by a large, pointy rock. In comparison, the rock's smaller fellows, positioned at random intervals beneath her body, were no more than minor discomforts. The cicada shells she barely noticed.

Hoping to escape the gouging of the large rock, she shifted her hips. Immediately Frankenstein's monstrous countenance loomed over her, blocking out the night sky.

Unprepared, Summer shrieked. A hand clapped down over her mouth, pinning her to the ground when she would have scrambled up and back.

"Shut up, damn it," growled a too horribly familiar voice. Summer recognized the dulcet tones of her captor. The face was his, too. Trapped again.

Defeated, she surrendered her fate to God and chance, closed her eyes, and lay limply in her uncomfortable bed of rocks and cornstalks and bug bodies. If he was going to kill her, let him do it now. She wasn't moving again.

The hand over her mouth cautiously lifted.

Summer didn't so much as bat an eyelid.

Human silence stretched moments into an eternity.

Without warning, her left breast was grabbed and squeezed.

"Get off me!" Outraged, Summer knocked his hand away, rocketed into a sitting position, and jerked herself backward on her rump. The still-running van behind her stopped her scoot to safety. Drawing her legs up to her chin, she glared at him.

Passively waiting for death was one thing, but submitting to sexual assault was something else.

"Thought that would get you," her captor said. He sounded smugly male, and all at once very normal. He was sitting cross-legged on the ground not three feet away, massaging his thigh again. Summer thought she detected an amused gleam in the single misshapen slit that was all she could see of his eyes, but with his features so distorted, it was hard to be certain.

In the dark, he was not quite so fearsome-looking. Probably because she couldn't see him all that clearly, of course. In a bright light, his face would doubtless still make her want to scream and run. Still, she wasn't as afraid of him as she had been at first. Maybe it was his barely discernible twinkle of amusement that had done it, or maybe it was because, for a few minutes there, they'd been allies as they'd raced away from goons with guns. Of course, there was always the possibility that she'd hit her head harder than she'd thought in the crash, and this puzzling lack of terror was the result of brain damage.

Whatever, it worked for her.

"Go to hell," she said with loathing. His swollen mouth quirked in what might—or might not, given the state of his face it was hard to tell—have been a fleeting, surprised smile. Her terror receded even farther.

"I've been, thanks. Now I'm back. Too many sewer-mouthed women there for me," he said. Summer didn't reply, just eyed him evilly.

After a moment he spoke again. "Your friends back there didn't seem too concerned about hitting you when they were shooting at me. Maybe you'd better think about that. At this point, a smart gal might consider switching sides. Come clean with me, and I'll see what I can do for you."

"I don't know what in blazes you're talking about." *In blazes*

was a phrase she frequently used. She was certainly not moderat-
ing her language because of something *he* had said. Sewer-
mouthed, indeed! Who cared what a monstrous-looking homicidal
maniac thought?

"Sure you don't."

"Those men are not my friends."

"Sure they're not."

"I never saw them before in my life."

"Sure you haven't."

"Damn it, I'm telling the truth!" See there? So much for moder-
ating her language.

"Sure you are."

"Who the hell are you, anyway?" If she felt like swearing, she
would.

He gave her a long look. "A cop. Kind of."

"A *cop*? *Kind of*? What the hell is a kind of cop?" Summer
almost hooted in derision.

"A kind of cop is somebody that it's bad news to mess with,
lady. When you got involved with this bunch, you fell in with the
wrong crowd. Know what happens to cop killers—or would-be
cop killers—in the great state of Tennessee? One way or another,
they wake up one morning dead."

"Do you think that I—" She broke off, rapidly reviewed the
evidence, and concluded that maybe he was deranged and maybe
he wasn't, but there definitely had been three men shooting at him
—no, at them. Something unsavory was going on, and, cop or not,
he needed to know she was not a part of it. "I am not a cop killer.
I am not a would-be cop killer. I am not even a would-be killer of
a kind of cop. I am a janitor."

"A *janitor*?"

"Yes, a *janitor*. You know, somebody who cleans up after everybody else? A janitor. That's me."

There was a pause. "Bullshit."

"It's the truth. I own Daisy Fresh Janitorial Services, and I was
just finishing up cleaning Harmon Brothers' funeral home when I
ran into you."

"Bullshit."

"I'm telling the truth," Summer insisted. "I haven't the slightest idea what's going on here—and I don't think I want to know. Whatever you're involved in, you can just include me out."

"I asked you where the rest of the gang was and you knew just exactly what I was talking about. You even told me where they were. If you're not involved in this, how'd you know they were out back?"

"It was a lucky guess."

"Yeah, right."

"It was. I swear it was. You scared me, and I told you what I thought you wanted to hear. I didn't even know there *were* any men. I thought you were deranged. I was *humoring* you." Summer took a deep, calming breath. "Look at me. This is a janitor's uniform, can't you tell? My God, do you think any self-respecting woman would voluntarily run around town in a pair of black polyester pants and a white nylon blouse with a daisy embroidered on the pocket?"

There was a pause. "Let me see some I.D."

"I don't have any I.D. I left my purse—"

"At the funeral home. Locked inside. With your car keys. Yeah, I believe it. I'll give you this, though: You think fast on your feet."

"You can look me up in any phone book in town. My name's in there, the name of my janitorial service is in there, and my voice is even on the answering machine if you want to call."

"Good idea. I'll just whip the old cellular out of my pocket and —oh, pardon me, these aren't my pants. I left mine back at the funeral home, along with my phone. Locked inside the building. Just like your purse. And keys. Guess I can't call and check out your story. What a shame."

"There are dozens of pay phones in Murfreesboro. All you have to do is drive into town, stop at one, and put in a quarter."

"Next time I feel real stupid, I might."

"You could do it right now. The van's right here."

"*If* it still moves, which it may or may not, and *if* I wanted to chance starting the chase up again, I could do that. But I don't have any intention of leaving here for a while yet. They didn't see us run off the road."

"How do you know?"

"Because if they had, your friends would be all over us by now."

"They're not my friends. I keep telling you that."

"And I keep not believing you. Guess I'm not a very trusting sort by nature."

"If you're a cop, you're not going to kill me." Summer was thinking aloud. The knowledge burst in her brain like a rocket on the Fourth of July. She felt almost giddy as relief sent her spirits soaring skyward. "I'm out of here."

She stood up, then was forced to lean against the van as the sudden movement made her dizzy.

"Oh no you're not." His hand shot out, fastening around her ankle like a shackle. "You're under arrest."

"What?"

"You heard me: You're under arrest."

"I'm under *arrest*? You can't arrest me!"

"I just did."

"You can't! I haven't done anything! Besides, you're just a kind of cop, if you're even telling the truth about that, which I doubt, and I don't think being a kind of cop, whatever that means, gives you the power to arrest anybody. What is a kind of cop, anyway? Sort of like a rent-a-cop? They have those at K mart at Christmas. To direct traffic. Or is a kind of cop more like a security guard? They can't arrest people, either."

"Jesus, are you finished? I'm a cop, okay? Just a cop. And you're under arrest."

"I don't believe you." She scowled down at him. "Show me some I.D."

"Funny." They both knew the answer to that one.

"I don't believe you're a cop at all."

"I don't believe you're a janitor, so we're even."

"Let go of my leg!"

"Make me."

Summer took a deep breath. "If you're a cop, I'm going to file a complaint. You held a scalpel to my throat. You punched me in the face. You grabbed my breast. You scared the daylights out of me. You'll be in so much trouble you'll never get out of it."

"Ooo, I'm quaking in my flip-flops."

"You should be. My father-in-law's the police chief here in town."

"What?" He appeared to think that over, then shook his head. "Yeah, sure. God, you do think fast, don't you? What are you, a pathological liar?"

"I'm telling the truth, damn it. Again."

"Right. I bet you don't even know the police chief's name."

"Rosencrans. Samuel T. Rosencrans." Her answer was triumphant.

A pause. "You could've read that anywhere."

"I could've. But I didn't. He's got a disgusting-looking mole under his left ear, and he smokes cigars. And the *T.* stands for *Tyneman.*"

Another pause. "Old Rosey's only got one son. Last I heard he was married to a twenty-five-old, drop-dead-gorgeous underwear model from New York."

"Lingerie model. Your information's out-of-date. But that's me."

Frankenstein eyed her up and down. "Yeah, and I'm Marky Mark."

Summer felt her temper heat. "So a few years have passed, and I've gained some weight. So what? It's still me."

"I thought you said you were a janitor."

"I am."

"A janitor who models lawn-jer-ee?" A jeer underlay the deliberately drawn-out mispronunciation.

"I used to model lingerie. Now I own a janitorial service." Summer spoke through her teeth.

"Yeah. Sure. I can see why you made the switch. Anyone would rather scrub toilets for a living than prance around in front of a camera in a bra and panties. I know *I* would."

Summer gave him a killing look. "Oh, shut up. And let go of my leg."

"Rosencrans or not, you're still under arrest."

"Fine. I'm under arrest. Now would you let go of my leg?"

"Getting to you, am I?" he said with smirk in his voice, rubbing his index finger suggestively along her shin. "I have that effect on babes."

"You're making me sick."

"I have that effect on babes, too." This time there was no mistaking the distorted grin, brief though it was. His finger stilled.

"I bet." She said it with relish.

"I warn you: Run, and I'll tackle you. I used to be a linebacker in high school, and rough is the only way I know how to play." He released her ankle and got to his feet. He wasn't all that tall, as she'd noted before, but he was definitely built like a football player. Or maybe the too-tight T-shirt just made his shoulders and arms and chest *look* formidable. Whatever. She had no doubts at all that he would tackle her if she ran, and it would hurt, so she stayed put.

"What high school?" Her question was truculent.

"Trinity." He named a Catholic high school in nearby Nashville that was famous for its football team.

"Oh, yeah? What's your name?" She'd known a number of kids who'd gone to Trinity. Guys, mostly. Nashville had been the place to hang out when she'd been a teen. Bright lights, big city, and only forty or so miles down the road.

"Steve."

"Steve what?"

"Calhoun." He sounded wary, and it was that very wariness that tipped her off. *Steve Calhoun.* He was more famous in the Tennessee mountains than Davy Crockett. Or maybe the correct word was *infamous.*

She must have been looking at him kind of funny, because he said flatly, "I see you've heard of me."

CHAPTER SEVEN

"Who hasn't?" Summer saw no reason to spare his feelings. Steve Calhoun was indeed a cop. A detective, to be precise, with the Tennessee State Police. Or at least he had been. She wasn't sure of his current status, because the newspapers had long since abandoned him as old news.

In any event, about three years before, he had been one point of the most notorious love triangle ever to explode over central Tennessee. His romance-gone-wrong had burst into public view when the woman with whom he'd been having an affair—a fellow detective's wife, no less—had hanged herself in his office. In police headquarters, in downtown Nashville. The fact that the dead woman had been an aspiring country singer on the verge of making it big added to the drama. So did the fact that the woman had left behind not a suicide note, but a videotape. The footage included sensational shots of herself and Steve Calhoun, her husband's lifelong best friend as well as fellow detective, in the throes of some very steamy sex. On a desktop, in the selfsame office in which she'd taken her life. According to the tape, she had killed herself when he'd broken off their adulterous affair.

TV had loved it. The papers had loved it. The story had even found its way into the *National Enquirer.*

Steve Calhoun had gotten his proverbial fifteen minutes of fame with a vengeance.

"Yeah, well, don't believe everything you hear. About half the stuff that was flying around then wasn't true."

"You mean half was?" Summer couldn't help it. The question just popped out.

The look he shot her was withering. "Don't be a wiseass, Rosencrans. I don't like wiseasses."

"Ooo, you're scaring me."

"Good. I like you better scared. At least you keep your mouth shut."

"And my name's not Rosencrans. It's McAfee. Summer McAfee. Lem Rosencrans and I are divorced."

"Smart guy."

"If I remember my scandals correctly, you got fired after—all that came out. So you're not a cop. Not even kind of. Not anymore. And certainly not in Murfreesboro. Which translates to, I'm out of here."

"Go on, Rosencrans. Try to leave. Make my day."

She looked at him. He looked back. Dirty Harry couldn't have topped that look—and Dirty Harry had had the use of both eyes. Folding her arms over her breasts, Summer made a huffing sound, leaned a shoulder against the van—and stayed.

"Glad to know you're not as dumb as you look."

Summer chose to ignore that. "So what were you doing on an embalming table in a funeral home in the middle of the night, anyway?"

"Haven't you ever heard of Harmon Brothers' early-bird special? Come in before you're dead, and they give you half off all their services."

"Ha-ha."

"I like a woman who laughs at my jokes."

Summer shot him a killing glance. It appeared to leave him unfazed.

"I'm serious. How did you get there? Were you in an accident, or what?"

"An accident. Right." He snorted. "Your friends beat the bejesus out of me, doused me with kerosene, and were firing up the crematorium in my honor when you decided to check my pulse. Good thing my head's harder than they thought, or by now my ass would've been french-fried."

"I keep telling you, they're not my friends. I don't have the faintest idea who they are." The unusual volume of the funeral home's air-conditioning was suddenly explained. The increasing roar hadn't been her imagination at all, but the crematorium being fired up. Summer recalled that it was located right next to the embalming room and shivered inwardly.

"You know, I almost believe you."

"Glad to know you're not as dumb as you look." This comeback earned her an acknowledging glint. "So who are *they*? The men who did this?"

"You tell me."

Summer drew in a deep breath. "Forget it. Just forget it. I don't care. If they're trying to kill *you,* they're probably the good guys. Anyway, they've got my vote. And now I'm going home."

She pushed away from the van in anticipation of doing just that —a walk of sixteen or so miles with only one shoe was nothing compared to the aggravation of remaining in his presence for another second, and the way she felt at that moment if he tackled her, he'd get his daylights punched out—only to have him rise to his full height and block her way.

"Rosencrans. Uh-uh."

"Go screw yourself, Frankenstein." She tried to dodge past him, only to be stopped by his hand on her arm.

"Frankenstein?" He—almost—sounded like he was on the verge of laughing.

"It's what you look like. And let go of my arm."

"Not—" He broke off, arrested. Summer heard it too: the thick, beaten-air sound of helicopter blades.

"A chopper." His voice was hard suddenly. The hand that gripped her arm tightened until it hurt. "Get in the van! Go!"

Summer had no choice. Before she could move, he grabbed her by the waist, lifted her off her feet, and practically threw her through the van's open door.

"Jesus, what do you weigh?" he panted, swarming in after her and using a hand on her rump to shove her off the passenger seat, where she had landed on all fours.

"Are you always this obnoxious, or are you making a special effort just for me?" Summer hit the floor between the seats with a force that sent a stab of pain through her right knee. Her left knee was spared simply because it didn't quite touch the ground. There wasn't room.

"Get down!"

The door slammed shut. He was on top of her, squashing her into the narrow space between the seats, covering her body with his. Summer lay half on her side, in miserable discomfort, suffocating from the smell of him, the heat of his body, his weight.

"You're not exactly a featherweight yourself, you know," she growled, trying to extricate herself and ending up flat on her back.

"Pure muscle. And everybody knows that muscle weighs more than fat."

"Yeah, right."

This time Summer was sure of his grin as the interior of the van was suddenly flooded with bright light. What on earth . . . ? A searchlight. Of course, the helicopter was equipped with a searchlight. Was it a *police* helicopter, then? Had someone heard the gunfire and dialed 911? If so, they were saved! All they had to do was jump out and flag it down! From the sound of it, it was almost directly overhead.

"It could be the police!" Summer wriggled and squirmed, trying to work free without success. Though he stayed atop with the tenacity of a barnacle, she did manage to inch backward till she reached the center of the van, where she lay panting on her back in the narrow space left between two stacks of cargo piled chest-high against either wall. Her flailing arms dislodged a furniture blanket, which slid over them with the suddenness of a dropped curtain. Instantly they were cocooned in suffocating darkness.

"Could be." His breath surged warm and moist against her neck as she clawed the musty-smelling blanket away from her face. Drawing in a lungful of fresh air, she shoved at his shoulder. He didn't budge. His chest crushed her breasts and his legs were heavy as logs against hers. He was as hard, and heavy, as a piece of furniture.

"Let me up! We need to make sure—and flag it down, if it's the police!" Her struggle to get loose only tangled the blanket more closely around them. Only her head and her arms were free. She tugged vainly at the heavy gray folds.

"I don't think you quite get the picture, Rosencrans. We—"

The implosion of the windshield interrupted him. Pebbles of glass ricocheted through the van like BBs outfitted with turbochargers. Summer cringed as they *ping*ed and rattled all around her. One stung her neck and she flinched, crying out.

Frankenstein cursed, wrapping his body more closely about hers, pulling the blanket over their heads. Suddenly she was extremely glad of his solid bulk atop her and the protection of the blanket.

The passenger window shattered as what sounded like a hailstorm pounded the sides and roof of the van. Whoever was in the helicopter was shooting at them. Definitely not the police.

"Who are those guys?" she moaned as kaleidoscopic visions of the cut-down-by-a-barrage-of-gunfire end of *Butch Cassidy and the Sundance Kid* danced in her brain.

To which he replied, "You tell me."

Under any other circumstances, she would have hit him. But it occurred to her with terrifying clarity that just at that moment he was all that stood—or lay, to be precise—between her and a bullet. Lots of bullets.

She didn't hit him. Instead she made herself into as small a package as possible, and lay very, very still. He curled protectively above her, shielding as much of her body as he could.

As suddenly as it had begun, the hailstorm ceased. After a moment, cautiously, Frankenstein stuck his head out of the blanket.

To Summer's relief, the light had vanished. The night was as dark and quiet as death.

Summer shivered at the comparison.

"You okay?" He was breathing heavily.

"Y-yeah." Except for the fact that her teeth chattered.

"We've got to get out of here," he said, dragging himself off her and throwing the blanket aside. He hauled her up with him by hooking a hand in the waistband of her slacks just above her belly button and lifting.

"Let go!" She batted his hand away even as he thrust her into the driver's seat. Glass was everywhere. She was sitting on a small mountain of it, and as she realized that she popped up again, mentally thanking God for the new tempered windshields. If they had been in an older vehicle, they would have been cut to smithereens by flying shards. With a series of quick swipes, she brushed most of the glass off her seat.

"Quit worrying about your butt and drive!" He thrust her back down and reached over to yank the transmission into reverse. The van didn't move.

"Why don't you?"

"Because when I can see at all I'm seeing double, triple of everything. Besides, you're good at it. You got us this far, didn't you?" He jammed his foot down on the gas. For no more than an instant the wheels spun furiously, and then the van shot backward.

"I'll drive!" Summer grabbed the wheel.

"That's a good girl." He was grinning, if she cared to term that teeth-baring, lopsided twist of his battered face a grin. Funny how unafraid she now was of him. He might look like he belonged in a horror movie, he might have hurt and threatened and scared her out of five years' sleep, but she knew as well as she knew her own name that Frankenstein wasn't going to murder her—though thanks to him someone else just might.

"We make a pretty good team, don't you think?" He shifted into drive and stomped on the accelerator. The van hurtled forward. Warm, bug-laden night air rushed in through the hole where the windshield had been. For one dreadful, pixilated moment Summer thought they were going to crash into the combine again.

Just in time she yanked the wheel to the right, and the behemoth's yellow metal framework flashed by.

"Good reflexes," he approved.

"Get your foot off the damned gas!"

If he heard that, he ignored it. They barreled over the uneven surface of the field, heading—Summer hoped—toward the hole in the fence through which they had originally crashed. The cornstalks formed a shifting curtain obstructing her view. The van mowed them down. Before its onslaught, they fell like dominoes.

Bursting through to the soybean field was a relief. At least she could see. The hole in the fence was there, to the left. With his foot on the gas they only partly made it, taking out another six feet or so of board fencing as they plowed through.

In the morning, there was going to be one hopping-mad farmer hereabouts.

But that wasn't her problem. Her problem—at least her immediate problem—was the lead-footed lunatic beside her. And the bullet-spitting helicopter that lurked somewhere out there in the wild, midnight-blue yonder. And the goons with guns.

And the eighteen-wheeler that roared straight toward them down Route 231.

"Get your foot off the gas!" she screeched again, even as they hit the ditch and were airborne. The van landed with a bounce on the blacktop—not a hundred feet in front of the oncoming truck. The wheel was yanked out of her hands. The van fishtailed. An air horn shrieked. Brakes screeched. Headlights blinded. Summer shut her eyes. As if her ears were registering sounds in slow motion, she heard the squealing, rending, thudding sounds of a crash.

"Jesus, you are one lousy driver."

Summer opened her eyes to find that they were still alive, still on the road, and speeding toward town. Gasping, she glanced in the driver's side mirror—the rearview mirror had perished along with the windshield—to find that the eighteen-wheeler now rested at a crazy angle in the ditch beside the road. Even as she watched, its door opened and the driver popped out.

He was shaking his fist and shouting after them.

"You almost got us killed!" Her voice was shrill, the glance she sent Steve Calhoun wildly accusing.

"Listen, Rosencrans, if we don't get the hell out of here, we *are* going to get killed. What do you think that was back there, a drive-by shooting?"

For once in her life, Summer was bereft of speech.

CHAPTER EIGHT

In minutes they were streaking toward another intersection, fortunately as deserted as the last. Murfreesboro was straight ahead, Nashville to the northwest, Chattanooga to the southeast. If they made a 360-degree turn, 231 headed straight into Alabama behind them. Since they were running at ninety-plus miles an hour on a road where the posted speed limit was forty-five, straight ahead seemed the best option. If possible, Summer preferred to avoid any more incidental brushes with death.

"Hang a left," he directed.

Toward Nashville, not Murfreesboro. Of course he meant to send them skidding on two wheels through that intersection, probably just for the heck of it. One thing she had already begun to suspect about Steve Calhoun: Like the young turks from *Top Gun,* he felt the need for speed.

"What, are you homesick?" She couldn't resist the jibe.

"Funny, Rosencrans. Just do what I tell you."

"Get your foot off the gas!"

He ignored her. The van rocketed toward the intersection at
what felt like warp speed. When she made no immediate move to
send them into a death-defying skid, he grabbed for the wheel.
Summer batted away his hand—and got mad. Reaching down, she
pinched the bare, bruised, hairy thigh closest to her so viciously
that he screamed.

And jerked his leg to safety. With his foot removed from the
gas, the van immediately began to slow.

"What the hell was that for?" He rubbed his thigh and glared at
her.

"I told you to get your foot off the gas. *I'm* driving, remember?"
Summer's foot was already firmly in possession of the pedal. Her
glance dared him to try to do anything about it.

"Vicious bitch." He rubbed his thigh some more. "Jesus, that
hurt. Hang a left!"

"I'm going to!" She did, applying the brakes judiciously until
they were safely through the intersection. Then, with a wary eye on
his lead foot, she accelerated northwest on 41.

Rolling fields of crops separated by wire-and-post fences and
the occasional stand of leafy trees flashed past. Warm air spiced
with insects peppered her face. The smell of manure was strong.
Propelled by the wind, a large bug went splat against her cheek.
Summer swiped at its slimy corpse with an expression of loathing.

"You do realize that there are bad men with guns chasing us,
don't you? If we don't go real fast, they're going to catch up."

"Oh, shut up." But Summer pressed a little harder on the gas,
and watched the needle creep toward ninety. Squinting against the
wind and the bugs, she strained to see the blacktop as it wound its
way into the equally black night.

"There's a gravel road up here somewhere that we need to find.
On the right. As dark as it is, it's going to be easy to miss."

"Maybe we should turn on the lights."

"Jesus, Rosencrans, you still don't get it, do you? We are trying
our damnedest to hide from men who want to kill us. That helicopter didn't just vanish into thin air, you know. Something made
it back off—maybe it saw the semi coming, or maybe there was
something else. But you can bet your bippy that it's looking for us

now. No telling how many cars are swarming out of Murfreesboro, and maybe from Nashville too, and God knows where else, after us. We don't have much time before they're all over this area like ants at a picnic. And you want to turn on the lights?" He shook his head. "Not smart."

"What did you do?" Summer asked in a hushed voice.

Frankenstein snorted. "Let's just say I got the wrong people totally pissed off, okay?"

"Who?"

"Look, does it make any difference? All you need to know is that whoever is after me is after you too, and they aren't real nice folks."

Oh, God. She'd already had ample evidence of that. "As soon as I get home, I'm going to fire some people," Summer muttered.

"What?"

"Never mind."

"Damn it, Rosencrans, I think you just passed the turn-off! Do you have to talk every blasted second?"

A distant sound could have been helicopter blades. They both strained to identify it over the rushing wind. Any reply Summer might have made vanished from her consciousness in that instant. Remembering the recent fusillade of bullets with which the helicopter had savaged the van sent a tingle of fear zooming along Summer's spine. With a single scared glance at the man beside her, Summer stood on the brakes, turned the van in a wide, bumpy circle that flattened grass on the far side of the pavement, and headed back the other way. Only slower. Where was that road?

"There! See?" He pointed.

Summer saw what looked like tire tracks cutting through knee-high grass to a wire fence, where they ended at a wide black ditch. In the dark it was difficult to be certain, but if this was his escape route, it sure was a short one.

"Are you sure?" Skepticism underlay the question.

"Pull off, will ya?"

From the sound of it, the helicopter, if helicopter indeed it was, was getting closer. With an inward prayer, Summer turned off the road onto the tire tracks. The van lurched over ruts and bumps.

Of necessity, she stopped the van about fifteen feet in, at the edge of the ditch, which now appeared more like a yawning gulley.

"What are you stopping for?"

"Possibly it's escaped your notice, but there's a ditch in front of us. Now what?"

"It's a cow-crossing, Rosencrans."

"Would you stop calling me that? My name is Summer *McAfee*."

Summer peered through the open windshield as she spoke. Now that she looked closer, she saw that the moonlight gleamed dully off black, evenly spaced iron bars that formed a ground level bridge over the chasm. As a born and bred country girl, she should have guessed. With fencing on either side, without the cattle guard there would have been a gate. Feeling foolish, she drove over it without a word.

Once across, the road surface did not improve. The van dipped and shuddered, following the scarcely visible trail to the far edge of the field, which was marked by more fencing that separated the pasture from what appeared to be dense woods.

The helicopter, if indeed it had been a helicopter, was very far in the distance now. Summer could barely hear it.

"Where are we going?"

"To a place I know."

"What kind of place?"

"Just drive, would you? Jesus. Do you yammer like this all the time?"

"Screw you, Frankenstein."

"Maybe later. When we have more time."

"In your wildest dreams."

"Rosencrans, believe me, my wildest dreams don't include you. More like naked blond triplets with forty-inch chests."

"I believe it."

"You should. It's true. Look out! That's a cow!"

Summer hit the brakes. There was, indeed, a cow, lying right smack in the middle of the path, placidly chewing its cud. A Black Angus, to be precise, which was a valuable beef animal the color of night. Only its moist eyes reflecting the moonlight revealed its presence. If Frankenstein hadn't seen it, she would have run right over it. Or into it. Somehow she didn't think the van would have made it past that cow. It was a very large cow.

"Drive around it." He spoke impatiently.

"What if we get stuck? Who knows what kind of condition this field's in? Get out and shoo the thing off the track."

"And give you the chance to drive off and leave me here? Uh-uh. No way."

Since that was precisely the thought that had niggled, just momentarily, at the edge of Summer's mind, she didn't say anything. Instead she honked the horn. The cow didn't budge. Frankenstein grabbed her wrist.

"Jesus, Rosencrans! Why don't you just send up smoke signals to tell them where we are while you're at it?"

"The name's *McAfee*. And I didn't think of that." She had been too busy pondering the pros and cons of abandoning him.

"I believe it." The way he said it, it wasn't a compliment. Summer yanked her wrist from his grasp.

A car whizzed past on Highway 41, headed for Nashville, its headlights slicing through the night. It was going way too fast. Summer tensed, and glanced over at the man beside her.

"Drive around it," he said again. Her suspicion as to the car's mission was reflected in his voice.

Without another word she drove around the cow, dodged a Grand Canyon–size rut and two of the cow's fellows lounging nearby, and bumped back onto the track. Another cattle grate marked the boundary between the pasture and the woods. As the van rocked across it, the sound that might have been a helicopter grew louder again. By the time they were under the leafy canopy, there was no longer any room for doubt. Their pursuer was back, almost directly overhead.

"Stop. It's more likely to see us if we move."

Summer stepped on the brake. The helicopter dropped low, its searchlight raking the field through which they had just passed. Summer turned in her seat just in time to see the cow they had dodged caught in its beam. The helicopter had more success than the van. With a spooked moo, the creature got to its feet and

galloped toward the opposite end of the pasture. The searchlight
followed it, flashing on a wave of heaving black hides as panic
infected the rest of the herd. For a moment the helicopter
hovered. The searchlight panned the field, illuminating grass and
milling, mooing animals. As suddenly as it had arrived the helicopter rose, turned, and headed north.

"That was close," Summer said. Sweat beaded her back, making
the cheap nylon blouse cling uncomfortably to her skin.

"Too close." He sounded a whole heck of a lot cooler than she
felt. "Come on, let's go."

Summer drove on, hands clenched around the wheel as the van
bumped and rocked down the rutted track. Highway 41 was left
miles behind, and the woods thinned out. Another cattle crossing,
another field, and they pulled out onto blacktop. Against the background of starry sky, slumbering farmhouses dotted the landscape.

Call her paranoid, but the mere act of emerging from beneath
the shelter of the trees onto a real road made Summer start to
sweat again. Fortunately the road appeared deserted, and, strain
though she would, she could detect no trace of sound to indicate
that the helicopter was nearby.

"Left," he directed.

Summer obeyed, then took a deep breath. A moth flew in her
mouth. She gagged and spat, finally succeeding in getting it out.

"Bugs are an acquired taste, I believe," he said.

"Like them, do you?" Disgusted, she wiped the moth-parts-
laden spittle from her chin.

"De-licious. Especially panfried . . ." He smacked his swollen
lips appreciatively.

"You're gross, do you know that?"

"I try." This was said with suitable modesty.

Summer didn't deign to reply. A few minutes later, she spoke
again.

"Don't you think we ought to stop somewhere and call the
police?"

He laughed.

"We could even stop at one of these farmhouses. I'm sure if we
knocked, they'd let us use the phone."

"I hate to burst your bubble, Rosencrans, but who do you think is chasing us?"

"What?"

"Yep."

Summer sputtered. "That's not possible. They shot at us. They were trying to kill us."

"See why honest citizens are always bitching about police brutality?"

That wasn't funny. "You're joking, right?"

"Uh-uh."

"Oh, my God!"

"My sentiments exactly."

Summer cast him a wild-eyed glance. "There's got to be some mistake. Sammy may have a prick for a son, but he wouldn't let his men shoot at innocent people!" A thought occurred to her. "All right, so maybe you're not so innocent. He still wouldn't let them just kill you!"

"Old Rosey may not know."

"You mean they're doing this without the proper authority? Then all we have to do is go straight to Sammy—I know where he lives—he'll put a stop to—"

"Whoa, Rosencrans!" This was said as Summer looked for a place to turn around. "Not so fast. It's not that easy. The problem is, at this point we can't trust anybody. Not even your esteemed father-in-law. Somebody—lots of somebodies—want me real dead. I'm just not entirely sure who, or why. But one thing I am sure of is this: Whoever it is won't twitch a whisker at killing you, too."

"You don't even know why they're shooting at you?" Summer was aghast.

Frankenstein shook his head. "Not—exactly." He hesitated, and shot her a glance. "A few years ago I stumbled onto something—something big. Then—everything happened, and detective work was suddenly the last thing on my mind. But I've had a lot of time to think since—hell, I haven't done much of anything else lately—and I came back to check something out. Tonight I got a little careless, and they caught me at it. And they did their level best to kill me."

"Who?" It was almost a moan.

"I told you, I don't know. Not for sure. It might not be the police, exactly. Maybe just one or two rogue cops are involved. But there's something going on, some kind of very large criminal operation. I was watching some kind of deal go down in the cemetery beside the funeral home just before I got hit over the head."

"Oh, my God!" Summer pictured herself scrubbing on, all unknowing, while mayhem and murder took place just yards away. Ghosts would have been preferable.

"Pull in here." The van had just topped a rise, and traveled about a quarter of a mile past a squat white clapboard farmhouse. The "here" Frankenstein indicated was another rutted track, but this time Summer turned onto it with alacrity. Visions of hostile cars swarming like army ants across the region's roadways took firm possession of her imagination. The helicopter had appeared to be following the highways, too. Under those conditions, the farm track they were bumping over suddenly seemed like a positive haven. When they once again pulled out onto blacktop, she felt her stomach clench.

"Turn left."

They topped another rise. On the other side, down in a bowl-like valley, tall pines swayed and smooth dark water gleamed in the moonlight.

"Where are we?" It was the first thing she had said for at least ten minutes.

He glanced at her. "Cedar Lake. Take a right at the next intersection."

Summer did, and found herself confronting seedy civilization: a motel advertising rooms for twenty-four dollars a night, a McDonald's, closed at this hour, another motel enticing travelers with "Free Cable!," a run-down outlet mall. A gas station/mini-mart at an intersection appeared to be the only establishment that was open. A single car waited in its parking lot. Next door, a grassy area with uprooted trees and idle heavy equipment spoke of ongoing construction. After that the road curved, following the contours of the lake.

"Turn in here." He indicated a wide, paved driveway that led up to a fenced enclosure. A double row of long, one-story warehouses made of corrugated metal was enclosed by the fence, which was at least nine feet tall and topped by a triple strand of barbed wire. The gate at the top of the driveway was equally tall and equally buttressed, and, unless he was a better climber than she was, impregnable.

"Punch in nine-one-two-eight."

The van had stopped at the gate. At Frankenstein's instruction, Summer glanced in the direction he pointed, to discover a black metal box on a pole. The box vaguely resembled a telephone without a receiver. Like a telephone, it had a number pad.

Rolling down her window—it seemed ridiculous to have to roll down a window when the rest of the van was open to the night, but hers was the sole survivor—Summer punched in the four digits. Faint beeps sounded as she touched each number. When she was done, she stared at the box expectantly. Nothing happened.

"What are you waiting for?"

At Frankenstein's impatient question, Summer glanced around to discover that the seemingly impregnable gate was swinging open.

CHAPTER NINE

The boatyard hadn't changed. As far as Steve could tell, not so much as a tossed Coke can had been moved in three years. The rusted-out pickup loaded with odds and ends parked alongside the aged Winnebago that its owner still hadn't found time to restore, the oceans of old rubber tires that somebody meant to use someday for something, the seen-better-days boats with hopeful FOR SALE signs in the windows were the same, or the originals' twins. As always, a few cars belonging to weekend boaters were parked beside the warehouses. Acres of rusty barrels still stood sentinel along the fence. As the van rolled through the gates and up the incline toward where the ground leveled off at the back, Steve was struck by such a strong sense of déjà vu that he was dizzy.

It was as if the world had suddenly spun many revolutions backward, and everything was as it had been before. Before Deedee had killed herself, and pretty much ended his life, too. When Deedee died, he lost not only her but his job, his wife, his daughter, and his best friend all in one dreadful stroke. He broke his parents' hearts; his father died of a heart attack six months later. He lost the respect of nearly everyone who knew him. He lost his own self-respect. Then, in trying to eradicate the pain with booze, he almost lost himself.

Deedee had been blond and pretty and about as big as a mosquito, and he had known her since she was thirteen. He and Mitch had met her at the same time, at the Dairy Queen where all the kids hung out. Since the place was crowded, choice of seating had been limited. He and Mitch had spotted a couple of empty stools at the counter, and he had sat down with scarcely a glance at the frizzy-haired blonde on the next stool. Her ice-cream sundae—hot fudge, his favorite—was served just as he sat, and that was what caught his attention. He must have been eyeing the confection hungrily, because she glanced up at him, smiled, and offered him a bite on a spoon. Surprised to find himself staring into a pretty elfin face with cerulean eyes and a wicked smile, he barely was able to summon the presence of mind to open his mouth. Deedee popped the ice cream in—and looked past him at Mitch. In that instant he lost her to his best friend.

Not that it was any big surprise. Every girl they ever met immediately looked past him at Mitch. Mitch was taller, leaner, smoother, handsomer. Girls were bowled over by him. Steve had gotten used to that by the end of first grade.

But there'd been something about Deedee—he'd minded, sort of, about Deedee. He never had been able to figure out why. There'd been prettier girls. And a whole heck of a lot of "nicer" ones. Deedee had liked to party, and when she drank she got even wilder than she was by nature. Maybe that was what had appealed to him so about her: her wildness. Fear was as foreign as Shanghai to Deedee, while his own natural disposition was about as far from wild as it was possible to get.

"Good old Steve," Mitch had always called him, with a clap on the shoulder and a hint of affectionate contempt. Good old Steve: that was him, all right. Always keeping doggedly to the path, always doing what was right and expected, always uncomplainingly pulling Mitch out of the frequent peccadilloes he fell into. Who had almost gotten caught replacing the American flag Mitch had stolen from atop the high school when they were teenagers? Good old Steve. Who had spent countless Sundays completing due-on-Monday assignments for both of them when Mitch had been too hung over from partying the night before to get out of bed? Good old Steve. Who had covered for Mitch with Deedee when Mitch had sneaked out with other girls behind her back, even after Mitch and Deedee were married? Good old Steve.

When he had joined the marines, he had taken their motto to heart: *Semper fidelis.* Always faithful. In his friendships, in his work, in his marriage. That was him. Good old Steve.

Until one day he wasn't faithful anymore. One day he succumbed to the lure of cheap booze and his best friend's unhappy wife and balled Deedee's brains out. That had been the beginning of the end.

Or maybe the end of the beginning. Because now he was back, like a risen Lazarus, to try to reassemble the pieces of his shattered life.

It had taken him three years, but he had finally seen it: the flaw in the scenario investigators had painted of the way Deedee had died.

She'd hanged herself in his office early one Sunday morning. His office, which he locked each night as faithfully as he did everything else. His office, to which Deedee had not had a key.

How had she gotten in?

"What is this place?" The question jolted Steve out of his reverie. Glancing over at the woman beside him, he was instantly reminded of the deadly turn his life had taken. Thanks to the double vision resulting from the beating they'd given him, he saw two of her, two blurry images that swayed apart and then together, threatened to merge and then split again. Two hazel-eyed, brown-haired, big-titted women whose features he had not yet managed to get a real good fix on. Two innocent bystanders who might still die tonight because of him. Or two supremely clever liars. He still hadn't one hundred percent made up his mind which.

Though no crook he had ever run into had yakked that much.

While one small, objective part of his brain hoped he didn't have a concussion, the rest of his intellect (which admittedly was not quite firing on all cylinders right at that moment) wrestled with what to do. There were options, he knew there had to be, but he couldn't think straight with his head pounding and the swelling that had once been his face throbbing and every muscle in his body feeling like it had been worked over with a tire iron—which wasn't particularly surprising considering that most of them had. The only solution that occurred to him was classic in its simplicity: Get the hell out of Dodge.

"I asked you, what is this place?"

For a moment there, Steve had almost forgotten his companion. "Boat warehouse."

"*Boat* warehouse? What the heck is a boat warehouse?"

The woman was a *talker*. Practically the only time she had shut up all night was when she'd been unconscious. If she wasn't careful, the thought just might give him ideas.

"A warehouse where they keep boats." If it hadn't hurt so much to wrinkle his forehead, he would have scowled at her.

"Oh, thanks. That tells me a lot."

Steve gave up. Clearly he was not going to be able to intimidate her with his facial expressions—a technique he had used before with good results—when he couldn't even move his face. "It's used for off-season storage. For people who don't want to keep their boats in the water year-round. It should be pretty much deserted this time of year."

"Do you keep a boat here?"

"A friend does. In winter. Right now, he's probably got it docked in front of his cabin on Cedar Lake."

"Is that where you're headed? To your friend's?"

Steve gave an unamused chuckle and for the moment ignored her hopeful use of the singular pronoun. "Rosencrans, at this point I'm not sure I *have* any friends. Stop up here in front of that last building, would you? If we're real lucky, they still keep the spare key in the same place."

Man, he hurt all over. Sliding out of the van—she couldn't go off and leave him because of the locked gate—he did his best to ignore the assorted stabs and twinges that assailed him when he moved. The charley horse in his thigh had hurt like the very devil, but it seemed to be easing up. The main thing was, no bones seemed to be broken—unless his skull was cracked, which, if the way it ached was any indication, it might well be.

Back about five years ago, Mitch had bought a thirty-two-foot Chris-Craft cabin cruiser for fifteen hundred dollars. Top of the line. Slept six. Mitch crowed about the great price, which Steve had agreed it was—just like Mitch to get the deal of the century— until he found out that the damned thing was thirty years old, made of wood, and didn't run. A classic, Mitch called it. Just needed to be restored. Guess who'd spent weekends and after hours for eighteen solid months helping his buddy replace boards and paint and tinker with the engine?

Yep. Good old Steve.

At Deedee's funeral, Steve had felt like the lowest worm alive. He could picture Mitch the way he'd looked that day, eyes red-rimmed from weeping, shoulders heaving in his dark suit, head bowed. Mitch's mother had stood beside him, clutching her fair-haired boy's arm. It had been January, and it was cold out. The wind was blowing. The sky was aluminum foil gray. There'd been hundreds of mourners at the graveside service—nothing attracted a crowd like scandal. Grief- and guilt-racked, Steve had been un-able to stay away. After the coffin was lowered into the frozen earth—a white sifting of frost lay like lace over the raw sides of the open grave where Deedee was laid to rest; he could picture the scene still—the mourners had started to disperse. Mitch was turn-ing away when Steve walked up to him. Hat in hand, his own eyes unfocused from sorrow and shame and lack of sleep, he'd meant to offer his friend an apology, condolences, his head on a plate if Mitch wanted it. Anything. He'd done wrong, but he'd never meant for Deedee to die.

For a second he stood right in front of Mitch. His best friend looked at him, simply looked at him, ignoring his outstretched hand, his stumbling words. The classically handsome face, the eyes of choirboy blue, could have been painted plaster for all the emo-tion they showed. Then Mitch's mother—he'd known her practi-cally all his life, too, and would have sworn she considered him almost a second son—put a hand on Mitch's arm, and the pair of them turned and walked away as if Steve were invisible.

A rebuke well deserved.

From that day to this, he hadn't set eyes on Mitch.

Two days after the funeral, he was fired. For conduct unbecoming a police officer. The following Saturday, while he was still asleep, his wife took their little girl and left. In the note he found stuck to the refrigerator, she informed him that she was filing for divorce.

His life was shattered. In the space of a week, everything that had made it worth living was gone.

The thought of putting his pistol in his mouth and pulling the trigger crossed his mind. As a solution, it would be both simple and effective. Oblivion would be a welcome end to his wrenching pain. But one day someone would tell his little girl what he had done. To be known as the daughter of an adulterous, scandal-ridden, disgraced cop was bad enough. To have her grow up as the daughter of a suicide would be worse. He could not do it to her.

He had done wrong, and he was being punished. Though he was no believer in karma, karma was exactly what it was. He deserved to lose his little girl, his wife, his best friend, his job. He deserved to lose his life, too, at least figuratively. Deedee had lost hers.

Which was why he hadn't fought, not his firing, nor his wife's petition for divorce and request for sole custody of their daughter. He'd signed every frigging paper they'd put in front of him, sent support checks for three frigging years, without complaint.

Because he'd known the punishment, the pain, had been earned.

With everything gone, he hit the road. That first night, in a cheap motel, he started to drink. He more or less stayed drunk for the better part of the next two and a half years.

Medicating the pain.

He had screwed around with his best friend's wife. He had done what, among guys, was absolutely taboo.

When he had regained his senses and told Deedee that he just couldn't do that to Mitch anymore, she'd pitched a fit. Deedee had been a pro at pitching fits. But he had never, ever once entertained the thought that she might kill herself. Deedee? Over him? Get real.

But she had. Jesus. But he had no answer—yet—to the riddle of how she had gotten into his office, to which she didn't possess a key.

The key to the warehouse was right where it had always been. Steve withdrew it from its hiding place, unlocked the door, and, not without some difficulty, shoved the rusty metal panel aside.

Just like the old days. When he glanced around, he almost expected to see Mitch grinning behind him. Grinning because, as always, Steve was doing the grunt work.

Or Deedee, who had accompanied them to the boatyard a lot.

But wait. Deedee *was* there. Her tiny, frizzy-haired frame seemed to materialize right in front of the van's smashed-in nose. For a fraction of an instant, no longer than the twinkle of a star, Steve could see her. She waved at him, waggling the red-painted fingers of her right hand just like she always did.

Then she was gone.

Steve blinked, shook his head to clear it, and stared at the spot where she had been. Of course she was gone. She'd never been there in the first place. The blows to his head were causing him to hallucinate, or something.

Weird.

Just like life was weird.

CHAPTER TEN

As Frankenstein fiddled around, Summer entertained the idea of gunning the van backward and leaving him to his fate, but the memory of the closed gate dissuaded her. Mainly because she couldn't remember the code, and he would almost certainly catch up to her while she sat in front of the gate frantically punching in numbers at random.

Besides, in the van she would be a marked woman. Whoever was searching for them knew the vehicle well.

A garage-sized door slid sideways, opening up the warehouse. Frankenstein turned, stared at the van for a moment as if lost in thought, then shook his head and beckoned her in.

She drove past him. Inside, the warehouse was as dark as a coal cellar. The darkness became inpenetrable as the door rattled shut behind the van. She couldn't see as far in front of her as the steering wheel. Under the circumstances, Summer dared to turn on the headlights. The beam illuminated a vast, echoing space, perhaps one and a half stories tall and about half the length of a football field. To her left loomed a large half-painted boat perched on a peeling trailer. A single lightbulb sprang to life as she braked the van. The bulb dangled from the ceiling by a cord.

Perhaps half a dozen boats ranging in size from an open runabout to the large cabin cruiser to her left were parked at random intervals inside. With the door closed, not even the warehouse's vast size could keep it from feeling cozy. For the first time in what felt like forever, Summer was reasonably confident that she was physically safe. The tension ebbed from her body like water going down a drain.

She slid the transmission into park, turned off the key, then leaned her head against the back of the seat. Allowing herself to go limp was such a relief.

Behind her, the double doors at the rear of the van opened. Frankenstein, up to no good. There was a moment of silence, then a between-the-teeth kind of whistle.

Against her better judgment, Summer looked around.

Frankenstein's head and shoulders were silhouetted by the light outside the van. His expression was in shadow, but she did not need to see where his eyes rested to realize what had prompted that low whistle: The van's cargo was a pair of glossy gray coffins.

Oh, God.

With the concealing furniture blankets crumpled in the aisle between them, the coffins were so obvious that Summer had trouble believing that she had ever escaped seeing them. But darkness and urgency and fear combined must have blinded her to the reality of the shrouded rectangular shapes. Now the van's inside light was pitiless in its illumination.

Oh, God.

Of course the van must have been delivering coffins. Nothing odd about that. After all, its destination had been a funeral home.

Oh, God.

There was nothing so inherently horrible about coffins, she told herself. No need to hyperventilate over their mere presence. She had merely to think rationally, and compose her nerves.

Oh, God.

Frankenstein hoisted himself aboard the van from the rear.

Light poured through bullet holes in the roof and sides, reminding Summer of the pierced-tin Christmas ornaments her mother had bought in Mexico and used on their tree every year. Two webbed black straps ran through metal loops set into the sides of the van. The straps were secured around the coffins, presumably both to hold them closed and to keep them in place.

Oh, God.

"What are you doing?" she asked, horrified, as he began to unfasten the straps.

"Checking."

Checking what was the obvious next question, but Summer realized she didn't really want to know. Still, she could not help but watch with a certain fascinated dread as he freed first one strap and then the other. Then he lifted a lid.

The way her life was going lately, she should have been prepared. There was a corpse inside the coffin. A young man in a dark suit, hands crossed piously on his breast.

Oh, God.

Summer's eyes snapped shut. She felt ill.

"What are you moaning about now?" Frankenstein growled.

Summer's eyes opened, and she glanced around again. Big mistake. He had the lid up on the second coffin. It was as occupied as the first. This time the body was that of a young woman. College-age, perhaps, with long dark hair, decked out in a pretty floral dress with a lace collar.

Oh, God.

"We've got to take them back," she said with conviction.

"Yeah, right." He was staring down at the corpse.

"We do! This is—sacrilegious, or something. They're *dead*."

He shut the lid. "Better them than us."

"What are we going to do?"

"I vote for heading for Mexico."

"I mean about the—the bodies!"

He sighed. "You are a worrywart, aren't you?"

"I don't consider myself a worrywart just because I'm upset that you've stolen two dead bodies!"

"We, Rosencrans. The operative pronoun here is *we*." The

strangled sound she made earned her an irritated glance. "And for God's sake stop moaning, will ya?"

"I am not moaning!"

"Sounds like moaning to me." He turned and clambered out the back, shutting the double doors with a slam that rocked the van. Summer expected him to come around to her door—she expected him to do *something*—but as minutes passed and she saw neither hide nor hair of him it became increasingly obvious that he was no longer nearby.

Oh, God. Had something happened to him? Had the goons who were chasing them found them? Had they taken Frankenstein out when he jumped down from the van? Was he even now lying on the gravel nearby, blood bubbling from a cut throat, while his killers waited to claim their next victim—her?

Oh, God.

Or had his end been supernatural in origin? Maybe ghosts took a dim view of body snatchers.

Body snatchers. As she thought of herself in that light, Summer moaned again.

"You sound like a donkey with laryngitis." The door beside her opened without warning. Summer screeched, and shot sideways away from it like a sprung rubber band.

Frankenstein surveyed her from the open door.

"Where have you been?" she gasped.

"Nature called. Come on, get out. I've found us a new set of wheels."

"What?"

But he was already walking away from the van. His limping gait was surprisingly fast. Summer had to scramble to catch up with him.

"Wait—we can't just leave them."

"Who?"

"The bodies!"

"Why not?"

His tone was so indifferent that Summer sputtered. "Because— because we just can't."

"I don't see that we have much choice. Unless you want to

bring them with us. I always looked forward to going on a double date with a couple of stiffs. Or would you rather try to bury them? I hear grave-digging's hard work."

"Would you be serious?"

"I am being serious." A slight quirk at one end of his swollen mouth alerted her to the fact that he smiled suddenly. "Serious as a grave."

"Oh, ha-ha."

"Glad to see you've kept your sense of humor."

Summer didn't even bother to dignify that with an answer. "We've got to do *something*—at least call somebody and tell them where they—the bodies—are."

He snorted. "Why not just tell them where we are while we're at it?"

"We should call the police"—a sharp shake of his head vetoed that idea—"or Harmon Brothers," another shake of his head, "or *somebody.*"

Frankenstein shot her an impatient glance. "Those people in there are already dead, Rosencrans. You want to join them?"

Summer shook her head.

"Me neither. So we don't call anybody, understand? We just keep our mouths shut, our heads low, and hightail it out of the great state of Tennessee."

"But . . ." As Summer followed him through an ordinary-size door at the far end of the warehouse, he flicked off the light. The fresh night air struck her like a threat. Outside, she felt exposed. Vulnerable. She looked anxiously skyward, searching for any sign of the helicopter.

"Couldn't we just stay here until morning?" Her voice was so small that she barely recognized it as her own.

He shut the door and tested the knob to be sure it was locked. "What do you suppose is going to be different in the morning? Do you think the bad guys vanish in a puff of smoke at daybreak? Not hardly. The bad guys'll still be bad—and they'll still be searching for us. So shake your booty, Rosencrans."

"Would you quit calling me that?" She addressed the question to his back. He was already a dozen paces ahead. Summer hurried to catch up. "Damn it!"

"What're you swearing for?"

"Fun."

"Whatever turns you on." He stopped in front of an ancient-looking black car and bent, feeling beneath its massive front bumper. The sound of the hood popping open was as loud as a gunshot to Summer's sensitized ears.

"What are you doing?" Glancing around, Summer wrapped her arms over her chest. The night had grown cool, but she thought it was nerves rather than temperature that was the cause of her sudden chill.

He opened the hood wide, pulled a coil of wire obtained God knew where from the back pocket of his cutoffs, and bent over the car's yawning mouth. "Connecting the battery to the coil."

"Why?"

"Jesus, Rosencrans, don't you ever shut up? I need to concentrate here."

"So who's stopping you?" But after that she seethed in silence as, following a couple of apparent false starts that had him swearing under his breath, he wrapped one end of the wire around a battery post and threaded it down through the engine. He dropped to the ground, turned rather clumsily onto his back, and scooted under the car. Minutes and a ton more curse words later he was out again, grimacing as he clambered to his feet.

"Get in." He shut the hood.

"But . . ."

"Just do it, would you?" He came around the car, opened the driver's-side door, and stood waiting.

"But—this is somebody's car."

"No kidding."

"You're stealing it."

"I'm trying to. Only you keep talking."

"Stealing a car is against the law. You could go to jail. *We* could go to jail."

"Just get in the car, Rosencrans." An ominous glance warned her against continuing to argue. It was clear he wasn't in the right humor to appreciate dissent. Not without severe misgivings, Summer swallowed her objections and got in.

The interior of the car was clean. A baseball cap and a couple of textbooks in the backseat attested that its owner was probably a male high school or college student. At the thought of making off with some kid's car, Summer felt another pang of conscience.

"I don't think we should . . ." she began.

"Don't think, okay?"

He slammed the door behind her and leaned in the open window. Seen up close and personal, his face looked awful. It was impossible to tell whether, under normal conditions, he could be described as a handsome man. Summer tried to recall whether or not she had ever glimpsed a picture of Steve Calhoun, and failed. Surely the papers had carried photos of him, but she simply couldn't remember.

"Look, this is a '55 Chevy. We can start it without a key. I know, because I used to drive one when I was in high school. The transmission's in neutral. I want you to keep it in neutral till it starts picking up speed down the hill. Then shift into first."

"But . . ."

"Don't talk, Rosencrans, okay? Just do what I tell you. When we get a good clip going, shift into first. Simple."

"But . . ."

"I'm gonna be back here pushing. If we do it right, the engine'll turn over and we'll have wheels. Wheels that nobody knows we've got. We can just cruise right past 'em out of Dodge."

"I don't know how to drive a stick shift."

"What?" He looked at her as if she had suddenly started speaking in tongues.

"I don't know how to drive a stick shift. I learned to drive on an automatic, and that's all I've ever driven."

"Jesus." He rested his head against the top of the window, and closed his one good eye. A second later, he opened it again. "You're gonna have to learn. Right now."

"I've never been very mechanical . . ."

"The alternative is that *I* drive, and *you* push."

"Oh."

"Yeah, oh."

"I'll try."

"Great." He took a deep breath. "Okay, listen. All you have to do, when you get ready to shift into first, is depress the clutch pedal first. See that third pedal over there on the other side of your brake? *That's* the clutch. Step on it, shift into first"—he reached in front of her to demonstrate with the black-tipped handle that stuck out of the right side of the steering wheel—"just like this. Hit the pedal, move the stick up and forward. Easy. Try it."

Summer did.

"See?" he asked when she had performed to his satisfaction.

"Easy." If her voice lacked conviction he overlooked it.

"Good. Let's do it."

"Wait!" Summer hoped the panic that infused her voice was audible only to her own ears.

"Hit the clutch, shift into first." He was already walking around to the rear as he called to her.

With both hands on the wheel, Summer was once again tense as a crouched cat. Slowly, laboriously, the car started to move. Gravel crunched. She turned the wheel so that they were aiming toward the gate. The road leading to it was downhill all the way.

The car began to pick up speed.

"Now!" he yelled.

Move the stick up and forward—a hideous grinding noise—no, step on the clutch first and then . . . She did it. Through the rearview mirror, she saw that Frankenstein was lurching along in a lopsided jog behind the car. Then the engine coughed to life, capturing her attention.

Alone in an unmarked car, she drove straight on down to the gate.

CHAPTER ELEVEN

"Death—the last sleep? No, it is the
final awakening."

—Sir Walter Scott

Being a ghost was not a whole heck of a lot of fun.

Deedee felt as though she were being borne helplessly along by a swift river current. Once she had drifted outside the window, a mysterious force had caught her up, propelling her to destinations unknown at speeds so fast that the stars above and lights below had melded into a gigantic sun-streaked torrent. She bobbed up at scenes from her own life, not of her own will but for some reason she didn't yet understand. The tiny clapboard house where she had lived as a little girl. The high school where she'd been cheerleader. The recording studio where, two months before she had died, she'd gotten the chance to sing backup for Reba McEntire because the regular girl was sick.

The highlight of her life.

They'd said she was good, the people in the studio. That she had *some pipes.*

If she had lived, she might have been a star.

That was what she mourned most about her lost life, she realized. The waste of her God-given talent before it could be recognized. She had had the voice of a honky-tonk angel, yet precious few had ever known it.

A honky-tonk angel. If she was an angel at all, that was the kind she was.

But she didn't think she was an angel. She wasn't sure, of course, but when she thought of angels she thought of heavenly beings with golden halos floating over their heads and big white wings and harps.

Angelic angels. She'd been many things in life, but angelic wasn't one of them.

Did Heaven have an angel opening for a hard-drinking, fast-living hell-raiser with three-inch nails and blue jeans so tight it hurt her to sit?

Maybe. But it didn't seem likely.

Instead she thought she might be a ghost. As a kid, she'd always thought being a ghost might be kind of fun. Floating through darkened hallways, moaning in the middle of the night, moving things out of their accustomed place—just in general scaring the socks off people. Fun.

But if she was a ghost, ghosting wasn't all it was cracked up to be. For one thing, though she seemed to be able to materialize—at least, the warm tingling that every once in a while pervaded her being along with a sense of the matter that was her rushing together and becoming solid made her *feel* like she was materializing —she could not materialize at will.

She just popped up, like a jack-in-the-box, and vanished as quickly. Her mother had been sitting on the tattered tweed couch in the living room of the house where she had grown up, watching *Roseanne.* Deedee had recognized her mother, recognized the poor shabby room, even recognized the program—and felt the tingling. All of a sudden her mother's eyes had turned toward where Deedee floated by the rocking chair and grown huge. She had screamed—and fainted dead away.

Just about the reaction to be expected from someone who had seen a ghost.

Her old buddy Steve—what had happened to his face?—at least

he hadn't fainted when she'd felt the tingling again outside the boat-storage place. But he hadn't waved back, either, when she had tried a tentative greeting. Instead he'd just stared at her, real hard. Maybe he hadn't seen her at all. She couldn't be sure.

There wasn't much she could be sure about, anymore.

But she did know one thing: There was some tie, like a huge invisible rubber band, that bound her to earth. In order to get to heaven, she had to break the bond.

But first she had to figure out what the bond was.

CHAPTER TWELVE

If Summer had remembered the code, she would have been gone. Out of the whole mess and headed for home. As it was, she sat glowering at the closed gate until Frankenstein opened the passenger door and slid in, panting.

"Nine-one-two-eight," he said.

Sulkily Summer punched in the numbers. The gates swung apart, and the Chevy bucked through the opening like a spastic kangaroo.

"Damn it, when you let up on the brake, you have to hit the clutch first!"

"I told you I don't know how to drive a stick!"

Somehow she got the car smoothed out. A glance in the rear-view mirror showed her that the gates had closed behind them. In response to his gesture, she turned left onto the road, retracing their route back through the small town. The lights of the 7-Eleven glowed on the right. Apparently the store was true to its neon advertising: OPEN 24 HOURS A DAY!

"You got any money?" He felt in the pockets of his cutoffs and came up empty.

"No." They both knew where her money was. In her purse, waiting with her bucket and vacuum cleaner by the funeral home's front door.

"Check out the gas gauge."

There was a hair less than a quarter of a tank.

"That'll get us maybe eighty, ninety miles." He glanced at the 7-Eleven speculatively. Summer's blood went cold as she wondered if, horror of horrors, he was thinking about robbing the convenience store for gas money.

"I'm not going eighty miles." That glance of his was the last straw. She had had it. Absolutely had it. She was not being a party to anything else dangerous—or illegal.

He either missed or ignored the implication in her words. "Pull in, will ya?"

"No!" Summer almost shrieked, and stepped on the accelerator for emphasis. The Chevy sputtered twice, then spurted forward. "No, no, no!"

"A thousand times no?" He looked at her as if she had suddenly sprouted an extra nose. "What the hell's the matter with you?"

"I will not be a party to robbing a convenience store!"

"I wanted to stop so I could take the wire out of the engine!"

"No!"

They reached the intersection that led out of town. Just past the traffic light Summer saw a small white sign identifying the road: 266. She knew where she was!

"Hang a right."

She glanced both ways down the dark, deserted strip of highway —and turned left. Just in time she remembered to depress the clutch. The Chevy lurched, but kept going.

"Hey, I said hang a right."

"No."

"What do you mean, no?"

"I'm going home."

"*What?*"

"You heard me."

"You're going *home?*"

"That's right."

"You mean to Murfreesboro?"

"That's right."

"You've gotta be out of your effing mind!"

"I'm going home." Summer set her jaw, clamped her hands around the wheel, and refused to look at him.

"Do you have a death wish or are you just plain stupid? Murfreesboro is where the bad guys are, remember?"

"It's where the bad guys *were.* They're probably spread out all over this part of Tennessee by now, looking for us. Anyway, they're looking for the van. You said so yourself. They won't recognize this car if they drive right past us."

"Cut the crap, Rosencrans, and turn around."

"It's *McAfee,*" Summer growled. "And I'm going home! I refuse to be a part of this any longer! Whatever you're involved in, it has nothing to do with me. I was doing my job, minding my own business, when you kidnapped me. *I* had nothing to do with murdering that man back there at Harmon Brothers'. *I* had nothing to do with stealing the van. Or the bodies. Or this car. *I've* never been involved in anything illegal in my life. The police aren't after *me.* Nobody has any reason to want to kill *me.*"

"Oh, yeah?" His voice was ominously quiet. "What about me?"

"What?" She glanced at him then.

"Maybe I do. Maybe you've just given me a reason. Maybe if you don't do what I tell you, I'll wrap my fingers around your neck and squeeze the life out of you with my bare hands. Did you ever think of that?"

She returned her attention to the road. "If you want to, go ahead."

There was a pause. Summer could feel his gaze on her. She had called his bluff, and he didn't much like it. She, however, felt perfectly confident in doing so. Whatever Steve Calhoun was, whatever scandal he might have been involved in, whatever crimes he might have committed, he was not a murderer. Or at least, she amended, remembering the van's original driver with a tiny inner shiver, he wasn't going to murder *her*. She was as sure of that as she was of her own name.

"What makes you think I won't do it?"

"I told you, if you want to, go ahead."

There was another pause. "Look, Rosencrans . . ."

"McAfee!"

"Whatever. Maybe I won't kill you, but whoever's after me will. They'll be able to find you, in Murfreesboro. Didn't you leave your purse in that funeral home? I bet it had your address in it, didn't it? On your driver's license? Sure it did. They'll find it, and they'll come calling. Looking for me."

"So I'll tell them you kidnapped me, used me to get you out of town, then let me go. I'll tell them I don't have any idea where you are. And it'll be the truth. I won't know. I don't want to know."

"They'll kill you anyway. Trust me, Rosencrans. They'll come after you, and they'll kill you."

"Then I'll get out of town!" She was so agitated that she let that Rosencrans pass. "My mother's spending a few weeks with my sister and her kids in California. I'll go to them. I'll catch the first plane out. I'll go home and change and pack a few clothes, and head straight for the airport. In Knoxville, not Nashville."

"And just how will you get to the airport? You don't have a car anymore, remember?"

"I'll call a cab! I'll take a bus! I'll *get* there, believe me!"

"You think they won't come after you in California?"

"No! I think they won't! I'll go to the police, if I have to! At this point, I'm still an honest citizen! They'll protect me. I'll go to the police in California. That's what I'll do."

"If you go back home, you may not live to get to California."

"That's what you say. Why should I listen to you? Nobody wants to kill me. They want to kill *you*. I don't know why. I don't want to know why. I even hope you get out of this with a whole skin, really I do. But I don't want any part of it. I'm going home."

"I don't suppose it makes any difference to you that I can't see to drive? How'm I supposed to manage until my vision gets back to normal?"

This blatant attempt to tap in to her store of pity didn't work.

"I don't want to sound callous, Frankenstein, but that's your problem." Summer hesitated, her sympathy zone touched in spite of herself. "If you want, you can hide out at my house. For a day or two. Just until you can see."

"Yeah, right. That's the first place they'll look."

"Then park the car and catch a bus. Or a train. Or a plane. Do what you want. I don't care. I'm going home."

For a few minutes he said nothing more. Summer decided that he had given up arguing and felt herself begin to relax. She was really tired. What time was it, four, four-thirty? Her body longed for bed. Talk about a hard day!

"You keep any money at your house?"

His words, spoken out of the blue, made her start. She glanced over at him suspiciously. "Why?"

"I was thinking maybe you could float me a loan. I'll need gas money."

"I keep a little money in a cup in one of my kitchen cabinets. Not much, maybe thirty dollars. You can have that."

"Thanks. I'll pay you back."

His unspoken rider was *If I get out of this alive.* Summer heard it as clearly as if he had said the words aloud. Guilt raised its bothersome head once more. She glanced at him, but he was staring straight ahead, out through the windshield.

"I've got a bank card."

"Yeah?"

"I can withdraw up to two hundred dollars at a time. You can have that money, too."

"Sure it wasn't in your purse?"

"I keep my credit cards in a safer place than that."

"Oh, yeah? Where?"

"In the freezer. Frozen into a tray of ice. That way I have to melt the ice before I use the cards. Sort of a built-in braking system, so I won't be tempted to spend what I don't have."

"Smart, Rosencrans. Money's tight, huh?"

Summer shrugged. "I get by."

"Anything you lend me, I'll see you get it back. I promise. Unless . . ." His voice trailed off.

"Unless you're dead, right?" she finished dryly. He was laying it on thick, and she knew he was doing it deliberately, but still the thought of him dead was beginning to bother her. Just as he intended, she was sure.

"In the morning I'll call my lawyer and have you written into my will."

"Funny."

He laughed. "Okay, so you won't get it back if I'm dead. Otherwise, you will. Trust me."

"I do." Summer was surprised to find that it was the truth. She knew that if she made him a loan, he would pay her back unless death kept him from doing so. He might be a kidnapping, car-stealing, scandal-ridden murderer, but she'd bet her life savings that he wasn't the kind of sleazeball who welshed on his debts.

"I appreciate that."

"You should."

Summer turned onto Route 231, which led straight into Murfreesboro. Her house was no more than fifteen minutes away.

"You sure you don't want me to take you to Sammy? He's not involved in anything dishonest. I'd stake my life on it," she said.

"Maybe you'd stake yours, but I'm not willing to stake mine. Thanks anyway."

A red pickup rumbled past, headed in the opposite direction. Its headlights kept Summer from getting a glimpse of the driver—but whoever was hunting them wouldn't be driving a pickup truck. Would they?

She was getting as paranoid as Frankenstein himself.

The car topped a rise, and the lights of Murfreesboro were suddenly before them. Not that there were many at that hour: a still-open Sav-a-Stop, a fire station, a couple of streetlamps, a traffic signal. As the Chevy approached the intersection where Summer needed to turn right, a police car pulled up at the light directly opposite.

Beside her, Frankenstein tensed. Summer tensed, too. For the first time in her life she wondered, was the officer in the car friend or foe?

She didn't like the uncertainty.

The traffic light changed, and the police car drove past them without pausing. Summer let out her breath and turned right. Being hunted was not a pleasant experience.

She was glad it was almost over.

Her house was located in Albemarle Estates, a small residential development about a mile off the main highway. It was nothing special as houses went—a modest two-bedroom brick ranch on a street of similarly modest two- and three-bedroom brick ranches— but she had qualified for the mortgage herself, come up with the down payment herself, made the monthly payments herself. That was something she was inordinately proud of, and her pride carried over to the house. It was the best-kept one on the block, its trim a pristine cream, its concrete porch and walk bordered by meticulously neat flower beds. Built in the postwar boom of the early fifties, it had a mature willow tree in the front yard and a profusion of well-cared-for bushes nestled up against the foundation.

The door to the one-car garage was shut, just the way she had left it. The front porch light was on, just the way she had left it. The curtains were drawn, the interior dark. Everything was quiet, still, peaceful. Just the way it was supposed to be.

The Chevy's engine suddenly sounded inordinately loud as they cruised along the sleeping street.

"Do me a favor, okay?" Frankenstein said as she indicated with a gesture which house was hers. "Pull around the corner before you stop, and we'll walk back. Just in case."

The way he said "just in case" had such a chilling effect on Summer's nerves that she did as he asked. A house with a FOR SALE sign in the front yard stood empty just beyond the turn. Summer pulled into its driveway, shifted carefully into park—she was getting pretty good, the gears didn't make a sound—then reached down to turn off the ignition.

Frankenstein watched her surprised fumble. "We don't have a key, remember? Anyway, we need to leave the engine running. Just in case."

"Would you stop saying that?"

"What?"

" 'Just in case.' You're giving me the willies. Do you really think someone's in my house?"

Frankenstein didn't answer for a minute. "No," he said finally, opening his door. "I don't think they're here—yet. I actually think you've got about twenty-four hours before they give up chasing us across the hinterlands and show up here. But I've been wrong before. And this isn't the kind of mistake you get to make twice."

So much for reassurance. Leaving the motor running, Summer slid out of the car.

CHAPTER THIRTEEN

"Why do I keep getting the feeling that I'm making a big mistake here?"

Frankenstein's muttered question seemed addressed more to himself than to Summer. With her hurrying to keep up, he moved quickly along the sidewalk, hands jammed in the front pockets of his cutoffs, shoulders hunched in what Summer assumed was an effort to ward off the predawn chill. The moon was low in the east, casting a cold, pale light over the slumbering subdivision. A brisk breeze swirled cicada shells out of their path. Somewhere in the distance a frustrated tomcat yowled. Otherwise, the night was absolutely silent except for the whirring of the cicadas, which was so omnipresent, Summer didn't even register it anymore.

"You won't get very far with no money for gas."

"That's what I keep telling myself. Know what myself keeps answering? You won't get very far dead, either." He slowed his pace with three houses still to go and stopped altogether in the lee of a large lilac at the far edge of Summer's next-door neighbor's yard. "Does everything look right? No lights on or off that shouldn't be? No curtains askew? Anything at all out of the ordinary?"

"Everything looks just like I left it."

"All right. Give me your key and wait here."

Until that instant the appalling truth had not occurred to Summer.

"I don't have a key," she said in a small voice.

He glanced at her. She suspected his expression would have been the epitome of disgust if she'd only been able to read it. As it was, his facial swelling obscured everything except the resignation in his voice.

"The key's in your purse, right?"

"Right."

"Why am I not surprised, I wonder. Why do you women have these love affairs with purses, anyway? What's wrong with a plain old pocket? At least you're not always leaving them behind."

Summer didn't dignify that with an answer.

"No spare key hidden under a fake stone in the shrubbery?"

"No."

"Any unlocked windows?"

"No. I'm very careful about that."

"Good for you. Any suggestions as to how to get in?"

"Well—my next-door neighbor has a key." Summer indicated the house that claimed the lilac.

"Wonderful. All you need to do is go knock on her door—let's hope she's an early riser, because it's not quite dawn—and ask her for your key. Of course, if she's very observant you'll need to think up some reason why your blouse is all ripped and you've got a bump the size of an egg on your forehead and you're missing a shoe and—"

"She's in Florida," Summer interrupted, remembering.

"That does a lot of good. Leaving a spare key with a neighbor who's in Florida."

"She's got school-age children and it's summer break and she and her husband took them to Florida. It's the first vacation they've taken in two years."

"I'm happy for them. You have any objection to me breaking a window?"

"Under the circumstances? No, of course not."

"Wait here."

Before Summer could say aye, yes, or nay, he disappeared around the side of the bush. Actually, waiting while he checked out her house was not a bad idea, especially if there were murderous types lurking about, but the whole chauvinistic bit rankled. Still, if someone had to wind up dead, better him than her, and feminist principles be damned.

She held fast to that notion as she craned her neck around the bush to watch the action at her house.

Only, as minute after minute ticked by, there was no action. *Nada.* Zip. Had he gotten in? *She* could have broken in in the length of time he'd been gone. Surely he was not going to leave her standing out here without a word for the rest of the night!

Her house appeared undisturbed. As far as she could tell, no lights had been turned on inside. The outside looked as deserted as it had when they first drove past.

Where was he?

Maybe he'd tripped over the sprinkler hose; she had left it stretched across the back walk to water the new border of yellow zinnias she'd just planted around the patio. Or maybe he was having trouble fitting through a window. His shoulders were broad, and her windows, conventional double-hungs, weren't that big.

Maybe he was rifling through her house.

Maybe he was at the wrong house.

Maybe the bad guys had him.

Maybe . . . but she could maybe herself to death, Summer decided irritably. She would give him about five more minutes, and then she was heading for the car and Sammy as fast as she could go. If Frankenstein didn't like it, that was just too bad. His prolonged absence was scaring her.

Goose bumps chased themselves across her arms. The wind blew, the lilac swayed, the cicadas whirred. Frosty moonlight waxed and waned, casting twisty, elongated shadows like reaching

fingers over the neat lawns and deserted street and sidewalk. A
tune began to intrude on the edges of her consciousness. Summer
found herself humming it under her breath, trying in vain to remember the words, the title. When they came to her at last, she
smiled wryly at the appropriateness of the song. It was Patsy
Cline's "Walking After Midnight."

Summer felt as if she were trapped in a bad horror movie complete with mood music. Waiting for the monster to put in an
appearance. Which, in a way, she supposed she was. At least she
was waiting for Frankenstein.

She didn't even have time to crack a smile at her own humor
before she saw him. Just a glimpse of him, slipping around the far
corner of her house. So he had not been able to break in yet.
Maybe the glass in her windows was proving more resistant than
either of them had given it credit for. Or maybe, as seemed more
likely when she thought about it, the last time she redecorated
she'd painted the windows shut.

In any case, if he was *still* outside, he definitely needed help.

Summer sidled out from behind the bush and slunk—there was
no other word for it—behind her neighbors' house. Scaling the
chain-link fence that enclosed her own backyard was the hardest
part. Her sneakered toe fit perfectly in the little diamond-shaped
openings, but the bare toes of her other foot hurt like heck when it
was their turn to climb.

Unlike her child-oriented neighbors' lawn, her own was an oasis
of velvety-soft fescue and colorful flowers. She spent so many
hours laboring on her yard that she didn't even like to think about
what that said about her life. With no husband or children to
distract her, and with her social life consisting of occasional evenings out with a small circle of female friends and her less than
sizzling relationship with the divorced dentist, she had put a great
deal of her spare time and almost all of her passion into her resi-
dence. She liked to think it showed.

The thick cushion of grass was cool and soothing beneath her
abused foot. Even in the dark, the zinnias' bright, bobbing heads
outlined the patio. Summer eyed them with approval as she
stepped carefully over a bank of glossy impatiens, skirted the small

water-lily pond that was last summer's project, and headed toward
the far side of the house. On impulse, she yanked a tomato stake
out of a raised bed as she passed it. As a weapon, the yard-long
stick wouldn't be worth a whole lot, but still it was better than
nothing. Not that she expected to need a weapon, but like the Boy
Scouts, she believed in being prepared.

Frankenstein must be trying to break into the window of the
spare bedroom, Summer decided. It was just out of her sight,
around the corner in the most private part of her yard, where the
fence formed a trellis for this summer's project, her Zephyrine
climbing roses.

Summer breathed in their spicy-sweet aroma as she stepped
around the side of the house. The delicate pink semi-double
blooms with their dark green foliage had flourished under her
care, and almost hid the fence from view. She had had such success with these new additions to her garden that next year she
meant to plant them all around the fence line. A tingle of anticipation at the thought provided the first pleasurable emotion she'd
had for hours.

But at least she had located the source of her displeasurable
emotions, she consoled herself as the pleasant sensation died away
in the face of stark reality. There he was, peering over the fence,
his chest crushing her poor flowers! Too bad they were thornless;
he deserved a few wounds for his carelessness. The Zephyrines
were delicate!

"Would you get off my roses?" she hissed at his back, bristling
in defense of her darlings. For emphasis, she poked him in the
backside with the pointed end of her stick.

"Yeow!" He clapped a hand to the part she had abused and
whirled to face her.

He was not Frankenstein! Summer's eyes rounded and her
mouth dropped open as the man brandished his own stick. Then
she saw to her horror that it was not a stick at all. It was a rifle—
and the business end of it was pointed right at her midsection.

How she had ever made such a mistake she couldn't fathom.
The guy wasn't even wearing shorts. If she'd taken just a moment
to think, she would have realized . . .

Chalk up another "if only" to add to her collection.

"Drop it." He indicated her stick with the muzzle of the rifle. Summer didn't really obey. What happened was that the tomato stake more or less fell from her suddenly nerveless hands.

"Well, well, well," he said. The predawn gloom obscured his features, but Summer knew from the tone of his voice that she was in big trouble. "What've we got here? Another pretty lady. How about you and me head on inside?"

She assumed that refusing was not an option. Her only hope was to think fast.

"I'm just checking on my neighbor's house," she lied, the words spilling out rapidly as fear settled like a rock in her stomach. "I know you must be the man she hired to watch over the property, but she's really particular about her roses and . . ."

"Shut up." His voice was brutal. He made a threatening gesture with the rifle. "And turn around. Now."

Summer opened her mouth, shut it again, and pivoted. Trying to con him into letting her go was clearly a waste of breath. All at once, the heavy perfume of the Zephyrines threatened to choke her. Briefly she toyed with the idea of bolting. Surely he wouldn't just shoot her in the back, in cold blood? An instant's reflection answered that question: Of course he would. But was he likely to fire and reveal his clandestine presence in this small enclave of closely packed houses? A gunshot would surely awaken someone, who would—what? Rush to her assistance? Call the police? Maybe just turn over and go back to sleep, putting the sound down to fireworks, or a backfiring car?

Was she willing to take the chance that he wouldn't pull the trigger?

Even if she bolted, he wouldn't have to shoot to stop her, she realized suddenly. Her own fence would do that. No way could she get over it before he caught her. Why hadn't she bordered her yard with hedge roses, as she at first had been inclined to do? Why had she chosen a four-foot chain-link fence, of all things?

To keep the neighbors' dog out of her flowers, that was why. Her last slim hope of escape was snatched away by the existence of a boisterous mutt that liked to dig.

And the worst part of it was, the dratted animal wasn't even home to bark and alert his owners to her plight. For the first time ever he was in a kennel while her neighbors vacationed.

To think of the nights she'd been awakened by that howling hound, and now, when she needed him . . . But that was the story of her life.

"Get a move on." Prodding her in the small of the back with the rifle, he herded her toward the sliding glass doors that opened onto the patio. When she stopped, he reached around her to tap on the glass. Nothing happened, and he gave an exasperated grunt. A moment later, he repeated the exercise, keeping the mouth of the rifle nestled against her spine all the while. This time the curtain shifted as someone peeped out. There was the click of the lock being turned, and then the door slid open.

Summer was prodded inside.

Her dining room, onto which the patio door opened, was dark. By the faint glow that filtered in from the kitchen, she saw at a glance that everything was just as she had left it. An oak table and chairs—not antique, but old, and lovingly restored—and a pine china cabinet that she had hand-painted to match the wallpaper made up the room's furnishings. Nothing had been disturbed, down to the centerpiece of freshly cut daylilies that rested in a fragile glass vase on the table and the two place settings of her good china that she had left ready for her regular after-church lunch with Jim, her dentist friend.

Not that she was likely to keep the date.

"Who's she?" The man who had opened the door was shorter than the first man, and his voice had the slurred drawl of the mountains. Definitely a local. Summer didn't think either was a thug from the funeral home, but in the dark it was hard to be sure.

The man who had brought her in shrugged. "She was poking around outside. She claims she's a neighbor."

"Take her downstairs."

"My husband will be wondering where I am, and . . ." Summer tried desperately.

"Shut up and start walking!" A shove sent her stumbling

toward the kitchen. The feel of the rifle in the small of her back kept her moving.

The light from her kitchen was so faint because it was beaming up from the basement through the partly opened door. Summer was forced toward that door by the rifle at her back. Behind her, the two men exchanged low-voiced conversation that she couldn't quite separate into distinguishable words.

Her basement stairs were gray-stained wood. She had brightened the concrete walls with a coat of white paint. Resting against the far wall were the washer and the dryer, with a basket of folded towels atop it. The other furnishings were an old but still functional TV—turned on mainly when her nieces and nephews came to visit—a rarely used exercise bike, and a couch and two chairs that had been bounced from the living room when she got new ones a year or so back.

Frankenstein sat sprawled on the couch, watching her descend. His hands rested on his lap. His wrists were bound together with gray duct tape. Fresh blood trickled from the corner of his mouth. Over him stood a thug with a pistol, who glanced up as Summer and her entourage appeared.

"Who's she?" the thug standing over Frankenstein asked him.

"Never saw her before in my life," Frankenstein answered. His glance darted to Summer, daring her to contradict him. He needn't have worried: she didn't feel the slightest inclination to do so. Glancing around the basement, she had discovered a tableau as horrifying as it was riveting.

Not far from the stairs but out of Summer's direct line of vision until she had nearly reached the bottom, a red-haired woman had been hog-tied to a kitchen chair. Summer's first thought was simply that that chair had no business being in the basement. It was a tall ladderback, purchased unfinished and then painstakingly stained dark green by herself, and it belonged to the set in the kitchen. Then she took a good look at its occupant, and all other concerns vanished from her mind. The woman slumped bonelessly forward, kept from falling only by the bonds that held her to the chair. Her head drooped so that her chin rested on her chest, concealing her face from view. Her tumbling hair was a two-tone sea of dark roots and red waves. The outfit she was wearing was identical to the one Summer had on: a Daisy Fresh uniform.

Except the front of the woman's blouse was dyed a dark, wet-looking crimson. The chair sat in a puddle of scarlet. It took a few seconds for Summer to realize that what looked like bright red paint spilled all over the woman and the floor was really blood.

With a sense of shock Summer identified the woman as Linda Miller, one half of her worthless Saturday night work crew. Summer was almost positive that she was dead.

CHAPTER FOURTEEN

"She was sneakin' around outside." The man whose backside Summer had made the monumental error of poking spoke from behind her.

"Oh, yeah?" The third thug's gaze swept over Summer again, darted to Linda Miller and then to Frankenstein. "*She* the cunt in the van, Calhoun?"

"I told you, I never saw her before in my life."

The third thug's eyes narrowed. Without warning he hit Frankenstein across the face with the butt end of the pistol. The blow made a sickening *thunk* as it landed, opening a gash across his poor abused cheek. Frankenstein's head snapped back, and he grimaced, but he didn't make a sound. Summer did.

"Don't hit him!" she cried, appalled. "Yes, I was in the van."

"Ah." The third thug smiled while blood welled into the jagged tear he had opened in Frankenstein's face. Summer watched with a sick feeling in the pit of her stomach as blood began to run down his swollen, discolored jaw. "So you live in this house, right? *You're* Summer McAfee."

"That's right." They must have found her purse.

Frankenstein shot her a warning look, but Summer couldn't see that whether or not she admitted her identity made much difference at this point, except that it might keep the goon with the gun from hitting him again. No matter what she did, it seemed pretty obvious that they were going to wind up dead. Hideous, unbelievable thought! She was too young to die! Think, she told herself desperately. Think of a way out. Only, she couldn't seem to come up with anything.

Now that she had admitted her identity, the thugs seemed to relax. The third thug—a bristly black mustache adorned his upper lip, matching the fringe of hair surrounding his bald dome— looked almost genial as he glanced over at Linda Miller's body. He was in his late forties, dressed in stained, loose-fitting jeans and an aqua double-knit sport shirt. His face was tanned and wrinkled from prolonged exposure to the sun. Incredibly, considering that the dark blotches on his jeans were most likely blood, he almost looked kind.

"Guess the cunt was tellin' the truth after all," he said. "She kinda looked like the picture on the driver's license, though, you gotta admit."

"I thought it was kinda funny that she'd be carryin' a TV out of her own house," said the second thug—the man who'd opened the patio door—as he propelled Summer down the remaining stairs. He was a short, stocky man, fiftyish, with a grizzled gray crew cut, dressed in gray slacks and a navy nylon windbreaker.

"You mean she really *was* burglarizing the place?" The first thug snickered. The sound made Summer glance behind her, then watch with fascination as his belly, which formed a slight paunch over the ornate western belt that cinched his jeans, shook when he laughed. Getting her first good look at him in a strong light, Summer wondered how on earth she had ever mistaken him for Frankenstein, even in the dark. Frankenstein might weigh a ton, but his physique was that of a football player: all solid sinew and muscle. This guy was broad, all right, but flabby. His hair was even the wrong color and style: auburn and long around the ears rather than close-clipped black. The only similarity she could see between the two men was that they were both a hair under six feet tall, and they both wore black knit shirts. The thug's was an expensive Polo. Frankenstein's was a ripped, too tight T-shirt sporting a picture of a beer-guzzling bullterrier above the legend "Rude Dog Rules."

She must have been blind to make such a mistake. Her concern for her roses must have temporarily unhinged her mind.

"Hell, no wonder we couldn't get her to say nothin' different. She didn't know nothin' to tell."

"Yeah, well . . ." The third thug shrugged. "We woulda had to kill her anyway. We just could've saved ourselves the trouble of tryin' to make her talk first. I *thought* she was one tough babe. I've never seen the man I couldn't break, let alone the chick."

The first thug shook his head. "Ya still shouldn't've killed her. Not till we knew she didn't know anything. If she'd been the right chick, we'd be up shit creek now."

"Hey, it was an accident, okay? She spit in my face and I lost it for a minute. Anyway, we could've gotten everything we need to know out of Calhoun here."

"Girls is easier. And more fun."

"Yeah, well, so now we've got another girl to work on. She your girlfriend, Calhoun?"

"Hell, no. I like my women young and blond. She doesn't know anything about this. She's a janitor, for God's sake. She was cleaning the funeral home where your pals dumped me when I pulled a knife on her and forced her to drive me out of there. You're wasting your time with her."

"He don't tell us the truth, we're gonna beat the crap out of him till he does," the third thug warned, looking at Summer. "You his girlfriend?"

"Yes." If it would save Frankenstein from another beating, Summer was willing to say anything. She was still trying to digest the mind-boggling notion that Linda Miller might have been burglarizing her house when she'd been killed. It was possible, she supposed. Linda was new in town and had worked for Daisy Fresh for only a few weeks. She and her cleaning partner, Betty Kern, had applied for the job together and asked to work together. Sum-

mer had seen no reason not to hire them. Their references had
been in order. Now she had to wonder if they had deliberately not
shown up for the Harmon Brothers job, a job they'd been told was
vital to Daisy Fresh, knowing that Summer herself would have to
take it because getting a replacement with no warning at that time
of night would be all but impossible. As a blueprint for burglary,
Summer had to admit that it was nearly foolproof. She felt a spurt
of anger at Linda for her treachery, but then one glance at the
bloody body tied to the chair replaced anger with pity and a sick
fear for herself. Whatever Linda had done, she didn't deserve to
be butchered. No one did.

Including herself and Frankenstein. Fear made Summer's heart
beat faster. This was unbelievable. It was too much. No way could
any of this be happening to *her*.

"See? Girls is easy," the first thug said.

"Yeah." The third thug sounded almost disappointed. In response to a jerk of his head, Summer was propelled over to the
couch and pushed down beside Frankenstein. Her leg brushed his
as she sank into the faded chintz upholstery. He didn't even glance
at her. His attention was all on the three thugs, who now stood
over them, a gloating triumvirate of toughs. Summer could feel the
rigidity in his body. He was waiting, waiting—but what, realisti-
cally, could he do?

It was time for the posse to burst in.

Where was Arnold Schwarzenegger when he was *really* needed?

More to the point, where was Betty Kern? Had she been in on
the burglary? If so, could she possibly have escaped and gone for
help?

"So you gonna be a smart guy and tell us where the van is,
Calhoun, or are we gonna hafta hurt your girlfriend first?" the
third thug asked genially.

Summer's eyes widened at the threat. She would tell them
where the van was in a heartbeat, if push came to shove. No way
was she going to get hurt to conceal the whereabouts of a
smashed-up, shot-up, dead-body-bearing van.

"I told you, she's not my girlfriend. If you want to hurt her, go
ahead." Frankenstein shrugged indifferently. Summer stiffened.

Beside her, Frankenstein was as taut as a coiled spring. He directed a distorted smile at the thug. His battered face seemed to sneer. Summer swallowed but didn't say a word.

"Maybe we'll hurt you instead, asshole." The thug slammed his pistol into Frankenstein's forehead. The sound of metal whacking into bone made Summer flinch. Her stomach lurched as Frankenstein's head snapped sideways. For an instant, as he blinked in the aftermath of the blow, Summer found herself looking into his eyes. Both eyes. Almost obscured by the swollen flesh surrounding them, they were nevertheless both open, and retained a surprising impact. They were cold eyes, she saw, dead eyes, with the irises almost as black as the pupils. They were not the eyes of anyone she would ever wish to befriend, or even know. Ordinarily they would give her the shivers. At the moment they glinted with pain and rage. And, she thought, silent warning: Say nothing.

But why? She wanted to scream the question, but instead she asked it silently. He returned her look without expression for another fraction of an instant. Then his mouth tightened, and he straightened. His gaze refocused on the man standing over him as casually, as easily, as if he got hit over the head with a pistol every day.

But his body was, if anything, more tense than before.

Then Summer got it. Whether she picked it up out of the air, as some sort of psychic message from his brain to hers, or whether she just plain figured it out she didn't know. But she got it. For some reason the bad guys wanted the van even more than they wanted Frankenstein, but they didn't know where it was. She and Frankenstein did. That knowledge was all that was keeping them alive. The whys and wherefores of it she didn't understand, but she knew that whatever they did to her she couldn't, for the life of her, break down. If she could help it. One look at Frankenstein's purple balloon of a face, one glance at Linda Miller, and she didn't know how long she would be able to hold out if they began to focus their efforts on *her*. Maybe a quick death would be preferable to hours of torture.

Get moving, Arnold!

Icy, shaking terror bubbled up inside her. She had to face it:

Arnold wasn't coming. There would be no last-second heroic rescue by the Terminator. This was real life.

Help.

The third thug reached for her hand and dragged it, resisting, from her lap. For a moment he smiled at her, stroking the soft skin over her knuckles with a rough-padded thumb. Summer felt as though a tarantula were crawling across her hand. She wanted to snatch it back, and scream, and scream, and scream.

The Lord helps those who help themselves. She was a Southern Baptist, bred up on Sunday school, and that tenet had been drummed into her from childhood. Her choir-leader mother had put it another way: Praise the Lord, but pass the ammunition.

The thug lifted her hand to his mouth and lightly kissed the back of it. His fellow thugs were grinning. Summer shivered with revulsion.

Please, Lord, she prayed, send some ammunition fast.

"It's up to you, sweetheart. You can tell us what we want to know right now, the easy way, or we can start breaking your fingers, one by one. I'll start with this little pinky. It won't take hardly a second—and it'll hurt a whole lot." He cradled her hand in both of his, stroked her fragile pinky with his thumb, then suddenly wrapped his big hand around it so that she could feel the strength of his grip.

Summer knew he could break her finger as easily as a twig. Hideous anticipation paralyzed her. She froze, waiting for pain.

"*Then* you can tell us. But make no mistake, you will tell us. Now, where is the van?"

"I told you, she doesn't . . ." Frankenstein growled, coming partway off the couch. Suddenly the business end of a pistol was shoved against his temple by thug number two, who looked as if he might enjoy using it.

"You sit on back down, now, boy," number two said, and Frankenstein slowly, reluctantly subsided.

"I'm going to tell them," Summer said in a shrill voice that she had trouble recognizing as her own, flicking a scared glance at Frankenstein. She then looked directly up at the man squeezing her pinky. The first thug hovered at his shoulder like an evil genie.

The second one continued to hold a pistol to Frankenstein's head. "I'll—I'll tell you anything you want to know. Just—just don't hurt me. Or him."

"Shut your stupid mouth," Frankenstein growled.

"Shut yours, or I'll blow your head off," the second thug answered, jabbing the mouth of the pistol viciously against Frankenstein's temple. Frankenstein grimaced and was silent. The thugs exchanged satisfied glances.

"So where's the van?"

For a moment Summer had to think. Frankenstein was her boyfriend, right? She couldn't call him Frankenstein. "St-Steve left it, you know? It wasn't running very well, because it was all shot up. He said a bullet must have pierced something in the engine. So he left it."

"Where? Where did he leave it?" As one they leaned toward her.

"In a field."

"What field?"

"I don't know. A field, okay? I'd—I'd have to show you." Summer tried to infuse a desperate cunning into her voice. "But only if you promise to let us go, after."

"Sure, sweetheart. You show us, we let you go." The soothing promise was about as believable as a crocodile's tears, but Summer managed a timorously relieved smile. She'd always been a good actress—once she had thought she might be able to make it a career—and under the circumstances she was ready, willing, and able to give the performance of her life. For her life.

"See? It wasn't so stupid of me to tell them."

She addressed that remark, adrip with a pathetic bravado, to Frankenstein, who glowered at her and growled, "Don't be a damned fool."

At least he wasn't stupid, her monster.

Hands grasped her upper arms, and Summer was hauled to her feet.

"No point in taking him. We can just waste him here." The comment, made by thug number two, was low-voiced, but Summer heard it. She made no pretense that she hadn't.

"You promised to let us go if I showed you! Steve too!"

"Sure, sweetheart, sure we'll let you go. Both of you. Soon as we get our van back. Shut up, you lughead." This was hissed at thug number two. Thug number three, the speaker, wrapped a hard hand around Summer's upper arm and propelled her toward the stairs.

"Bring him," he ordered, glancing over his shoulder.

"But . . ."

"She might be lying. She might not remember. Whatever. We don't want to burn any bridges until we're sure."

So the thugs weren't as stupid as all that. Summer's spirits, which had started to rise, sank again. But at least she'd bought them some time.

Summer was just starting to climb the stairs when she heard it: the click, click, click, of someone, or something, in heels or taps or some other odd kind of footgear, walking across the kitchen linoleum toward the basement door.

Arnold?

The cavalry?

Betty Kern?

Almost without realizing it, Summer stopped climbing and held her breath. Behind her, the thugs and Frankenstein stopped too.

Everyone froze, listening.

CHAPTER FIFTEEN

A hand clamped over Summer's mouth. She was dragged backward down the stairs, then set on her feet again. The five of them, thugs and victims, clustered in a tight little group at the base of the steps, craning their necks in a futile attempt to peer into the darkness beyond the sliver of light cast by the barely ajar basement door.

A pistol pressed hard against Summer's temple. The third thug's hand still squashed her mouth. It tasted strongly of beer. Summer loathed beer. Under less dire circumstances she would have gagged.

Frankenstein faced her, a pistol held to his head, too, compliments of the second thug. The concrete floor felt hard and cold beneath Summer's one bare foot. The mouth of the pistol felt colder against her temple.

"Check it out," the third thug muttered to the first.

Summer and Frankenstein exchanged tense glances. The first thug cautiously crept upward toward the door. He kept his back pressed to the concrete wall of the stairwell. His pistol was drawn and ready.

The curious clicking footsteps stopped.

Summer realized she was holding her breath.

The first thug reached the top of the stairs and listened hard. Silence.

Summer dared to hope. In her imagination, a whole squad of friendly policemen was crouched in her kitchen, ready to spring to the rescue.

Policemen in high heels or tap shoes? She didn't think so.

Okay, then, Arnold.

The notion of the Terminator in pumps was almost enough to make her smile even under the circumstances.

She would settle for Betty Kern. Heck, at this point she would settle for anyone she could get.

The first thug glanced down at them. Summer's captor removed his hand from her mouth to make a violent shooing gesture. The first thug visibly swallowed, then reached out and swung the basement door wide. Summer licked her dry lips and waited.

Nothing happened.

A moment later the clicking started up again. The first thug hugged the wall, his pistol extended at arm's length, aimed at whoever appeared.

Summer stopped breathing.

Suddenly an eight-inch-tall mop of fawn-colored fur moved into the pool of light, and clicked to the edge of the stairs. Bulging chocolate eyes focused on Summer.

"Muffy!" she moaned.

The tiny pink-satin bow that adorned the top of the Pekingese's head quivered. Other than that, and the liquid eyes, the dog looked like a mobile hairball. If she noticed anyone besides Summer, she gave no sign of it. Instead she started down the stairs, hopping delicately from step to step, completely ignoring the gunman she bypassed.

"It's just a goddamned dog!"

Grand Champion Margie's Miss Muffet, now retired from the ring, was not *just* a dog. She was Summer's mother's cherished darling, and the winner of more ring-wars than Mike Tyson. For the last ten years, everywhere that Margaret McAfee had gone, Muffy had gone too, by plane, train, automobile, and cruise ship. The only reason Muffy was not at that moment in California with her mistress visiting Summer's sister Sandra was that one of Sandra's boys had recently developed a violent allergy to doggy hair. Or so Sandra said.

Summer had been elected to baby-sit. Er, doggy-sit. Thanks, Mom. Thanks, Sis.

She could almost see her older sister grinning at her. Muffy was not exactly a popular houseguest. She had other unfortunate habits besides shedding.

"That pooch sure scared the crap out of Charlie!" The goons' tension dissolved in a burst of jocularity at their point man's expense.

"What kinda pussy are you, Charlie?"

"Pussy's the word, all right. Me-ow. Scared of a little *doggy*."

"Shut up, you morons!" Charlie was not amused. He scowled as he descended from the top of the stairs in Muffy's wake.

"Come here, pup, pup, pup, pup!" The thug guarding Frankenstein snapped his fingers at Muffy. She went right to his feet. Summer could have strangled her with her hair bow as she submitted with regal dignity to having her ears scratched. She might have been more forgiving if the thug had not kept his gun pressed into the base of Frankenstein's spine the whole time.

"Nice doggy," the goon crooned.

Damned useless animal. Why couldn't she have been a Doberman?

"Let's go." The third thug turned businesslike again. The second thug straightened up from petting Muffy. Charlie paused two steps from the bottom of the stairs.

"Move, you." The third thug prodded Summer with his pistol. Hopelessly, Summer started to obey.

"Shit!" the second thug shrieked. Summer jumped a foot straight up in the air. She was not the only one, but she was the only one whose expression was not murderous when she landed.

"Damned dog pissed on my foot!"

Summer glanced down. Everyone glanced down. The hems of the second thug's gray slacks were damp. A puddle spread rapidly around his Florsheimed foot. Dignity unimpaired, Muffy was already hopping back up the stairs.

Urinating on anyone she disliked was one of Muffy's unfortunate habits.

Thugs one and three guffawed. Summer smiled. All hell broke loose.

Charlie went sailing through the air, courtesy of Frankenstein's hands in his belt. He flew with a flailing bellow, and missed Summer by millimeters as he crash-landed. The other two thugs were not so fortunate. Charlie mowed them down like bowling pins.

"Run!" Frankenstein bellowed. No gentleman he, he had already leaped over Muffy and was halfway up the stairs. The thugs cursed and scrambled to regain their feet and their guns.

Summer sprang after him. She paused only to scoop up Muffy —she really couldn't leave her mother's precious darling to the mercy of a trio of murderers. A pistol went off as she swooped, sounding like an explosion in such cramped quarters. Something smacked into the wall just above her bent head, sending out a shower of what felt like sand. A bullet! If she hadn't bent to retrieve Muffy, she would have been hit!

With Muffy tucked beneath her arm, Summer leaped up the remaining two stairs and dived through that doorway like a quarterback sneaking a keeper over the goal line.

The thugs were already barreling up the stairs.

Summer's head crashed into the wall opposite the basement door. She saw stars as she ended up sprawled on her stomach. Muffy squirmed out from beneath her and licked her face. Ungratefully, Summer swatted her away.

The basement door crashed shut. Frankenstein pushed the button that locked the knob. The bad guys were locked in the basement! They were saved, saved, saved!

"Cheap-ass lock," Frankenstein grunted as the knob began to rattle. For added security, he snatched a chair from the trio that still remained with the kitchen set and wedged it beneath the knob.

Summer scrambled to her feet and stared at the door with a pounding heart. The air was thick with muffled curses and threats as the thugs lunged against it from the other side. Watching the thin panel quake beneath their determined assault, Summer began to revise her initial jubilation.

They weren't saved yet.

"You got a gun in the house?"

"No." Summer was a staunch advocate of gun control. Besides, they scared her.

"Figures."

"We could call the cops . . ."

"Who the hell do you think's in the basement? Come on, let's go!" Tearing at the duct tape around his wrists with his teeth, Frankenstein bolted toward the nearest door. It led to the garage.

A fierce banging rattled the basement door. With a single longing glance at her kitchen phone—it had been programmed to dial 911 at the touch of a single button—she snatched up Muffy and fled after him.

He had to use his foot to shove aside something that blocked the door. A dark, motionless form, sprawled on the white linoleum.

Betty Kern, Summer discovered as she raced after him. Dead, without a doubt. Beside the body lay the mahogany box that contained the silver her mother had given her for her wedding. Forks, knives, and spoons were scattered across the floor.

So much for help from that direction.

When Summer appeared at the top of the shallow flight of steps, Frankenstein had already found and pushed the button that opened the automatic door. Dawn's gray light spread across the garage as he ducked beneath the rising panel. There was a car in the garage—and it was not hers.

The car was a late-model navy Lincoln Continental. Summer knew Lincoln Continentals. Her mother had one, though hers was bright yellow.

The racket from the kitchen—muffled thuds and curses—told

her that the thugs were still locked in the basement. This would take a few minutes—did she dare take the time?

The thought of the ancient Chevy being pursued by this sleek baby decided her. She *would* take the time.

All but dropping Muffy, who grunted her indignation as she landed on all dainty fours with rather more force than usual, Summer ran to the car, released the catch, and raised the hood. It took only seconds to rip out the spark plug wires.

A gunshot followed by the sound of splintering wood was her signal that time had run out. Clearly they had decided to shoot their way free. Summer hit the button that operated the garage door and sprinted beneath it as it started to close. Muffy ran at her heels, and Summer scooped her up again. As she gained the street she looked this way and that, but Frankenstein was nowhere in sight.

He had probably abandoned her and Muffy to their fate. The no-good son of a . . .

Still she ran down the street. Dead center, toward where they had left the running car.

Without warning the Chevy careened around the corner and roared toward her. Low and black and bewinged, it gave new meaning to her mental image of something that moved like a bat out of hell. Mindful of Frankenstein's warning that he couldn't see to drive, Summer leaped for the edge of the road just as the car's breaks squealed. The Chevy came to a rocking halt about five feet beyond where she had just stood.

Yet another way she might have died on this nightmarish night.

The passenger door opened. "Jesus, Rosencrans, what took you so long?"

Explanations and recriminations could wait. Clutching Muffy to her bosom, Summer flung herself inside.

She didn't even have time to close the door before Frankenstein stomped on the gas. Flung back against the seat, Summer clawed at the vinyl for purchase and prayed she would not be thrown out onto the pavement. Muffy, no fool, crawled under the seat.

"Shut the door!" Frankenstein roared.

Summer shot him a killing glare. Clinging to the seat back for all she was worth, she dropped a handful of spark plug wires that she didn't remember hanging on to in the first place and reached for the wildly flapping door. Her perch was precarious at best, and if he went round a bend—but she caught the handle and slammed the door shut.

For a moment she felt as limp as a cooked noodle.

Summer slumped in the seat, her head down, her hands curled in her lap. She noted with a flicker of chagrin that her hands were black with grease. How the mighty are fallen, she mourned on behalf of her once much-praised fingers.

They were roaring past her house just as the thugs burst through the front door. The three charged out onto the front lawn and watched wild-eyed as the Chevy tore past.

At the sight of them Frankenstein must have put the pedal all the way to the floor, because the Chevy peeled rubber like a good fifties car should. They raced to the end of the street, and took the corner on two wheels.

As she was flung against the door she had just closed, Summer didn't even bat an eyelash. She congratulated herself on getting positively used to flirting with death.

They skidded left out of the gates that marked the entrance to Albermarle Estates. The objects on the seat between them happened to catch Frankenstein's eye.

"What the hell's that?" he asked, indicating the little pile of twisted black wires. With his vision, they probably looked like snakes. Snakes from hell. To match the car. A bat out of hell carrying snakes from hell.

Summer giggled.

He glanced at her. Both his eyes were visible again, though neither opened wider than a slit. She only hoped he could see.

"Keep your eyes on the road," she admonished him. Not that it would probably do much good, but at least he hadn't crashed them. Yet.

"What are they?" He really did sound perplexed.

"Spark plug wires," Summer explained, settling deeper into her seat. Then, at his astonished glance, she added, "To keep them from following us. The nuns did it to the Nazis in *The Sound of Music.* Hey, I like movies."

Frankenstein glanced at her again. His lips twitched, and then he started to laugh.

CHAPTER SIXTEEN

Their luck ran out on Route 165 just south of
Tellico Plains. Or, rather, their gas did.

Summer was driving. It was full daylight by this time, but she
was so tired that she could barely focus. Her hands, which she had
wiped as well as she could on her pants, were no longer black with
grease but merely faintly gray, with black rims around the nails.
She couldn't look at them without feeling queasy. Beside her,
Frankenstein frowned down at a map he had found in the glove
compartment. For the last fifteen minutes he'd been trying to use
it to plot the escape route that afforded them the best possible
chance of avoiding detection. Something, either his blurred vision
or the same exhaustion that plagued Summer, was making it an
uphill task.

"We want to keep heading south on 165. We should run into a
gravel road running east–west in about half an hour. I can't find it
on the map, but I've been up this way before. I know it's there."
His voice was rough-edged with weariness.

Putt. Putt. Sputter. Putt. The Chevy seemed to be having a coughing fit. Summer frowned and pushed on the gas. For an instant the car responded. Then it gave another consumptive snort and started to slow down.

"Jesus, we forgot about the gas!" Frankenstein sounded as horrified as she felt.

Summer stared down at the gas gauge in stupefaction as the Chevy's speed slowed to a crawl. How could they have forgotten something so important? But what could they have done even if they had remembered? It hit Summer like a baseball bat between the eyes: They didn't have any money. She had forgotten to retrieve the thirty dollars from her house.

All that for nothing.

"Pull off the road."

They were in the mountains now, and the road—all the roads—were uphill. Steep, forested slopes slanted skyward on Summer's left; on her right was a sheer drop of perhaps a thousand feet. Up ahead, more mountains rose out of the early morning mist. Snow caps blended with drifting white clouds in the distance.

A hawk dipped and swooped overhead as Summer pulled off onto the rocky shoulder. They were about halfway up a tortuous two-lane mountain road with no sign of civilization in any direction. They hadn't spotted another vehicle since they'd passed a coal truck skirting Tellico Plains.

"Now what?" Summer asked, shifting into park—she'd really gotten very good at shifting—and setting the emergency break before the Chevy could roll downhill.

Frankenstein shrugged and opened his door. She had pulled to the left, across the northbound lane, so the car would hug the mountain rather than perch precariously on the edge of the cliff.

Summer got out too, absently tugging on her broken bra strap to get her pertinent assets back where they belonged. Muffy crawled out after her, slunk to the edge of the road, and threw up in the tall grass.

Muffy had always been prone to travel sickness.

"Now we walk." Frankenstein already had the back door open. Besides textbooks, and the baseball cap, the backseat yielded four cans of unopened beer remaining in a plastic ring-pack, a zip-up hooded sweatshirt, and a pair of high-topped basketball shoes. From the looks of them, they were at least size eleven.

"Must be a big kid." Frankenstein gave the shoes a cursory glance and set them alongside the beer, cap, and sweatshirt at his feet.

"Walk!" His previous remark just registered on Summer's consciousness. She was so tired, she could barely stand, much less contemplate putting one foot in front of the other. "You've got to be kidding!"

"Nope. Unless you can fly." Frankenstein turned and headed back the way they had come. Too weary to do anything except lean against the car and watch him retreat, Summer was relieved when at last he bent, picked up something from the roadside, and headed back toward her. For a moment there she had feared she and Muffy were being abandoned.

She was almost too tired to care.

"What's that for?" she asked when he was once again within hearing range. He was carrying a rusty metal rod about three feet long.

"To break into the trunk. To see if there's something in there we can use."

He inserted one end of the rod in the crack by the lock. After a few mighty heaves—Summer was impressed with the way his biceps bulged beneath the short sleeves of the T-shirt when he bore down—the metal on both sides of the lock was bowed and bulging.

But the trunk was still locked.

Summer began to grin.

Except for the new cut in his cheek, Frankenstein's face didn't look quite so fearsome this morning, or maybe she had grown used to the way he looked. Both his eyes were ringed with truly magnificent shiners, but they were open wide enough so that she could actually discern the color of his irises without having to squint. His facial bruises ran the color gamut from purple to yellow to green. So when what little normal-hued facial skin he still possessed flushed bright red with annoyance and exertion, she merely admired this cheerful addition to an already impressive array of colors.

"What are you laughing at?" he snarled when his dozenth effort to pop the lock failed.

Summer told him, and added helpfully, "Looks to me like what you need is a can opener."

Frankenstein shot her a killing glare. Summer grinned at him. He gave a downward heave on the rod—and it bent almost double.

But the trunk was still locked.

Summer giggled. Frankenstein swore. Withdrawing the rod from the crack, he stared at its twisted shape for a bitter moment before throwing it aside.

"Jesus!" he bellowed, without apparent provocation. Summer jumped in reaction to the shout, then followed the trajectory of his outraged gaze.

Muffy trotted daintily away from his foot.

"Goddamned dog peed on my foot!" He banged his fist down hard on the trunk. The trunk popped open.

Summer couldn't help it. She laughed so hard she had to sit down on the ground. She laughed so hard that when Muffy crawled into her lap all she could do was bury her face in the dog's talcum-scented fur to try to muffle her cackles. She laughed so hard that her sides ached, and she thought she might die from being unable to catch her breath.

Then she caught a glimpse of Frankenstein's sour expression, and laughed some more.

"She does that," she gasped semiapologetically when she could spare enough air for speech.

"She does that? The dog goes around peeing on people's feet and all you can say is, she *does* that? Jesus."

"She doesn't much like men—and anyway, she saved your rear back at my house. And she got the trunk open."

"*I* got the trunk open."

"You wouldn't have gotten it open without Muffy's help."

"Out of gratitude I might let her live, then." Frankenstein finished wiping his foot on the grass at the edge of the road and headed back for the trunk. He disappeared from view as he rummaged inside.

From the safety of Summer's lap Muffy barked once, a delicate little yap.

"What's she barking at?" Frankenstein's head emerged from the trunk.

"I think she's saying she's hungry."

"She's *saying* she's hungry? Give me a break. You're not one of those dotty women who treat their dog like a kid, are you?"

"She's not my dog. She's my mother's. And she's not dotty. My mother, I mean. Not Muffy." Fatigue was tangling her tongue.

"She's not much like you, then. Your mother, I mean." Frankenstein seemed to get the drift of her speech remarkably well. His eyes appeared briefly over the top of the trunk. "You don't live with your mother, do you?" He sounded faintly alarmed.

"No, I don't. She moved to Santee, South Carolina, with my dad when he retired. He died five years ago. She still lives in Santee, but she travels most of the time."

"So what are you doing with the mutt?"

"Baby-sitting." Summer made a face. "My sister Sandra—Mom's visiting Sandra—says her oldest boy is allergic to dog hair. Personally, I think she's lying. Muffy doesn't like Will, her husband."

"I just bet Will doesn't think much of Muffy, either."

"Probably not."

Frankenstein slammed down the trunk, only to have it bounce up again, narrowly missing hitting him in the nose. He jumped back and shot Summer a look that dared her to grin.

She grinned anyway.

"Get off your lazy butt and get over here and help me with this." He sounded disgruntled. Summer's grin broadened.

"Help you with what?"

"We're going to push the car over the cliff. Any questions?"

About a million, but Summer only managed to sputter, "W-why?"

"Because I think it'll be fun. Why do you think? They saw it, that's why. They can identify it. They find it, they find us. We would have had to get rid of it pretty soon anyway. There's probably a BOLO out on it by now."

"A BOLO?"

"Be on the lookout for. I told you, those guys back there are cops. At least, one of them is: the one with the mustache. He works for Cannon County. I used to see him around. Name's Carmichael. He knows me, too."

Summer shivered. She was suddenly no longer amused. "Are you sure?"

"Sure as a date with a hooker. Now, want to help me push this car?"

Not really, Summer answered mentally, but she stood up anyway. Frankenstein opened the driver's door and put one hand on the steering wheel. Summer walked behind the car and braced herself against the back bumper. She didn't enjoy pushing, but she had done it before. The '66 Mustang she had driven all through high school had had a carburetor problem. The engine had died almost every time she stopped at a traffic light. Until she saved up enough to get it fixed, she had done a lot of pushing.

"Yo, Rosencrans!"

Summer peered around the side of the car. It was impossible to see over it because of the defiantly upright trunk lid.

"We're on a hill. I'm getting ready to put the transmission into neutral. That tell you anything?"

Summer pondered.

"Get out from behind the car, doofus. Push from the front. That way, when it starts rolling backward, you won't get run over."

Good point. Too tired even to take offense at being called "doofus," Summer moved to the front of the car.

"Ready?"

Summer nodded.

"I asked if you were ready?" It was a bellow.

"Yes!" Summer bellowed back, after checking that Muffy was safely ensconced in the grass. Muffy was sprawled on her belly, her head on her paws, watching alertly. From the look of her, nothing short of a dish of Kal Kan was going to get her to move.

Smart dog, Summer thought as her own stomach rumbled.

"When I say let go, let go! Got that?"

Summer nodded again. Then, remembering that he couldn't see her, she yelled, "Yes!"

Frankenstein muttered something that sounded vaguely uncomplimentary under his breath. Then the car started to roll backward.

Very little pushing was required. The Chevy started slowly, but as Frankenstein maneuvered it across the road it picked up speed. At the end it was really rolling, so fast that Summer had to trot to keep up.

"Let go!" Frankenstein yelled. Summer already had. He leaped away from the car and Summer watched, fascinated, as it sailed over the edge. For one glorious moment, it hung suspended against the backdrop of mountains and sky and trees, looking for all the world like a hideously overweight bat. Then its back end pitched downward, and it dropped from sight.

Seconds later the crash came, or rather a series of crashes. Then silence. No explosion. Nothing spectacular at all. The Chevy didn't even catch fire.

Of course, they'd been out of gas.

"Can't see it from the road." Satisfaction was plain in Frankenstein's voice as he glanced around at her. He still stood on the rocky shoulder, looking down. His eyes flickered over her once, then moved beyond her up the road.

"There's a car coming, Rosencrans. Get out of the way."

Summer glanced over her shoulder. A white Honda had just come around the bend. It was bearing down on them cheerily. She walked to the side of the road to stand beside Muffy and the jumble of items Frankenstein had removed from the Chevy.

Her heart began to pound. The Honda was getting closer—surely it couldn't be the goons again. She was getting mighty sick of the goons.

Suddenly Frankenstein was beside her.

"Do you think they . . ." she began, glancing anxiously up at him.

"Shut up," he said, and slid one arm around her shoulders and the other around her waist. Twisting her so that his back was to the road and her head was on his shoulder, he covered her mouth with his.

CHAPTER SEVENTEEN

The earth didn't move. Bells didn't ring. Stars didn't explode inside Summer's head. Wrapped tightly in Frankenstein's arms, tilted backward, she clung to a pair of very broad shoulders to keep from falling on her butt, suffered the feel of hard, warm lips mashed against hers, and waited the kiss out. He didn't even use his tongue.

It was clear that Frankenstein's mind, like her own, wasn't on what he was doing.

Finally he lifted his head, glanced cautiously up and down the mountain, and set her back on her feet.

"All clear."

He sounded as unruffled as if he'd been kissing a department store mannequin. To Summer's amazement, his unconcern pricked her vanity.

"Good." If her voice was cool, well, it was better than being hot. And hot was what she was starting to feel. Hot with disgruntlement. Not that she meant to let him know it. After all, she hadn't been floored by his kiss either. And if he had tried to use his tongue, she would have bitten it!

"It was just tourists. A family. The backseat was chock-full of toys and kids." He grinned at her suddenly. "When they saw us lovebirds, the mom and dad averted their heads. I think they even speeded up. Mustn't shock the kiddies."

That kiss wouldn't have shocked Shirley Temple. Summer was still ruminating on it—had she lost her looks to that extent? was he gay?—as he bent over the pile of items by the road.

No, he couldn't be gay. The scandal with his friend's wife precluded that. It must be her. Something about her just didn't turn him on. Summer couldn't have felt more affronted if he'd called her a foul name. In fact, she would have preferred it.

"Hey, at least we eat." Frankenstein held up an unopened eight-pack box of peanut butter snack crackers for her inspection. Summer eyed them sourly. Muffy responded with more enthusiasm. At the sight of the box, she came to her feet and yapped.

"Later," Frankenstein told her, and dropped the box back on the pile.

Besides the crackers, the trunk had yielded a gym bag containing an orange muscle shirt, black nylon shorts, white athletic socks rolled into a ball, another pair of enormous sneakers, and a basketball. There was also a tattered quilt, a tire iron, and a roll of breath mints. Combined with the map, and the items from the backseat, it was quite a haul.

Summer reflected that her dentist friend wasn't real hot for her either. She'd had an IUD inserted on his behalf, and hardly needed it. Face it, she told herself, you are thirty-six years old. Over the hill. Long in the tooth. Not a sex kitten anymore.

That she didn't want to have sex with Frankenstein, wouldn't have sex with him if he begged her, if he offered her a million dollars like Robert Redford had to Demi Moore in that stupid movie *Indecent Proposal,* was beside the point. For her pride's sake, she wanted him to want her. She was not required to want him back.

And if that didn't make any sense, that was just too bad.

The scowl on her face would have terrified a bull moose.

Frankenstein paid no attention. He was busy bundling everything except the basketball, cap, and tire iron back into the bag. He bounced the basketball on the pavement once or twice, his expression wistful. Finally he heaved it over the cliff, watching its downward trajectory with what looked like real sorrow. Then, without so much as a word to her, he clapped the cap—it was black, with *Bulls* written in red across the front—on his head, picked up the bag and tire iron, and headed into the forest.

"You coming or not?" he paused at the edge of the trees to demand over his shoulder when Summer just stood there glaring at his back.

"I'm missing a shoe," she told him, only then remembering that pertinent fact herself. Apparently the monster didn't hear. He was moving away, already just one more shadow among the dark trunks.

A rumbling warned Summer that another vehicle was headed in her direction. Snatching up Muffy, muttering imprecations under her breath, she hurried after Frankenstein.

The forest floor was as prickly and mushy and unpleasant under her bare foot as she had thought it would be. For a moment or so, as she followed him deeper and deeper into the trees, she could barely see. Finally her eyes adjusted to the gloom.

She found herself in a primeval forest. It was beautiful, lushly green, with vines snaking up from the ground to twine around gnarled branches and sunlight slanting down in shimmery columns through openings in the leafy canopy overhead. It was also eerie. There was a kind of hush in the air, a sense of time having stopped. Summer had the feeling that she had stepped through the looking glass into another world. A world where she—and Frankenstein and Muffy—were very much the intruders. A world not meant for humans, but for creatures like the bushy-tailed squirrel who watched her warily from an overhead branch, or the lizard who scrambled across a rock as she passed it. A place where the golden empty cicada shells that clung to the rough gray bark had eyes that could see, and the droning music made by their former occupants grew louder with each step she took deeper into their domain.

She had never been a nature enthusiast. The forest gave her the jitters.

"Would you *wait*?" she exploded at Frankenstein's disappearing back, and practically ran to catch up with him. It was amazing how fast he could move even with his limping gait.

"Jesus, you're slow." He glanced down at her in disapproval as she came panting up beside him.

Summer was too winded to do more than grit her teeth. Muffy, for all her deceptively small size, weighed a ton. And the trek, so far, had been all uphill.

She set the dog on the ground and plowed on beside Frankenstein. Muffy followed reluctantly.

"What now?" she asked.

"What do you mean, what now? Now we walk."

"Where to? Do you have a plan? Or do we just walk until we fall off the end of the earth?"

"Jesus, you talk a lot." He stepped up the pace.

"Just tell me one thing: Why should I stick with you? I'd probably be safer on my own." She stopped walking and stood, arms akimbo, glaring after him.

Frankenstein stopped too, turning to face her with a shrug. "It's your call, Rosencrans. You might be safer on your own. *If* you think you can find your way back to civilization without me, and *if* you think they won't catch up with you as soon as you do and try to pry my whereabouts out of you. I don't want to rain on your parade, but if I were you I'd think back on what the bad guys did to those two other women just because they happened to be in your house. Just because they thought that one of them was *you*."

Summer shivered. She had been doing her best *not* to remember the fate of Linda Miller and Betty Kern. Every time she recalled Linda's limp, bloody body, the question that popped into her mind was: Had it hurt much, to die like that?

Of course it had hurt.

Summer shied away from the thought. It was too horrible. Her protective barriers went up once more. She would not think about it. If she did, she feared she would curl up into a whimpering little ball right there and then, and refuse to budge ever again.

"You think I'm taking you with me just for the pleasure of your company, Rosencrans?" Frankenstein's voice was hard. "If you do, think again. Now that we're on foot, I'll get where I'm going a heck of a lot faster if I leave you and that mutt of yours behind. I'm letting you tag along because I owe you. You wouldn't have gotten involved in this mess if it weren't for me. So I kind of feel responsible for you now. You want to take over responsibility for yourself, feel free."

He turned and lurched off through the trees.

As his words percolated through her brain, Summer stared after him for a moment. Then, galvanized by the memory of the two women who had died in her place, she trotted after him.

"Could you at least tell me where we're going, please?" she panted meekly when she caught up.

He didn't seem at all surprised to see her. He didn't seem particularly pleased, either.

"My dad and I had a fishing camp up in these mountains, okay? That's where we were headed before we ran out of gas, which wasn't such a bad thing, now that I think about it. We're probably safer on foot. They won't expect that; they'll be watching the roads. The camp's about a three days' walk due east. Nobody ever went there but the two of us. I figure we can hide out for a few days while I try to think this mess through. There's got to be a way out. I'm just too tired to see it."

"Maybe we should . . ." But Summer found herself talking to his back as he set off again. Clearly he was not interested in her suggestion, which involved calling her sister who was a lawyer in Knoxville. But then, she decided as she trailed after him, she didn't really want to get her sister involved in this, anyway. People who got involved in this seemed to wind up dead.

A fishing camp, she thought. He was taking her to a fishing camp. At least he had a destination in mind.

Taking a deep breath, she decided to follow where he led. What else was she going to do?

Some time later, his attention apparently drawn by her minutes-long silence, he glanced around at her. His pace slowed as he watched her hobbling to catch up.

"What're you limping about?" he asked.

"I only have one shoe."

He kept walking, but at least allowed her to close the gap. "How'd you lose the other one?"

The thought of bopping him over the head with the nearest solid object occurred to Summer, but that would be even more exhausting than explaining. Clearly he had not noticed that she had been only half shod throughout their entire acquaintance.

"Don't ask." She wasn't up to explaining either.

A plaintive whimper from behind them made Summer glance over her shoulder. Muffy, who'd been trailing farther and farther behind, now sprawled flat on her belly in the leaves.

"Come on, Muffy," Summer coaxed.

Muffy wagged her tail.

"Here, Muffy." Summer stopped walking and snapped her fingers. Muffy didn't budge.

"Jesus H. Christ," Frankenstein groaned. "I have to be out of my mind, saddling myself with Chatty Kathy and her fleabag. Why the hell couldn't you have left the damned mutt back at your house? They wouldn't have tortured *her*."

"I couldn't leave Muffy," Summer said, shocked.

"Then either get her to walk or carry her." Frankenstein moved off again.

"Come on, Muffy. Here, Muffy. Please, Muffy." But Summer's cajoling was in vain. It was obvious Muffy had no plans to move again.

Summer went back to fetch her.

They walked until Summer's legs ached. The last straw came when she stubbed her bare toes on a large rock that, thanks to the carpet of fallen leaves, she hadn't seen protruding from the trail.

"That's it," Summer said through her teeth, and dropped to the ground, not caring any longer if Frankenstein left her or not. Stretching her legs out, she massaged her injured toes while Muffy panted in the leaves beside her. When the pain lessened, she leaned back against a tree and stared up into its ruffled branches, trying clear her mind of everything except pleasant thoughts.

Frankenstein's battered face leaning over her got in the way of her concentrated effort to chill out.

"What's with you?"

Summer glared up at him. "I stubbed my toe. I have not had any sleep for twenty-four hours. I'm hungry. I'm scared out of my wits. I have badly chafed wrists, a bumped head, a bruised jaw, an aching rib cage, a broken bra strap, and a lost shoe. To top it off, I'm stuck here in a primeval wilderness with a murderer who looks like something out of a monster movie while even worse murderers hunt for me so that they can kill me. That's what's with me."

"Is your toe all better?"

Summer nodded.

"Then do you think we could get going again?"

"I'm not taking another frigging step."

Frankenstein looked down at her for a long, thoughtful moment.

"Suit yourself," he said, and headed off again.

Wait! That was not how it was supposed to work! He was supposed to realize that she was really, truly exhausted and sit down with her and reassure her and feed her some peanut butter crackers and offer to carry the damned dog.

He was *not* supposed to abandon her in the wilderness with nothing but a hairball for protection and vicious killers on her trail.

"Damn you, Steve Calhoun," she said to his retreating back as she struggled to her feet. By the time she scooped up Muffy and headed after him, he was almost out of sight.

He disappeared, finally, under an outcropping of rock. It jutted about six feet straight out from the mountainside and was about eight feet off the ground. Vines and bushes grew densely in front of it so that inside it was almost like a cave, Summer discovered as she followed him beneath the overhang. He was sitting on the ground, cap resting beside him as he rummaged through the gym bag, when she dropped Muffy and wilted at his side.

"We can rest here awhile. I don't know about you, but I'm about out on my feet." He barely glanced at her as he wrestled the quilt from the bag. Summer, so out of sorts and out of breath that she couldn't even talk, eyed him evilly. *He* was out on his feet? What about her?

"Want to sleep or eat first?"

"Sleep? We get to sleep?" This prospect so pleased her that she temporarily forgot a lot of her animosity toward him. "Where?"

A grin crooked his mouth. "Right here, Rosencrans. What were you expecting, a Holiday Inn?"

"Here?" Summer glanced around. "Out in the open? There might be bears, or wolves, or . . . anything."

"After murderers, bears and wolves sound pretty tame to me. Besides, I don't think they have wolves in the Smokies."

Summer noticed he didn't say anything about bears. She was about to point this out when Muffy yapped and crawled into her lap.

"She's hungry," Summer reminded him. "I guess that means we eat first."

"If you think I'm sharing what little food we have with a *dog,* you've got another think coming."

"She saved your life," Summer pointed out.

"Thank you," Frankenstein said to Muffy. "Now go out and catch yourself a nice, juicy squirrel."

"She's not that kind of dog. She's a Grand Champion, for heaven's sake. A show dog. My mother treats her like a child. I don't think she's ever been outside before without a leash."

"Tough," Frankenstein said, and tossed Summer a pack of crackers. "We've got exactly eight packs of crackers, four beers, and a roll of breath mints between us and starvation. Then *we'll* be catching squirrels."

There were six crackers to a cellophane-wrapped package. With Muffy's pleading eyes on her, Summer ripped her package open with her teeth. What Frankenstein said made sense, in a callous, coldhearted way. They needed to save every single scrap of food for themselves.

She passed Muffy a cracker anyway.

Frankenstein, munching his own cracker, watched with blatant disapproval.

"Women," he muttered, shaking his head.

"We saved your ass," Summer responded, including Muffy in that *we.* "More than once, I might add."

To underline the point she passed Muffy another cracker.

"Want a beer?" Apparently having decided to let the matter of Muffy and the crackers rest for the moment, he tore a Stroh's from the ring-pack and held it out to her.

"I hate beer." Summer accepted it with a grimace.

"I quit drinking beer a while back myself, but unless you see a handy spring it's all we've got."

Summer grimaced and popped the top. She was really thirsty, or she wouldn't have done it. Even the smell of beer was usually enough to turn her stomach. But she put the can to her mouth and drank. On top of the buttery, peanuty taste of the crackers, the warm beer was wet. That was the best she could say for it.

"I don't see how people drink this stuff," she said, wrinkling her nose and passing the can to him. "Here, you may as well have the rest. I only took a sip."

"Yeah, well, I guess enjoying a beer just takes practice. What are you, some kind of goody-two-shoes teetotaler?" He accepted the can and looked at it for a moment, hefting it in his hand, his expression unreadable.

"As a matter of fact, I am," Summer said, offended by his sneering indictment of sensible people who chose not to indulge in alcohol. "What are you, an alcoholic?"

"Yep," he said, and held the can out to her without tasting its contents. "You want any more?"

Stunned by his admission, Summer shook her head.

"Sure?" he asked. Summer nodded. He shrugged and stood up to pour the rest of the beer out in the grass by the cave entrance. She was still staring at him as he dropped down beside her again, then crumpled the can in his hand and stuffed it back in the gym bag.

"You can stop looking at me like that," he said with a touch of grim humor as he met her gaze. "I didn't drink it, did I? And I'm thirsty as hell, too."

Discomfited, Summer lowered her eyes and busied herself breaking her last cracker into tiny pieces to feed to Muffy, who licked her fingers appreciatively at the treat. When she looked up again, Frankenstein was spreading the quilt out on the rocky ground. It was the kind of quilt that one might keep in the back of the car for picnics, machine-made in a double wedding ring design. The background was cream, while the rings were formed with small, flower-printed squares of mauve and slate-blue cotton. The quilt was tattered around the edges, with a hole in one corner, and so faded that at first glance it was hard to distinguish the mauve from the blue.

As Summer watched, Frankenstein lay down and rolled himself up in the quilt like a hot dog in pastry. Only his head, which nestled on the gym bag, was visible.

His eyes closed. To all outward appearances, he was well on the way to falling asleep.

"Hey, what about me?" Summer demanded, outraged.

His eyes opened. He frowned at her for a long moment, then silently spread his arms, looking rather like a bird about to take flight as he opened the quilt for her. His message was unmistakable: Here's the bed; if you want to use it, you're going to have to share it with me.

Quickly Summer reviewed the alternatives. They were few, and unattractive. At the moment what she needed more than anything was sleep. She was so tired, her eyes felt grainy. If she had been a flower, she would have drooped long since.

Scowling, she slipped off her remaining shoe, tugged reflexively on her bra strap, and crawled into his arms.

They closed around her, pulling her close. Within seconds her back nestled against his chest, her head was pillowed on the gym bag next to his and she was cocooned in his warmth and the quilt.

Under the circumstances, to feel as safe as she suddenly did was absurd. She knew it, but she felt safe anyway.

His steady breathing stirred her hair. From the sound of it, he was asleep almost the moment she lay still. As she drifted off in turn, Summer smiled a little. She suddenly had an irresistible mental picture of herself trying to explain to her mother just exactly how it was that she had wound up sleeping with Frankenstein.

CHAPTER EIGHTEEN

Steve slept deeply and dreamlessly. When he opened his eyes at last, it was to find himself looking at Deedee.

Impossibly, she seemed to be hovering some six feet above him, stretched out horizontally, lying on her back on the ceiling in fact. His eyes traveled over her with disbelief. She was wearing cowboy boots, skintight, faded-out blue jeans, and a leather motorcycle jacket. Her frizzy blond hair spilled over her shoulders and around her face, which sported a beaming smile framed in lots of red lipstick and a pair of bright blue, heavily mascaraed eyes.

Definitely Deedee.

But Deedee was dead.

As he remembered that, a cold thrill of horror ran down his spine.

She waggled her red-tipped fingers at him.

Steve yelped and sat bolt upright. At least, he would have sat bolt upright if he hadn't been all entangled in a sleeping woman and a tourniquet-like quilt.

"Bad dream?" murmured the woman—Rosencrans—groggily, batting thick, mascaraless eyelashes at him as she tried to fight free of sleep. Sleep won. Within a matter of seconds she was once again out like a light.

Even now that he was half upright—he was leaning back on his elbows in a semi-sitting position, the best he could do under the circumstances—she still cuddled against his chest, seemingly oblivious to his pounding heart beneath her ear.

A bad dream, he echoed her words silently. Yes, of course, that was what he'd just had. Sneaking a quick, spooked glance at the rocky ceiling, Steve realized that was all it could have been. There was nothing above his head but rock, and moss, and a spiderweb.

Deedee was *dead,* for chrissake.

He'd never had a nightmare like that in his life. A waking nightmare. At least, he thought he'd been awake. Maybe he hadn't. Maybe he had dreamed the whole thing and only awakened when he had bolted upright.

Jesus.

He hadn't been asleep in front of the boat warehouse.

Maybe he had a concussion. Maybe, despite his rapidly clearing double vision, his eyes were playing tricks on him in a highly macabre way. Maybe recurring visions of Deedee were going to be his punishment for the rest of his life.

In the three years since her death, he had never once had a vision of Deedee. If these vividly real images were a kind of punishment, why were they cropping up now?

Who the hell knew?

He needed a drink.

It wasn't the first time he had felt the fierce craving since he had sworn off alcohol six months ago. What it had done to his mind and his body, to say nothing of his soul, over two and a half years no one would believe. Booze had nearly destroyed him a second time. He'd fought the fight of his life to get off it and stay off it.

There had been a moment there when he'd been tempted to tell himself that one beer wouldn't harm him. The grace of God—and Rosencrans's sarcastic inquiry as to whether he was an alcoholic— was all that had saved him. He'd be battling the craving for booze for the rest of his life, he realized. It was a battle that he meant to win. One rejected beer at a time.

Settling back down on his less than comfortable bed, re-arranging the woman in his arms so that she wasn't quite strangling him as she slept with her head on his chest and her arms looped around his neck, Steve tried to dismiss what he had seen. He needed to go back to sleep while he had the chance. It had been a hellish forty-eight hours. His mind needed rest to think; his body needed rest to heal.

When he closed his eyes, he should have been thankful that his worry over what he had or hadn't seen on the ceiling was quickly replaced. The problem was what replaced it. Lying there trying not to think of anything at all, he found that his mind was beyond his control. His body, too. With every breath he drew, he grew more keenly aware of the gender of the person sprawled across him. Definitely female. Definitely round, curvy, desirable female. Her tits were burning twin holes in his chest.

With the best will in the world not to do so, Steve recalled how they had looked naked: beautiful, rose-tipped white breasts, so satiny smooth they gleamed in the moonlight. Dolly Partonesque breasts. The stuff-of-male-fantasies breasts.

Some men liked legs, some men liked asses. He was a breast man, himself.

He remembered how it had felt to squeeze one.

Booting the memory from his mind, he concentrated on falling asleep.

The more he tried not to think about exactly what it was that felt so soft and warm and arousing atop his body, the worse the sensation got.

He ended up with the first sober hard-on he'd had in three years.

Steve gritted his teeth and opened his eyes. Since sleep was clearly impossible, the thing to do was think. Work at the puzzle. Try to figure out exactly what was going on, who was behind it, and how he—and she—could get out of it in one piece.

It was useless, he admitted minutes later. He couldn't keep his mind off sex. It had been a while since he'd had any, and, physically, the woman in his arms was just the kind he liked: lushly full and feminine.

This morning he had discovered that she had the softest lips in the world. Lucky he had had enough self-control not to do anything about it.

Under the circumstances, sex with Rosencrans was a complication his life did not need.

All at once the back of his neck prickled. He had the distinct sensation that he was being watched. Unable to help himself, he cast a wary glance at the ceiling.

No Deedee.

Of course no Deedee. He felt both foolish and foolishly relieved.

Until he noticed the dog. It was sitting beside their makeshift sleeping bag, its ridiculous beribboned head cocked to one side and its bulging eyes fixed on something behind him.

Steve turned his head so fast, he damned near cracked his neck.

From the corner, Deedee waggled her fingers at him.

Steve gave a hoarse cry and leaped to his feet, woman, quilt, and all.

She vanished. Deedee vanished. Right before his eyes. Only she didn't actually vanish, of course, because she'd never really been there in the first place.

Shaken, Steve glanced at the dog. She had lost interest in whatever had first attracted her attention and was now placidly scratching an ear.

Damned mutt.

"Is it time to go?" Rosencrans was awake again. He looked down into sleepy hazel-brown eyes that blinked dazedly up into his, noted the straight nose, the creamy texture of her skin, and the wide, well-remembered softness of her lips. Now that he was getting his vision back he could see that she was a damned attractive woman—no, a damned *pretty* woman—even dazed, dirty, and disheveled. She was leaning heavily against him, her hands linked behind his neck, letting him support her weight. He felt the shapely warmth of her in his arms, against his body, and found his explanation for the sudden unnerving visions of Deedee.

They must have been brought on by guilt. Because Rosencrans was the first woman he had wanted, stone-cold sober, since Deedee's death.

CHAPTER NINETEEN

"We need to get out of here." Frankenstein's words were so urgent that they pierced the fog of grogginess that surrounded Summer.

"Why?" Were the bad guys on their trail? Coming immediately fully awake, she struggled against the quilt that suddenly felt to her like a straitjacket, desperate to be free.

"Because we need to." Reaching behind his neck, he unclasped her hands and gave them back to her. Humiliated to discover that she had been clinging to him—*clinging* to him, of all things— Summer withdrew her hands and her body from all contact with his and busied herself with extracting herself from the quilt.

He seemed as anxious to be free as she.

"Is someone coming?" Fear infused her voice and was evident in the quick looks she shot at the mouth of their den. "Did you hear something? See something?"

"No." Frankenstein folded the quilt. He opened the gym bag and pulled some things out before stuffing the quilt in.

"Then what's going on?" Something in his manner was downright scary. He was cold, impersonal, abrupt, unfriendly. That wasn't so surprising, but there was something else as well. He almost seemed—afraid. What had happened while she had been asleep, for goodness' sake?

"Nothing's going on. We need to get a move on, is all. Here, put these on. You can't go around out here in that janitor outfit. You'll stand out like a sore thumb."

Frankenstein stood and thrust a handful of garments at her. His eyes as they met hers were hostile. Summer was bewildered. What was wrong? What had she done?

Taking the things from him, Summer saw that he had passed her the basketball shorts and muscle shirt.

"I can't wear this," she said, holding up the muscle shirt. Even to a cursory glance, which was all she had given it, it was obvious that the shirt was not made for a woman. Its deep, scooped neckline, narrow straps, and enormous armholes would leave her effectively shirtless from the waist up.

"What do you mean, you can't wear it? If the color or something doesn't suit you, that's just too bad."

Summer got the impression that he was deliberately being as nasty as he could be.

"It's not the color, stupid. It's the way it's made. See?" She held the shirt up to herself. The hem reached well past her thighs, the bottom two thirds had ample material—but the top, where it counted, was hardly there.

Frankenstein's frown told her that he saw what she meant.

"Here," he said, pulling off his own shirt and handing it over. "Trade me."

Summer accepted his T-shirt, passed him the muscle shirt, and tried not to look with too much interest at broad shoulders, a well-muscled, hairy chest, and a compact waist with just the faintest suggestion of love handles puddling over the sides of the too snug cutoffs.

His left shoulder and side might be be abloom with purple-to-yellow bruises, but the underlying body was powerfully built.

Summer had always been attracted to big, muscular men.

He pulled the shirt over his head and jerked it into place. The word *Nike* leaped into prominence across his abdomen. His shoulders and upper chest remained essentially bare. His eyes met hers.

Lest he somehow manage to read her thoughts in her eyes, Summer averted her gaze.

"Hurry up, will you?" he said, picking his cap up from the ground and walking outside, taking the gym bag with him. Muffy padded after him.

Left alone, Summer shed her Daisy Fresh uniform and scrambled into the basketball shorts and T-shirt. The shorts were black, made of flimsy nylon, but fortunately were cut to be baggy and fit her reasonably well, stopping just a few inches shy of her knees. With a quick glance at the entrance to their hideaway, Summer slipped out of her bra and made a hurried, but secure, knot in the strap. Putting it back on, she was pleased to rediscover how it felt to have secure support on both sides.

"You done yet?" Frankenstein, speaking from just outside the entrance, sounded impatient. Summer dragged the T-shirt over her head. It was a trifle snug over her bosom and hips, but by yanking at the hem she was able to stretch the material enough so that she thought it looked reasonably decent.

Now if she could only shower, scrub her teeth, and brush her hair . . .

"Almost," she called, combing a hand through her tangled hair, which straggled around her face and down her back. It was as fine and straight as corn silk, and at the moment felt about as limp. Summer wished vainly for fifteen minutes alone with a showerhead, shampoo, a hair dryer, a fat round brush, and some mousse. Her hair might be plain, ordinary brown, but it could look pretty good when she tried.

Would he have kissed her with more enthusiasm if he had ever once seen her with makeup and her hair done?

Summer made the best of things by weaving a single braid that would hang down her back. The only problem was how to secure the end. Since her blouse was ruined anyway, she decided to tear a strip from that and tie it around the braid. Which was harder than she had thought; she had to gnaw through the material with her teeth first.

Frankenstein came in while she was chewing on her blouse.

"You can't be that hungry yet," he said.

Summer made a face at him, ripped the blouse, and secured her hair.

"How do I look?" she asked, gesturing at her outfit.

"Like you've been camping about a week too long," he said, and thrust the pair of high-topped black sneakers at her.

Summer eyed them, but shook her head. "I can't wear those. They're miles too big."

"Beats going barefoot."

"You wear them, and I'll wear the flip-flops."

"Look, Rosencrans, we're going to be hiking for miles. Miles, do you understand? You can't hike in flip-flops. You could turn an ankle, and if you do I'll be damned if I carry you. Or you could step on a broken beer bottle, or a snake. You could . . ."

The snake did it. "Give them to me."

He did. Summer saw that the athletic socks were inside. With a grimace she sat and pulled them on. As she did, she saw that he was donning the other pair. White low-tops, sockless.

"How come you get the low-tops, and I get the high-tops?"

"Because the shoes fit me. They don't fit you. I gave you the high-tops so you could tie 'em tight around your ankles so they wouldn't fall off."

Good point. Good idea. Summer did as he suggested. By the time she finished, he had already gathered up her discarded clothes, stuffed them into the gym bag, picked up the tire iron, and headed outside again.

He was gazing into the distance, his mouth unsmiling, his eyes shaded by the brim of the baseball cap, when she joined him. He was clearly out of sorts about something. For her even to be able to tell that much about his expression, she realized, the swelling in his face had to be going down. She wondered again what he would look like when he was back to normal. Would he be handsome? Cut and bruised and blood-streaked as his face still was, it was impossible to say.

She wished he would kiss her again. With enthusiasm, this time, just to see what kissing Frankenstein would be like.

"What're you looking at?" His gaze swung around, catching her eyes on him, and his response was pugnacious. Summer turned pink, embarrassed by her own wayward thoughts. He scowled.

"You need to wash your face," she managed to say, and was proud of herself for the coolness and quick thinking of her response.

"So do you," he answered, and swung off uphill without another word.

Summer had had about enough of his surliness. She wasn't catering to it any longer. Head high, she turned and marched in the opposite direction.

Muffy, torn, sat on her furry bottom, looked from one separating human to the other, and whined piteously. Summer ignored her, too.

When she emerged from the shelter of a nearby bush, business completed, she was secretly relieved to find Frankenstein waiting beside Muffy, arms crossed over his chest, shoulder propped against a tree, cap brim pulled low over his eyes. She hadn't thought he would just walk off and leave her, but she hadn't been entirely sure. Now she was.

Hostility radiated from him as she approached. Twelve hours earlier, the mere sight of the monster wearing such a glower would have terrified her. Now, safe in her new certainty that he wouldn't leave her, she felt at ease enough to glower back.

"Ready now?" he asked with deep sarcasm.

"Yes, sir," she answered with a mock salute, and had the reward of seeing his scowl deepen.

"Here. We can eat as we walk."

He tossed a pack of crackers at her, swung around, and headed off again. Or maybe *stalked* was a better word.

CHAPTER TWENTY

The sign hammered into a tree where the trail forked said HAW KNOB, ELEV. 5,472 FEET. The arrow pointed straight ahead.

When Frankenstein headed east instead, Summer heaved a sigh of relief. Serious mountain climbing at this point would, she feared, just about do her in.

"Woof." Chocolate doggy eyes looked up at Summer pleadingly. Muffy squirmed in her arms. Not bothering to set her down —Muffy had already firmly established that she would not walk— Summer shifted her weight to the other arm, and shot a dagger look at the broad masculine back some dozen feet ahead.

The man was tireless. They'd been walking without a break for what seemed like days. It was twilight now, and she for one was exhausted. Her feet hurt: the too big shoes rubbed blisters on her heels even through the thick socks. Her arms hurt: Muffy, for all her smallness, weighed a ton. Frankenstein's callous suggestion was that if Summer grew tired of carrying her, she should just pitch her over a cliff; *he* didn't offer to carry her.

And Summer refused to ask.

Her fondest wish was that Muffy would pee on his foot again. But the dog couldn't even do that if they didn't stop.

An insect bite on the side of Summer's neck itched, and she scratched it dispiritedly. It was one of about two dozen she had collected. As the sun set, the mosquitoes had come out to dine.

Never in her life had she thought to find herself envying a mosquito, but at least they had something to dine *on*.

Summer was so hungry that she ached with it. Her stomach was so empty that it felt like it was collapsing. She pictured it as a deflating balloon.

There were three packs of crackers left. Frankenstein had already announced that they would have to be saved for the morrow. Summer's head understood; her stomach emphatically did not.

"Woof," Muffy pleaded.

"Hush," Summer said, nuzzling her suddenly tortured nose against Muffy's fur. She knew what had prompted that forlorn bark. She smelled it too: food.

Up ahead, to their left, was a lodge. Frankenstein was carefully skirting it, anxious to avoid as many people as he could. He was right, of course. The less attention they attracted, particularly given his battered state, the better, but still the aroma pulled at her like a magnet: woodsmoke and grilling steaks. Yum.

Her mouth watered. Her stomach growled. Muffy whined. Sympathetically, Summer scratched behind her ear.

Muffy shook her hand off. What she wanted was not love, but *food*.

Up ahead, Frankenstein forged on through the trees, looking to neither the left nor the right. Of course, he was beyond feeling anything as human as hunger.

He'd been cranky all afternoon. If Summer had had any better choices, she would have left him high and dry hours ago.

Only she didn't have any better choices.

She and Muffy were stuck with Frankenstein.

A couple strolled hand in hand out of the darkness to her right. They saw Summer moving through the trees nearby and gave a friendly wave. Summer waved back and watched them as they continued toward the lodge. She was traveling perpendicular to the path on which they trod; up ahead, Frankenstein had already crossed it. A quick glance showed her that he had been all but swallowed up by the darkness ahead. If she wasn't careful, she would lose him in the dark.

Slowing without conscious thought, Summer watched enviously as the couple crossed a small, decorative bridge that led to the lodge's parking lot. Beyond them, a car pulled in, its headlights illuminating several of its already parked fellows, and picking up the bright madras plaid of the woman's sundress. Her companion wore a pale blue sport coat and tie and held her hand. Clearly they were going in to dinner.

Summer ached to be in that woman's shoes. Not for the sake of the man, or the dress, but for the dinner. Imagining the meal the woman would soon consume threatened to bring tears to her eyes.

All at once Summer realized that Frankenstein was completely out of sight. She increased her pace, and tried to keep her mind off food.

It was impossible. Her nose was mercilessly tantalized. Her gaze kept slipping sideways. The lodge was lit and so were several cabins to one side of it. Through the uncurtained windows, Summer could see the silhouettes of people inside the buildings. The couple she'd been watching reached the stone terrace. Another couple moved toward them, and they shook hands all around. Then they went inside—undoubtedly to have dinner.

By chasing after Frankenstein, she would be leaving behind what she was rapidly coming to think of as the last outpost of civilization. The tantalizing smell of grilling steaks beckoned her back.

Frankenstein didn't care if she starved.

She could turn around, right that very minute, and become part of civilization again simply by joining the people at the lodge. Their company would be infinitely preferable to that of a grumpy murderer who had hardly deigned to glance at her for hours. A murderer who was on the run for his life—and whose very existence endangered hers. Without him, no one would ever have displayed the least inclination to kill her.

Which was the only reason he was letting her tag along with him. The knowledge was galling.

But even if she did opt for the lodge, Summer thought, she had no money for food or a room. Bruised and unkempt as she was, her appearance would attract attention. She could ask for help— but what help could, or would, those innocents give her? They would certainly call the police.

Summer shivered. She wasn't quite sure whether she believed Frankenstein's assertion that the police were the bad guys—but she wasn't quite sure she didn't, either.

One thing was certain: She didn't want to find out the hard way.

Gritting her teeth against civilization's devilish allure, Summer kept walking. Muffy whined. Trees whispered in the wind. Frogs croaked and crickets chirped. The cicadas hummed. A car horn honked in the distance. The smoke-borne smell of the steaks grew fainter. So did the hum of voices.

Good-bye, civilization! Summer's stomach growled a sad farewell. Muffy seemed to droop in her arms.

She almost bumped into Frankenstein, who was waiting beneath a tree for her to catch up.

"If you can't keep up, you're on your own," he growled as she blinked at him in surprise, and turned and stalked away again. Scowling at his retreating back, Summer followed wearily.

Soon there was no trail. Instead he forged his own path through the undergrowth. In the gloom Summer stumbled over rocks and tree roots she couldn't see. The pace he set was killing. As the lodge receded to nothing more than a fond memory, Summer grew increasingly afraid to let Frankenstein out of her sight.

It would be just her luck to lose him far from the succoring lodge.

"Slow down," she gasped at his back after a while.

He kept walking.

"I can't keep going at this pace."

He kept walking.

"I'm starving."

He kept walking.

"Can't we at least take a break? It's the middle of the night."

He kept walking.

"Asshole," Summer muttered under her breath, and kept walking too.

The wind moaned through the trees. A loud crack somewhere nearby was followed by a crash and a resounding thud.

Summer shot forward like a rabbit flushed by a hound and grabbed Frankenstein's arm.

"What's the matter with you now?" He sounded grumpy as ever.

"What was that?" She was too apprehensive to care.

"What?"

"That sound."

"A falling branch. What did you think it was?" His face was in shadow as he glanced down at her. Feeling foolish, Summer dropped his arm.

"I don't know. A bear, maybe. A hungry bear, wanting Muffy and me for dinner."

He grunted derisively, muttered something under his breath that sounded like "I should get so lucky," and started walking again.

Summer stared after him, affronted. He was almost out of sight when she hurried to catch up. She vowed that she'd let herself be eaten by a dozen bears before she spoke to him again.

In unfriendly silence they waded through streams, climbed over downed trees, and stomped through clearings. Summer tripped on fallen limbs and got snared by brambles, and kept walking. The night smelled of damp leaves, horse manure, and, more faintly, flowers. Delphiniums? one part of her mind wondered abstractedly. Or maybe lily of the valley? There was definitely a hint of honeysuckle.

Muffy's weight dragged on her arms, making her back and shoulders ache. Several times she set the dog down and moved off, only to have to return for her when Muffy adamantly refused to budge.

"I ought to leave you," she muttered the third or fourth time this happened.

Securely cradled in warm arms once again, Muffy licked Summer's chin.

What time was it? Summer wondered. Midnight? One or two a.m.? Was Frankenstein going to walk all blasted night?

She had to pee. She was afraid if she stopped for long enough to relieve herself, Frankenstein would disappear. She was going to have to break down and call to him—but she wasn't sure she had enough wind left.

With a yap Muffy leaped from her arms and took off through the trees.

It was so unexpected that Summer could only gape after her.

Up ahead, Frankenstein just kept walking.

"Hey!" she called. Then, more loudly, "Yo, Frankenstein!"

He stopped, looked around. She beckoned wildly, though she wasn't sure that, dark as it was, he could see. Apparently he could, or at least he got the gist of her urgent gesture. He retraced his steps.

"What now?" He sounded positively poisonous.

"Muffy took off."

"What?"

Summer repeated herself, pointing in the general direction in which Muffy had disappeared. He swore.

"We've got to get her back. Just like the car: they find her, they find us. They couldn't possibly *not* identify her. She's so ridiculous-looking, she's got to be one of a kind."

"She is not ridiculous-looking!" Tired as she was, Summer managed a spurt of indignation on Muffy's behalf.

"Just help me find the damned dog, okay?"

But Muffy was nowhere in sight.

They split up, beating through the trees on a vaguely parallel course, calling softly for Muffy.

Their only answer was the sudden hoot and rushing flight of an owl overhead. Apparently they had disturbed its hunting. When it was no longer within sight or sound, Summer got up from the crouch into which she had dropped at the owl's advent and started walking again. With every other step she glanced cautiously upward and all around. Who knew what other creatures might be lurking nearby?

Summer smelled it first—smoke. She slid across to Frankenstein, who had paused. He smelled it, too. Together they advanced through the woods in the direction of the aroma, cautiously. If it had attracted them, perhaps it had attracted Muffy.

Through the trees they saw the outline of half a dozen tents, silhouetted by a roaring fire. Three men and a flock of youngsters in uniforms sat around the campsite. One of the men was talking. Whatever he was saying had the children transfixed.

Boy Scouts on a camp-out, probably swapping ghost stories. Summer recognized the uniforms and smiled.

They were also roasting hot dogs and marshmallows on sticks over the fire.

As Summer realized that, her stomach gave a mighty growl.

"Hey, look! Something's stealing our things!"

"It's a coon!"

"It's a possum!"

"It's a bear!"

"Grab the crossbow!"

"Crossbow, hell! Grab the rifle!"

To a man, the Boy Scouts and their leaders leaped to their feet and dashed toward where Summer and Frankenstein watched them through the trees. Just ahead of the pack streaked a small, furry creature that looked for all the world like a diminutive Cousin Itt. A white plastic grocery bag bounced along the ground beside it. The handles were clutched in its mouth.

CHAPTER TWENTY-ONE

Frankenstein snatched up Muffy and the bag, and ran. Summer ran, too. With a tribe of whooping Boy Scouts in hot pursuit, they crashed through the forest in great leaping bounds. Foot snagged by a wayward vine, Summer went down. To her surprise, Frankenstein came back for her. Grabbing her hand, he hauled her to her feet and dragged her along after him.

Gradually the sounds of pursuit died away.

Summer developed a stitch in her side. Pulling her hand from Frankenstein's, she slowed to a walk, pressing her hand to her side, and finally stopped altogether.

"I'm not taking another step." She spoke with finality. It was an effort to breathe.

"You're not very athletic, are you?" he said disapprovingly, turning to frown down at her.

"No, I'm not. If you'd wanted Jackie Joyner-Kersee, you should have kidnapped *her*. I'm sure she would have been delighted."

"You know, you're a real pain in the butt."

"You're not exactly a little ray of sunshine yourself, Mr. Macho Man," Summer snapped back, glaring up at him from her bent-over position.

To Summer's surprise, he grinned. It was the first smile she had seen on his face in hours.

"Slumped over like that, you look kinda like the Hunchback of Notre Dame."

"Then we make a fine pair of monsters, don't we, Franken-stein?"

He laughed. Summer eyed him less than fondly. While she carried nothing, he was loaded down with gear. The gym bag was slung over his right shoulder, and the tire iron and grocery bag dangled from his right hand. Muffy was tucked under his left arm like a football. Muffy alone weighed a ton, Summer knew. And the blasted man wasn't even breathing hard.

"All right, that was a pretty good run. You've earned a rest. Besides, your dog fetched supper."

"Is it food?" All thoughts of disliking him forgotten, Summer glanced longingly at the bag.

"Look for yourself." He passed it over.

Summer looked. The sack contained three unopened packages: hot dogs, buns, and marshmallows. A yellow plastic cigarette lighter, price sticker still affixed, slid along the seam at the bottom.

"It's a feast," she said, awed.

Frankenstein took the sack back. "Come on, let's go find a place to cook it."

Summer groaned. "I'm telling you, I can't walk any farther. Not another step."

"Not far. Just till we find somewhere where we can light a fire without burning the forest down. Don't quit on me now, Rosen-crans. Maybe our luck's turning."

"McAfee," Summer corrected weakly, but he was already on the move again. Taking a deep breath, relieved to discover that she could, Summer grudgingly followed. Not so much Frankenstein, but the food.

After about a quarter of an hour they came to a wide, rippling stream that looked shiny black in the darkness. Summer was so

tired that she would have walked right into it if Frankenstein
hadn't stopped at the edge. Instead she walked into him. Her nose
bumped against his broad back.

"Over there," he said, pointing to the other side as, rubbing her
nose, she stepped out beside him. "We can build a fire and spend
the night."

Thank God.

Across the water lay a rocky area strewn with boulders. It
stretched for about forty feet to where a tall cliff crowned with
pointy-topped pines cut across the skyline. Flinty pale against the
night sky, the cliff looked as if it had been hewn from limestone.
Crystals imbedded in the rocky sides gleamed dully in the moonlight.

Frankenstein waded into the water. Taking a deep breath, pressing her palm against her still bothersome side, Summer followed.

In contrast to the seventyish temperature of the air, the water
was cold. Icy, as a matter of fact. It swirled about her ankles and
her calves, and rose toward her knees. Ahead, Frankenstein
splashed toward the opposite shore. Reassured, Summer saw that
even in the middle of the stream the water barely passed his knees.

She would not drown. She would not even get the hem of her
shorts wet. She took the opportunity to stop and scoop up sand
from the pebble-strewn bottom to scrub her hands and face.

As she rinsed away the sand with more icy water she felt better.

Frankenstein had reached the bank while she was attending to
her ablutions. He took off his cap, set it, Muffy, and the gear down
on the bank, and turned back to lend her a hand. At least, she
thought that was why he was turning back, and she splashed forward to meet him. Her dislike of him softened still more, blunted
by his concern for her.

He stopped some two feet away, bent double, and thrust his
head beneath the surface of the water.

Summer was so startled by the unexpectedness of his action that
she lost her footing. The sole of her too big sneaker slid on a
mossy rock, and for a moment she teetered wildly. Then, with a
startled cry and an enormous splash, she went down.

Her mouth was still open when the water closed over her head.

The suddenness of it, the shock of finding herself totally submerged in icy water, caused her to panic. She choked, flailing like
a chicken on the chopping block.

A hand caught the front of her T-shirt and dragged her upward.
Her head broke the surface of the water, and she coughed and
gagged and spat as she tried to fill her waterlogged lungs with air.
Soaked to the skin, she was hauled to her feet and steadied with a
warm hand on each elbow. Glancing up, she saw Frankenstein's
grinning, dripping face.

He deliberately held her at arm's length so that she would not
get his clothes wet.

"If you laugh, I'll kill you. I swear I will," she said through
gritted teeth and a curtain of sopping hair.

He laughed.

Summer thought about kicking him. With her luck her foot
would fly out from under her and she would end up taking another dunking.

She thought about punching him, but she figured he'd dodge.
She'd probably end up in the drink again that way, too.

Either way, he'd laugh even more.

She turned and stomped toward shore. Her water-filled shoes
felt like they weighed about a hundred pounds each.

Squelching up onto the bank, dripping and shivering, Summer
wrapped her arms around herself. She must have been quite a
sight, because Muffy took one look at the apparition arising from
the stream and started backing away.

Behind her, she thought she heard a snicker.

Over her shoulder, she threw Frankenstein a glare that should
have toasted his toes.

Was she ever mad! Mad at him, mad at herself, mad at the
world! If Heaven had planned the whole sorry last twenty-four
hours as some kind of cosmic entertainment, well, she would like
to kick Heaven right in the teeth!

She was also freezing her buns off.

"Here," Frankenstein said, sounding faintly choked as he pried
one set of her frozen fingers from her arm and thrust the quilt into

it. "Go get out of those wet clothes before you catch pneumonia. I'll start a fire."

Casting him a venomous glance, Summer, clutching the quilt, retired behind a large boulder with what dignity she could muster.

When she emerged sometime later, swaddled in the quilt like a papoose, her wrung-out clothes held stiffly before her, her wrung-out hair twisted in a soggy coil down her back, she was relieved to discover that he was paying her not the least attention. His back was to her as he worked to blow life into a flickering flame that licked halfheartedly at a pile of twigs. Muffy was stretched out like a small fur rug at his side.

Summer hung her clothes from branches, careful to snag them securely so that they would not fall during the night. She turned her enormous shoes upside down to dry atop a rock. By the time she had finished, Frankenstein had the fire going and was threading hot dogs onto a stick.

Food. Nothing less than that would have enticed her to approach the fire—and him.

She was very conscious of being naked beneath the quilt.

"Here," he said as she approached, and handed her another stick that skewered four marshmallows. Regarding him warily, Summer sank cross-legged to the ground. The quilt unexpectedly parted in front, baring an embarrassing expanse of pale inner thigh. Shooting a quick look at Frankenstein—thank God he appeared to be staring into the flames, oblivious—she hitched the soft cotton closer around her body. Modesty restored, she too focused on the fire and concentrated on roasting her share of dinner to a turn.

He ignored her. She ignored him.

The wind, still warm from the day, blew softly across the clearing. Flames danced around the small pile of sticks as it passed. Overhead, stars twinkled, ringed in by a fringe of towering pines.

Frankenstein was about a yard away, and, like her, he sat cross-legged on the hard-packed earth. Try as she would to pretend he was not there, he loomed large in her peripheral vision.

His wet hair glistened seal-black in the firelight. The right side of his face, the side that was nearer her, was not as badly damaged as the left. There was still some bruising, but most of the swelling seemed to have receded. It was possible to discern that he had high, rather flat cheekbones; a straight, high-bridged nose; thin lips; and an obstinate chin. The natural color of his skin was slightly sallow, she thought. As an adolescent he must have suffered with acne, because his cheek bore faint traces of scars.

Not a handsome man, she decided smugly. And remembered that disinterested kiss.

He glanced at her. Ringed by twin shiners, his eyes were as black as his hair. They were guarded eyes, dangerous eyes. The eyes of a man who was not afraid to die—or kill.

One glance from those eyes should have made her shiver in her shoes. Which, she discovered to her surprise, it did. Only not from fear.

She glanced away hurriedly, so that he would not think she was looking at him. When her gaze stole back to him, he was once again staring into the fire.

Summer found herself admiring the breadth of his shoulders, bared by the orange Nike shirt and gleaming in the firelight, and the rippling muscles in his arms. Beneath the tight cutoffs, his thighs and calves were well muscled, too, and well furred as well. The deep neck of his shirt revealed that his wide chest was liberally endowed with swirls of silky black hair.

He wasn't handsome, but he was masculine. Intensely, powerfully masculine. The sheer force of that masculinity was sexier than mere handsomeness on its own could ever be.

As she came to that conclusion, Summer found herself meeting his gaze. For a second, no longer, their eyes locked and held. Then, as casually as if nothing momentous had occurred, Frankenstein shifted his attention back to the hot dogs he was roasting over the fire.

Summer, on the other hand, felt like she had just been struck by lightning.

How was it possible to be cold, scared, and starving—and yet at the same time wildly attracted to the man who had caused all three?

When he didn't even seem to realize that she was a woman?

By the time the marshmallows were done, Summer felt as grumpy as he had acted all day. She was also so ravenous that she couldn't even wait for the marshmallows to cool. Instead she pulled one from the stick while it was still bubbling hot, and popped it into her mouth.

And promptly burned her tongue.

"Oh! Ah!" she gasped, and gulped desperately at the beer Frankenstein obligingly passed her. With her tongue cooked to a crisp and the cloying sweetness of the marshmallow acting as a barrier, the beer was not half bad.

"I thought you hated beer," he observed when at last she lowered the can.

"I do." Her tongue still tingled. She waggled it experimentally.

"No beer parties in college?" He carefully pulled a hot dog from the stick.

"No." Summer shrugged. "No college." With rapt interest she watched as he balanced the stick by the fire, split a bun and tenderly placed a hot dog therein.

"None at all?" He took a huge bite.

"Nope. Hey, how about me?" Indignantly she reached for the stick he had put down, which still held three hot dogs. He was obliging enough to trade the package of buns for a marshmallow.

"How come?" He ate the marshmallow whole.

"How come what?" Summer took her first bite of hot dog. It tasted wonderful, fantastic, divine. If she'd been writing for a *Mobil Travel Guide,* she would have awarded it five stars.

"How come no college?"

"I went to New York to model instead. As a teenager I took classes at a modeling school in Murfreesboro—they cost an arm and a leg, let me tell you—and modeled part time. After high school graduation, the school set up some interviews for me with some agencies in New York. One took me on, and the rest, as they say, is history. I always thought there'd be plenty of time later for college. I was wrong." She took another bite out of her hot dog: ambrosia.

"So how long did you stay in New York?"

Muffy was approaching him flat on her belly, her tongue lolling, her tail wagging abjectly. She gave a delicate little yap, and Frankenstein scowled at her. Then, to Summer's surprise, he broke off a third of his hot dog and handed it to her.

"I modeled till I was two months shy of twenty-five. Not high fashion stuff like I had hoped—lingerie, for catalogues, mostly, and some hand work. Lingerie wasn't as big then as it is now, and hands weren't big at all. I made a decent living, went to a lot of really neat parties, and enjoyed myself in general. Then all at once there were other girls, younger girls, who were in demand. Just as suddenly as that"—she snapped her fingers—"it was over. I was too old. So I came home."

Snapping her fingers had been a mistake. Muffy did her crawling-rug imitation in Summer's direction. Summer fed her part of a marshmallow.

"How long ago was that?"

"Eleven years."

"So you're thirty-six."

"Sounds awful, doesn't it?" Summer took another bite of hot dog and tried to pretend she didn't care. She did. Getting older was not something she had been prepared for. No longer being young and reasonably gorgeous had required a lot of adjustment. Getting up in the morning and counting the crow's feet around her eyes, having to use her mascara wand and then a rinse to color the gray hairs that increasingly appeared among the brown, was not something she had ever expected would happen to her. But of course it had.

She was glad getting over it was all behind her, which it was.

Except when a man, especially one who interested her as much as Frankenstein was beginning to, seemed to feel that she possessed not one iota of sex appeal. Then getting older stung all over again.

CHAPTER TWENTY-TWO

"Thirty-six sounds pretty good to me. I'm thirty-nine."

"Men are different. Given the chance, I bet you'd date twenty-year-olds." Disgust laced Summer's voice.

"Nope. I like my women old enough to know better, but young enough to do it anyway."

Summer snorted. "Ha-ha."

He grinned and pulled another marshmallow from the stick.

"So what happened after you came home? By home you do mean Murfreesboro, I take it."

Summer nodded. "I was born in Murfreesboro, and when New York stopped happening I came home to Murfreesboro. Don't you know that, however far they may wander, Tennesseeans always come home?"

"I think I may have heard that somewhere." Frankenstein bit into his second hot dog with as much evident enjoyment as he had attacked the first. "You came home to your family? Parents, brothers, sisters?"

"Mom, Dad, older sister Sandra, younger sister Shelly. I was the one in the middle. The headstrong one who never would listen. Dad used to say I always had to learn things the hard way. He wanted to send me to college; I took the money and went to New York instead. My sisters, on the other hand, chose college. Sandra's a medical technologist out in California now, happily married for fifteen years, with four gorgeous children. Shelly lives in Knoxville. She's a lawyer, happily married for nine years, with three gorgeous children. Then there's me: a divorced, childless janitor."

Summer laughed, but there was no humor in the sound. Her sisters had sensibly chosen to follow the paths their parents had mapped out for them; Summer, on the other hand, had defied all advice to reach for a star—and in the process gotten her fingers badly burned.

"At least you had the courage to try." This comment, coming from Frankenstein, from whom she would have expected some kind of joke at her expense, startled Summer. After a moment spent twisting the notion this way and that, she looked at him with real gratitude. Never had she thought of her choice in quite that way, and to do so eased a hard little knot of regret that had been festering for a long time inside her.

Before she could comment, he continued: "So what did you do, a New York lawn-jer-ee model, back home in Murfreesboro?"

Summer smiled a little. "I got married, what else? To the police chief's handsome doctor son. Despite the little hitch of his being Jewish, my parents were thrilled. Despite the little hitch of my being Baptist, *his* parents were thrilled. I was even thrilled—for a while. It wore off."

"What happened?" He sounded surprisingly sympathetic.

Summer bit into her hot dog. "He married the lingerie model, not me. When he found out that my natural weight was some twenty pounds heavier than it was when he married me and my hair didn't curl unless I put curlers in it and my lips weren't naturally red without lipstick, he freaked."

"Oh, yeah?" Frankenstein responded to Muffy's rug routine by tossing her a section of bun. "So you got a divorce, huh?"

"Not right away. I wish I had. He spent five long years trying to turn me back into the woman he thought he had married. Someone who was feminine, sexy, and glamorous twenty-four hours a day. I spent five long years letting him. More fool me." Without meaning to, the bitterness Summer had thought was long behind her crept into her voice. The things she had done for Lem! She had dressed to the teeth, kept a perfect house, cooked meals from scratch, entertained his friends and colleagues with the slavish attention to detail of a frigging Martha Stewart—and spent a lot of time watching movies on the VCR while Lem worked all the hours God sent. She had been slowly going crazy with unhappiness, and all the while, to please him, she had dieted to the point of starvation. Sometimes, when she couldn't stand it any longer, she would wait until Lem was out of the house and stuff herself with anything she could find—ice cream, bread, candy bars she had hidden just for that purpose. Then she had inevitably been sick. Sick to her stomach, yes, but also sick with shame for not being able to be the girl Lem thought he had married. As Lem had told her time and again—practically every time he'd seen her eat a normal meal, in fact—he hadn't realized he was marrying a hog.

With Lem, she had always felt like a hog.

Frankenstein looked her over thoughtfully. "More fool he, I'd say. For an old bag of thirty-six, you're not half bad."

Summer gave him a sudden, dazzling smile. "I don't know what you're after, Frankenstein, but keep on buttering me up like that and you just might get it."

He grinned. "It was a compliment. I swear."

"That's what they all say."

"Have a marshmallow. Maybe it'll sweeten you up."

"Maybe."

They split the last toasted marshmallow. Summer savored the sticky confection as it melted on her tongue, then mourned its passing. Frankenstein must have felt the same way, because he licked the gooey residue from his fingers when his half was gone.

"So what happened after you finally got a divorce from what's-his-name?"

"Lem. Dr. Lemuel C. Rosencrans, urologist. Are you really interested in hearing the rest of my life story?"

"There's no TV. Got nothing better to do."

Summer made a face at him. "Okay, I got a divorce. With no-fault divorce, and without any children, and since Lem was already a doctor when I married him, and since we had no equity to speak of in our house, I ended up with practically no money. Which was a shock. I'd never known before what it was like to have to worry about what I was going to eat the next day. My parents were living in Santee by that time and my dad was ill. They were sick about the divorce. I didn't want to burden them any more than they were already burdened. My sisters were married and moved away. It was me, on my own. I was determined that I was going to make it, with no help from anyone. Only, I didn't have any education, or training for any type of job. I'd been a lingerie model—try finding a job with that kind of reference in Murfreesboro—and a housewife. I'd gotten too old and fat to model underwear and I no longer had a husband or a house. But one thing I did bring out of my marriage: By golly, I knew how to clean. So I started cleaning other people's houses. And Daisy Fresh was born. It's supported me ever since, and it's grown every year."

Frankenstein swallowed the last bite of his hot dog. "I don't know how to tell you this, Rosencrans, but that's quite a success story."

His comment pleased Summer inordinately. "Thank you."

"So by now you've got what's-his-name out of your system, I presume. What about new boyfriends?"

"I'm seeing someone. Jim Britt, a dentist."

"Serious?"

Summer hesitated, then decided to tell the truth. "No."

"Good."

She looked at him carefully. "What do you mean, good?"

"I'd hate to think of you turning back into some doctor's little housewife." His expression was bland.

"That will never happen again in this life, believe me. I've learned my lesson." Summer shuddered theatrically, watching with regret as he folded the top of the marshmallow bag to guard against temptation. About a dozen marshmallows still remained inside. Prudence dictated that they, and the remaining hot dogs, buns, crackers, and breath mints, be saved for the future meals. "If we're playing Twenty Questions, I have a few for you: Did you go to college?"

"Yup. Eastern Kentucky University. Majored in law enforcement. But not right out of high school. First I joined the Marines."

"On purpose?" Most of the fortyish men she knew had spent their formative years doing their best to avoid the service.

He grinned again. "Yeah."

"Why?"

"Let's just say I was a sucker for that *the few, the proud* crap."

"Really?"

"And I didn't want to get drafted. I thought I'd come out better if I joined before they nabbed me."

"Did you? Come out better, I mean."

"I'm still in one piece, so I must have. Although a lot of my friends managed to ride out the waning years of the draft in the National Guard."

"Were you in Vietnam?" Her voice was hushed, and she looked at him with renewed respect.

He grinned again. "No, but I sweated it for a while there. Just about the time I got out of basic, they started bringing troops home. I was never so thankful for anything in my life. I spent most of my hitch in North Carolina. Which meant I kinda lost my chance to be a big war hero."

"At least you didn't die."

"That's how I've always looked at it."

"Did you—*are* you married?"

"Divorced." His tone was easy. No roadblock went up at all.

"When?"

"Three years ago. When my life went to hell in a handbasket. Along with everything else that happened, my wife left me. Took my daughter with her."

"You have a daughter?" Somehow the idea that he might be someone's dad hadn't occurred to her.

"Yep. She's thirteen now. I've seen her exactly three times since she was ten." The bitterness in his voice told her how sensitive the topic was. "She doesn't want to see me. Blames me for everything that happened, including the divorce. Says I ruined her life. The kids at school make fun of her because she's my kid."

"I'm sorry." Her own memories of the past dulled in the face of his imperfectly concealed pain.

"Yeah. Me too."

"So your wife divorced you over—what happened?" Trying to be delicate, Summer's tongue stumbled over the last words.

"You mean my little bout with adultery? Oh, yeah."

"I'm sorry," Summer said again. The words were inadequate, she knew, but she could come up with nothing better.

"I'm not. Not anymore, not about the divorce. We were never good for each other. She used to tell me I never really loved her, and she was right."

"Did you meet her in North Carolina?"

He shook his head. "Elaine's from Nashville. I met her after I got out of the Marines. She was two years younger than me, and we were married for eleven years. Maybe three of 'em good ones. She used to be jealous of every woman I said two words to. And I never cheated once, I swear on the Bible. Not until . . ." His voice trailed off. Summer understood what he didn't say.

"What was her name?"

His glance at her was unreadable. He didn't pretend not to know whom she meant. "Deedee."

"Did you love her?"

"Deedee?" He was quiet for a moment, his eyes reflective. "I was crazy about her from the time we were teenagers. Then I finally got what I'd been hankering after for twenty-two years— she and I in a red-hot affair—and it wasn't what I expected at all. We were oil and water, not compatible a bit. But I loved her. Yeah, I loved her. In the end, it wasn't enough. Not for me. And not for her."

The raw anguish in his voice as he finished warned her to leave the subject alone. When Frankenstein suddenly busied himself by breaking one last hot dog into pieces for Muffy, she tactfully got to her feet and retired into the darkness with a murmured excuse about heeding nature's call.

When she returned, he didn't look up at first. He was squatting by the fire, his attention focused on feeding sticks to the flames. As she watched him without, she thought, his being aware of it, he picked up a freshly opened beer that was waiting beside him and took an enormous swig.

Summer remembered what he had said about being an alcoholic, and felt a twinge of alarm.

He must have felt her eyes on him then, because he glanced around. Her gaze went involuntarily to the beer can he still held.

Knowing that she watched, he put the can to his lips and took another long swallow.

"Quit worrying," he advised her when he was done, wiping the back of his hand across his mouth. "You wouldn't want me to die of thirst out here in the wilderness, would you?" He grinned suddenly at the expression on her face. "Besides, it's water. I filled an empty can up at the stream."

"In that case, I hope you don't get dysentery." It was hard to keep her tone as light as she knew it needed to be. She felt such enormous sympathy for him that it took a huge amount of dissembling not to let it show.

He would hate it if he guessed she felt sorry for him. Summer knew it instinctively, as surely as she knew that in life there would always be taxes and death.

Her flippant rejoinder made him grimace. "Jesus, I never thought about that."

"Too late now."

Without warning, Summer yawned so widely that her jaws cracked. With her stomach full, she was out on her feet. She needed sleep in the worst way. Then she glanced at Frankenstein, suddenly ill at ease.

He was busy repacking their remaining supply of food, wrapping it in the white plastic bag and then unzipping the gym bag, to, she assumed, stow it away. When she yawned, he grinned at her.

"Looks like bedtime for you, Bonzo."

Bedtime for Bonzo, indeed. She was agreeable. There was just one teensy little problem.

They only had one quilt between them. And she was wearing it.

CHAPTER TWENTY-THREE

"Need some jammies?" Frankenstein fished in the gym bag and held out something. Summer recognized her own Daisy Fresh uniform with relief. The clothes might be less than fresh, but at least they were clothes. She wouldn't have to sleep naked after all.

"Thanks." Summer accepted the garments and retired behind a rock to pull them on. Without underclothes, her bare bottom clung to the polyester pants, and her breasts hung unconfined beneath the thin nylon of the blouse. Glancing down, Summer saw that her nipples thrust visibly against the cloth.

She pulled the quilt back around herself, and felt better. Not quite so hideously exposed.

When she emerged from behind the boulder, she saw that he had zipped himself into the hooded sweatshirt and dragged the gym bag over to a spot near the fire. He was stretched out flat on his back with his head resting on the bag and his arms crossed over his chest.

His eyes were closed. They flickered open as Summer hesitantly approached.

"Good night," he said.

Summer watched in disbelief as his eyes closed again. From the sound of his breathing, within seconds he was asleep.

Good night?

Clearly she did not have to fear the consequences of sharing a quilt with him. He was quite content, no, eager from the look of him, to sleep alone, braving the chill night air rather than share a quilt with her.

He had not been so particular earlier in the day. Had he somehow divined that she was growing increasingly attracted to him? Did he fear being attacked in his sleep?

Summer's face burned.

She glanced around at the darkness outside the flickering circle of light cast by the fire and shivered. Anything could be out there.

Nevertheless, she was not going to debase herself by begging to sleep with Frankenstein.

Clutching the quilt closer, Summer dropped to her knees, brushed a reasonably grassy spot free of rocks and twigs, and lay down. Clicking her tongue at Muffy, she swooped the dog up when she approached and cuddled her close beneath the quilt.

Muffy sighed and snuggled. Summer no longer felt quite so alone.

Closing her eyes, she willed herself to go to sleep.

Paradoxically, now that she wanted to, Summer found that she could not. Curled into a fetal position not far from the fire—or Frankenstein's feet—with a wad of quilt for a pillow, Summer tried everything to make herself drowsy, from counting sheep to imagining the flowers she would plant in next summer's garden. Nothing worked. Her mind was awake and busy; her emotions seesawed between affront at Frankenstein's lack of interest and fear at her surroundings.

Frankenstein had not even so much as shot her a suggestive look all through their meal. He must have known she was naked beneath the quilt, but clearly the knowledge had not disturbed him in the least.

Screech!

Summer's eyes snapped open. What was that sound? Glancing around, she could see nothing moving outside of the dancing flames and Frankenstein's rhythmically rising and falling chest. Beyond the small circle of light cast by the fire, the darkness was impenetrable.

The sound must have been made by an animal—a *small* animal, she hoped—somewhere far away in the woods.

Her lids started to droop again. *Why* hadn't Frankenstein made a pass at her? Most men, given the circumstances, wouldn't have hesitated. Had anxiety over their predicament sapped his sex drive? Was he too blamed tired after their endless trek?

The thought that he was too much of a gentleman to take advantage of the situation occurred to her, only to be dismissed with an inner hoot.

Frankenstein a gentleman? She didn't think so.

Crack!

What was that? Summer's eyes sprang open again. Once again there was nothing to be seen except the rocks, the fire, and Frankenstein. Muffy was snuggled beneath her chin, fast asleep. Her fur tickled Summer's nose, but not for anything would she have evicted her sleeping partner. Though the comfort Summer took from the dog's proximity was largely illusory and she knew it, still it made her feel better to have Muffy near.

If there was a bear prowling nearby, how much help would Muffy be?

At least she would bark, Summer told herself. I hope, honesty compelled her to add.

In her experience, Muffy barked only when trying to make herself clear on the subject of food. Oh, well, maybe she would think a prowling bear was something to eat.

More likely the bear would decide to make a meal of Muffy.

Summer's lids closed again. Sleep, she ordered herself. Sleep. With the best will in the world, though, sleep would not come.

Was she just not Frankenstein's type? she wondered. Did he not find her attractive? Men used to fall all over themselves around her.

Used to being the operative statement.

Despite his joking comment to the contrary, Frankenstein probably did prefer firm-bodied, empty-headed twenty-year-olds.

A thirty-six-year-old woman with crow's feet and a soft, well-rounded body might not turn him on.

Most men didn't have the sense to prefer hard-earned wisdom and a measure of life experience to blind, giggly adoration, either.

The bottom line was that most men thought with their dicks. Clearly Frankenstein's dick was not thinking of her.

Which, Summer told herself fiercely, was just fine with her.

And on that note she finally fell asleep.

Sometime later, a hoarse cry jerked her awake.

Summer sat bolt upright, heart pounding. It was still dark as pitch. Had she been asleep long? She had no idea. All she knew was that she was suddenly scared to death.

Someone had screamed.

Glancing around, she saw that Frankenstein was on his hands and knees, face ashen, staring fixedly at a point just beyond the fire. It didn't require a genius to deduce that the cry that had awakened her had come from him.

"What is it? What's wrong?" Visions of bear attack danced in her head as, dragging the quilt and Muffy with her, she scrambled across the few feet of rocky ground that separated them. Frankenstein didn't even glance at her as her shoulder and hip butted against his side.

"Look—look there!" He pointed into the darkness.

Summer looked, but saw nothing except the shadowy images of swaying branches. Like him, she was on all fours. Side by side, they stared at something just beyond the light.

"What? What is it?" Summer's heart pounded. Her throat grew dry as she searched the shifting shadows for whatever menaced them. To put such fear into Frankenstein, it had to be a werewolf, at least. Or the bad guys.

"Don't you—can't you see her?" His voice was hoarse, horror-filled.

"Who? See who?" Her eyes practically popped from her head as she peered in the direction he pointed. Whatever kind of danger lurked just beyond her sight, if it was awful enough to horrify Frankenstein then it was awful enough to horrify her. She was ready, willing, and able to be terrified on faith alone.

"Deedee." The name emerged as a croak.

Deedee? Who was Deedee? Gasping with fear as her eyes bored a hole through the night, Summer tried to remember. Wasn't Deedee the name of the woman who . . . ?

"Deedee's dead!" she burst out.

"Don't you think I know that?" The look he turned on her was savage. "But she's here—look! Oh, my God, she's here!"

He sounded shaken. Glancing at his face rather than the empty night, Summer realized that he must have had a nightmare. Of course, that was the explanation. The only explanation. Come to think of it, he'd had one before.

"Good God, you scared me to death." Giddy with relief, she sank back on her haunches.

"Damn it, look at the dog!"

The urgency in his voice brought her up on her hands and knees again. Knowing it was ridiculous, Summer looked—and felt cold chills race down her spine. Muffy stood just inside the ring of light, tail and ears erect, staring at exactly the same spot where Frankenstein's gaze was fixed.

The same spot where he claimed to see the long-dead Deedee.

Could both of them really be seeing a ghost?

Nonsense! There was no such thing.

If there's something strange . . .

In the shadows beyond the fire, something was taking shape. Summer's eyes widened. Her breath stopped. Beside her, Frankenstein was as still as stone. Like hers, his attention was riveted on whatever was moving about just beyond the circle of light.

Muffy stood with ears and tail alert, staring.

. . . in your neighborhood / Who ya gonna call?

Summer's heart pounded. Was she really, truly, about to see a real, live (or whatever) ghost?

There—she was not mistaken—*a solid shape had materialized just beyond the light and was moving toward them.*

Ghostbusters!

Muffy yapped, Summer screamed, Frankenstein yelped, and the thing took flight.

Summer watched, mesmerized, as a trio of white-tailed deer leaped in almost perfect unison over their campsite and fled into the night.

"Jesus." Frankenstein was breathing hard. He glanced back at the spot that had so fixated him before. "She's gone."

Spell broken, he collapsed on his back, his hands pressed to his face. Summer knelt at his side.

"What do you mean, she's gone? Of course she's gone. She was never there. You idiot, you scared the stuffing out of me." Summer punched him in the arm. She had been so frightened that her breathing was still unsteady.

"Hey, that hurt!" Frankenstein caught both of Summer's hands when she would have punched him again. "I have a bruise there!"

"It was a bad dream!"

"A bad dream." Frankenstein's hands tightened around hers. She met his eyes and saw that they looked haunted. "You didn't see anything?"

"I saw some deer."

"Jesus."

"You had a nightmare."

"I think I'm losing my mind." He closed his eyes. "You don't believe in—ghosts?"

Summer shook her head, though of course he couldn't see. "Don't be silly."

"That's how I feel." He groaned. "So why do I keep seeing Deedee?"

"You've seen her before?"

"Yeah. Oh, yeah." His eyes opened again.

"When?"

The look Frankenstein gave her was shuttered. "Before."

"When you cried out in your sleep earlier, for instance?"

"Yeah."

"Then it was a bad dream. Just like tonight was a bad dream. What you have to ask yourself is, what brought it on?"

Frankenstein laughed, sounding unamused. "That part I think I've managed to figure out."

"Oh, yeah?"

"Yeah."

Summer waited, but he didn't seem inclined to be more forthcoming. "So tell me."

"Rosencrans, believe me, you don't want to know."

"Yes, I do."

There was a sudden glint in his eyes. "Sure?"

"Sure."

"Positive?"

"Would you quit being ridiculous and tell me?"

"Okay. Remember, you asked for it." His hands shifted to her wrists, shackling her. "I only see Deedee when I get a hard-on."

"What?" Summer couldn't believe her ears.

"You heard me. And I only get a hard-on when I think about making it with you."

Summer tried to snatch her hands away. He hung on. No wonder he was gripping her wrists so tightly! He was worried about being punched again! And with good reason! "You no-good, lying, aggravating son of a . . ."

"I'm telling God's own truth," he said, and moved one of her clenched fists down to rest atop his fly to prove it.

Summer went suddenly very still. Beneath the tight, zipped-up denim, the rock-hard bulge was unmistakable.

"See?" he asked softly. And he wasn't laughing.

Summer met his gaze and caught her breath. The passion that burned for her in those deadly black eyes was real.

"Frankenstein—"

"I think you'd better call me Steve," he said with a suggestion of a laugh, and drew her down into his arms.

Summer went willingly, lying across his chest as his arms slid around her back. Her own arms crept around his neck.

"Steve," she breathed, watching his eyes.

They glinted at her.

"That's better," he said, and rolled over with her, so that she was lying on her back and he was leaning above her, propped on his elbows. Hands on his shoulders, Summer looked up into that bruised, battered, decidedly unhandsome face, and felt her insides turn to jelly.

Then Steve lowered his head and kissed her.

CHAPTER TWENTY-FOUR

This time the earth moved. Bells rang. Stars exploded in Summer's head. His mouth was hard and hot and, surprisingly, very gentle. His tongue touched her lips, slid between her parted teeth, and claimed her mouth. A warm, strong hand found her left breast, closing over it through the thin nylon. Summer's senses swam.

Shaking, she kissed him back with abandon, eyes closed, arms locked around his neck. When his hands parted the ravaged edges of her blouse to stroke her bare breasts, Summer arched her back to offer him greater access. When his mouth left hers to slide down her throat and close over one pebble-hard nipple, Summer clutched the back of his head, pulling him closer as he switched his attention from one eager nipple to the other.

Never in her life had she felt passion like this.

Impatient with his clothes, her hands wormed under his sweatshirt and muscle shirt to clutch his back. His skin was warm, smooth. The muscles beneath were strong. Summer stroked those hard contours, glorying in his strength. Her palms slid down along his spine to burrow beneath the waistband of his cutoffs.

"Jesus." Frankenstein—Steve—pulled away, sitting up suddenly and yanking both shirts over his head in a single fluid movement. Summer looked at his broad shoulders, at the wide expanse of his chest with its wedge of curly black hair, at the hollow of his throat and his flat male nipples and the neat circle of his navel spilling over the waistband of his shorts, and felt her mouth go dry. She wanted him. Oh, how she wanted him!

He fumbled with the metal button that fastened his shorts. Brushing his hands aside, Summer freed it herself. Then she found the metal tab of his zipper and pulled it down.

Hiding coyly beneath the white cotton of his Jockey shorts, the burgeoning evidence of his desire for her thrust through the open V of the zipper.

Summer caught her breath, and ran her forefinger down the length of the bulge.

"Rosencrans, you're blowing my mind," he said. Then, before she could even think about reminding him that under the circumstances her name was Summer, for heaven's sake, he was on top of her, his mouth on hers, his hands between them fumbling for the fastening of her slacks.

There was no fastening. The cheap polyester pants had an elastic waist. Discovering that, he moved on. His hand slid down inside her pants, over her soft stomach to the nest of hair between her legs. Summer forgot to breathe as he caressed her with knowing fingers.

He found the small nub that ached for his attention, and proceeded to caress it until she was almost mindless. She was spiraling higher and higher . . .

All at once he froze. His fingers stilled at their task. His body, which had been pressing rhythmically against hers, went rigid. Summer whimpered, writhed, thrust herself pleadingly against his hand, begging him without words to continue. He didn't move.

Her eyes opened. He was not looking at her. With his hand down her pants and his arm around her back and her body quaking beneath him, pantingly available for his delectation, his head was raised and he was staring off into the dark.

"Steve . . ." Summer whispered, lifting herself a few inches off the ground to press her bare breasts suggestively against his chest. The contact between her throbbing nipples and his hard, hair-roughened muscles felt so good that for a few seconds she almost forgot he wasn't paying attention.

"She's clapping," he said suddenly.

"What?" Entwining her arms around his neck, flattening her breasts against his chest, Summer kissed the side of his neck.

"Jesus H. Christ, I've got to get out of here." Pulling her arms from around his neck, Steve leaped to his feet and zipped up his shorts.

"What?" Summer fell back to earth and stared up at him, bewildered.

"Come on, we've got to go."

"What are you talking about?" she wailed. He snatched his muscle shirt from the ground and pulled it over his head.

"Put that on," he said, throwing the hooded sweatshirt at her.

"What is *wrong* with you?" Sitting up, Summer regarded him with disbelief. He was bundling up the quilt and stuffing it inside the gym bag.

"Damn it, will you get dressed?" His glanced raked over her. Summer was very conscious suddenly of how she must look, black-polyester-clad bottom planted in the dirt, her blouse hanging open so that her ripe, rose-crested breasts were bare to his eyes, knees bent, hair tousled around her face, eyes no doubt bright with passion.

Slutty. That was the word she was hunting for.

Embarrassed suddenly, she drew the edges of her blouse together, fastened the few remaining buttons, then reached for the sweatshirt and zipped herself into that for good measure.

"Here. Hurry up." While she was thus occupied, he had retrieved her damp clothes from the branches where they'd been hung to dry. The *here* was uttered as he dropped her shoes and socks beside her. Summer blinked at them with disbelief as he bundled her bra and panties inside her shorts and shirt, and stuffed them into the bag.

"You've got to be kidding. We're really going?"

"Get your shoes on!" It was a muted roar. Hostility radiated from him like rays from the sun.

"Well, screw you, Frankenstein!" Outraged, Summer snatched up the still-damp socks and yanked them over her feet. He was pulling on his own sneakers as she laced herself into the squishy, too big basketball shoes.

Even her outrage didn't seem to touch him. It was if he had switched off—no, forgotten, really—the passion that still pulsed through her veins with a life of its own.

"I'll carry the dog. Let's go." On his feet now, Bulls cap firmly on his head, Frankenstein kicked dirt over the fire. Then, to Summer's burgeoning fury, he headed off into the dark without another word to her, or even so much as a glance over his shoulder to make sure she was following.

How dare he treat her so badly? Summer fumed as she stomped after him. Not quite having the nerve to teach him a lesson by stomping in the opposite direction doubled her anger. To jump up in the middle of the most explosive lovemaking session she had ever experienced and run off into the night for no good reason that she could discover was about the most infuriating behavior she had ever encountered.

She would be damned if she spoke to him ever again.

With Frankenstein in the lead and setting a killing pace, they plunged down gulleys and up hillsides, skirted piles of fallen rock and one very pungent cloud of *eau de skunk,* all in the pitch-dark. The ground grew squishy beneath the fallen leaves as they passed an underground spring, and patches of mud sucked at Summer's shoes. Branches creaked eerily with every passing breeze. The sharp smell of pine needles and the more muted scents of earth, leaves, and mold replaced the smell of skunk.

Finally the sun rose, and misty wisps of vapor floated up lazily to greet it. Fingers of fog crept through the woods and kept going. Birds trilled. The cicadas sang.

Dawn gave way to full morning, and gradually the air warmed.

The droplets of moisture that had sparkled in the sunlight like jewels beneath the trees dried up. Squirrels came out to breakfast.

Summer wanted breakfast.

Ahead of her, Muffy tucked under his arm like a football, Frankenstein just kept on going and going and going like a human version of the blasted Energizer Bunny.

She knew what ailed him, now that she had had time to think the whole fiasco through. Right in the middle of making love to her, he had imagined that he saw Deedee again.

Which didn't sit in her craw very well at all, any way she looked at it.

Eyeing his broad back evilly, Summer began to hum.

If there's something strange . . .

Since she had met him, that idiotic tune had practically become her theme song.

As she followed him, she hummed. He walked. She hummed a little louder. Still he walked. She hummed very loudly indeed.

Back stiffening, he started to slow down.

". . . in your neighborhood / Who ya gonna call?"

She was singing now, softly. But the words were unmistakable. Frankenstein stopped walking and pivoted to glare at her.

Summer stopped too, cocked her head to one side, grinned, and continued:

"Ghostbusters! Na na na na na na na! Na na na na na na na!"

"Are you making fun of me?" He sounded as if he couldn't believe she would dare.

"Me?" Summer stopped singing and shook her head, trying to look innocent. He stared at her hard for a moment, then swung around and started off again.

Summer started after him. *"If there's something strange . . ."*

"Would you please stop singing that damned song?" Annoyance was plain in the glance he threw over his shoulder at her. He sounded as if he were struggling very hard to hold on to his temper.

"I'm sorry. I didn't realize it would bother you," Summer said, saccharine-sweet. When he was face-forward again, she added wickedly, *"I ain't afraid of no ghosts!"*

"Damn it, Rosencrans! Shut the hell up!" Having apparently given up on holding on to his temper, he practically vibrated with anger as he wheeled to face her.

Summer snickered. She couldn't help it.

"You can just quit laughing, too."

"I'll laugh anytime I damned well please. And I'll sing if I want to, too," she answered cordially, and took up singing again.

"Would you stop?" he roared. Muffy started at the sudden explosion of sound, and with an impatient glance he set her on the ground. Summer, from the safety of a good ten feet away, kept singing.

"Na na na na na na na!"

"Damn it, Rosencrans, I'm warning you!" His fists were balled on his hips and his eyes shot warning sparks at her.

"Why does that song bother you?" she asked, grinning. "Just because you think you're being haunted by your own private ghost is no reason to take it personally."

"Why, you—" He bit off a word that Summer was certain was most uncomplimentary, but his eyes said it for him. His fists were no longer balled on his hips. His hands hung loosely down at his sides, his fingers flexing and unflexing as if he ached to wrap them around her neck. Bared by the sleeveless shirt, the muscles of his bare arms tensed until they bulged like the rolling hillsides they had just traversed. The brim of his Bulls cap shaded his eyes.

Summer knew that by referring to his obsession with Deedee, she could be accused of hitting below the belt, but she didn't care. It was time that Mr. Macho Man realized how ridiculous the whole ghost bit was.

"I ain't afraid of no ghosts," she sang tauntingly.

Steam practically came out of his ears. His whole body tensed.

"That's enough, Rosencrans," he said through his teeth.

Summer grinned at him. *"If there's something strange / In your neighborhood / Who ya gonna call? Ghostbusters! Na na na—"*

She never made it through the last few *na*s. With a bellow of rage he divested himself of tire iron and gym bag and dived for her. With a shriek, Summer turned to run. She hadn't made it two paces before his hand closed around the back of her neck.

"Feeling brave, are you?" he asked as he whirled her around to face him, his hands on her shoulders. "Go on, sing it again. I dare you."

Summer looked up into the hard, furious, bruised and battered face. She saw the danger signals in the snapping black eyes and the tight-clenched jaw.

And she lifted her chin and started to sing, *"If there's something strange . . ."*

His hands tightened on her shoulders threateningly. His black eyes blazed. If ever a man had had murder written all over him, at that moment Frankenstein was that man.

CHAPTER TWENTY-FIVE

Summer was unimpressed. "What are you going to do, strangle me?"

"By God, I'd like to." He sounded like he was on the verge of breathing real fire.

"Intimidation won't work," Summer told him, and twinkled tauntingly up at him. "Unlike you, I'm no scaredy-cat."

"*What?*"

"Scaredy-cat," she repeated softly, then added, *"I ain't afraid of no ghosts!"*

"Shut the hell up!"

"Na na na na na na na . . ."

"Arghh!" It was a growl of pure rage, and for a moment Summer was almost afraid. His hands tightened on her shoulders—and then he jerked her against him, tilted her head back with one hand imbedded in her hair, and brought his mouth crushing down on hers.

It was the first time she had ever been kissed by a man wearing a Bulls cap. There was symbolism in there somewhere, she was sure.

Summer opened her mouth to take a deep, shaken breath, and his tongue invaded the warm, sweet cavity like a conquering army. Her knees quivered at the onslaught. Her head was forced back. Her mouth was being mercilessly, ferociously possessed, and there was not a thing in the world she could do to stop it.

That being so, her arms slid up around his neck.

This was why she had taunted him so mercilessly. This was what she wanted.

"Steve . . ." she whispered into his mouth. Then she was kissing him back with a passion hotter than any fire. His arms slid around her back, her shoulders, crushing her to him.

"God, Rosencrans," he groaned in answer, and a small laugh shook her as she twisted in his arms to pull her mouth free.

"Summer," she told him, her lips just inches from his. "My name is Summer."

"Summer," he murmured obligingly while his eyes blazed down into hers. A faint smile curved his mouth. "Beautiful, sexy Summer."

Entranced beyond words, Summer lifted one hand from its death grip on his shoulder to lightly stroke the rough hair at the nape of his neck. She tweaked the cap from his head and watched as it dropped to the ground. He didn't appear to notice. His eyes remained fixed on hers.

"Kiss me, Steve," she whispered, her mouth reaching for his again even as she spoke. Plastered against him, she felt him shudder. She heard the sudden, harsh indrawing of his breath as she touched his mouth with hers. Then something happened. He glanced up, growing still, holding himself a little away from her. Summer could feel the sudden resistance in his body.

Deedee. Was he having visions of Deedee?

She meant to wipe Deedee clean out of his head.

"Steve—kiss me. Please." Shameless. That's what she was—shameless. But she wanted him, fiercely, hungrily, more than she had ever wanted anything in her whole life.

And she was willing to fight for what she wanted.

With one hand burrowing through his short crisp hair, she pulled his head down. She brushed her lips against his, softly, tantalizingly, and slid her tongue inside his mouth. She caressed his teeth and the roof of his mouth with her tongue. She touched his tongue with hers, stroked it, tried to coax it to come out to play. She nibbled at his lips.

And still he didn't respond.

She rubbed her pelvis up and down against the hard bulge in his pants.

He drew in a harsh, shaken breath, and suddenly he was looking at her again. Torment blazed from his eyes.

"Make love to me," she whispered. "Pretty please."

"Oh, God, I want to," he groaned, as if the admission condemned him to eternal hellfire. When she lifted her face he took her mouth.

It was a kiss so devouring that Summer closed her eyes and surrendered her soul.

She'd won. She knew it. Top this, girl, she taunted the absent Deedee even as her consciousness reeled under the onslaught of her senses and then stopped being heard from at all.

His hand came up to crush her breast. Summer could feel the heat and strength of it even through the layers of her sweatshirt and blouse. She arched her back, clinging close, trembling all over. He bent her back over his arm, kissing her as if he could never get enough of the taste of her mouth. Shuddering jolts of electricity rocketed through her body as he unzipped the sweatshirt and brushed it aside and then jerked open her blouse. When his hand closed over her bare breast she gasped at the sheer pleasure of it. Her nipple was stiff beneath his cupping palm. He tweaked it lightly between his thumb and forefinger. Summer gasped into his devouring mouth.

Only her arms wrapped around his neck held her upright as he abandoned his hold on her waist to cup her breasts with both hands. His mouth ate hers greedily as his hand stroked and molded, cupped and caressed.

Summer felt as if she were falling. She *was* falling. No, she was rising, being swept off her feet in more ways than one, as he picked her up in his arms. Summer opened her eyes to find his bruised jaw hard and taut and his black eyes alight as he carried her off through the trees cradled against his hard chest.

Pressing her mouth to the bristly underside of his chin, Summer clung to his wide shoulders and surrendered to the unaccustomed sensation of feeling small and helpless and entirely feminine. He carried her easily, as easily as if she weighed nothing at all. She'd known he was strong, but this display of effortless he-manism was impressive. His strength turned her on. She didn't say a word. She couldn't because she was beyond speech. But her eyes spoke for her. They were heavy-lidded with passion, alight with desire. *She* was alight with desire.

She had never felt this way about any man in her life. To find herself, at thirty-six, gaga over Frankenstein was incredible.

Clinging to him, Summer held tightly as he walked yards into the trees, until the delicate scent of flowers reached her nostrils and, glancing around, she saw that he had found a leafy bower. Kudzu, the invasive Japanese vine that was rapidly overrunning the south, covered the ground and the underbrush and the trunks of trees and everything else that did not move on a regular basis for as far as the eye could see. Creamy honeysuckle trumpets burst through the conquerer, winding upward around the lower branches of a circle of sturdy elms. The homely golden faces of dandelions appeared here and there across the carpet of vines. Vivid purple violets nestled cozily amidst the ground cover. Summer caught her breath as Steve bent to lay her down in a bed of flowers and dark green leaves.

As a romantic setting, she thought, it was perfect. He couldn't have done better if he had ordered it from central casting.

Then he came down on top of her, and she quit thinking altogether.

His kiss was hard and hot and slow, and almost unbearably sexy. It made the blood pound in her ears.

When he lifted his head at last, she was gasping for air.

"I'm hard as a spike," he murmured, smoothing her hair back from her face with hands that were less than steady.

"So what are you going to do about it?" she whispered back with a tiny, tremulous smile.

"What do you want me to do?"

"This." Summer took his hand and placed it on her breast. She pressed his hand to her, loving the warmth of his strong, masculine palm. Her nipple swelled almost painfully beneath his touch.

"Ah," he said. He watched her intently as his hand caressed her softness. The feel of his hand against her skin made her want to writhe. She wanted to feel it everywhere on her body—wanted to feel him everywhere on her body. She wanted him to make love to her until she begged him to stop. She remembered how he had touched her before, remembered the ecstasy he had given her with only his caressing fingers, and felt a hot, heavy throbbing start up between her thighs.

She wanted him to touch her there.

"Is that all?" His voice was hoarse, but a funny kind of half-smile quirked his mouth. How could he smile when she was going out of her mind for want of him?

She meant to drive him out of his mind, too.

"No," she whispered, and caught his wrist, sliding his hand down. "I want you to touch me here, too."

She put his hand between her legs.

He sucked in his breath. It was a rough, ragged-sounding inhalation.

"And I want to touch you here." Her voice was soft, barely above a whisper. Husky with desire. Her hand went to the front of his shorts. Closing her hand over his straining flesh, denim and all, she squeezed.

"Baby, you go right ahead." It was a growl, emerging from between clenched teeth and for a moment she obliged him. His hand pressed hard and hot between her legs. Then he was moving, shifting positions, sliding down her body. Through the barrier of black polyester his mouth pressed against the V between her legs and his hands closed over her bottom, his fingers seeking out and tracing the crevice between her soft cheeks.

Summer stopped breathing as he opened his mouth against the rough cloth covering the apex of her legs. Her heart pounded so hard it sounded like a jackhammer in her ears. She could feel the damp heat of his mouth burning her through the polyester. He opened his mouth more, pressing his lips and tongue and teeth against her, nibbling at her, biting her. Summer moaned, her fists clenching on the cool crispness of kudzu and violets, releasing the flowers' haunting scent to dance with the aroma of honeysuckle and sex in the air.

Steve lifted his head for an instant and met her gaze, wildfire in his eyes. Then he yanked her pants down around her knees and repeated the exercise, finding the the secret nub that ached and throbbed with need and caressing it with the hot, wet slither of his tongue.

Summer cried out. Of their own volition her thighs tried to part, to give him greater access to the part of her that wept for want of him, but her pants bound her at the knees. She lay flat, crushed by his weight, helpless to do anything to relieve her sweet agony as he brought her to the brink of ecstasy and beyond without even parting her legs.

"Oh, stop. Don't stop." Summer's hands closed into tight fists on the short strands of his hair, meaning to pull his head away. He reached up, caught her wrists, and brought them down, pinning them to the ground on either side of her undulating hips. She was left utterly defenseless. He was turning her into a writhing, needful, hungry object, reducing her to an abject, pleading *thing.*

"Don't stop!" Summer's eyes were shut tight, and she moaned as his tongue and mouth took her higher and higher. That she was bound at the knees, held down by his body, unable to escape his potent brand of sexual torture made it all the sweeter. Made it unbearable, in fact. Never in her life had she imagined feeling anything like *this.*

She came with a shudder that made her cry out, and brought her arching up off her bed of leaves to press against his mouth.

When it was over, when she was herself again, Summer opened her eyes to find him watching her. His black eyes glittered, his battered face was hard and set, and his lips were fused into a straight, implacable line.

"Now it's my turn," he said, and then he was on his knees above her. With quick, savage movements he removed her shoes and socks, yanked her pants the rest of the way down her legs, ex-

tracted her from her blouse, pulled his shirt over his head and
shucked his shoes and shorts and briefs. Summer was too weak in
the aftermath of passion to do more than watch as he stripped
them both.

She noted again that he had just the kind of body she liked—
solid and muscular and covered with a profusion of hair.

Then he was coming down on top of her. The weight of his big
body crushed her into the ground. She discovered a pebble somewhere in the vicinity of the base of her spine. He was urgent and
she was willing, but her own urgency was spent.

Or so she thought, until he kissed her breathless and suckled
her breasts and parted her legs with his thighs. He let her feel him,
hard and hot and pulsing, just touching the place where he could
enter anytime he chose. But he chose not to come in.

Instead he played with her until she was once again as taut and
quivering as the overtightened string of a violin.

Then he entered. Slowly. He was hard and fiery hot and filled
her to bursting. He kissed her mouth with slow, fierce passion,
kept her still with his arms around her, and held himself deep
inside her for long, slow seconds.

By the time he pulled himself out and then slid in again, Summer was on fire. She would have done anything he wanted. Anything . . .

She told him so.

His hands braced on either side of her rib cage, he stiffened his
arms until his weight was almost completely off her. Their only
point of contact was where their bodies joined. Slowly he moved
in, then out, then in again, until she lifted her hips with involun-
tary anticipation each time. Then he bent his head and took a
swollen nipple in his mouth.

Summer groaned.

He lifted his head and smiled then, a slow smile that acknowledged her passion, relished it, and promised more. The smolder-
ing depths of his black eyes held all the knowing wickedness of the
serpent.

"Steve . . ." she whimpered, pleading for an end. His eyes
flickered, and then he was lying atop her once again, wrapping his

arms around her and holding her to him and taking her with hot, fierce urgency back to a fever pitch of passion. Only this time he came with her. When he pushed her over the edge, he fell, too. His hoarse shout joined with her cry as they hurtled through space together.

It was a long, long time before he roused himself enough to roll away.

CHAPTER TWENTY-SIX

"The soul, like the body, lives by
what it feeds on."

—Josiah Gilbert Holland

She was starting to get the hang of this ghost
thing, Deedee realized.

At first it was disorienting to be always popping up here, there,
and everywhere, without, she thought, much rhyme or reason.
She'd found herself in the living room of her childhood home
again, where she discovered her mother and her aunt Dot, who
had lived together since both were widowed within a twelve-
month span eight years before, trying to contact her via, of all
things, a Ouija board.

"I tell you I saw her. Just as plain as I'm seeing you," her
mother was saying.

"I'm not sayin' you didn't, Sue. All I'm sayin' is, this Ouija
board ain't pickin' her up."

"Maybe you just don't know how to use it."

"I've been usin' Ouija boards all of my life, so I guess I know
how to use one. A Ouija is what advised me to marry Jett, you
know, when I would've taken Carl Owens."

"*That* don't recommend 'em much to me," her mother said.

Indeed, Aunt Dot's fights with Uncle Jett were legendary. Deedee had almost forgotten about them.

This time, try though she might, she couldn't seem to material- ize. But she could take control of the pointer.

"I-M-O-K-A-Y . . ."

"Would you look at that?"

"Are you pushin' that thing, Dorothy Jean?"

"You know I wouldn't do that! Oh, my heavens!"

"I-L-O-V-E-Y-O-U-M-O-M."

"Deedee! Ohmigod, Deedee! It's my baby! Deedee, Deedee!"

"Sue, calm down! Sue, ask her what happened that night! Ask her, quick!"

Deedee's mother and aunt, work-reddened, unlovely hands poised on either side of the plastic pointer, frantically pushed the felt-tipped wedge around the board. But Deedee was already be- ing sucked away.

When next she surfaced it was on a Nashville soundstage. A pretty blonde of maybe twenty-five, wearing headphones and a scarlet mini, was crooning into a microphone.

Deedee found herself watching the singer from the Plexiglas- walled control booth, where two men listened, frowning, to what Deedee considered a reed-thin voice.

"We need more volume out of her, Bill."

"Well, we ain't gonna get it. That's everything she's got. It doesn't matter, anyway. We can fix it. Hell, with the equipment we've got we can fix anything."

"She's scheduled to sing on *Nashville Live* Saturday night. 'Ag- ony' is already number eighteen with a bullet. Nobody's ever heard her sing live before. The critics are gonna be after her with knives if we don't get her to punch it up."

"Hell, I would if I could, and you know it. This little gal's pretty, and she sings okay, but you and I both know she never would've got the first whiff of a recording contract if she wasn't married to Hank Ketchum."

"You gotta admit, marryin' the head of Jalapeno Records was one hell of a career move. Too bad I didn't think of it."

"I don't think he would've proposed, in your case. Anyway,

Ketchum signs our paychecks, so we'd best shut up." Bill pressed a button and spoke into a mike. "Hallie, honey, try to hold those high notes just a little longer, would you? And see if you can put more emotion into it. Pretend your dog just got run over."

"I'll try, Bill."

"Thanks, Hallie. That's all I ask. Wanna take it from the top?"

"Okay."

Bill pushed the mike button again, signaled to the musicians, and sank back in his chair. "For *Nashville Live,* we're just gonna have to surround her with a lot of background singers, and hope for the best."

> *"Hurtin', I'm hurtin' so bad over you*
> *What did you think I would do?"*

The two men in the control booth came erect in their seats, stared hard at the blonde at the mike, and looked at each other in disbelief.

"Well, bust my britches! The girl *can* sing!"

"Hot damn! We're in business!"

Onstage, Deedee fought to retain control over the vocal cords she had appropriated, and gave the song her best. Following the words on the TelePrompTer, singing from the depths of her soul, she felt closer to Heaven in those few minutes than she ever had in her life—or death.

> *". . . Just lie down and die—that's not me*
> *Still, I am in agony."*

As the last notes died away, Deedee felt the familiar sensation of being sucked away. Vainly she tried to hold on.

She wanted to stay. . . .

The voice boomed out of the control room.

"Hallie, honey, that was just fine! Just fine!"

Once again in control of her vocal cords, Hallie answered breathlessly, "Thanks, Bill. Something just came over me . . ."

But Deedee missed the rest of the exchange. She was hurtling through the maelstrom once more.

When she came to rest again it was night, and she was in a small, tidy country cemetery. Her husband was crouched beside a grave.

Perched cross-legged atop the tombstone, Deedee leaned way forward—being a ghost allowed her to do that kind of thing without falling on her nose, she had discovered—and read the inscription:

TAYLOR
DEIDRA ANN CUMMINS
Born JANUARY 21, 1958—Died MAY 15, 1992
Love Is Eternal

Mitch was crouched beside *her* grave.

Deedee regarded the bent blond head and wondered if Mitch had thought up the inscription. She guessed so; it sounded like Mitch. Certainly her mother would never have come up with anything so poetic.

She had loved Mitch desperately from the time she was thirteen until almost the moment she died. They'd had their ups and downs—some ups, a whole lot of downs—but she had always loved him.

Now she looked at him with fresh vision. Love really wasn't eternal. At least, not in this case.

Mitch glanced up then, and for a moment Deedee wondered if he could see her. She hadn't felt the tingling that signaled when she had materialized, and he didn't scream or faint or even turn pale, so she guessed he couldn't.

But she could see him. He was as handsome as ever, his blond hair wavy, his blue eyes keen, his lightly tanned features classical. He looked like he had lost weight since she'd last seen him, but then at six feet one he'd always been lean, so she couldn't be sure.

Kneeling beside her grave, dressed in slacks and a windbreaker, he was the very picture of the grieving widower.

Except for the fact that his hands were covered with earth. A shovel lay beside him, and her grave, while thick with grass, looked raw, somehow. Too raw for a three-year-old grave.

It had been freshly sodded.

What're you up to, Mitch Taylor? she thought fiercely. Even as she felt the tingling, even as his eyes widened, she was sucked away.

This time, when she stopped, it was a hot, sunlit afternoon. At least, it was hot and sunlit outside. She was in a cave, floating up near the ceiling, staring down at a sleeping couple entwined in a quilt on the ground about six feet below.

The man was Steve—his face still looked like hell; the woman she didn't recognize. But they seemed mighty cozy together.

Deedee was watching them with interest when Steve opened his eyes.

He saw her. She could tell right away. So she waved at him, just to say hi.

He let out a bellow and sat up. Startled, Deedee lost control of her atoms and vanished.

When she got hold of herself again, she was in a corner of the same cave being stared at by a weird-looking little dog. Steve was once again lying down, with the woman cuddled on his chest. Steve was awake. The woman wasn't.

The woman definitely wasn't Steve's wife, Elaine.

That was kinda surprising. Except for the fling with her, Steve had always been a straight arrow. Deedee doubted if he'd ever cheated on Elaine before. She would have added "or since," but evidence to the contrary was right under her nose.

Despite the attraction she knew he'd always felt for her, she had had to work pretty hard to seduce old Steve. She was ashamed to admit that she had done it deliberately, to teach Mitch a lesson. Mitch, who would unzip his pants with alacrity for any bitch in heat, had sorely needed a lesson.

Her husband had been embroiled in another in his endless series of hot-and-heavy affairs when she'd decided to get even with him by getting it on with Steve. After fourteen years of marriage, Deedee had grown wise to the ways of Mitch; she knew all the signs. And she also knew that Steve was one of the few people on earth of whom her husband was genuinely fond. Mitch, handsome conniver and people-user that he was, generally stayed friends with people for just as long as he needed them. But his friendship with Steve had survived three decades. Between the two men there was a true bond.

Steve, being Steve, had lost his head over her for about three weeks, and then started suffering the tortures of the damned.

He couldn't deal with the guilt of having cheated on his wife, to say nothing of cuckolding his best friend.

He'd always been such a Boy Scout.

Which was one reason she was so fond of him, Deedee supposed. She wasn't in love with him, hadn't ever been, but she loved him. Like a brother, or something.

As the song—countless songs—said, she'd done him wrong. Real bad wrong.

That, she thought with a sudden flash of insight, was why she was still earthbound.

She couldn't go to Heaven until she had righted that wrong.

CHAPTER TWENTY-SEVEN

Steve lay facedown in kudzu, breathing in the scent of mold, feeling the damp chill of the ground beneath the vines seeping into his bones.

He was almost afraid to look up. The last time he'd checked, before he had completely lost his head, Deedee had been swinging from the branches of the huge elm just to the left of his outflung hand, hanging upside down by her knees as she gave him a thumbs-up sign.

Remembering, it was all Steve could do to repress a groan.

He *was* losing his mind. He had to be.

Or maybe his subconscious was trying to tell him something. Maybe these recurring visions of Deedee were its way of re-minding him to stay focused. His mission was twofold: First, he had to stay alive long enough to figure out exactly why everybody and his brother wanted to kill him and what to do about it; and second, he had to discover how Deedee had gotten into his office that fateful night.

Getting sidetracked by a woman was the last thing he needed.

What man had ever been able to think straight when his brain was intoxicated with thoughts of pussy?

So they had had sex. Good. Maybe he'd gotten it—and her—out of his system for a while.

A soft, wet mouth nuzzled his ear. God, was she hot for him again already? Steve wondered, and felt his member begin to stiffen in response.

All right, so maybe he hadn't gotten it—and her—completely out of his system. Maybe he was already hankering after another go-round.

He'd get over it. He had to.

Cool it, he cautioned himself sternly. At this moment, going all mushy-brained—and brick-dicked—over the woman could be the death of both of them.

He was not going to allow himself to think of sex again until they were safe.

He glanced up, scowling, to warn the temptress in no uncertain terms about the inadvisability of doing any more nibbling on his ear.

The eyes he encountered were not a warm golden hazel, but chocolate brown and bulging. As he stared into them, the mutt to whom they belonged tilted its head inquiringly, panting with execrable doggy breath right in his face. With a shudder of revulsion, Steve realized just exactly who had been licking his ear: He'd been given a hard-on by a dog!

"Shit!" He sat upright, dug his palms into his eyes to try to clear his brain, and snuck a wary peek at the thick canopy of branches overhead.

No Deedee. Thank God.

Steve drew a relieved breath, then glanced over at the woman who was stretched out in all her naked splendor against the deep glossy green of their kudzu bed.

The least she could do was lie on her stomach, he thought resentfully as his member, under no illusions this time, rose to instant attention.

Given a taste of what it craved, the damned thing was proving insatiable.

But she did look good. Summer. The name suited her a lot better than Rosencrans, which was why he'd better stick to calling her Rosencrans. Her eyes were closed. Her lashes lay in beautiful semicircular sweeps against her cheeks. Dozing, she looked flushed and satiated and content, just exactly like a woman was supposed to look in the aftermath of passion. Clearly she had forgotten, temporarily, that they were on the run for their lives. For all the anxiety she exhibited, she could have been lying on the smoothest sheets, the thickest mattress, at the best hotel in the country.

Sex was a great stress reliever. He had discovered that for himself long ago.

It was also an excellent stress inducer, at least in this particular case. The longer he looked at the object of his desire, the more stress he felt.

The obvious answer, of course, was simply not to look at her. But he couldn't quite do that.

Naked, she was beautiful. One arm curved up and around to pillow her head. Her armpit was exposed, white and vulnerable. The urge to crawl over to her and press his mouth to that enticing area was almost irresistible, but from somewhere he found the strength to resist.

Her dark brown hair fanned out over her bent arm to form a kind of a halo around her face. Her nose was straight, the nostrils slightly dilated as she breathed. Her lips—wide, tender lips that knew how to kiss—were parted. He wanted to press his mouth there, too, but again he managed to keep himself under control.

Her creamy skin sported numerous bruises—he felt guilty as he acknowledged them. Each one, directly or indirectly, could be attributed to him.

The discolorations emphasized rather than detracted from the sheer allure of her milky skin. Milky skin that had felt like warm silk under his hands.

With the best will in the world not to do so, Steve mentally stroked that skin with his gaze. Now that his vision was back to normal, he could appreciate properly her full womanly shape. *Voluptuous* was the only word that did justice to the jutting fullness of her breasts and the roundness of her hips, to the curve of her belly and waist and the long, delectable length of her legs.

She had small feet. He was a sucker for small feet.

Just looking at her made him so hard that he had to grit his teeth to keep from doing anything about it. What made it worse was the knowledge that she was his for the taking. He could do anything he liked with her.

She had told him so.

With a muttered curse Steve shot to his feet and snatched up his briefs.

"Steve?" His nemesis sat up, blinking the sleep from her eyes, still as naked as a babe but a hell of a lot more enticing to look at. She made not the slightest attempt to cover herself as she watched him yank his briefs up his legs, followed by his shorts. Even though he determinedly refused to look in her direction, just the memory of her rosy nipples and mink-brown bush and all the hills and valleys between drove him mad.

"Get dressed," he said harshly. He should never have brought a woman along. But what choice had he had? None. The knowledge didn't help. Gathering up her clothes in a quick grab, he tossed them at her.

"Is something wrong?" She sounded hesitant, confused. Her voice was a throaty, sexy contralto—why hadn't he ever before noticed just how sexy it was?—and it immediately conjured up memories of the cries she had made during sex.

Could dicks break? Because his felt as if it were going to, crammed inside the too tight shorts as it was. Keeping his back to her, he pulled at his fly in a vain attempt to relieve the pressure, and reached for his shirt.

"We've got to get moving." He knew he sounded hostile, but he couldn't help it. He felt hostile. The whole damned situation was impossible. Here he was, facing the distinct possibility of a woefully shortened life span, saddled with a chatterbox woman and her sissy mutt, with what felt like the whole damned population of the bad-guy hall of fame after him and a ghostly vision tormenting him at every turn, and all he wanted to do was get his rocks off—again. And again. And again.

With her. With Summer.

Damn it to hell. What a hell of a situation.

"So you're one of those," that sexy voice said with cold disdain.

"One of whats?" He still had his back to her, pulling on his shoes.

"One of those wham, bam, I-won't-bother-to-thank-you-ma'am types."

"What?" That did it. He had to glance around at her. She had one knee raised, the other curled beside her, and looked about as sexy as any woman he had ever seen as she sat naked among the dark green leaves and purple flowers and gray-barked trees of their bower, looking down her nose at him.

"I should have guessed," she said witheringly, and stood up, walking past him with regal dignity.

His breathing suspended as desire grabbed him by the balls. His eyes were riveted on her backside as she walked, naked, through the forest, her lush ass swaying, her spine straight, her hair flowing around her shoulders.

God, what an ass!

Shades of Lady Godiva!

"Where are you going?" he asked, feeling as if he might strangle on the very act of speaking.

"I'd rather wear shorts. It's getting hot, or haven't you noticed?"

He had definitely noticed. He had to reach inside his own shorts for a quick adjustment before he was bent double with pain.

Gathering up her shoes, socks, clothes, and dog, he followed. By the time he reached her side, she had extracted her bra and panties from the gym bag he had dropped, and donned them. The garments were plain white, sturdy and sensible rather than seductive. The bra had a knot in one strap.

So why did they turn him on?

Hell, everything about her turned him on. If he wasn't careful, he was going to catch himself getting excited over her damned sissified dog.

The animal licked his wrist. Alarmed, he put her down.

"Now that we've got *that* out of our systems, maybe we can put our heads together and figure some way out of this." Her gaze, meeting his as he straightened, was a cool challenge. She stepped into the nylon shorts as if he weren't even there, pulled them up her legs, adjusted them around her waist, and then, to Steve's mingled relief and regret, pulled the black T-shirt over her head.

She filled out that T-shirt so well that even the bull terrier adorning it seemed to be panting with lust.

She might have *that* out of her system, but he didn't. In fact, he had the distinct feeling that the poison was spreading.

"Yeah. Right." His reply was lame. He recognized that himself, but he couldn't help it. He could hardly think, much less talk. With a curl of her lip, she reached over and took her shoes and socks from his hand and dropped them to the ground. Then, picking up the gym bag, she heaved it at his midsection.

"Catch!"

"Whoa!" Steve caught the bag with a grunt. She had thrown it hard. Eyeing her narrowly as she sank to the ground to pull on her shoes and socks, he supposed he should consider himself fortunate that she had not thrown the tire iron at him instead.

Milady was clearly p.o.'d.

"You *have* thought beyond what happens once we get to your fishing camp, haven't you?" she asked scathingly, wrapping long shoelaces around her ankles and tying them. "Going up there to think isn't much of a plan. If you don't mind my saying so."

Wait a minute. Unless she could come up with something better, he did mind her saying so.

Steve was just about to tell her that when she stood up, scooped up her ridiculous beribboned mutt, and strode off.

Leaving him to gather up the gear, snatch up his cap and settle it on his head, and follow. He didn't much like following, he discovered. It wasn't his style.

Especially when the leader he was following had a mouthwatering tush that gave him a pang with its every come-hither swing.

CHAPTER TWENTY-EIGHT

"What did you mean, wham, bam, whatever?" Frankenstein asked out of the blue. He sat on the ground, his back propped against a tree, one leg stretched out before him, the other raised and bent at the knee. The damned symbolic Bulls cap was pulled low over his eyes. They had stopped to eat—peanut butter crackers and water, and a raw hot dog for Muffy—beside the clear green water of a rippling creek. It must have been late afternoon— Summer had lost all track of time, so she couldn't be sure, but it felt like late afternoon. Sun slanted down through the trees, dappling the ground and the rock on which she sat. The day had been hot, maybe ninety degrees, but the forest had protected them from the worst of the heat. They got humidity and gnats instead. The combination, in her opinion, was worse.

Sweat beaded Summer's forehead. Her hair, unwashed now for almost three whole days, felt rank. She didn't even like to think about whether or not she smelled. Her leg itched, and she scratched the large red insect bite on her calf absentmindedly.

"I don't know what you're talking about." Still furious at herself
for almost tumbling headlong into another disastrous relationship
with another disastrous man, Summer replied coldly. It wasn't
only herself she was furious at, either. Every time she thought
about how uninhibited she had been with him, the things she had
said and done and felt, she wanted to cringe. Even more humiliat-
ingly, when she remembered the things he had done to her with
his hands and mouth and body, she couldn't help it: She felt a
little thrill. That thrill made her mad all over again.

Then, while she had still been basking in the glow of the most
fantastic lovemaking session she had ever experienced, he had
made it clear that it had meant absolutely nothing to him. *She*
meant absolutely nothing to him.

He'd been horny, and he'd wanted sex. That was the simple
truth. Once he'd gotten what he wanted, he had lost all interest in
her. He hadn't even had the good manners—or good sense—to
pretend otherwise.

She didn't know why she had been surprised.

"What you said—back there. You said I was another one of
those wham, bam, something-thank-you-ma'am types." His voice
was carefully neutral. Good thing. It wouldn't have taken much to
make her fly at him like an enraged blue jay.

Summer stopped chewing and swallowed. "Oh, God, you're not
one of those men who has to rehash things every time you have
sex, are you? What do you want, applause?"

She was pardonably pleased when his eyes narrowed. "I just
want to know what you meant."

"Not a thing." She drank water from her well-rinsed beer can.
Under the circumstances, the taste of beer would have been the
last straw. She would have been violently ill. "Forget it."

"I don't want to forget it."

"What are you, part bulldog? Can't you just let it drop?"

Apparently not put off by the edge in her voice, Frankenstein
shook his head. "Nope."

Summer scowled at him. "All right. If you really want to know,
I'll tell you. My ex-husband was like that. He wanted sex when he
wanted it, and he would sulk for days if I didn't instantly oblige. I

learned that it was easier just to do it, you know, rather than put up with his pouting. So we'd have sex—it usually took about five minutes—and as soon as it was over he'd jump out of bed, run for the shower, and get on with his life. Wham, bam, I-won't-bother-to-thank-you-ma'am, see? And that would be the last I'd get of any kind of love or romance or even simple human kindness out of him until he got horny again. At which time the whole process would be repeated. Know how I could tell when he was getting horny? He'd drink a beer. The only time he ever did." Summer looked down at the can in her hand, and grimaced. "I hate the taste of beer."

"I'm not your ex-husband."

"No, you're not, are you?" Summer smiled at him, but it wasn't a nice smile. She wasn't feeling particularly nice at that precise moment. "So I don't have to put up with that kind of crap from you, do I? And I won't." She took another sip of water, and said what she had been thinking for the last few miles. "I've decided to call Sammy."

"What?" Frankenstein almost choked on his own water.

"You heard me. I've decided to call Sammy. I don't know how you think *you're* going to get out of this mess alive, and to tell you the truth I don't particularly care. But I am going to call my ex-father-in-law, of whom I am still very fond, who also happens to be the Murfreesboro Chief of Police, to come and get me. You may not trust him, but *I* do."

Frankenstein stared at her. Summer ate her last cracker with elaborate unconcern. Over the past few hours her thinking had grown crystal clear. Further involvement with Steve Calhoun and his problems was a recipe for disaster on all fronts. He could break her heart. He could get her killed. It had taken her a while to develop wisdom, but, by golly, she had at last developed it. One thing she had learned over the course of her life was that she had to take care of herself; nobody else would.

Certainly not Frankenstein.

"You can't do that."

"Oh yes I can. Try to stop me."

"It could very well be suicide."

"So could staying with you. I prefer to take my chances with Sammy."

Frankenstein gulped some more water. "Too bad. It's not in the cards."

"What do you mean, it's not in the cards? It's in the cards if I want it to be in the cards. You don't tell me what to do."

"Somebody needs to. You're about as good at taking care of yourself as that ridiculous dog."

"Oh, yeah? I hate to point this out to you, but both Muffy and I seem to be better at taking care of ourselves than you are at taking care of yourself. We didn't get ourselves into this mess: you did. The whole world's chasing us because of you. You're the problem here, and I've decided that in order to fix the problem, Muffy and I need to get away from you."

"Wait a minute. This is all because you're mad at me about what happened this morning, isn't it?"

"I don't know what you're talking about."

"Oh yes you do. You're mad because we had sex."

"I am not!"

"You are too."

Summer took a deep breath. "I am not mad at you because we had sex."

"No, you're mad because we had sex and you enjoyed it."

Summer felt her cheeks heat. "Pretty full of yourself, aren't you, Frankenstein? What makes you so sure I enjoyed it?"

"I know when a woman has a good time during sex."

"Oh, yeah? Well, you had a good time too."

"Yes, I did." He met her fuming gaze full on. "I had a fantastic time. You were great. Is that what you want to hear? Is everything all better now?"

"I don't want to hear anything at all from you." Summer poured the rest of her water onto the ground and stood up.

"I don't know what you're so bent out of shape about. *You* came on to me, if you recall. You wanted it, you got it. So why don't you quit acting like an outraged virgin?"

"I did not come on to you!"

"Oh, yeah? *Kiss me, Steve.* What was that? *Touch me here.* Sounds like coming on to me to me."

"Maybe I was just trying to distract you from the little ghost you're so afraid of. Did you ever think of that? Was that the problem at the end, by the way? Did you think you were seeing Deedee again?" Summer said that last in a mocking falsetto—and she struck home. She could tell it by the clenching of his jaw, and the sense that, if humans could give off steam, he would be.

They glared at each other. Muffy, watching, burrowed her nose beneath her paws. Neither of the human combatants payed her the least bit of attention.

"Fine," Frankenstein said suddenly, his jaw jutting. "If that's what you want to do, it's fine with me. Call your father-in-law. Maybe the time he and his buddies take to try to make you talk will give me just the extra hour or so I need to get away. Maybe I'll get really lucky, and they'll make sushi out of the mutt, too."

"You leave Muffy out of this!"

"With pleasure." He got to his feet, cramming the remains of their lunch into the gym bag. "Come on, Rosencrans. You want to take your chances with the law, I'll help you find a phone."

Good. That was just what she wanted. A phone.

"There's a campground about five miles south of here," Frankenstein continued, shouldering the gym bag and tucking the tire iron under his arm. "Or at least there used to be. Come on, baby, let's take you to Papa. It'll be a relief to get you off my hands."

Frankenstein stomped off. Summer was left to pick up Muffy and follow.

If she hadn't been so darned mad, by the time they reached the outskirts of the campground she would have had second thoughts about the advisability of what she meant to do. His crack about making sushi out of her and Muffy had hit home. She kept remembering Linda Miller and Betty Kern.

But she couldn't back down now. She was too darn mad at him. Anyway, despite anything Frankenstein said to the contrary, she was making the only sane decision. She was (almost) sure of it. Sammy loved her like the daughter he had never had. He would never hurt her. She was as certain of that as it was possible to be certain of anything.

The sound of children laughing was Summer's first clue that they had reached their destination. Hearing it, Frankenstein stopped walking and propped a shoulder against a tree, waiting for her to catch up.

"This is it," he said laconically as she came up to him. "Hiawatha Village. We used to camp here sometimes when I was a kid. Go to the manager's office—it's in the middle of the campground. I'm sure you can talk somebody there into letting you use the phone. I'd loan you a quarter, but I'm fresh out."

He seemed to be in a hurry for her to leave him. Looking ahead at what seemed to be a play area still some distance away through the trees, Summer hesitated. Should she do this?

"Getting cold feet?" he asked. Or maybe *sneered* was a better word.

"You can come with me," she said. Angry as she was with him, she hated to think of him being left out in the woods all alone, with murderers on his trail. "Sammy's not part of this. I know it in my bones."

"Believe me, Rosencrans, your bones have got no intuitive powers. They're good for jumping and not much else."

That was it. That was the last straw. Summer straightened her spine, lifted her chin, and started to walk away without so much as a good-bye.

"Rosencrans!"

Summer glanced back. Having unzipped the gym bag, Frankenstein held her wadded-up uniform in one hand. As she looked at him, he heaved the garments at her.

She almost dropped Muffy as she grabbed for the clothes. Catching them clumsily, she stuffed the ball he had made of them under one arm. Aping Frankenstein, she had Muffy clamped under the other one.

"Sure you don't want to change your mind?" he asked as their eyes met for a brief moment.

Summer shook her head. "Sure you don't want to change yours?"

Frankenstein shook his head, then lifted a hand in a salute. Summer ignored niggling second, third, and fourth thoughts, turned her back on him, and started walking away.

She was doing the right thing. She knew it, even if her pesky heart did not.

"Yo, Rosencrans!"

She looked back at him again.

"You've got great tits and a great ass. If we both get out of this in one piece I might just give you a call."

Before she could reply, he turned and strode off through the trees.

Summer found herself well and truly alone. Suddenly every tiny noise was magnified: the hum of the cicadas, the harsh squawk of an angry blue jay, the excited laughter of the distant children. The forest seemed suddenly bigger, darker, more menacing.

Muffy whimpered. Summer bent her head to rub her nose against the dog's fur. At least she wasn't *quite* alone.

The knowledge didn't make her feel appreciatively better. She was conscious of an enormous sense of loss. For a moment she almost feared she might cry. She, who never cried.

Summer clamped her teeth together so her lips would not tremble. She was better off without Steve Calhoun. Leaving him behind was the first step to disentangling herself from this mess.

No man was worth her life.

Clinging to that thought, Summer walked through the trees past the playground where children played on ancient swings and more children rode plastic animals on springs cemented to the ground and still more children swarmed over a decrepit-looking jungle gym.

They, and their tired-looking parents, paid her no mind at all.

She kept walking, past pickup campers and RVs and tents. People went about their business, none of them paying the least attention to her. In front of one tent, a couple and their sulky-looking teenage son sat in molded plastic chairs. The couple argued while the boy snapped his fingers in time to the music that apparently poured through the headphones that he wore.

"Excuse me, could you point me toward the manager's office?"

Summer asked the woman, who broke off her argument with her husband to stare suspiciously at Summer as she approached.

"Up that way," she said, jerking her thumb in the direction of a gravel road. "But, honey, I gotta warn ya: This campground don't allow no dogs."

"Thank you." Summer beat a hasty retreat. Something about the way the woman looked at her made her uneasy. Again she got the feeling that maybe, just maybe, she had made a mistake.

Maybe she should have stuck with Frankenstein after all.

She had made the right choice, Summer reassured herself stoutly as she headed down the gravel road toward, she hoped, the manager's office. One phone call to Sammy and her troubles would be over. He would come and fetch her and take her somewhere safe and feed her and provide her with a bed and a bathtub and . . .

Showers. She was walking past public showers.

Summer's head swiveled as that fact hit home. The sign on the concrete-block building's blue-painted door was unmistakable: WOMEN'S SHOWERS.

Before she saw Sammy, before she bearded the manager in his den and begged for the use of his phone, she could have a shower.

She could be clean!

That woman had probably been staring at her so strangely because she looked like a close cousin of the Creature from the Black Lagoon.

Not for long.

Unable to resist the lure of hot water, Summer headed for the showers.

Inside, the building was deserted, probably because early evening was an awkward time for showering for most normal folks. The concrete walls were painted white, and the tile floor was an off-shade of blue. If the grout was moldy and mildew adorned the corners, why, to Summer's mind it didn't detract one iota from the sheer beauty of her surroundings. Dented blue lockers, grayish white shower curtains, and a mirror with a crack running across its upper right corner looked to her deprived eyes like fixtures that would have been right at home in Buckingham Palace.

So what if it smelled damp and musty? She was actually in a real live bathroom!

Muffy wriggled, and Summer put her down. Muffy sniffed the air suspiciously, then pressed close against Summer's ankles.

Summer paid no attention to her. Instead, she went into a toilet stall, made use of the facilities—real toilet paper was such a luxury that she almost kissed the roll—and then searched the eight shower cubicles for soap. In the fourth one, she got lucky. Not only was there a sweet-smelling white rectangle left behind in the soap dish, there was an entire makeup kit in a clear plastic zippered case on the flimsy white shampoo shelf that dangled from the showerhead.

Manna from heaven!

Summer thrust her wadded up Daisy Fresh uniform onto a bench outside the shower cubicle. As she did so, a clatter attracted her attention. Glancing down, she saw that a cigarette lighter lay on the floor beneath her clothes. *The* cigarette lighter. The yellow Bic that had seen her and Frankenstein through their adventures. Thrown carelessly into the gym bag, it must have gotten caught up in her clothes.

How would Frankenstein start a fire tonight without that cigarette lighter?

She would not worry about him, Summer told herself stoutly. He would just have to manage on his own for the time being. Maybe Sammy could fix things for him, too.

He had been eager enough to have her leave him.

But she wasn't going to think about Frankenstein. Not now. Now she was going to have a shower and maybe put on some makeup, and then, when she was clean and human-looking again, call Sammy.

Sammy could sort this whole mess out. If anyone could save Frankenstein, it was Sammy.

She picked up the cigarette lighter, tried not to trip over Muffy as the dog followed her into the shower, and unzipped the makeup kit. The cosmetics it contained were drugstore brands, inexpensive but adequate: a pot of Cherry Smackers lip gloss, a tube of mascara, purple—*purple?*—eye shadow, powder blush in a namby-pamby shade of pink, and a pressed-powder compact, luckily translucent. She had a feeling that the makeup kit belonged to a teenage blonde. But it was hers now. Finders keepers.

There was also a small brush and a purse-size can of hair spray. Who could ask for anything more?

Adding the lighter to the bag's contents and zipping it closed again, Summer turned on the hot water and blissed out.

Half an hour later, she stood fully dressed in front of the cracked mirror. She had washed her hair as well as her body with the sweet-smelling soap, and then brushed the damp strands around her fingers until the ends gave up and curled. After fixing the reluctant curve with a spritz of hair spray, she turned her attention to her face. The bruise on her forehead was turning yellowish—which just brought out the gold glints in her eyes, she consoled herself as she flicked mascara onto her lashes. A dab of powder on her nose—not for anything would she use that appalling pink blush, and, anyway, after two days spent outdoors without sunblock she certainly didn't need the color—and she was almost done. As a final touch, she applied gloss to her appreciative lips.

If Frankenstein could only see her now.

Muffy, who had fled the shower at the first hint of spray but who once again hugged her ankles, yapped once.

Summer glanced down at her. Her tail was erect, and her ears were, too. Turned the opposite way around from Summer, she faced the door.

Glancing up, Summer was just in time to watch through the mirror as Charlie, the thug from her basement, stepped through the shower room's door.

He was still wearing the same ornate western belt.

CHAPTER TWENTY-NINE

Moving slowly, almost of their own volition as her mind all but ceased to function, Summer's hands fumbled among the cosmetics spread out on the sink. Lip gloss, powder compact, mascara, hair spray . . .

Charlie met her gaze through the mirror. He smiled, revealing yellowing teeth. Muffy growled. Suddenly weak-kneed, Summer resisted the almost overwhelming urge to whirl to face him. Her stomach pressed hard into the edge of the sink. Her hands continued their frantic search.

"Remember me?"

Summer didn't answer. She couldn't. Calm, she told herself fiercely. I must remain calm.

"Of course you do," Charlie answered for her, and chuckled. "Where's Calhoun?"

He ambled toward her, his eyes watchfully scanning the room. It must have been obvious after just a few seconds that Summer was alone, and as he relaxed a swagger entered his gait. So confi-

dent was he that he had her trapped, he didn't even bother to
make a point of displaying the wicked-looking switchblade that he
grasped in one hand.

"I don't know." Her voice was reedy with panic. Her heart
pounded. Her lips parted as she fought for breath. Terror, raw and
numbing, threatened to overcome her senses.

Stay calm, she cautioned herself again.

"Sure you don't."

"I don't. We—split up a while back."

Charlie shrugged. "You don't want to tell me now, that's cool.
You'll tell me later—and believe me, it's more fun that way. At
least, it is for me. *You* might not think so."

His gaze met hers through the mirror. He smiled again.

"Hey, you sure clean up nice. Mind, I thought you were real
pretty even down in your basement."

Oh, God, his eyes were crawling all over her body through the
mirror. Summer felt unclean. Was rape as well as torture and murder on his agenda? Whatever happened, she would not go quietly
into that good night. She would fight.

She didn't know if she had the strength to fight. Fear rendered
her muscles as flaccid as spaghetti. Why, oh why, had she ever left
Frankenstein?

Charlie covered the twenty or so feet separating them in what
seemed to Summer like the blink of an eye. And yet, he didn't
appear to hurry at all.

Now that he was close behind her, his paunchy belly almost
touching her back, she grew light-headed with fear. But, she reminded herself, he would not kill her where she stood. He needed
her to find the van—and Steve.

That knowledge pumped a modicum of courage into her veins.

Her fingers wrapped tightly around the items she had sought
and found.

"It's gonna be my pleasure getting you to tell me everything you
know." His hand, warm and stubby-fingered, closed over the back
of her neck. A spasm of revulsion shivered along Summer's spine.

Charlie glanced down at the floor suddenly, his expression ugly.
"Oh, no you don't," he said, and before Summer realized who, or

what, he was talking to, he drew back his foot and kicked something viciously. "You won't piss on *my* foot."

The brown fur mop that was Muffy flew through the air, crashing with a piteous yelp into the tile beneath the sink.

The distraction provided Summer with the opening she needed.
Jerking free of Charlie's hold, she threw herself to the left—and
tripped over Muffy, who scuttled for safety uttering high-pitched
yelps.

Summer fell heavily, landing on her elbow and hip. For a moment the pain of hitting her crazy bone against the tile floor almost
paralyzed her. She barely managed to hang on to the items in her
hands as electrifying tingles shot up and down her arm. Flopping
like a fish, she turned onto her back.

"So you want to play, bitch?" Charlie was coming toward her,
an ugly smile on his face. He loomed over her, swooping down.
"I'll play."

He waved the knife inches above her face. He leered at her, his
face ugly, menacing. Long hairs grew out of his nostrils, and he
had a scar on his chin. Gathering all her courage, ignoring the
lessening tingles in her arm, Summer raised her clenched fists and
brought them together over her chest.

The Bic lighter was in her right hand. Summer flicked it, and a
tiny flame shot up. Almost simultaneously she depressed the nozzle butting into her left thumb. The nozzle belonged to the pink
metal cylinder of the purse-size hair spray.

The sickly sweet scent of hair spray reached Summer's nostrils
milliseconds before the stream of aerosol mist hit the flame.

"What the . . . ?" Charlie began.

With a muted roar, a tongue of fire shot two feet in the air.
Charlie, leaning down, was caught full in the face. He screamed,
dropping the knife and staggering backward, hands clutching his
face, as the smell of burning filled the air. Summer released the
nozzle, watching with horrified fascination. What she could see of
his face behind his hands was bright red. Tiny flames licked at the
edges of his hair.

Summer didn't wait to see more. Still clutching her homemade
flamethrower, she scrambled for the door on all fours. Muffy was

ahead of her, then underneath her, running too. Summer got tangled up by the little dog, and almost fell flat on her face.

"You bitch! I'll kill you for that, you bitch!" Sobbing, face uncovered now, Charlie lurched after her, arms opening and closing like giant pincers as he grabbed for her. Apparently his vision had been affected; it was obvious he could not see clearly. Staggering in her wake, he looked like an apparition from hell. Charred skin hung in long strips from his face. The surface that remained was pulpy and raw. His eyebrows and lashes were gone. The flames that had danced along his hairline were now extinguished, leaving little wisps of smoke in their place.

Dodging his clutching arms, Summer fought to bite back a scream. Screaming could do her no good. It would only alert Charlie's pals, who, she was sure, lurked somewhere in the vicinity.

"I'm gonna kill you!" It was an unearthly howl. Summer's hair stood on end. She reached the door and climbed it, scrabbling for the knob. He seemed to really see her then. His eyes focused on her. Terrified, Summer nevertheless managed to turn the knob. She yanked opened the door just as he lunged for her, and bolted —smack into a solid masculine chest.

For an instant after the collision she was shocked speechless. Hard male hands grasped her shoulders, hurting her as they held her captive. Hysterical tears rose to her eyes, making her vision swim. Despair rendered her both blind and numb. She could see nothing, feel nothing.

That she had almost escaped made her recapture seem even more cruel.

"Bitch!" The howling thing that was Charlie came charging through the door. With a push her captor shoved her aside. Summer fell to the ground, scraping her knees on the gravel path that circled the building but not caring as she clawed at the grass to get away. God was affording her one more chance at freedom, it seemed, and it was not for her to question the whys and wherefores of his gift.

Summer staggered to her feet, glancing fearfully over her shoulder as she prepared to run for her life—only to see Frankenstein bring the tire iron down on Charlie's head with all his might.

She would recognize that Bulls cap anywhere.

Thwack! Charlie dropped like a felled tree. He toppled backward, his head striking the metal door with a resounding thud on the way down, and lay still.

"Take that, you bastard," Frankenstein said, standing over him.

"Steve, oh, Steve!" Summer had never been so glad to see anyone in her life. She stumbled toward him, collapsing against his chest. His arms, including the one that still held the tire iron, closed around her. He hugged her tight. Summer felt something that might have been his lips brush the top of her head. "Oh, Steve!"

"Are you all right?" He held her a little away from him, looking intently down into her face.

Summer took a deep breath, nodded, and collapsed into his arms again.

"What happened to him?"

She glanced up to discover that he was staring down at Charlie's ruined face.

"I—I did it." Her teeth chattered with shock.

"*You* did it? Jesus, what did you do?"

It was only then that Summer realized she still clutched the lighter and hair spray. "I—I—this," she stuttered, holding out her hands so that he could see the evidence.

"You lit his cigarette or styled his hair?" he asked dryly, relieving her of her weapons. He turned them over in his hands, studying them.

"I burned him."

"You *burned* him?"

"If you spray the hair spray over the flame, it makes a kind of flamethrower. I saw it on *F/X2*."

"*F/X2?*" He sounded totally at sea.

"It's a movie." She was shaking. His arms came around her once more, holding her close against his comforting warmth.

"Jesus." He glanced down at Charlie again, then back at Summer. There was awe in his face. "Rosencrans, you are something else."

A whimper came from the other side of the closed door.

"Muffy!" Summer would recognize that sound anywhere. Steve bent to shove the hair spray and lighter into the gym bag at his feet, then obligingly pushed the door open. The little dog, now limping on her hind leg, came out, skirting Charlie's inanimate body to crowd against Summer's ankles.

"He kicked her," Summer said, picking Muffy up.

"Oh, yeah?" Steve glanced down as Charlie stirred and groaned, and started to sit up. "That's for Muffy," he said grimly, bringing the tire iron down on Charlie's head. Charlie fell back as if he had been poleaxed. He landed so hard that his head bounced; then Steve hit him again, across the chest. Summer winced instinctively at the sound of the blow. "And that's for Summer."

"Stop!" Summer couldn't stand it. "You'll kill him!"

"He was trying to kill us, remember?" Steve said. "Anyway, I never kill people in cold blood. I just aim to put him out of commission for a while."

Steve was hefting the tire iron skyward for what Summer suspected might be another blow just as a blond teenager in skintight jeans and an older, heavyset woman in Lycra bicycle shorts and an oversize pink T-shirt came around the corner of the building.

"I must have left it in here . . ." the girl was saying, only to break off as she saw Steve and Summer staring at her with Charlie sprawled at their feet. The woman saw them at the same time and clutched the girl's arm, stopping her in her tracks. Both their eyes went wide as saucers, and their mouths gaped, as they stared.

"We were just leaving," Steve said hastily, snatching the gym bag from the ground near his feet and pulling Summer with him as he headed away from the transfixed pair. Summer went willingly. The girl and her mother began to back away, then turned and ran in the direction from which they had come.

In the distance Summer heard sirens wail. She glanced over her shoulder in the direction of the sound. A navy Lincoln Continental nosed into view, moving slowly toward them down the gravel road that bisected the campground.

A navy Lincoln Continental . . . She knew that car!

"It's them," Summer said urgently, but Steve had already seen. He grabbed Muffy from her, tucked her under his arm, caught Summer's hand, and pulled her around the corner of the shower building out of sight of the car. Then he ran.

Her fingers entwined with his, Summer ran too, as if all the demons of hell were after her. Which, in a manner of speaking, they were.

Even as they left the campground behind, the sirens grew louder. They ran through the trees, leaping small bushes and fallen logs, until they found a path that seemed to lead straight uphill. Keeping up with Frankenstein in full flight was hard, but terror gave Summer's feet wings, and her lungs strength. Besides, she was deathly afraid to let go of his hand. Not for anything did she mean to get left behind.

At last they paused for breath on top of what Summer had thought was a small rise, both of them bending almost double as they gasped for air. Muffy, set on her feet, immediately collapsed with a groan, and lay panting as though she had run every step of the way, which she emphatically had not.

Glancing around, Summer was surprised to discover that the small rise was in actuality a stone-faced cliff, and they were perched near the edge of it, overlooking the campground below, spread out like a child's playscape. She was even more surprised to see the blue lights of at least half a dozen police cars, minuscule at that distance, flashing in front of a squat building that she took to be the women's showers.

"I never even called Sammy," she said, puzzled. Had all those cops shown up because the girl and the woman from in front of the showers had reported a beating? But that was impossible. She had first heard the sirens while the women were still in sight.

"You didn't need to." Steve reached into his back pocket and drew something out, which as he unfolded it Summer recognized as the front page of the morning newspaper. "Look at this."

He handed it to her. Summer looked and gasped.

There, in full color on the front page, staring back at her, were three remarkably clear photographs: Steve, herself, and Muffy, whom the caption grandly identified as Grand Champion Margie's Miss Muffet.

The headline over the pictures, set in inch-high boldface type, read: CALHOUN, GIRLFRIEND, DOG SOUGHT IN CONNECTION WITH DOUBLE HOMICIDE.

Jaw dropping, Summer scanned the accompanying story. She, Muffy, and Steve were the subjects of a statewide manhunt after the bodies of Linda Miller and Betty Kern had been found in her home. The police were working with two possibilities: Either she and Steve, whose fingerprints had been found at the scene, were partners in crime, or he had taken her, and her dog, hostage. In any case, citizens spotting any of the three were asked not to try to apprehend them but to call police. They were considered armed and extremely dangerous.

"Where did you get this?" Summer asked, dumbfounded.

"In the manager's office. I decided you were making a mistake, so I came looking for you. You weren't where I expected you to be, but the manager was. So was this. He was reading it when I came through the door. I had to take him out."

"Oh, my God! You didn't . . . ?" She glanced at him, her thoughts immediately turning to murder.

"No, I didn't," he said dryly. "I told you, I don't kill people in cold blood. I just put him to sleep for a while. *He* never had a chance to tell anybody, and nobody else saw me. I made damned sure of that. Somebody must have recognized you or the dog—I told you, she's so weird-looking she attracts attention—and called the police."

"I asked a woman the way to the manager's office," Summer said, remembering. "The way she looked at me—it must have been her!"

"Probably." He was looking down at the scene below. People, at that distance appearing no bigger than ants, were beginning to crowd around the police cars.

"Maybe we should go back," Summer said hesitantly, looking too. "After all, they *are* the police . . ."

He shook his head. Summer didn't argue. As far as she was concerned, her safety now lay with Steve.

CHAPTER THIRTY

They were still standing there, watching the tableau far below, when a miniature pickup truck pulled up slowly to park beside the police cars. A man got out and was almost immediately joined by two uniformed police officers.

The man and the officers walked around to the back of the truck, scattering the gathered crowd. The man climbed up into the truckbed, did something, then jumped down again.

This time he was accompanied by a pack of leashed dogs.

Summer could hear shrill echoes of their cries from where she stood. Muffy came upright, her head cocking as she stared down.

"Jesus. They've brought in dogs."

A third cop walked up to the group around the animals, and passed a bundle of what looked like cloth to their handler. The man took the bundle, bent and offered it for the dogs to sniff.

"Did you leave anything in the shower room?" Steve was folding the newspaper back into its small rectangle.

Summer thought. "The—the makeup kit. Uh—and my uniform! My Daisy Fresh uniform! Do you think they're letting those dogs smell my uniform?"

"I'd say so," Steve answered grimly, and returned the folded newspaper to his back pocket.

Even as Summer looked down again, the handler loosed the dogs. There were five brown and black hounds, and they scattered, sniffing the ground. Seconds later one of them, near the building, set up a howl.

"He's found the trail."

The other dogs rallied to their leader, and all five of them streaked in a pack for the woods, baying at the top of their lungs.

"Oh, God, what do we do? Do you have a plan?" Summer looked wildly at Steve.

"Yeah," he answered, bending to scoop up Muffy and then grabbing the gym bag and Summer's hand. "Run like hell."

Some plan. But Summer didn't say it. She didn't have a chance. With Steve dragging her along behind him, it was a struggle to breathe, much less speak. The baying of the dogs was a distant, but potent, spur. Her feet barely touched the ground, she ran so fast. She almost seemed to be floating—probably because she felt light-headed.

Summer didn't know whether that was from the altitude, hunger, or fear.

They ran down a gulley full of brush, which sported a trickle of water at its bottom. Halfway down the mountain, the gulley suddenly made a sharp left, and turned into a full-blown creek.

Steve splashed into the icy water, yanking Summer after him. She slipped on the smooth brown stones that covered the creekbed, and went down on one knee, disturbing a school of minnows, which scattered.

"Ouch!" A rock jabbed into Summer's knee, but she had no time to suffer properly. Steve was already hauling her upright.

"Why do we have to run through a creek?" Summer wailed as she rubbed her damaged kneecap. The way it felt at that moment, she would never be able to walk again, much less run.

"Because dogs can't track through water." Steve paused for

about two seconds, just long enough to glance down at her leg and ascertain that she was not seriously injured. "I don't think."

"Oh, great. *You don't think.* That's reassuring. I hope you're right."

Without bothering to reply, Steve jerked her into motion again. With the surefootedness of a goat, he bounded through the ankle-deep water. Slip-sliding, cursing, and praying with every step, Summer splashed precariously after him.

The sounds of the dogs grew fainter.

Finally, about the time Summer's lungs and heart threatened to burst, Steve clambered out of the creek and collapsed facedown on the ivy-covered bank. Summer, falling on her stomach beside him, fought to breathe.

Muffy, lying on her side like a creature exhausted when she hadn't run so much as a step, even had the temerity to pant.

Summer didn't have the strength to do more than glare at the pampered pooch.

"Catch your breath. We can't stop long," Steve advised her, drawing in deep lungfuls of air.

"Where are we going? Are we still heading to your fishing camp?"

Steve shook his head. "That was Plan A, and it's scrapped. If the police are going to scour these hills with dogs, they'll find it in two shakes of a lamb's tail. Now we're on to Plan B."

"What's Plan B?" Summer asked with deep misgiving.

Exhausted as he was, Steve managed a brief grin. "I'm working on it, okay? Let's go!"

Summer groaned, but he was inexorable. He was on his feet again, dragging her up with him, making her run even though her legs were still shaky from the last marathon. The sun was at their backs as they raced downward through the forest. It was just beginning to dip beneath the majestic purple peaks. At any other moment, Summer would have been most appreciative of the hot magenta and neon orange pinwheels swirling across the western third of the sky. Under the circumstances, she spared the dazzling beauty of the heavens only a cursory glance—and hoped.

Could dogs continue to track in the dark? Surely even dogs had to rest sometime.

A dirt bike roared toward them from the east. It literally flew into sight, jumping over the top of a hill and skittering semi-sideways down the slippery mountainside. A lone man was aboard, a young-looking man in jeans and a leather jacket.

Steve slowed, and Summer slowed with him.

"What now?" she gasped, ready by this time to see a bad guy behind every tree.

Steve looked at her, grinned, and let go of her hand.

"Plan B," he said, and jogged toward the oncoming motorcycle.

It skidded to a flourishing halt in front of him, and the driver climbed off. Summer watched warily as he propped the bike on its kickstand, turned off the engine, took off his helmet, and clapped Steve on the back. He even patted Muffy on the head.

He knew Steve. He was friendly. How on earth . . . ?

Summer approached with caution. In her experience, if something seemed too good to be true, it usually was. And an ally arriving out of nowhere certainly seemed too good to be true.

Steve was grinning as he turned to beckon her in. The man beside him was more sober-faced. He was about Steve's age and height, but leaner. His complexion was swarthy, and his hair was as black as oil and straight. Summer realized that he was Native American.

"This is Renfro. Renfro, Summer. Here, put this on."

Renfro nodded at Summer as Steve passed her a bright yellow helmet that he unstrapped from the rear of the bike, then turned worried eyes on Steve. "Leave the dog with me."

Steve, putting on the helmet that Renfro had worn, shook his head. "Nah. There's half the state and a pack of dogs besides chasing us. They catch you with the dog, they'll know you helped us. That wouldn't be good for your health."

"I'm not worried." Renfro was strapping the gym bag and tire iron on the back of the bike.

"Thanks anyway, buddy. And thanks for coming. I owe you."

"Big time." Renfro smiled then, flashing even white teeth as he finished his self-appointed task. "As usual."

Steve laughed. "How will you get back?"

Renfro shrugged. "Walk. Thumb a ride. Catch a bus. Call my dad. I'll manage."

"If you run into the posse hunting us . . ."

"They won't bother me. I'm hiking through the forest. What's to bother? If the dogs attack me, maybe I can sue." He said it hopefully, with a wide grin. Summer realized that it was meant for a joke. She smiled.

"You have your helmet on?" Steve turned to look at her critically, tugging on the strap beneath her chin to make sure it was tight. His helmet was in place. She almost missed the Bulls cap, which he had tucked into the gym bag.

"Oh, I almost forgot." Renfro dug in the pocket of his jeans and brought forth some folded bills. "Forty dollars. It's all I had in the shop."

"Thanks, man." Steve accepted the money, stuffed it in his own back pocket. "Take care."

"You too."

Steve kicked up the stand, straddled the bike, and motioned for Summer to join him.

"What about Muffy?" She looked down at the hairball at her feet.

"You'll have to hold her. Try to keep her out of sight. Maybe you can stick her under your shirt."

Summer picked up Muffy, lifted the hem of her T-shirt, and tucked the little dog inside. Then she climbed awkwardly aboard the motorcycle. It was about the size of an adult's bicycle, but thicker. There were pegs for her feet, she discovered, and a metal bar against which she could rest her back.

Perched on the narrow black vinyl seat, she felt about as secure as a cat on a high wire.

Renfro grinned broadly, surveying them. "You look like the all-American family. Dad, Mom, baby-to-be"—he patted the bulge in the tummy area of Summer's T-shirt that was Muffy—"on a Yamaha. Maybe they'll use you in an ad."

"See ya, Renfro." Steve kicked the starter. The bike roared. Renfro waved, and they were off.

Summer had never experienced such a bone-rattling ride in her life.

If she could have, Summer would have clung to Steve with all her strength as they careened over the uneven ground. But Muffy, who was not taking kindly to this new mode of transportation, was between them. She needed one arm just to hang on to Muffy. The other she clamped around Steve's waist.

They went up and then down the mountain, heading north rather than continuing in the easterly direction they had been traveling on foot. The bike skittered sideways on wet leaves and unseen rocks and roots so many times that Summer got used to feeling they were going to hit the dirt at any minute. Twice, when they came over a hill, she was treated to beautiful vistas of mountains rolling away into the distance, each crowned with its own halo of clouds. The scenery was straight out of a movie. The dangers were more real. Steep, heavily forested slopes ended without warning in craggy precipices. Sometimes the ground just seemed to stop, falling away in breathtaking drops of hundreds and even thousands of feet.

So far, Steve had managed to avoid taking them over any of those drops. But Summer wasn't optimistic. Lately, she'd felt like a character on the old television show *Hee Haw:* If it weren't for bad luck, she'd have no luck at all.

Beyond fear finally, Summer screwed up her eyes against the wind, held Muffy close, and hung on for dear life as they dodged trees and rocks and roots at speeds she was sure neared seventy miles an hour. Early on, she realized there was nothing she could do to make her precarious perch any safer. Her life, and Muffy's, were in Steve's hands. She could only pray that he knew what he was doing—and that they would not zoom over a rise and find themselves sailing over a cliff.

Surprise, surprise.

Around them the world was growing darker. Lengthening shadows lay across the ground like prison bars. They crested another rise. The back tire came off the ground. In the distance, where Summer's eyes fixed in sheer self-defense, mountains rose out of darkening air.

Without warning the bike shot into the sky like a bucking bronco. This time, both wheels left the earth. Summer screeched, clamped both arms around Steve's middle—Muffy, squashed between her stomach and Steve's back, couldn't have gotten free if she'd wanted to—and shut her eyes. When the bike landed, bouncing, they were on pavement, racing uphill.

"You're going to kill us!" she screamed in Steve's ear.

"This is fun!" he roared back.

Fun. Of course, to him, it would be. *I feel the need / the need for speed* . . . He was suffering from Top Gun-itis again.

"Is it even legal to ride this thing on the road?" Summer yelled.

"Hey, this baby swings both ways: on-road or off."

Whatever that meant. Summer decided not to worry about it. Men and their macho toys were beyond her understanding at the moment.

It was a two-lane highway, and judging from the mist that crept across it, they were very high now in the mountains. Summer shivered, but not from fear, or the eeriness of her surroundings. Her shorts and T-shirt offered scant protection against the rushing air. She was growing thoroughly chilled.

But they seemed to have eluded their pursuers, at least temporarily. There were other vehicles on the road, a few cars, some campers. Vacationers all. No cops. No bad guys. With their helmets on, riding a motorcycle none of their pursuers knew they had, Summer thought—hoped—that she and Steve were to all intents and purposes invisible. Just two more tourists, vacationing in the mountains.

"Where are we going?" Summer screamed. The wind blew her question back in her face.

"I don't know. Maybe Mexico," Steve yelled back.

Mexico? She didn't want to go to Mexico! Anyway, they were heading north, not south!

She opened her mouth to tell him so, and promptly swallowed a bug. Gagging, spitting, she decided to hold her peace until they stopped.

Surely they would stop soon. The constant vibration was making her butt numb. She shifted on her narrow seat, but that brought no relief.

Ridiculous, when one was running for one's life, to worry about minor discomforts, Summer knew. But she couldn't seem to help it: her butt was numb and her legs were cramped and her feet were going to sleep and she was freezing. The wind in her face never stopped. Cold and bug-laden, it beat against her skin, numbing that, too.

And she was hungry. Starving, actually. As a diet, running for one's life was proving drastic but effective. Maybe she could make an infomercial and market it and get rich.

A green sign by the side of the road read APPALACHIAN TRAIL. Below it, a small brown woodchuck stood on its hind legs, sniffing the air. Ahead, as far as the eye could see, stretched miles of blue-green forest and dozens of mountain peaks, rising up out of the mist one after the other. The vista was beautiful, glorious—Summer realized that she was seeing the Smokies in all their natural splendor.

Her instinctive mental response to that edifying bit of knowledge was, Yippee.

As night descended, the traffic thinned out. Glancing behind her, Summer watched the twin white dots of car lights heading down the mountain. Except for an ancient blue camper just in front of them, they were alone on the mountaintop.

Streaking through the dark, clinging like a monkey to a man she hadn't even met three days before, Summer was assaulted by a sudden pang of homesickness. She missed her mother. She missed her sisters. She missed her nieces and nephews. She even missed her brothers-in-law, with whom she didn't always see eye to eye. What she wouldn't give to be safe in her own house, warm and cozy and well fed, with all of this just a terrible nightmare from which she would soon awaken!

She was suddenly, searingly conscious of the man to whom she clung. Would she really wish Steve Calhoun to be nothing more than a figment of her dreams? If she could, with a wave of her hands, make him vanish along with the situation he had gotten her into, would she?

The answer was disturbing: no. She might wish away the circumstances, but not the man.

It occurred to her, in the near meditative state brought on by cold and wind and discomfort and unceasing vibration, to wonder why she wouldn't wish away a man who had kidnapped her, terrorized her, brutalized her, and exposed her to numerous threats to life and limb, and who might still easily be the death of her. He was not her type at all. She wasn't one hundred percent positive what her type was, but she was positive that he wasn't it.

He wasn't even handsome, for goodness' sake. Lem, with all his faults, was at least handsome. Steve Calhoun was rude and crude, liked violence and speed and danger, made jokes at her expense, admitted to a (supposedly former) drinking problem, and was hung up on a ghost. He was also notorious, unemployed, wanted by the police, and on the run for his life.

He was, by no stretch of her imagination, her idea of what a Knight in Shining Armor should be. She had always, secretly, hankered after a Knight in Shining Armor.

But he had come back for her, there at the campground. That was something. A very big something.

She couldn't be falling in love with him.

Could she? If she was, she was putting Heaven on notice right that minute that she would consider it just one more in a long line of life's little dirty tricks.

By the time night fell so conclusively that Summer was hard put to see her hand in front of her face, the camper had pulled off. Probably to make camp. At least, she assumed that was what campers did. She had never been camping in her life, and if this experience was any example of the pleasures of outdoor life, she didn't foresee taking it up anytime in the near future.

Would they ever stop? There was a lot to be said for physical misery as a means of taking one's mind off one's troubles, she would be the first to agree, but enough was enough. If they didn't stop soon so she could straighten her cramped muscles, Summer feared she might never walk again.

Except for the beam of the motorcycle's headlight cutting through the mist that now rolled across the road in great waves, there was no light at all. No moon. No stars. No streetlights. Complete darkness.

Summer wondered about the cliffs that fell away from the roadside to her left, about the complete lack of guardrails, and about how high up they were. One wrong move and they would find themselves hurtling out into nothingness. She had a sudden ridiculous picture of herself, Steve, Muffy, and the motorcycle as E.T. and Co., soaring into space to cycle in front of a full moon. There were just two things wrong with that vision, she thought: Number one, tonight there was no moon at all, and number two, the motorcycle could not fly. Instead they would crash and die. . . .

It was an effort, but the ache in all her muscles helped: Summer finally managed to dismiss that last cheering thought from her mind.

Muffy whined, and Summer patted her consolingly. The little dog had actually settled down in her warm bed of tummy and T-shirt with surprising docility. Despite the pat, Muffy whined again, and Summer got the message: Muffy needed to go potty.

She leaned forward to yell in Steve's ear.

"What?" he yelled back.

"Muffy has to pee!"

"So hold her out over the side!"

Funny. Very funny. "Will you stop?"

"As soon as I find a place."

They rode on for a bit. Muffy whined, Summer patted, the motorcycle rolled. Talking to Steve was at least something to do, even though hearing and being heard over the roar of the engine and rush of the wind required considerable effort. Summer leaned forward again.

"Do you have any idea where we are?"

"I know exactly where we are."

"Well, where?"

"We're lost!" he yelled back, and laughed like a hyena.

Summer would have punched him in the side if she hadn't been afraid of those waiting cliffs.

CHAPTER THIRTY-ONE

Why Steve finally decided to stop where he did, Summer couldn't tell. He merely pulled off the road onto a pitch-black overlook just like every other pitch-black overlook they had passed.

Far be it from her to question a gift from the gods, though, she thought, and climbed on shaking legs from the back of their metal steed while the climbing was good. She'd ridden horseback a lot in her girlhood. The way she felt now was saddle-sore times ten.

Muffy immediately squatted beside the motorcycle.

Summer had to fight the urge to do the same. Instead, she staggered off into the dark.

The wind blew unceasingly, growing colder with every minute. Summer glanced around at the black shrouded vista of mountains and trees and moonless sky, and shivered. For once, the cicadas were silent. Maybe they had crawled back into the ground for another seventeen years—or maybe they had frozen solid, as she felt she might do. But there were other living creatures in the forest. Summer could hear their rustlings. As she took care of business in the lee of a tree not fifteen feet from where Steve wrestled with the motorcycle, she had the sensation that a million unseen eyes were watching her through the dark.

Probably thinking, Dinner!

Summer nearly broke her neck scrambling to rejoin Steve and (relative) safety. While she had been otherwise occupied, he had put the motorcycle up on its center stand and was, as she returned, unhitching the gym bag from the back. Muffy, her hair bow piteously askew, huddled at his feet.

She's as afraid of this place as I am, Summer thought, and, not without a few painful twinges, stooped to gather the dog up into her arms.

Muffy rewarded her with a lick on the chin.

"We may as well spend the night here. As dark as it is, it's too dangerous to go on."

Hear, hear. But Summer didn't say it. Instead she followed Steve into the trees.

"I have a question for you," she said as, at Steve's direction, she gathered sticks for a fire. "Did your friend Renfro show up like that by accident?"

"Does Michael Jordan have hair?" Kneeling on the ground, Steve was clearing a circle of nature's debris all the way down to pure earth for the fire.

Summer had to think about that. "No," she said at last.

"Exactly."

Her brain was so fried from the events of the day that she had to think about that, too.

"Are you trying to say that Renfro showing up was *not* an accident?" she asked finally, carrying her pile of sticks over to him and flopping at his side. She was chilled to the bone. Reaching over, she unzipped the gym bag and dragged the sweatshirt from its depths.

"You got it." While she pulled the sweatshirt on, he examined the sticks carefully, discarded a few, and began to arrange the others in a neat pile. The fleecy sweatshirt did nothing for the twin columns of ice that were her legs. She extracted the quilt from the gym bag and wrapped that around herself, too.

"Did you contact him with smoke signals or ESP?" She couldn't help it. She *felt* sarcastic. She also felt like she was coming down with a cold. With her luck, it would probably turn into pneumonia. Not that the prospect concerned her particularly. At this point, pneumonia was way down on her list of things to worry about.

He sent her a sidelong glance. "I used the phone in the manager's office. After I saw that newspaper, I knew that hiding out at the fishing camp wasn't a good idea. We needed to put a lot of miles between us and everybody who was hunting for us, fast. I've known Renfro since I was a kid. He used to go fishing with me and my dad a lot, and sometimes we'd ride dirt bikes. He's a motorcycle nut, always has a bunch of them around in various stages of repair. He runs a souvenir shop with his dad on an Indian reservation about twenty-five miles from Hiawatha Village. When I called him and told him where I was and what I needed, he said no *problemo.* He'd already read the papers, and from what I gathered he wasn't all that surprised to hear from me. So when we had to run for it, we ran in the direction I knew he'd be coming from. And there, in a nutshell, you have Plan B."

"It worked," Summer admitted, inching closer to the cone-shaped pile of sticks as he ignited them with the always useful Bic. She didn't think she would ever be warm again in her life.

"My plans always work," Steve said with a smirk.

"Oh, yeah? Then what's your plan for getting us out of this? I don't think Mexico is such a great idea."

Steve dug in the gym bag and came up with what was left of their food. He zipped the bag up again, and leaned back against the convenient trunk of a tall pine. "I don't think so either," he said, threading limp-looking hot dogs on a stick and passing it to Summer to hold. Summer tried not to think about the various kinds of food poisoning that could lurk in meat that had gone unrefrigerated for at least a day, and held the stick out over the fire. Dangerous or not, she was going to eat those hot dogs. She was starving.

In her fur rug mode again between the two humans, Muffy yapped. Summer and Steve exchanged glances. Steve passed Muffy a slightly-the-worse-for-wear peanut butter cracker.

"I've been thinking about it," he continued, arranging buns on a rock, which he shoved close to the fire. "Running is not the solution here. Now that they've set it up so that we're wanted for murder, every police force in the whole U.S. is going to be looking for us. If they think we've crossed state lines, the FBI will be after us. If they think we've left the country, Interpol will be after us. The way our luck is running, we'll probably be featured on next week's *America's Most Wanted*. The good cops—and they outnumber the bad by a wide margin, believe me—are now our enemies just as much as the bad cops—and the bad guys who are not cops. The good cops will either arrest us and send us back to where the bad cops can get to us, or, if we resist, shoot to kill. That's what I would do in their case. That's what any cop would do."

"Shoot to kill?" Summer echoed faintly. Steve nodded and began to thread marshmallows onto a stick.

"You've got to realize, we're the bad guys now," he said. "We're criminals, wanted by the police."

"Oh, my God!" Summer was appalled. "Maybe we better call a lawyer. My sister's one; then there's the guy who handled my divorce. He didn't do such a good job, to tell you the truth, but maybe he could recommend . . ."

Steve was shaking his head. "We don't need a lawyer. One thing we don't have to worry about is beating criminal charges. If we're caught, we won't ever make it to trial. Depending on who catches us, we might or we might not even make it to jail."

"Oh," Summer said in a small voice. The reality of their situation was scary.

"Pay attention; you're burning the hot dogs."

Her thoughts recalled to the demands of the present, Summer quickly turned the hot dogs. Steve was right, the side that was now on top was black and bubbly. Good thing she liked her hot dogs that way. Heck, at this point she liked her hot dogs any way at all.

"So what do we do?" Summer couldn't see a whole lot of options. But maybe, she consoled herself hopefully, she was just tired.

"I think our best bet is to go back to the boat warehouse. We need to find out what is in that van that everybody wants so much. If it's what I think it is, we contact the media with our story. If we can get the media behind us—and we have a good shot at it, they seem to love police-scandal stories—then we should be reasonably safe." He glanced at the hot dogs, shook his head, and removed the stick from her hands. "I think they're done." The dryness in his voice was probably due to the fact that their dinner was as black as a cinder.

"But we know what's in the van. Dead bodies are in the van." Summer accepted a hot dog, wrapped in a slightly stale-feeling but warm bun, that he passed her.

"Baby, believe me, they're not chasing us to hell and back just so they can pay their respects to the dead." Steve bit into his own hot dog. Muffy whined. Summer absentmindedly broke off a bit of bun and fed it to her. "If there wasn't something that they want very badly in that van, we'd already be dead. And it's not those bodies."

"What do you think it is, then?" Summer tried to remember the interior of the van. She hadn't seen anything besides the coffins and their contents, but then she hadn't really looked.

"Drugs, probably. It could be any number of things, but drugs would be my guess. Coke or smack, maybe. Not grass, it takes up too much room." He removed a marshmallow from its stick and put it in his mouth whole. Then he popped open one of their two remaining cans of beer, and passed it to her. The other can, she saw, rested on the ground beside his leg. It was already open. Summer eyed it askance.

"I hate beer," was all she said.

"Drink it."

She accepted the can with a grimace, propping it against her leg. Steve took a long swig from his can. There was so much else to worry about that Summer couldn't summon more than a flicker of dismay over her self-confessed alcoholic's apparently nonchalant consumption of beer. If the can even held beer. She was beginning to know him well enough to suspect it did not.

"Water?" She hazarded a guess, cocking a brow at the can.

He looked at her in some surprise. "What makes you think that?"

"It is, isn't it?"

"Yeah."

"Thought so." Her lip curled in satisfaction. She hadn't been mistaken in her reading of his character.

"Think you're pretty smart, don't you?" he asked.

"Yeah." She had to smile. "Where'd you get it?"

"I drained out the beer and filled the cans up with water from a tap at the campground when I came looking for you. See the little hole in the lid? Easy. As long as you plug the hole with something. In this case, bubble gum."

"You mean mine's water, too?" Summer glanced at her can with genuine excitement.

He nodded. She grinned at him and took a big swallow. The water was lukewarm and had a faintly metallic edge, but still it tasted wonderful. She drank again, then returned to the matter at hand.

"Could you, please, tell me how you wound up in the funeral home the other night? Everything seems to have started then."

Steve shook his head and devoured another marshmallow. "No, everything didn't start then. It actually started more than three years ago. This is something to do with the case I was working on when I—when Deedee died."

He looked pensive suddenly, or as pensive as it was possible to look when licking marshmallow goo from one's fingers.

"Go on," she said a tad irritably. Deedee was beginning to get on her nerves.

"You want to know the whole thing?" His glance was inscrutable. "All right. It was supposed to be confidential, but under the circumstances I think you deserve to hear it. Hell, maybe you can help me figure it out. So far, I seem to be missing something. The key." He laughed and fed Muffy the badly charred end of his hot dog without her even having to yap for it. Muffy gobbled up the morsel greedily.

"You know I am—was—a detective with the Tennessee State Police." It was as much a question as a statement, and Summer nodded.

"About three and a half years ago I was asked by my superiors to investigate possible corruption in a small-town police department." He glanced at Summer, hesitated, and swigged his water. "Hell, you might as well know that it was the Murfreesboro Police Department. Chief Rosencrans made the request. It seemed that the corruption—the alleged corruption—was so widespread in his department that he needed outside help in rooting it out. They weren't sure which, if any, of their own guys were clean."

"Then doesn't that prove that Sammy's not involved? All we have to do is contact him and . . ." Summer broke in eagerly.

Steve shook his head. "It doesn't prove a thing. Did you ever hear of bluff and double bluff? Just because Old Rosey asked us to investigate doesn't mean he wasn't involved. Maybe he just thought initiating the investigation himself would be a good way to obscure his involvement in what was going on. Hell, I don't know. When you've been a detective as long as I have been—was, whatever—you learn never to take anything at face value. Just because it looks like a cow, and sounds like a cow, and smells like a cow, doesn't mean that it *is* a cow, if you follow me."

Summer thought about that and nodded. Exhaustion was taking its toll. Her brain was not the sharpest it had ever been at that precise moment, but she was pretty sure she got the main idea: Maybe Sammy was a good guy, and maybe he wasn't.

"Anyway, I investigated, and I concluded that there was something rotten in Murfreesboro. Something really rotten. Those guys were being paid off by the bushelful—but by whom? And why? This was a hush-hush investigation. Nobody was supposed to know about it but my immediate superior and Chief Rosencrans. All the action seemed to center around Harmon Brothers funeral homes. Something was going down on the premises—a big-time drug operation, I'm fairly certain, though I never had a chance to prove it. Whether the funeral home people are involved, or just the premises themselves, I'm not certain. I suspect at least some of the people—employees or owners—have to be in on it, or they'd be filing complaints about strangers coming and going at odd hours at their cemeteries. No complaints were filed. I checked. I also got whiffs that some high-society types around the state might be involved. Some politicians might be involved. And some cops might be involved. I was just getting pretty deep into it—and then Deedee died."

"She committed suicide," Summer said softly, wanting him to face it. He glanced over at her, his expression suddenly harsh, intent.

"Did she? That's that they said. Hell, there's a good case for it, at least on paper. We did have an affair, and I did break it off kind of abruptly. But would Deedee hang herself over that? I always did find that hard to believe. I just can't see Deedee killing herself over me. I can't see her killing herself at all. Deedee wasn't the type. She was—vibrant, I suppose, for want of a better word. She was the type to grab life with both hands and twist its tail until it gave her what she wanted."

"Maybe you just don't want to see it." Summer thought, hoped, that if she pressed him to get everything that had happened out in the open, it might have a healing effect. It was time and past that Deedee's ghost was laid to rest. "Didn't she leave a suicide note, or, er, videotape?"

"Yeah." The tips of Steve's ears reddened. He took a sip of water and cast Summer a sidelong glance. "Somebody—I can't believe it was Deedee; you can bet your life *I* never saw the camera if it was—videotaped us, uh, doing it. There was some pretty steamy footage on that tape—I know, because during the course of the investigation into whether or not I should be fired they made me watch it three times. Deedee was—a free spirit. She liked to try different things. Like being tied up, or having sex in unexpected places."

"Like on your desktop." Summer's voice was dry. She knew she was idiotic to resent any sexual encounters that he might have had before he even met her, and sexual encounters with a dead woman were certainly no threat—but she resented them, anyway. Because, she decided, to Steve, Deedee was very much alive. He even had visions of her ghost.

She was shocked to realize how much she needed for him to put Deedee, living or dead, right out of his life.

"A fan of the *National Enquirer,* are we?" he asked, cocking a sardonic eyebrow at her.

"Actually, I think I saw it on *Hard Copy.*"

"Jesus." Steve picked up his can as though to take a drink, then set it down again without doing so. "After the first thrill of making it with Deedee wore off—I'd had the hots for her from afar for years, you understand—I started to feel guilty as hell. There was Elaine. She was my wife. We were in love when we got married, or at least *I* was in love. I can't speak for her. By the time the kid was born, the flame had flickered out. Still, we kept going through the motions. Don't get me wrong, Elaine was—is—a good woman, a good mother. I'm not going to say otherwise to try to justify what I did."

He picked up the can and this time guzzled about half the contents. When he put it down, he wiped his mouth with the back of his hand and glanced at her. His eyes were unreadable, shiny black disks in the dark. "Even worse than Elaine, there was Mitch. Mitch is—was—my best friend. We went to kindergarten together. We went to elementary school together. We met Deedee together, when we were in high school. Mitch was the quarterback on our football team. I was the center. The only thing we didn't do together was join the Marines. He went to college instead. But when I got out of the service, I went to college too, and ended up in the state police with Mitch. He made detective the year before I did. Hell, when Elaine and I bought our house in Nashville, he bought one right down the street. He was there at the hospital passing out cigars the night my daughter was born. We hung out together. We were tight, tighter than a lot of brothers. I screwed my best friend's wife. It was indefensible. I know it, believe me."

He broke off. His jaw hardened, and Summer was treated to a view of his stony profile as he stared into the fire. After a moment, as though he felt the weight of her unspoken sympathy, he slanted a brooding look her way.

"Deedee and Mitch had been married forever, and he'd been screwing around on her for years. Maybe she'd been screwing around on him, too. I don't know. How can anybody know? Anyway, this time he was involved in an affair that Deedee seemed to think was pretty hot and heavy. She needed a shoulder to cry on, and whose better than mine? We'd been friends, all of us, for so long. I never meant what happened to happen. It just did. I was drinking one night, and she was lonely, and—it happened." He covered his face with his hands suddenly. "God, if I could only take it back. Just that one moment. If I could only take it back, I would."

Looking at him, looking at the broad shoulders slumped now in defeat, at the bowed head, at this strong man suddenly brought low in an attitude of utter despair, Summer realized the sad truth: She *was* in love with him.

God help her.

And she couldn't stand to see him hurting. Even if his pain was caused by his grief for another woman, she had to do what she could to ease the sting.

She crawled over to him and wrapped her arms, quilt and all, comfortingly around his shoulders.

And pressed her mouth to the unshaven, sandpaper roughness of his cheek.

His hands fell away from his face. His head lifted, turned, and his black eyes bored into hers with blast furnace intensity.

CHAPTER THIRTY-TWO

Except for the orange glow of light cast by the flickering flames, the forest was dark as pitch. Shadows from the fire leaped and danced like pagan phantoms among the black trunks of trees. The wind moaned in the treetops. Small animals scurried and squeaked.

Summer studied the fathomless black eyes, the unhandsome, powerfully magnetic face, the wide shoulders, the rough black hair.

She was in love with this man. The thought was so scary that it almost made her sick—but it was exhilarating, too.

He tilted his head and kissed her mouth.

Summer closed her eyes. It was a tender kiss, a sweet kiss, and the emotions it brought with it were so intense, she wanted to cry.

Then, without warning, he broke off the kiss. Summer opened her eyes, bewildered, as he drew back.

"This is a mistake." His voice was unsteady.

Hurt, Summer started to draw away in turn. But then she remembered that this was Steve, proud, unreachable Steve, whom she loved. Steve, who had been hurt and was still hurting. Steve, who needed her.

Instead of giving up, she tightened her arms around his neck. Closing her eyes, she lifted her head and found his lips with hers. When her mouth touched his he did not pull away, but neither did he respond. She might as well have been kissing a statue as she rubbed her lips sensuously against his weather-dry mouth.

He was resisting her. Why? Because of Deedee. Summer knew it instinctively. She and Deedee were locked in battle for Steve's soul.

Never mind that Deedee was dead.

His lips stayed stubbornly closed against hers. Summer, who had never deliberately set out to seduce a man in her life, did now. She traced the outline of his mouth with her tongue, probing at the line where his lips joined. She could feel every muscle in his body stiffen as he fought against responding.

"Make love to me, Steve," she whispered against his mouth. Even his neck was rigid with resistance as she stroked its nape with gentle fingers, trying to coax his head down.

"For both our sakes, I need to keep a clear head," he said, sounding strangled. Summer smiled at him and crawled into his lap, adjusting the quilt so that it cocooned both of them. Her arms wrapped around his neck. His raised knees and long, muscular thighs on the one side and warm abdomen and wide chest on the other made a nice cradle for her bottom. Her breasts brushed his chest. His hands, quite of their own volition she was sure, found and tightened on her waist.

"You don't need a clear head tonight."

He could have put her off his lap easily. Summer knew he could; she had experienced his strength before. And he was certainly ruthless enough not to care about hurting her if ridding himself of her was truly what he wanted. But it wasn't. She knew it wasn't.

"Summer . . ." Despite his protests, those black eyes were fixed on her mouth.

"Shhh." Summer put a finger to his lips to silence him. She

couldn't stop looking at him. She was so close to him that she could see every mark, every bruise, every scar on his skin. She could see, individually, the thousands of stubbly hairs that made up the rough black shadow that darkened his jaw, the faint puffiness that still distorted the right side of his face, the yellowing edges of a deep purple bruise on his forehead, the discolored circles around his eyes. The gash over his cheekbone was just starting to heal; so was the one at the corner of his mouth. His battered state should have lessened his appeal, but, oddly, it didn't. He looked like a weary gladiator, this man she loved, she decided as she absorbed everything about his face from the bushiness of his black eyebrows and the bump in the bridge of the harsh blade that was his nose, to the unexpectedly tender curve of his lower lip above a mulish jaw.

"Look, I don't want to get involved. . . ." His breathing was uneven. Summer smiled at him tenderly.

"I don't either, but I think it's already too late." She moved then, lifting her mouth toward him at the same time as she drew his head down to hers. He let her pull him down—she was under no illusions that he could not have stopped her if he chose—but that was all the encouragement he gave her.

Summer closed her eyes and touched her lips to his, softly at first, in a butterfly kiss that tantalized. No response. Coaxing, her mouth stroked his, begging, promising. Still he resisted—but the sudden harsh indrawing of his breath told her all she needed to know.

This was a battle she was going to win.

He felt big and warm and solid against her. Summer snuggled closer, shifting so that she was half lying against his chest, her breasts pressed close against the hard muscles there, her arms locked around his neck.

He opened his mouth to say something—make some other protest, no doubt—but she forestalled him by sliding her tongue inside his mouth.

He stiffened as if all his muscles had tightened in a single spasmodic jerk. Would he fight to the end, this gladiator of hers? Summer drew back her head, her lids opening languorously. The black eyes blazed down at her, as scorching as the embers of their fire. She kissed him, softly, briefly. Still he didn't surrender. Summer smiled at him as her breasts nuzzled into his chest. His eyes narrowed and his jaw hardened. Summer could feel the momentary cessation in his breathing.

Then, "To hell with it," he muttered thickly, and his mouth came swooping down on hers.

He kissed her as if he were starving for the taste of her mouth. His lips and tongue alternately caressed and plundered, while his arms locked around her waist and back, holding her as if he never meant to let her go. Summer met his greediness with her own need, her arms wound tight about his neck, her head thrown back against his shoulder. She felt suddenly weak, as if all her muscles had turned to jelly. She doubted that she could sit up on her own if he should release her. Not that there was any chance of that. She could feel his passion building like steam in a pressure cooker; already she was being seared by its heat. He had taken over the kiss completely; she merely followed where he led.

When his mouth left hers at last to slide hotly across her cheek to her ear, Summer moaned. He nipped the tender lobe, his teeth arousing rather than punishing, then kissed the soft skin below it.

"I want you," he murmured, his breath warm against her ear. Uttered in a hoarse, ragged voice, the phrase was incredibly sexy. Summer began to tremble.

"I want you too." She threaded her fingers up through his hair and pressed her mouth to the warm hollow below his ear. She could feel the racing of his pulse against her lips.

He was leaning back against the trunk of the pine and she was lying against his chest, her legs curled around his, the quilt covering them both. His hand slid up to cradle the back of her head as he tilted her so that his mouth could have easy access to the softness of her throat.

Summer closed her eyes against a momentary glimpse of bats swooping after insects across a night-dark sky and refused to allow herself to remember where they were or why. She blocked out everything except the feel of Steve's hands and mouth and body. He was what she wanted, what she needed—just Steve.

His mouth traced its way down her neck, nibbling and sucking and licking at the soft column. Finally he reached the throbbing hollow at the base of her throat. He stopped there for a moment, his lips pressed against her skin. She could feel the hardness of his mouth, the roughness of his unshaven jaw, the warm wetness of his tongue as it lazily explored the soft depression. Then one large, warm hand found her breast.

Summer's head swam. Her nipple hardened instantly, pressing against his palm through the layers of sweatshirt and T-shirt and bra. He found the eager bud, stroked it with his thumb, then took it between his fingers, gently rolling it back and forth. The pleasure was so intense that Summer gasped.

She was suddenly starving for the feel of his skin against hers. Her hands slid down his chest, burrowing under the Nike shirt, reveling in the feel of the hard, hair-covered flesh. She stroked his chest, his belly. He was warm, so warm—all she wanted was to get closer to that warmth.

Her questing fingers encountered the waistband of his shorts. She found the button, freed it, tugged the zipper down. His mouth burned the skin of her neck, his hand on her breast went suddenly rigid, and she got the impression that he had ceased to breathe. Then her fingers slid beneath his briefs, across his tightening abdomen, to close around the huge, hot, hungry part of him that was made for her possession.

"Jesus!" As her fingers closed on him he groaned, then groaned again. Suddenly he was rolling with her, flipping her onto her back with such urgency that she lost her bearings and had to cling to his shoulders as the only solid things in a shifting world. They were tangled, momentarily, in the quilt. With a muttered oath, he jerked free of it, casting it aside. Then he was on top of her, his body hard and heavy, his breathing coming in fast, ragged pants. His mouth fastened on hers with a greedy passion that stoked an answering fire in her. Summer kissed him back hotly, wanting his lovemaking with a fierceness that she would never, before this day, before Steve, have believed herself capable of feeling.

With the tiny part of her brain that was still functional, she realized he was what she had been seeking for years. A man who needed her; a man to love: Steve.

His hands were unsteady as he undressed her, and Summer had to help him. Unable to get the sweatshirt zipper all the way down, he gave up and jerked the garment over her head. Summer was still wearing her T-shirt and bra, and, impatient, he merely tugged those out of his way, leaving them twisted beneath her armpits. As his fingers found her breasts, closing over the soft mounds in a grip that should have hurt but didn't, she moaned and forgot all about trying to help him work the fastenings on her clothes. He kissed her breasts, and she thought she would die with the sheer exquisite pleasure of it. Then suddenly, abruptly, his hands and mouth were removed. She opened her eyes to discover that he had left her to tug off his shorts, his shirt, his shoes. Hands shaking, she sat up to help him, running her mouth greedily over his body as they both pulled at his clothes.

When he was done, it was her turn. He yanked her T-shirt and her bra over her head without bothering to unfasten the latter. His hands found her breasts, and he bent his head to kiss her, but she eluded him.

She had different prey in mind.

With her hands on his shoulders she pressed him down on the smooth, slick carpet of fallen leaves, kissing his neck, running her mouth over the warm, hair-roughened skin of his chest, nibbling at his tightening abdomen, on the way to her prize.

When she found him with her mouth, he groaned. He was huge and hot and hard as she kissed him, licked him, swallowed him whole. His muscles clenched, his eyes closed, and for a moment, as she took him higher and higher, she reveled in her power. He was hers, all hers, and she was claiming him.

Then his hands tangled in her hair, pulling her away from him, pulling her up. He turned with her, flipping her onto her back and yanking down her shorts and panties with a quick series of near-frenzied movements. Her shorts and panties were about her ankles, and she still wore her shoes, but he couldn't wait to strip her properly. With a groan he came down on top of her again. Her knees parted of their own volition and her arms wrapped around his neck as she welcomed him. He thrust home with hard urgency, and Summer gasped. His answering growl enflamed her. She rose and fell with her own urgent need as he moved in, then out, then in again in a relentless, driving rhythm. Her head was thrown back, her mouth wide open as he took her, and she took him, too. Her nails dug deep into his muscled back; her thighs squeezed his hips. She was mindless with pleasure, delirious with it, trembling with it. There was no room in her head for anything except the wonder of her own need—and the knowledge that this was Steve.

His hands closed over her buttocks, lifting her so that he could thrust more deeply inside her, and with a harsh groan his mouth clamped over the tender nipple of her left breast.

Summer could stand no more. Pleasure more intense than anything she had ever imagined burst gloriously inside her.

"Oh, Steve! Steve! *Steve!*"

She shuddered and clung, crying out her joy into the endless dark. He responded with one final, savage thrust and his own harsh cry, shaking as he held himself inside her.

Then, with the suddenness of a passing storm, it was over.

Summer lay limply on the ground, conscious of a steadily increasing litany of discomfort. There was a hummock of grass between her shoulder blades. Her legs were freezing. The big lummox collapsed atop her weighed a ton.

And it was starting to rain.

CHAPTER THIRTY-THREE

"I t's raining." Summer kissed his bristly cheek.

"Mmm?" Steve didn't open his eyes, didn't lift his head, didn't smile at her, didn't *move*.

"I said it's raining." A fat drop plopped on her nose to underline the point. She shoved at his shoulder. "We're going to get soaked."

His eyes opened then. The dangerous black depths glinted at her for a moment, and then he stirred, kissing her nose. "You're beautiful," he said.

"So are you," she answered, smiling.

"I bet you say that to all the guys." He fluttered his eyelashes at her in exaggerated flirtatiousness.

"Nope. Only the handsome ones."

He laughed. "I've been called lots of things in my life, but never handsome."

"Obviously you've been hanging out with the wrong kind of woman."

"Obviously."

Another drop splattered on Summer's forehead. Suddenly Muffy was there beside her, whining, peering anxiously down into her face. Summer wasn't sure, but she didn't think Muffy had ever been out in the rain before.

"Damned voyeuristic mutt," Steve muttered. "Bet she watched the whole thing."

He rolled off Summer and sat up, knees bent, arms resting on his knees as he cast what appeared to be a wary look around, seemingly paying particular attention to the lower branches of nearby trees. For what? Summer wondered, and then she figured it out.

The fire hissed and sizzled as another few raindrops hit.

"Looking for Deedee?" Summer asked sweetly, sitting up and restoring her shorts and panties to their proper position. Steve glanced at her, narrowed his eyes, pursed his lips, and finally nodded.

"I think she's haunting me."

Summer couldn't help it. Despite the half-joshing tone of his voice, she saw red. She hadn't won the battle to lose the war!

She grabbed a pine cone from the ground and heaved it at him. It caught him on the chin.

"Hey!" he said, rubbing his chin and looking surprised. "What was that for?"

Summer threw another one. It hit its target too. Then she scrambled to her feet and loomed over him, catching him by both ears and dragging his head around, glaring down into his upturned face with her nose no more than six inches from his.

"I don't want to hear another word about Deedee! Not so much as another syllable, understand?"

For a moment he looked almost alarmed. Then he grinned, reached up, grabbed her around her waist, and pulled her down onto his lap.

"I like my women jealous," he said, and kissed her. His hands found and fondled her bare breasts. He was naked and she was half so and his kiss was setting her afire. . . .

A shower of raindrops broke them apart.

"It's going to storm," he said, lifting his head to the distant sound of thunder. "We've got to find some kind of shelter."

"What do you suggest?" She knew as well as he did that there was no shelter around for miles.

"Pack everything up but the quilt. I've got an idea."

Summer got dressed, then did as he told her while he pulled on his cutoffs and shoes and vanished into the trees. In the distance lightning flickered briefly across the sky. The wind blew more raindrops across the clearing. Their fire sizzled and danced. It was going to pour at any minute.

"Come on." Steve reappeared, kicked out the fire, grabbed the gym bag and Muffy, and headed back into the trees. Somehow Summer didn't think a forest was the best place to be during a thunderstorm, but, hugging the quilt to her bosom, she followed.

She would follow those broad shoulders to hell and back.

Beneath a sheltering grove of what, from the smell of them, seemed to be cedars, he had thrown together a crude shelter consisting of one picnic table turned upside down atop another one—this, Summer presumed, was to make doubly sure the rain didn't drip through the cracks in the top—with pine branches leaning against the sides.

"Give me the quilt."

She passed it to him, and he crawled beneath the picnic table to spread the quilt on the ground. Raindrops began to fall in earnest. Summer joined him in a hurry. When they were settled, they lay spoon fashion, cocooned in the quilt, with Summer's T-shirted back snuggled against Steve's bare chest, and his arms around her waist. Their heads rested on the gym bag. Their shoes, and Summer's socks, sat side by side near one jury-rigged wall.

Thunder rolled ominously. Rain began to fall in a steady stream. Muffy whined and looked with piteous entreaty at Summer. Summer pulled the little dog against her chest and wrapped the quilt around her, too.

The three of them were unexpectedly cozy in their makeshift shelter with the rain coming down all around but not touching them. The air was cool, and damp, and smelled of rain and leaves. The patter of raindrops hitting the top of their shelter was soothing. With Steve's arms around her, Summer was warm and dry, and, despite the circumstances, felt curiously content.

"Tell me about your dentist friend." Steve's voice was a low rumble in her ear. Summer slanted a glance back over her shoulder at him, smiling to herself.

"He's a very good dentist," she said demurely.

"Do you sleep with him?"

"That," Summer said, wriggling around so that she was facing him and then tweaking his nose, "is none of your business."

"Oh, yeah?"

"Yeah."

"You planning to see him again?"

"You mean if we survive this?"

"That's what I mean."

Summer eyed him. "Maybe."

"Maybe?" His black eyes narrowed.

"Depends on if I have a reason *not* to see him again."

"Like what kind of reason?"

"I don't know—like maybe if there was somebody new in my life."

"Is there?"

"Mmm."

"That's no answer."

"It's the best you're going to get."

"Oh, yeah?" He kissed her mouth, his lips warm and leisurely and entirely proprietary. "Know what? I think there's somebody new in your life."

"I thought you didn't want to get involved."

He smiled lazily at her. The effect of that smile at such close quarters was devastating. "I don't. But like you said, I think it's already too late."

"Really?"

"Uh-huh."

"You're involved?"

"Looks like it, doesn't it?"

"So what about Deedee?"

Steve sighed, and rolled onto his back, bringing with him Summer, the quilt, and Muffy, who was tangled up in it. Muffy, indignant at being treated with so little consideration, wriggled out the end of the cocoon to hunch indignantly just inside the shelter. Neither human paid the least attention to her.

"Baby, I think you've got hold of the wrong end of the stick where Deedee's concerned. We never had the kind of love affair that you seem to think we did. What was between us was never meant to be a forever kind of thing. She and I both knew that all along. All right, so I keep thinking that I see her. I can't help it. Damn it, I know she's dead, and I don't believe in ghosts. So you want to hear the only explanation I can come up with?"

"What's that?" Summer, lying sprawled atop him securely swathed in quilt, lifted her head, folding her hands on his chest and propping her chin on them as she looked down into his face.

"I never saw her before I met you. Not once, in the three years since she died. I think I'm seeing her now because of guilt over the way I feel when I'm with you."

"Really?" Summer looked down at him hopefully.

"Really."

"So how do you feel when you're with me?"

Steve grinned. "Horny."

Summer pinched his chest. He yelped, rubbing the injured spot.

"Is that all?" She glared at him.

"Hey, it works for me."

Summer pursed her lips and rolled off him, crossing her arms over her chest and presenting her back to him with a flounce.

"What more do you want?" he protested, leaning up on one elbow to peer down into her averted face.

"From you?" Summer laughed. "Not a thing."

"Now you're mad at me." He dropped a kiss on her ear. She elbowed him sharply in the chest. He grunted, cringing, and then leaned over her again.

"I suppose you want me to tell you that I think we've got something special going here. That with you and me, maybe it is a forever kind of thing. Is that it?"

"I don't want you to tell me anything. I don't even want you to speak to me. I—"

"Well," he interrupted, his breath warm as he spoke into her ear. "That's just what I think."

It took a moment for that to sink in.

"What?" She turned over so that she could see his face. He smiled at her, rather ruefully, she thought.

"You heard me," he said.

"Repeat that."

"Not on your life."

"Steve Calhoun, are you trying to say that you've fallen in love with me?"

"I guess."

"You *guess*?"

At the indignation clear in her face and voice, he backtracked hastily. "All right, I know. I think."

"You *think*?" This time it wasn't indignation she felt. It was outrage, pure and simple.

"Jesus, Summer, what do you want?"

"I want you to tell me, straight out, that you've fallen in love with me, if that's what you're trying to say."

He stared at her without speaking for a moment. They were facing each other, lying on their sides swathed in the quilt, their heads inches apart on the blue nylon gym bag. Summer, rigid with temper, had both arms crossed firmly over her chest. Steve reached down, grasped both her hands with his, and pulled them, not without some token resistance on her part, free. Then he carried them to his mouth, and pressed a kiss against the knuckles of both hands.

"I think that maybe, just maybe, you were sent to rescue me from outer darkness," he said quietly. "When I first encountered you, in that funeral home, I didn't really care if I lived or died. Now I do."

"Steve," she whispered, touched to the heart by his words, and the infinite tenderness in his black eyes.

"Hush," he said. "Let me finish, now that you've got me started. For years, I haven't been able to look into the future with any kind of hope or joy. Now, when I think of a future—of being with you in my future—I feel both. Does that mean I've fallen in love with you? Who knows? But I'm willing to give it a shot—if you are."

"Oh, Steve." Looking searchingly into his eyes, Summer realized how sincerely he meant what he said. Her heart swelled. They were two people, damaged by life, who had somehow found in each other what they needed to heal their wounds. And that was a miracle. There was no other word for it. Summer snuggled closer, freeing her hands to stroke his bristly cheeks, trace the hard line of his mouth, tenderly touch the healing bruises. "If you can't come right out and say it, I can: I'm in love with you."

"Yeah?" He gave her a curious, lopsided little smile.

"Yeah," she answered softly, and kissed his mouth.

Peering in through the makeshift shelter's entrance, a not-quite-ready-for-prime-time angel gave a rousing cheer.

Which neither of the two principals to the conversation heard. Though Muffy did, and cocked her head in wonderment.

CHAPTER THIRTY-FOUR

That night, the heavens celebrated. Thunder roared approval. Lightning cracked in laudatory bursts across the sky. Rain pelted down in never-ending applause. Summer and Steve, wrapped up in the quilt and each other, heard none of it.

She told him the truth of what it had been like to be married to Lem, about the bulimia she had developed as a result, about how hard it had been to heal herself and become whole again.

He told her about how he'd been drinking too much for years, about how, when his life had exploded in his face, he'd gone off the deep end and lit out on the bender to end all benders: a lost weekend that had lasted for nearly three years.

She told him that Lem had left her to marry his twenty-two-year-old nurse.

He told her that grief over the mess he'd gotten himself into had caused his father's death.

And they held each other, and cried, and laughed, and made love—and healed.

"So what made you decide to come back?" Summer asked sleepily several hours later, as the tale of Steve's wanderings over the last three years came to a close.

He was lying on his back and her head was cradled on his shoulder. The ground was hard. The air was cold. Pine needles prickled through the quilt in places to jab her most sensitive parts. Summer didn't care. Naked, swathed in the quilt and warmed by the blast-furnace heat of Steve's body, she felt blissfully, foolishly happy. Beneath the palm she had pressed to Steve's hair-roughened chest, she could feel the steady beat of his heart.

"To Tennessee, you mean?" One hard-muscled arm was tucked beneath his head and the other was wrapped around Summer's shoulders. As he spoke, his gaze was fixed on the raw planks of their makeshift ceiling. Summer immediately thought of him imagining Deedee lurking around up there somewhere, but dismissed the suspicion as unworthy. She had a gut feeling that Steve wouldn't be seeing Deedee anymore. At least, she added to herself fiercely, not if he knew what was good for him!

"Well, as I told you, I was out in Nevada. My credit cards and my savings had taken me a long way, but by this time I was about broke. I woke up one afternoon in a whorehouse—Mabel's, where the motto is The customer always comes first. There was a girl beside me, and we were both naked—ow, don't punch me!—but I couldn't remember how I got there, or a single thing we'd done. She was a hell of a good-looking girl, too."

Steve smiled reminiscently, then yelped as Summer gave a punishing yank to a captured twirl of his chest hair.

"Jesus, you're vicious." He slanted a glance down at her, grinned, and continued. "I couldn't even remember what day it was. So I asked her, and she said Christmas Eve. That made me feel kind of sick. So I got up, got dressed, and went back to the hotel I'd been staying in. It was a cheap hotel, twenty-five bucks a night. They changed the sheets maybe once a week." He took a deep breath. "So I started thinking about Christmas, and I picked up the phone and called my daughter. I hadn't talked to her for a while, because every time I called Elaine said she didn't want to talk to me. But this time my daughter answered. I said I loved her,

Merry Christmas. She said, 'I hate you, Daddy,' and hung up the phone.''

The pain in Steve's voice was as tangible as his heartbeat beneath Summer's palm. She ached for him, snuggling closer, kissing the side of his neck in silent sympathy.

"Children always say that to their parents. I know my nephews and nieces do." It was poor comfort, Summer knew, but the best she could offer.

"I know." He sounded tired. "But it was like she'd slapped my face. It shocked me into taking stock of myself. I saw the sorry thing I'd become—a dirty drunk sleeping with whores—and knew I had to make some changes. I took a shower, cleaned up, shaved. Then I went to church—it was a little Methodist church, sitting up on a hill in the middle of that podunk town—and I—well, hell, I prayed. Then the whole congregation started coming in. It was Christmas Eve, remember. There was a candlelight service. I stayed for that, too. When it was over, I knew I had to do my best to put things right in my life."

Summer listened, spellbound, to the deep rumble of his voice. His heartbeat was slow and steady beneath her hand.

He went on: "I quit drinking, there and then, cold turkey. With God's help, I haven't had a drink from that day to this. I got tested for AIDS. I was clean, you don't have to worry. Then I headed home, meaning to do my best to earn my daughter's forgiveness. On the way back, I started to think things through. Right after Deedee died, I was too shocked to see real clearly, but since I had quit drinking the fog was beginning to lift. I had a hard time believing that Deedee had committed suicide—you would have had to know Deedee to understand—but I hadn't questioned it, before. Now I started to. She'd left behind that videotape, remember. Besides the, uh, sex, it also had her saying that she was going to kill herself because I was breaking off with her to go back to my wife. Hell, I never said that. I never *left* my wife, and I broke off with Deedee mainly because of Mitch. She knew that, had a screaming fit about it in fact. So what she said on the tape just didn't fit." He hesitated for a minute, frowning up at the ceiling. "And then there was the key."

"What key?"

"The key to my office. It was a temporary office in Nashville, one I was using just while I worked on the investigation I was telling you about. I'd only been in it about a month. Because of the sensitive nature of the case, I had the locks changed on that office when I moved into it, and I locked it every single night, no exceptions. I locked it the night Deedee died in there. So how did she get in? She didn't have a key. There was only one, and it was either in my pocket or locked in my desk drawer at home every single minute of every single day. She and Elaine had never much liked each other—maybe Elaine sensed that I'd always had a soft spot for Deedee, I don't know—so Deedee was hardly ever at my house. She couldn't possibly have sneaked the key out of my desk drawer while I was asleep or anything like that. She hadn't been inside my house at all since we started sleeping together, I know. My office was locked, and she didn't have a key. So what did she do? Break in? Deedee weighed about ninety pounds, and she was anything but mechanical, and anyway there were no signs of a break-in. So how did she get into my office to hang herself? And why would she do it there, and leave behind that videotape, anyway? She was gonna be dead by the time it was found, so the only one it would hurt was me. Deedee was mad, but I don't think for a minute that the last act of her life would have been to deliberately cause trouble for me."

"So what are you saying? That you don't think she killed herself?"

"I don't see how she could have. But if she didn't, who killed her, and why? The only possible reason to take her out the way they did was to do harm to me, but why, if somebody's aim was to harm *me,* didn't they just kill me and have done with it? Shooting me would have been a hell of a lot easier than going through the whole elaborate setup somebody had to go through if Deedee was murdered. I can't make sense out of it. I couldn't when I first started trying to work it out, and I can't now. There's a piece of the puzzle missing, and I can't find it. So I decided the only thing to do was go back over the investigation I was working on when she died. Inch by inch, lead by lead, fact by fact, looking for something, anything, that I might have missed the first time around. That's what I was doing outside that funeral home that night, and that's how we ended up here."

"Because of Deedee," Summer said thoughtfully. "I'm starting to feel like I know her."

"She would have liked you." He grinned down at her suddenly. "She was an ornery, fiesty little fighter, and she liked those qualities in other women. She always said Elaine was a wimp. I don't think she thought Elaine was good enough for me."

"It sounds like she was right." Summer realized that she was talking about Deedee like she was an old friend. In fact, she was almost beginning to feel that way. Steve talked about her with affection and nostalgia—but not love, she was beginning to understand. Or at least, not the kind of love he offered her. Maybe she'd been wrong. Maybe Deedee was not a threat. Maybe she never had been.

They were silent for a few minutes. Then Summer said softly, "Do you really think we have much chance of getting out of this alive?"

Steve slanted a glance down at her. "Baby, we *are* gonna get out of this alive. Trust me."

She did, but, but . . . but she couldn't think about anything at all when he was rolling over with her and kissing her like that. And maybe, she thought with her last dim glimmer of intelligence, that was precisely what he had in mind. Then she gave herself up to his hands and mouth and body, and didn't think again for a very long time.

Dawn broke early. The rain had stopped sometime during the night, and the sunrise was beautiful—a fat orange sun painting the sky gorgeous shades of pinks and purples, so that the mountains were wreathed in lavender clouds and the tips of the piney forests were touched with rose. Puddles lay everywhere, and vapor drifted across the ground to rise toward the sky as if an invisible bride were climbing heavenward, trailing behind her yards of gossamer wedding veil.

Summer saw all this because the spot where she and Steve had spent the night was beside a true scenic overlook, with only a low stone wall between them and an unfettered view encompassing miles of mountain and valley and sky. Perched on the rim of the mountain, they crawled out of their shelter and came face-to-face with a breathtaking panorama of beauty. A vast wooded valley lay below, punctuated by a small bright lake. The sheer grandeur of the scene spread out before them should have embued them with awe, or at the very least a little appreciation. Steve gave their brave new world a single cursory glance and headed straight for the motorcycle, which he fussed over as tenderly as if it were his bride and this was the morning after their wedding. Dirty, rumpled, and disgruntled, Summer watched his ministrations to his machine with a darkling eye.

Heaven *would* have to send her a knight who lavished more care on his steed than his beloved.

Steve had kissed her awake as soon as the first creeping tendril of light found them in their shelter. Summer had returned his kiss sleepily, but her body had been warm and willing, primed by the passion that had blazed between them through the night. She had wrapped her arms around his neck, offering herself up to his hands with a voluptuous sigh.

Then, instead of starting the morning in the lusty fashion she fully expected after the night they had spent, he had squeezed her breast, smacked her bottom, and told her to get dressed: he wanted to get an early start.

So much for romance.

Thus, Summer admired the dawn while perched on top of a picnic table near the stone wall, while Steve labored over the stupid motorcycle. She and Muffy sat there alone, on what appeared to be the edge of the world, sharing the last of the peanut butter crackers. Not far away, Steve whistled with cheerful tunelessness while he wiped spark plugs on the end of his shirt and replaced them in their sockets. For his breakfast, he had chosen to polish off the marshmallows as he worked. Apparently, Summer reflected dourly, the excessive sweetness had gone to his brain.

When the spark plugs were connected and the seat was dried and the gym bag was packed and secured to his satisfaction, Steve at last turned his attention to his female companions. His eyes widened as he caught the expression on Summer's face.

"Are you always this grumpy early in the morning, or is this my lucky day?" he asked with a maddening grin.

"Are you always this cheerful early in the morning?" she responded with a poisonously sweet smile. "If you are, we may want to rethink this whole relationship."

"That's my little ray of sunshine," he said, laughing, and came over to drop a kiss on her mouth. His mouth was warm, his beard scratchy. Summer responded simply because she loved the fool. Then she realized he was stroking her lips so sensuously with his tongue because he was seeking cracker crumbs, and she pushed him away.

"Hey," he protested. "Last night you liked kissing me."

"Last night is history, pal."

"Is that your way of saying that the honeymoon is over?" He grinned. "Not on your life, Rosencrans."

"Oh, yeah?"

"Yeah." He moved close again, his hands finding her waist and pulling her over to the edge of the picnic table, where he positioned himself between her knees. "Kiss me, beautiful."

Her hands were on his shoulders. He had pulled her to the very edge of the picnic table, and her spread thighs gripped his hips while her feet in their giant sneakers dangled into space. Their position was suggestive in the extreme, and Summer wasn't sure she was in the mood for what it was suggesting. She was tired, hungry, dirty, scared, and out of charity with him just at that moment—so of course he had to start thinking about getting laid.

Men!

She looked at him with her head cocked a little to one side as his eyes glinted at her with something that was not quite a smile in their depths. The swelling had left his face, though the bruising and a pair of beautiful shiners remained, and she was able to see without distortion the rugged features of the man she loved. His cheekbones were high and flat, his jaw square, his lips on the thin side. His skin was pitted in places. His nose was a harsh blade. His was a hard face, a tough face, a give-no-quarter face—and she was entranced by every square inch of it.

He was big, dark, dangerous—and hers. No matter how out of sorts she felt, just looking at him gave her a thrill.

She scowled at him. He repaid the compliment by sliding his hand suggestively up her thigh. His fingers toyed with the elastic around the leg of her panties, then slipped inside.

She batted his hand away.

"I thought you were in a hurry to get on the road," she reminded him, although the heat from his hand had communicated itself to her and she was in no great rush herself.

"Ah, well," he said, smiling faintly. "I think there may be a slight change in plan."

The sun was well up in the sky before they finally got under way.

The night had done nothing to cure her saddle-soreness, Summer discovered as they headed back in the direction from which they had come. As soon as the vibration started up again, her bottom began to ache. By the time an hour had passed, her feet were asleep, her back felt like it was breaking, and there was a nagging pain in her calves. She rested her head between Steve's shoulder blades and tried to forget about her discomfort.

Finally she realized that that was impossible. She realized something else, too: Concentrating on how bad she felt at least kept her from feeling afraid.

They were headed right back into the lions' den, and Summer wasn't sure that was a really good idea.

She was so worn out, she couldn't make up her mind what she thought they should do. At last she gave it up. Trust me, Steve had said. For better or worse, that was what she was going to do.

She leaned back, flexing her neck, hoping to at least ease the ache at the base of her skull. Muffy lay across her lap beneath her T-shirt like a rag doll. The poor dog, innured to misery by this time, confined her protests at this uncomfortable mode of transportation to an occasional low moan. The day was growing increasingly hotter, the helmet was giving Summer a blinding headache, and she felt like moaning herself.

The only thing that kept her from it was the conviction that the situation was only going to get worse. She might as well save her moans for later, she decided, when they might be truly needed.

It was terrifying to consider that she—and Steve—might die today. So she concentrated on her aches and pains, and refused to think at all.

It must have been about three p.m. when Summer saw it: A small biplane, tracing lazy patterns through the soft blue sky, trailing a long white advertising banner behind it. She had often seen such planes with their messages about all-you-can-eat specials and two-for-one drinks from the beaches of Florida. She was vaguely surprised to find one soaring above the thickly wooded Smoky Mountains. It looked out of place, incongruous somehow, and she watched it curiously.

Finally it drew close enough so that she could just make out the message on the banner:

Steve. Where's Corey? Call 555-2101.

Summer gasped, staring, and read the message a second time. Then she poked Steve hard in the ribs.

CHAPTER **THIRTY-FIVE**

"**C**orey's my daughter," Steve said, his voice hoarse. He was standing by the edge of the road staring after the plane, which was disappearing behind a cloud-bedecked peak. Summer's arms were around his waist. He didn't have to spare her a glance to know that her eyes, fixed on his face, were wide with concern.

After Summer had directed his attention to the plane and its banner, he had nearly run off the road as he read the message once and then again.

There was absolutely no doubt that that message was aimed at him.

Corey. They had taken Corey. He thought of his daughter, a little plump, a little shy, with soft brown bangs that were always falling into her eyes and unbecoming plaid pleated skirts required by the parochial school she attended, and then remembered: The picture of her that he had held so long in his heart was Corey at age ten. She was thirteen now, a teenager, God help him. She would have changed.

They would hurt Corey, torture Corey, kill Corey, to get at him.

Adrenaline pumped through Steve's veins, bile rose into his throat, and his heart gave a sickening leap.

Oh, God, why had he never considered that they might go after Corey?

In his agitation, he nearly drove them over a cliff. Only Summer's horrified screech recalled him to the present in time.

Shaken to the core, he pulled to the side of the road, parked, and dismounted. Summer dismounted, too, holding him while he watched the plane vanish into the distance. With all his heart he longed for an M-16, to shoot the thing down; for an arm as long as a giant's, to pull it out of the sky.

Where is she? he wanted to scream, but did not, because it would do no good. The plane was beyond hearing, beyond his reach. He could not throttle whoever was in it into revealing Corey's whereabouts, into giving her back. He could not destroy them for daring to touch her. He could not do anything. He was helpless, stranded on the side of a damned mountain, while the daughter he had endangered suffered and perhaps died.

Stop it, he told himself fiercely. They would not kill her until they got what they wanted: the van and him. At the moment, Corey was their ace in the hole. She might be scared—all right, she had to be scared to death—but she was okay.

He had to keep telling himself that. If he didn't, he would go to pieces. And he couldn't go to pieces. He had to think. He couldn't outgun them, couldn't outfight them. He was one man, against their many. And the vicious bastards had his daughter.

He had to outthink them.

"I memorized the number," Summer said softly. "Do you think we should go find a phone?"

"I know the number. It's my ex-wife's. Yeah, we need to get to a phone." He glanced down at her then. She still wore the yellow helmet—Steve only just then realized that he still wore a helmet himself—and beneath it, her eyes were very wide and very worried. Her arms around his waist were soft with comfort. Her face was as white as he felt.

He looked down at the best thing that had happened to him in a long, long time and thought he should have known. Life, for all its uncertainties, had started looking too damned good again as of the previous night. Happiness had been handed to him like a gift, all wrapped up in a woman with a body that made him pant and an inner strength that earned his respect and a heart as soft as her skin.

He should have known it was too good to last. Heaven wasn't through punishing him yet.

Just not with Corey. Please, God, not with Corey. The fault was his, and his alone. Please, please, he prayed, don't take it out on the kid.

"I'm all right," he said, doing his best to reassure Summer though he knew it wasn't true. He wasn't all right. He felt as if he had received a blow to his solar plexus and was still disoriented as a result.

But he had to get all right. This wasn't the time to lie down and die, to howl at the moon and beg God and Heaven for mercy. This was the time to fight, damn it. To fight as he had never fought in his life, for Corey and Summer and himself.

In the last few days his life had been given back to him. No matter how little he deserved the gift, if he could help it he wasn't going to let anyone snatch it away again.

There had to be some way to win.

Winner take all, babe: The phrase popped straight out of nowhere into his head. It was a favorite refrain of Mitch's. Steve could remember Mitch saying it on many, many occasions throughout their life. The two of them had played each other at chess, cards, football, golf. Mitch had always known how to be ruthless, to do what he had to do to win. Steve, on the other hand, had played by the rules. When he had won, it had been an honorable victory, well deserved. That had always mattered to him, though Mitch had sneered.

The guys who held Corey captive would not play by the rules. Playing with them would be like playing with Mitch all over again. Only this time, whatever it took, Steve meant to play to win.

He couldn't bear to contemplate any other possibility.

"I'm all right," he said again, and bent his head to plant a quick, hard kiss on Summer's mouth. "Come on, let's go find a phone."

They found one, some forty-five minutes later, at a tiny mom-and-pop gas station–grocery store combination on the west side of Clingmans Dome. Summer, who had been holding Muffy, passed the dog to him as she went in to get change to operate the pay phone. Renfro's forty dollars would pay for quite a few long-distance calls.

There were tourists in the store, tourists arriving and leaving the parking lot by car and van and camper, but Steve thought, hoped, that the helmets and motorcycle would serve as effective disguises. It was no part of his plan to be arrested now. To do so would be to endanger Corey as well as Summer and himself.

To that end, knowing that Summer wouldn't like it when she discovered what he had done, he removed the quilt from the gym bag and thrust Muffy inside instead. With the bag partially unzipped so that the dog could breathe, it made a perfectly adequate carrying case.

At least, in his own estimation. Muffy kept trying to poke her head out. Every time those silky brown ears and that idiotic hair bow appeared, he thrust them back down again. He started to feel like a kid playing with a jack-in-the-box. If the situation hadn't been so deadly serious, it would have been ludicrous. When the pink satin ribbon came off in his fingers he stared down at it for a moment, wondering why he hadn't thought of removing it before. At least the animal wouldn't be quite so idiotically conspicuous without her bow.

Although the dog looked ridiculous enough without any adornment at all.

When Summer at last emerged from the quaint wooden store, she carried a brown paper sack in one hand. He glanced up as the screen door swung shut behind her, lifting one hand to shield his eyes from the glare of the bright afternoon sun.

Looking at her in her loose black T-shirt and shorts, with the too big high-tops laced tightly around her ankles and her face innocent of all makeup, Steve thought he had never seen a woman who better suited his notion of what one should look like. She had a natural beauty, a very feminine, unfussy beauty even in a motor-cycle helmet and some kid basketball player's clothes, that suited him right down to his toenails.

Her breasts jiggled and her hips swayed as she descended the pair of rough plank steps and walked toward him across the gravel parking lot. Steve knew that she was probably unaware of that. Still, it gave him pleasure to watch her, distracted him momentarily from the terrible anxiety that threatened to eat him alive.

"I got sandwiches," she announced as she approached, shooting a quick glance at a middle-aged couple in khaki Bermudas who had just exited their car and were walking toward the store. "Ham and cheese on rye. And apples. And Cokes."

The couple passed by without sparing them a second glance.

"Did you get change?" Steve couldn't help it. His voice was tense, and there wasn't a thing he could do about it.

"Yes." She reached into the sack and withdrew a handful of bills. "We've got twenty-five dollars left. Put it in your pocket."

"You did get quarters?" he asked, knowing that she had, knowing that he was being impatient but unable to stop himself. He had to find out what had happened to Corey, had to make that call right away or he would go out of his mind. He stuffed the bills in his pocket as she had directed and held out his hand for the coins.

"I got eight dollars' worth. That should be enough, don't you think?" Fishing in the sack, she came up with a handful of quarters.

"Keep your eye on the mutt." He took the quarters from her hand, pocketed them and a second handful, thrust the gym bag with its reluctant occupant at her, and headed for the phone. It was in a silver and blue kiosk attached to the side of the building, near the air hose and the rest rooms. A woman was emerging from the ladies' room even as he walked toward it.

She was sixtyish, frumpy, and looked at him without interest. He barely even noticed her.

He had to take off his helmet to make the calls. He was so agitated that he didn't even care that without it he was more vulnerable to being recognized.

Dropping quarters in the slot, he dialed the well-remembered

number: 615-555-2101. He should know it: it had been his number for almost a decade.

A computerized voice in his ear advised him that the call required two dollars and ninety-five cents. He dropped three dollars'
worth of quarters into the slot, stuck the rest into his pocket, and
held his breath.

"Hello?"

At first, because of the tension that roughened it, he didn't
recognize the low voice on the other end of the wire as his ex-
wife's.

"Who is this?" he asked sharply.

"Steve? Steve, is that you?" Relief made her sound shrill. He
had forgotten the way her voice tended to break and squeak when
she got excited or under stress.

"Yeah, it's me. Corey . . ."

"Oh, Steve, they took her! They came and took her! Oh, my
God, Steve, I never thought it would come to this! I . . ."

There was what sounded like a scuffle, a man's curse, a woman's
cry and a blow. Steve had long since quit feeling anything much
for Elaine, but at the thought that some thug was hurting her
because of him, his gut tightened.

"Calhoun?" The voice that came over the wire next was low,
guttural—a man's.

"Who is this?"

"Doesn't matter, does it? What matters is, we got your little
girl."

"If you hurt her, I'll . . ." Steve could feel blood drumming in
his ears. He felt murderous—and helpless. He wanted to threaten
and beg at the same time. But neither approach would help Corey.
He checked himself with an effort.

"You won't do shit." The man chuckled.

"I'll kill you." Steve couldn't help it. Conviction made the
words cut like a knife.

"Take a chill pill, man. We ain't gonna hurt your kid—if you
cooperate. Where's the van?"

In the time between when he had seen the banner and found a
phone, Steve had worked out the fundamental elements of a plan.

Basically, he aimed to get every law enforcement officer he had ever known, plus a sprinkling of the media for insurance, in the same place as Corey and the thugs. Which would require some careful coordination on his part. Fortunately, local interest in him was still keen, as he had discovered when he first came back home to Nashville. His fifteen minutes of fame hadn't quite worn off yet. The reporters he needed undoubtedly would be thrilled to be in on another chapter in the deathless saga of disgraced cop Steve Calhoun, and he felt fairly confident they would show up where he told them, one armed with a notebook and photographer and the other with a camera crew. Appetite whetted by the thought of being in on a huge, career-enhancing drug bust, his old boss Les Carter of the state police would be there, too, unless of course Les was dirty. In which case he might still show, but as a hired gun for the wrong side. Ditto with Homer Tremaine of the FBI and Larry Kendrick of the DEA. It wasn't a great plan, there was a lot that could go wrong with it, but at least it gave them a chance. Any chance was better than none.

If he told the thug on the phone where the van was, Corey and Elaine would have no chance at all.

"I ain't stupid, man," he said, talking the goon-lingo he had learned during his years as a cop. For some reason, goons responded better to their own kind of street talk. They seemed to lose a small measure of their suspicion of anyone who spoke the way they did.

"I think you're plenty stupid, man," the voice responded. "Anybody who would steal from us is stupider than a block of wood. Don't be even more stupid by holding out on us. Remember, we got your kid."

Like he was going to forget. Steve took a deep breath, tried to keep his murderous rage within bounds, and spoke into the receiver. "We can do a trade: my kid for the van."

"That's the idea," the voice said, sounding a shade friendlier. "Just tell us where it is, and we'll bring your girl home to Mama."

Yeah, right. And Santa Claus would come at Christmas.

Steve shook his head, then realized the thug at the other end of the phone couldn't see. "Here's the deal, man. You bring my kid to a spot I'm gonna tell you about. I'll meet you there. You let her go, and I'll stay and take you to the van. How about that?"

There was a moment's silence. "What spot?" the man asked.

Steve heaved a silent sigh of relief. They were going to go for it. Maybe, just maybe, they would all get out of this alive yet.

Hope joined deadly fear in an adrenaline-based surge of pure energy through his veins.

He put his hand over the mouthpiece and took a deep, steadying breath, glancing down at Summer, who had come up beside him while he was still fumbling to get the quarters into the slot. Her eyes were huge beneath the rim of her yellow helmet as she watched him, the gym bag with its restless cargo held gingerly in her arms. Muffy's chocolate bug-eyes peered over the blue nylon zipper at him.

Summer smiled encouragingly.

Steve removed his hand from the mouthpiece, and gave the thug a location, putting into motion the plan that was either going to free them all—or be the death of them.

"The van ain't there. We checked."

"You just bring my kid there, and we'll talk some more. If she's not there, you can forget about finding that van."

"She'll be there."

"You bring my ex-wife, too. I want both of them there, unharmed. You got no call to hurt either of them."

"You plannin' on havin' a fuckin' party?" The man sounded disgruntled.

"My kid and my ex-wife for the van. If either of 'em aren't there, you can go to hell."

"They'll be there." It was grudging, but it was agreement.

Steve breathed a little easier. "If you want that van, they better be. It'll probably take me about three, three and a half hours to get there. If you get there before me, you wait."

"Oh, we will." The man chuckled. "Calhoun, if you love your little girl, don't be too late."

He hung up. Steve slowly removed the receiver from his ear and stared at it.

"But once they have you, they'll never let Corey go," Summer objected urgently. "They'll kill you both. And Elaine too. And me."

Steve put the receiver back on its cradle, stared at it for a minute, then reached in his pocket for more quarters.

Before he dropped them into the slot, he turned to plant a quick hard kiss on the softest lips he had ever known.

"Rosencrans, you're just gonna have to trust me for a few minutes more. Then I'll tell you what I've got in mind."

CHAPTER THIRTY-SIX

They were parked at a picnic area about five miles farther down Clingmans Dome. All of them, including Muffy under the table, wolfed ham and cheese sandwiches. The humans guzzled Cokes. Muffy drank water from a puddle. The food tasted so good that not even Steve's recital of his plan could completely spoil Summer's appetite. Nor could her guilt over having set in motion a Plan B of her own. While Steve had been in the men's room, she had called Sammy. Not that she meant to tell Steve.

"So you called the DEA—and the FBI—and the newspapers . . ."

"And my old boss at the state police. Don't forget him." Steve took another enormous bite of his sandwich. "And WTES-TV, too."

"A TV station?" Summer cocked an eyebrow at him.

"I want everything that happens to be as public as possible. The more witnesses, the safer we're going to be. Everybody I called, I know personally. Just on my say-so, they're coming. One or more

of them might be dirty, but I don't think so. We're just going to have to take that chance. This is a drug deal, I'm willing to bet my ass, a big-money drug deal gone seriously wrong when we stole that van. That brings the DEA on board. The bastards kidnapped my daughter. That brings in the FBI. Les Carter, my former boss, is on board because he authorized the original investigation and, despite the fact that he's a tough S.O.B., I trust him. Rudd Guttelman of the *Nashville Sentinel* practically supported himself for a year writing about me and Deedee. He oughta be on hand for the aftermath. And Janis Welsh of WTES won a prize for local reporting about me. She's got a reason to want to be there, too."

Steve took another bite of his sandwich. Summer had had to argue quite fiercely to persuade him that they needed to eat before they did anything else—their last meal had been the breath mints around noon—but now that they had stopped by the road he was eating hungrily.

Watching him devour his sandwich brought a pang to her heart. Poor man, if ever she got the chance she was going to take a great deal of pleasure in making sure he got three square meals a day.

A memory of how she had cooked for and fussed over Lem in the early days of their marriage crept from her subconscious, reminding her that she had vowed never to provide such services for a man again. But she was in love, and she couldn't help it. Summer decided wryly that she just must be a little Suzy Homemaker at heart.

"What if one of the people you called *is* involved in this?" she asked to distract herself. Sammy wasn't, she reassured herself fiercely. If they had to trust somebody—and the time had come when they did—Sammy was the one she would choose every time. But still she didn't tell Steve what she had done.

"I was in the Marines with Kendrick of the DEA. *He's* solid as a rock."

"He's not the only one, is he?" Summer wished she had never brought up the possibility that their prospective rescuers might be bad guys, too. It was making her queasy.

Steve ran a hand over his face. "Hell, I think they're all solid. They are all what I would call people of integrity. It's impossible for me to imagine any of them being corrupted by drug money. But you never know. Anything's possible. People go wrong every day. Cops go wrong. We've already identified Carmichael as a cop, and I'm ninety-nine percent certain that your pal Charlie and the other goon from your basement will turn out to be cops, too. There are gonna be others. Higher-ups. That's why I called people I know personally. Friends, or former friends. And the media, too. For insurance."

"But why tell them—everybody—to meet at Harmon Brothers, of all places? Why not just have everybody converge on the boat warehouse and be done with it?"

"I chose Harmon Brothers because it's easy to find. God forbid that anybody should get lost. And because there's a lot of empty acreage there, without a lot of civilians around. And because the van isn't there. Remember, once the bad guys find out where that van is, they don't need us. Corey, being of no more use to them and being able to identify them and testify, if it ever comes to that, will be killed. So will Elaine. We'll be hunted down. If I sent the goons to the boat warehouse, and they beat us there, or something went wrong and our posse didn't show, we would have played our last card. They would have the van, and we would have zilch. As it is, by keeping the location of the van back, I have an ace in reserve. If things go right, when we show up in Harmon Brothers' parking lot, the thugs should be there with Corey and Elaine—and suddenly we should find ourselves swimming in assorted cops, feds, and reporters."

"And if things go wrong, they still don't know where the van is," Summer added softly.

"You got it."

"Plan B?" she asked.

He grinned. "Always. I always, always, have a Plan B."

"You're brilliant," she said, smiling at him as she finished the last of her sandwich. Not so much because she thought so—which she did—but because she could tell he was worried. And that he didn't want her to realize it. So she would pretend to be totally confident in his scheme just to give him peace of mind.

Just in case, though, there was always Sammy. God, she hoped she wasn't wrong about Sammy.

"You're besotted." His smile was lopsided as, meal finished, he stood up and came around to where she sat on the opposite side of the picnic table to drop a kiss on her mouth.

"Probably," Summer admitted, following him with her eyes as he straightened and crossed the grassy picnic area to toss his trash in a tall mesh wastebasket. He still looked like he had come out the loser in a barroom brawl. His skin around his eyes remained defiantly purple; the gash on his cheek was healing, but it was indubitably there. The left side of his face sported more colors than a rainbow. The right side wasn't much less showy.

His broad shoulders and muscled arms sported a wash of sunburn to add interest to their own bruises. He still limped slightly on his left leg.

He was dirty, unshaven, a little smelly—and her heart swelled with love every time she looked at him.

If anything happened to him, she would want to die.

She said a little prayer for him, for herself, for all of them as she gathered up the remains of her own meal and followed him to the trash can.

"Summer." He was standing beside the motorcycle as she walked up to him. His helmet was on the seat waiting for him to put it on. Hers was in his hands. There was a certain agitation evident in the way he passed the thing back and forth between his hands.

She looked at him inquiringly.

"I'm not taking you with me."

"What?" She frowned, not understanding.

"Now that everything is in place, now that the hunt's been called off and all the bad guys are converging on Murfreesboro, you're safer without me. I'm gonna drop you off at the first reasonably well-populated place we come to, and I want you to call your sister in Knoxville to come and get you. If you'll give me her number, I'll call you there tomorrow and let you know how things went."

Summer stared at him. "Not on your life!"

His lips twisted into a wry smile. His eyes were both warm and rueful as they met hers. "Now how did I know you would say that, I wonder?"

"You're not leaving me!"

"Listen," he said quietly. "I'll be safer without you, too. You're just one more person for me to worry about when the going gets rough. My goal is to get Corey—and Elaine—safely away from the goons. If you walk into the lions' den with me, then you're just one more person I have to keep safe. One more distraction. See what I mean?"

Summer did see. Instinctive protestations bubbled to her lips only to die unuttered. He was right; there was nothing she could do to help him now, and much she could do to hinder him. The only smart, sensible thing to do was to stay behind.

She would never have guessed how terribly hard it was to agree not to put herself in mortal danger.

"I see what you mean," she said in a tone as neutral as she could make it. Inside, her heart screamed and wept.

He put her helmet down on the vinyl seat beside his, reached out and took her face in his hands. "I just found you," he said quietly. "I don't want to lose you again."

It was the sweetest thing anyone had ever said to her.

Summer's arms went up around his neck. She pressed herself close to his hard, warm body. Tears welled up in her eyes, but— heroically, she thought—she fought them back. Crying would not help either of them.

"I don't want to lose you either," she whispered against his weather-dry lips.

"Baby, I'm harder to lose than a bad penny," he said with a crooked smile. Then he kissed her.

It was infinitely slow, and sweet, and tender. Almost as if he was saying good-bye.

When Steve lifted his head at last, and she reluctantly opened her eyes, Summer's vision was blurred with unshed tears. But just momentarily. As her vision cleared, her eyes widened. Over Steve's broad shoulder she saw that a police car and two other vehicles, a white Ford and a navy blue Lincoln Continental, were pulling onto the gravel shoulder of the road not two hundred feet away. Her gaze skipped right over the Ford. The flashing blue light of the police car mesmerized her. The navy blue Lincoln terrorized her. She was unable to move, unable to say a word; frozen with fear.

Steve must have sensed her horror, because, before she could choke out so much as a syllable, his head swiveled toward where she was staring.

"Jesus," he whispered, releasing her and grabbing for the nearby bike. For a moment Summer thought he meant to leap aboard the motorcycle and make a run for it through the forest. Her muscles tensed as she prepared to leap with him.

But it was already too late. The cars had stopped, and men, some uniformed and some not, spilled from their depths.

"Freeze!" a uniformed officer shouted, leaning over the just-opened door and snapping a pistol into two-handed position atop the closed window. Its barrel was pointed directly at Steve. "Get your hands in the air!"

But Steve wasn't looking at that man, or the other uniformed officer who popped up on the opposite side of the patrol car, his gun pointing across the roof of the car at them too. He wasn't looking at the middle-aged man in a white shirt and tan Sansabelt slacks who was standing beside the Ford, talking excitedly into a cellular phone, either. He was looking at a balding man with a black mustache who emerged from the driver's side of the van. The man appeared unarmed, but as he stepped down the breeze caught the edge of his tan linen sport jacket and Summer saw that he was wearing a shoulder holster complete with shiny black pistol.

One of the thugs from her basement. Summer recognized him at once. The one Steve had identified as being known to him, as a cop. What had he said the man's name was?

Not that it mattered. A thug by any other name was still as deadly.

Another man walked around the van to join Black Mustache. This guy was short, stocky, fiftyish, with a graying crew cut. Like his partner, he was dressed in a sport coat and slacks, although his

were navy and gray, respectively. On his feet he wore shiny tasseled loafers.

Summer wondered if they were the same ones Muffy had chris-
tened.

"Fuck," Steve said under his breath, and lifted his hands into
the air.

CHAPTER **THIRTY-SEVEN**

"Get your hands in the air! You, lady! Get your hands in the air!" The uniformed cop's order was a staccato bark.

Summer, unused to being on the wrong end of a policeman's pistol, held her hands up, palms pointing outward, at about shoulder level. She felt like a spectator, not a participant, in events that had no reality.

As if she were caught up in a really, truly, hideously bad dream.

Her most rational thought was, These guys constitute a major spanner in Steve's plan. Even her little insurance policy would not help in this case.

"Get those hands *up!*" The cop screamed.

"She's not armed," Steve called. "We're not armed."

"Get them *up!*"

The second uniformed cop, pistol wavering dangerously, slid on his heels down the small hill that separated the roadway from the picnic area while the first stayed on top of the hill and kept them covered. Summer, her hands at eyebrow level now in imitation of

Steve's, just out of instinct sidled a little closer to Steve for protection.

Of course there wasn't anything he could do to protect her now.

"Don't move!" The second cop stopped about a yard away, the mouth of his pistol aiming first at Steve, then at Summer, then at Steve again. He seemed nervous, and more frightening because of it, as his buddy came down the hill, his pistol at the ready too.

"Both of you, hit the dirt! Now!"

"The lady is the daughter of Murfreesboro's police chief. She's not with me of her own free will. Go easy on her, will you?"

"I don't care if she's the daughter of the President! I said hit the dirt!"

"It's okay. Lie down on your stomach on the ground. Keep your hands where they can see them." This quiet instruction from Steve was vaguely reassuring. He didn't sound panicked. He didn't sound as if he were on the verge of despair. He sounded calm, cool, and collected.

Maybe the two guys in uniforms were good cops. Maybe they would take them to jail and thus save them from the bad cops. Summer clung to that thought.

Following Steve's example, Summer dropped rather awkwardly to her knees then lay flat on the ground. It was damp from last night's rain, and the leaves were slippery wet beneath her cheek and knees and hands. With her head turned to one side, she watched as one of the uniformed cops ran his hands swiftly over Steve's prone body, patting him down. Then he dragged one of Steve's hands down behind his back, snapped a handcuff around it, and secured the other the same way.

Seconds later the same procedure was being performed on her. The young cop's hands ran over her everywhere, touching her in places he had no business touching. Thankfully, though, the search seemed to be entirely impersonal.

Summer's wrist was grabbed and dragged behind her back, and seconds later she, too, was handcuffed. The metal was cold and unfamiliar-feeling around her wrists. In a few minutes, she thought, being shackled in such a way might start to feel uncomfortable.

Steve was already on his feet and being marched toward the patrol car when Summer was half lifted, half dragged upright. In minutes she was being helped up the hill. Ahead of her, Steve slipped and almost fell on the slippery slope. Summer remembered his lightning-fast move in her basement, and for a few seconds waited hopefully for all hell to break loose. It didn't. Steve was dragged to his feet and shoved up the hill in Summer's wake.

"Get the dog," Black Mustache ordered abruptly. They were the first words Summer had heard him say.

"Yes, sir." One of the young cops scowled, but obediently went to pick up Muffy, who backed away, yapping at him like a Fury.

Apparently Muffy had more intelligence than Summer had given her credit for. She was learning to tell the bad guys from the good. Or vice versa. At this point, Summer had no idea which was which.

"Come on, doggy. Here, doggy," the young cop coaxed. Muffy growled, the first hostile sound Summer had ever heard her make. Her respect for the little dog, already far higher than when Muffy had arrived for her visit, increased again.

"What's the damned thing's name?"

Summer didn't reply. A hand gripped the back of her neck, hard. She glanced around to discover Shiny Shoes' grayish eyes on a level with her own.

"He asked the dog's name," Shiny Shoes said softly.

"Muffy," Steve answered for her as he was hustled past. "The dog's name is Muffy."

The guy in the Sansabelt slacks approached Summer, cellular phone bulging from his breast pocket, pad and pencil in hand. "Miss, can I ask you a question? I'm James Todd of the Bryson City *Post*. Were you really kidnapped, or . . ."

"This isn't the moment, buddy," Shiny Shoes growled.

"Steve didn't kill those women in my basement. He did," Summer said clearly, nodding toward Shiny Shoes behind her as she seized this heaven-sent opportunity to talk to a real live reporter. *He* was surely not involved in any of this.

"Him?" Todd looked with lively interest at Shiny Shoes, who shook his head at him and tightened his grip on Summer's neck.

"Talk to her later," Shiny Shoes said, and dragged Summer away.

As she was shoved toward the patrol car, she heard the snap of fingers behind her. Glancing back—not easily, because Shiny Shoes' hold on her neck could more properly be described as a death grip—she saw that one of the young cops was bent over, snapping his fingers at Muffy, calling her by name.

"Put them in the Lincoln," Black Mustache said. He stood with his arms folded across his chest, one foot resting against the Lincoln's front fender as he watched the proceedings with an eagle eye.

James Todd approached him, pad and pencil at the ready. "And you are?" he asked hopefully.

"No comment," Black Mustache snapped, and moved toward where one of the uniformed policemen stood with Steve.

"Hey, kid, I said put them in the Lincoln."

The cop getting ready to push Steve down into the back of the patrol car glanced up at Black Mustache, surprised. His hand was already on top of Steve's head. "They'll be more secure in the patrol car, sir."

"Do what you're told," Black Mustache snapped. The two uniformed cops—one had finally succeeded in snagging Muffy—glanced at each other, gave the impression that they exchanged invisible shrugs, and escorted Steve toward the Lincoln. With Shiny Shoes' hand still on her neck, Summer trailed behind.

Summer had a gut feeling that if she got inside that car, she was going to die.

Shiny Shoes opened the rear door and released her neck at last. A hand settled atop Summer's head. Seconds later she was pushed down into a plush velour seat. A combination shoulder/lap belt was pulled across her body. With her hands cuffed behind her back, she was as securely bound as if they had tied her to the seat. Steve, equally trussed up beside her, looked grim, Summer saw to her dismay. Muffy, set inside by one of the young cops, scuttled across the gray-carpeted floor to vanish beneath the front seat.

Smart dog. Summer only wished she could do the same thing.

The rear door closed. She, Muffy, and Steve were locked in the backseat together. Black Mustache and Shiny Shoes had yet to get in the car. The trunk opened, and both uniformed policemen walked past, lugging the motorcycle between them. From the way the car rocked, it was hefted into the trunk. The trunk was secured with something, but it would not close all the way. If she twisted around, Summer could see that it remained slightly open. She assumed the motorcycle's front or rear tire must be sticking out.

"What do we do now?" she whispered to Steve.

His reply scared her. "Pray," he said.

An explosion from behind the car, quickly followed by a second and then a third, widened Summer's eyes and snapped her head up. Goggle-eyed, she watched through the front passenger-side window as James Todd, who had been talking into his cellular phone again while he peered in at them, started to topple forward. The phone dropped from his hand like a stone. A neat black hole punctuated the space between his eyes. A thin trickle of blood was just beginning to run down the bridge of his nose as he fell from sight. It hit her with the force of a revelation: He'd been shot!

Of the young policemen there was no sign.

"Jesus," Steve said, and closed his eyes.

Only then did Summer realize that the two young policemen had been shot too.

She guessed that made them the good guys.

It was a heck of a way to find out.

Shiny Shoes and Black Mustache got into the car. Shiny Shoes took the driver's side, dropping a palm-size object onto the dashboard with a solid-sounding thunk. The object slid toward the junction of dashboard and windshield before Summer could get a good look at it.

"What's that?" Black Mustache asked as Shiny Shoes shut the door and started the car.

"Cellular phone. I've been wanting one for a while."

"A cellular phone? You don't mean to tell me that—damn it to hell, Clark, you are one dumb shit! If you use that phone, they can trace it to you. If you don't use it, and it's even found in your possession, your ass is burned. It belongs to that reporter, you lughead! How're you gonna explain how you got it? That'll finger you for his murder right there!"

Clark glanced over at his partner. "I didn't think of that," he said shamefacedly. Reaching for the phone, he added, "I'll throw it out."

"Damn right you'll—no, wait a minute." Black Mustache pursed his lips thoughtfully. "I've got an idea. Leave it. Just don't use it."

Clark obediently withdrew his hand and concentrated on driving. As the Lincoln gained speed, leaving behind the scene of the carnage, Black Mustache leaned an arm across the back of the seat and twisted around to grin at his prisoners.

"You shouldn't have done that, Calhoun," he chided with a reproving shake of his head. "Killing cops is not nice."

"They were just kids, Carmichael. What'd you have to do that for?" Steve asked.

Carmichael—of course, that was his name—shrugged. "One of 'em—Geoff Murray—knew me. He used to date my daughter. Some people back there at the grocery store called the local yokels to report that they thought some armed and dangerous fugitives— that's you two—had been there and left. Apparently the reporter heard it on a police scanner and hurried over to get in on the big scoop. It was just pure bad luck for those dudes that you were recognized at that grocery store, and more pure bad luck that young Murray was the cop who showed up at the scene just as we got out of the car to take a look at the area around the telephone." He shook his head, then waggled a forefinger at Steve. "Oh, by the way, it was pretty dumb of you to make that call. We had your ex-wife's phone tapped and as soon as you made it, zingo, we had you."

"That still doesn't tell me why you killed three men."

Carmichael shrugged. "When Murray recognized me, what was I gonna do, give him a chance to start thinking about how he ran into me up here, checking out a grocery store that he was also checking out? For two fugitives who later wound up dead? With him out of the picture, nobody has a clue that Clark and I were here. Besides, that reporter was nosy."

The careless prognostication of her and Steve's fate sent a chill racing along Summer's spine. But had she ever doubted for an instant that Carmichael meant for them to wind up dead?

Not since their encounter in her basement.

"Did you hear what that bitch back there said?" Clark growled, jerking his head in Summer's direction. "She told that reporter that I—that we—killed those cunts at her house."

"Well, we did," Carmichael said, and grinned.

"But she told him! And he's a reporter!"

"Don't go ballistic, Clark. He's dead, remember? He ain't gonna tell nobody nothin'."

"Oh, yeah," said Clark, and subsided.

"I had to cover my ass," Carmichael continued to Steve. "Much as it goes against the grain to waste fellow cops. Oh, well, Murray was a prick to my daughter anyway." He chuckled suddenly. "You'll get the blame for this, Calhoun, and when I blow your head off later tonight I'll wind up looking like a hero for catching a cop killer. They'll even find that reporter guy's phone on your body. With that evidence, it's an open-and-shut case. Pretty stupid of you to keep the phone, they'll say, but it sure makes a tidy package. Funny, ain't it, how life tends to work out? Even Clark's dumb-ass goof winds up helping the program."

There was a moment's silence. Then Steve spoke: "I've got a deal with some buddies of yours. But I guess you know all about that."

Carmichael grinned. "Oh, yeah, you mean the deal where you show up at some funeral home and tell everybody where you hid the van and then we give you back your daughter and you all ride off happily into the sunset?"

"That's the one."

"Ain't gonna happen," Carmichael said cheerfully. "At least, not like it's supposed to. You're gonna tell me where the van is, and I'm gonna make sure you're telling the truth. Then I'm gonna kill you like the interfering asshole you are."

"If you're going to kill me, why should I tell you where the van is?"

"Because I can make you hurt an awful lot before you die.

Because I can make the lady here hurt even more. Because we've got your daughter, and if you're real nice and make this real easy, we might still be able to just let her go."

"Yeah, and pigs might fly."

Carmichael laughed. "Hey, you shouldn't be so cynical. I'm really a nice guy at heart. I've got daughters of my own, four of 'em. I don't want to hurt a little girl that don't know nothin' about nothin'. Not even your little girl, Calhoun."

Summer got the chilling feeling that he enjoyed hurting people. Any kind of people. She thought of Corey Calhoun, of the two cops back there on the road, of James Todd and Linda Miller and Betty Kern, and felt sick. Her diagnosis was that, cop or not, Carmichael was primarily a sadist who enjoyed hurting people for its own sake.

Not an ideal criminal to be held hostage by.

"If I give you the van, what guarantee do I have that my daughter won't be hurt?"

"Just my word as a gentleman."

"That makes me feel a lot better."

"Watch your mouth, Calhoun."

There was a moment's silence. Then Carmichael said: "Look at it this way. You don't tell me where that van is, you *know* your daughter's gonna die."

Summer could feel the sudden tension in Steve's body all the way across the seat. The thought of anyone hurting his daughter drove him nuts. She'd already seen ample evidence of that.

"Why are you doing this, Carmichael?" Steve asked quietly. "Man, you're a cop. Doesn't that mean anything to you?"

"Not diddly-squat. I don't get paid enough for it to mean anything."

Steve's eyes narrowed. "Since you're going to kill me anyway, mind telling me what's in the van that you all want so much?"

Carmichael frowned, then shrugged. "Hell, I don't suppose it makes any difference if you know: money. Fifteen million smackeroos, to be precise. Cash. Moola. Hidden in the lining of the coffins, stuffed in the satin pillows, even tucked right inside those nice little dead bodies so it would sail right through customs. You

did find the bodies, didn't you? Bet they gave you quite a turn."
He snickered.

"They did," Steve said ruefully. Summer couldn't believe the
almost friendly tone he was taking with a maniac who meant to kill
them. "I guess the shit hit the fan when I took off with your van
full of money."

"Everybody went apeshit." Carmichael nodded in agreement.
"We had a rendezvous with some bad dudes scheduled for that
night, too. You heard of the Cali cartel? Out of Colombia? We
were supposed to give them the cash. They already gave us the
dope. A play-or-pay deal. They weren't real pleased when we had
to tell 'em that you stole their money."

Carmichael picked up his pistol suddenly and took bead on
Summer's forehead. Her eyes widened in horror as she stared into
the tiny black mouth. She was going to be shot just like that cop
was shot. There would be a tremendous blow shattering her forehead and a little black hole would appear and then—how long
would it take her to die?

"They gave us seventy-two hours to get the money back. Which
means we got till about two a.m. tomorrow morning. You can tell
me where that van is now, or I can speed things up by blowing
your lady friend away. I owe her one anyway, for Charlie. He's in
the hospital, by the way, his face cooked to a crisp. I know he
wishes he could be here with us right now." Carmichael smiled at
Summer. She felt her blood turn to ice. His eyes flicked to Steve.
"It's up to you, Calhoun."

There was an instant of silence. Steve and Carmichael locked
gazes in a silent duel of wills. Summer stopped breathing.

Then, "Head for Cedar Lake," Steve said. "The van is in a boat
warehouse on the west side of Cedar Lake. I think the warehouse
is called Watersports Sales, Service and Storage."

"I wouldn't've shot her yet," Carmichael said, sounding both
surprised and a tad put out as he lowered the gun. Summer's
impression that he was a man who enjoyed hurting people was
reinforced. He sounded disappointed that Steve had given in so
easily, as if he'd been robbed of a pleasure he'd been anticipating.
"Not here in the car. Think of the mess."

"I didn't think you cared about mess, Carmichael," Steve said tiredly, and rested his head back against the rolled edge of the luxuriously upholstered seat.

Summer glanced at him. He was staring out the window, his face bleak and set. She was both relieved not to be dead and horrified at what he had done. For her sake, he had revealed the location of the van. But now that the bad guys knew where it was, Steve no longer had his ace in the hole.

What had happened to his philosophy of always having a Plan B?

At the moment, she thought, any plan at all would do.

CHAPTER **THIRTY-EIGHT**

It must have been about eight p.m. when they reached Cedar Lake. They had stopped once, when Clark made a brief call from a pay phone at a service station and then went inside to use the men's room.

Sitting in the back of the Lincoln, which was parked at the side of the white-painted concrete-block cube, Summer again waited for Steve to do something. Surely her he-man had a trick or two up his sleeve—but he just sat there. Carmichael, turned sideways in the front seat so that to a casual onlooker it would appear as though he was talking to the two passengers in the back, kept them under the gun the whole time. Then Clark got back in the car, nodded at Carmichael, and they were off again.

By the time they got to Cedar Lake, Summer's hands were numb from the handcuffs. Her shoulders ached from being forced to stay in one position for so long. Her neck ached for the same reason. Shifting uncomfortably in her seat, Summer discovered that physical suffering did not always distract one's thoughts from fear, after all. She was miserable—and she was afraid.

It was rapidly approaching twilight when they made the turn that took them alongside the lake. The sun was still up despite the relative lateness of the hour because it was midsummer, but the town was luminous with the rosy glow of summer evenings in Tennessee. As the Lincoln drove past the all-night grocery where —was it only four days ago?—Summer had refused to stop, past the construction site that was once again idle as working hours were over, Summer felt her pulse begin to speed up.

In a very few minutes they would reach their destination—and Carmichael would no longer have a reason to keep them alive.

Looking out the window at the serene surface of the lake, its gentle ripples touched by fire from the setting sun, Summer thought she had never seen such an incongruously tranquil setting. The few boats that were still zipping across the water gave the scene the look of a happy vacation paradise. As she drank in the beauty of the waterscape, a quote popped out of nowhere into Summer's head: This is a good day to die.

Her modern sensibilities immediately screamed: *Not.*

"Which way, Calhoun?"

Steve, roused from his silent contemplation of the world outside the windows, gave directions. Beside him, Summer could feel her skin turning clammy. How could he be so coolly detached when they were soon to be shot?

Summer started to say her prayers: *Now I lay me down to sleep* . . . No, not that one—*Our Father, who art in Heaven* . . . Not that one either. She was so frightened, she couldn't even summon a cogent prayer. Instead she settled for Please, God, please.

There it was: the boat warehouse. It looked different in daylight, was Summer's first impression. More prosperous, with the double rows of corrugated buildings gleaming silver-pink in the light of the setting sun; and more security conscious. She could see that the fence surrounding the huge complex was a good twelve feet tall, with a triple strand of barbed wire surrounding the top.

But it looked just as deserted in the shimmering golden light of a Wednesday twilight as it had in the inky predawn hours when she had seen it last.

"This it?" Carmichael's question was aimed at Steve, who hadn't said a word for the last hour and a half.

"This is it."

Summer glanced at him and felt her fear mushroom. He looked tired. Deathly tired. Like the game was played out, and he knew he had lost.

But wait, she told herself: maybe he was merely pretending to be defeated. Maybe he had somehow managed to slip his hands out of the metal cuffs and was waiting to launch into some Ninja Turtle–esque moves when the thugs stopped the car and opened the back door.

Maybe . . .

As the Lincoln pulled into the driveway that led up to the closed gate, another vehicle—a maroon and silver van—pulled in behind them. For a moment Summer felt a leap of hope.

Could this possibly be rescue? Please, God, please . . .

"They're here," said Clark to Carmichael, nodding with satisfaction. Carmichael glanced past Summer's shoulder out the rear windshield.

"Now we're gonna have a party," Carmichael said to Steve, smirking.

"What do you mean?" Steve stiffened, staring at Carmichael with the first real interest he'd shown in a long time.

"Your little girl's right behind us. For her sake, you better have been telling us the truth. That van better be here."

"It is," Steve said grimly. To Summer's horror, she saw that beads of sweat had broken out along his brow.

Dear God, did he really not have any tricks up his sleeve? Maybe she'd better try to come up with some herself, quick.

"Hey, you need a code to get in," Clark said as he stopped the car and rolled down the window. "Anybody know the code?"

"You better know the code," Carmichael said to Steve. He lifted the gun and pointed it at Summer again.

"I know it—just let me think—uh, nine-oh . . . uh . . . four-seven."

Clark punched the numbers in. Nothing happened.

"That's the wrong code!"

"Wait! I know it—it's in my mind—just let me think—try nine-two-eight-one . . ."

There was a moment's silence as Clark's stubby fingers attacked the keypad again. Then, "Nothing's happening," Clark said.

"I must have got the numbers in the wrong order. Jesus, let me think . . ." Steve chewed his lower lip.

"You better think fast, or we'll blow your lady friend to hell. Then we'll start on your little girl."

"Nine-one-eight-two . . ."

Clark punched in the numbers. Again they waited.

"No!"

"Damn it, Calhoun . . . !" The pistol pointed at Summer suddenly aimed right smack at the center of her forehead. She froze, not even daring to glance at Steve. He had not had trouble remembering the code before . . . Squinching up her eyes, she clung to Carmichael's previous reluctance to make a mess in the car, and prayed.

"Try nine-one-two-eight."

"You better hope this one's right," Carmichael said ominously while Clark punched the numbers into the keypad. "If it isn't . . ."

The gate started to move.

Carmichael lowered the pistol. Summer slumped in her seat.

The Lincoln slid past the opening gates, closely followed by the van.

"Which building?"

"The last. On the left."

Steve was really going to give them the van. Summer had wondered if he might at least make them search the complex for it. Surely in the course of their search they would run into somebody —but, of course, if they ran into just an ordinary somebody, and not a squad of armed police, that somebody would be dead, and she and Steve would not be any better off.

The Lincoln pulled up in front of the warehouse and stopped. The aluminum building was closed up and deserted—just like all the rest.

Where is everybody? Summer wanted to scream.

"The van's in there?"

"Yes."

"How do we get in?"

"That panel there—in front—is a sliding door. The key's to the left, hidden under a loose piece of siding."

"Get out and show me."

Carmichael got out of the car, came around and opened Steve's door. Leaning in, he released the belt, and dragged Steve out.

Summer held her breath, waiting for Bruce Lee. What she got was a tired-looking man meekly leading his would-be murderer to the key.

Of course, he was protecting her and his daughter. How could he put up a fight without endangering them?

Summer tried not to panic over her hero's lack of heroics. What was Steve Calhoun anyway but an ordinary man? He was not a superhero. What was called for in this instance was—

Arnold! Oh, where was the Terminator when she needed him?

The door to the warehouse slid sideways with a rusty creak. From the outside, the cavernous interior appeared as black as pitch.

In response to a jerk of Carmichael's head, Clark got out, and opened the door for Summer. As he leaned across her to release her belt, she shrank back. He was ugly and mean and he smelled— briefly she entertained the notion of sinking her teeth into his neck.

But what would that get her but a fat lip, or worse? She wasn't yet in any position to try to escape.

The seat belt came loose, and Summer was dragged from the car. Weak-kneed, she almost collapsed when she first tried to stand, only to find herself yanked upright. As Clark dragged her impatiently toward the yawning darkness, Summer heard the crunch of feet behind her. Glancing over her shoulder, she saw two toughs gripping the arms of a brown-haired teenager who stumbled unhappily between them.

Corey Calhoun had bangs, a round, pale, tear-streaked face, and a just-budding body clad in a rose-pink T-shirt and purple flow-ered shorts. Her legs were tanned and bare. White sandals were on her feet. In that one quick glimpse before Summer was dragged into the warehouse, she saw that the child looked scared to death.

It took a few moments for her eyes to adjust to the darkness. When they did, she saw that Steve was standing over by the small wooden runabout that had been in the warehouse at the time of their last visit. Carmichael was beside him, glancing around.

Corey, dragged into the warehouse in Summer's wake, apparently saw her father at the same time.

"Daddy!" she cried. Pulling free of her captors, she ran to lock her arms around Steve's waist and burrow her face into his chest.

Steve, with his hands cuffed behind his back and a pistol pointed at his head, could do nothing to comfort his daughter. But the expression on his face as he looked down at that bent brown head made Summer want to weep.

For Steve, for Corey, for herself.

"Are you all right?" Steve asked the girl softly as Clark herded Summer over to join the little group. "They didn't hurt you, did they?"

Corey shook her head, though she didn't lift her face from Steve's chest. "They didn't hurt me. But Daddy, I'm so scared!"

"It's okay, baby," Steve said. "Everything's going to be okay. Don't be afraid."

Even if he was lying and she knew it, just hearing Steve say the words made Summer feel better too.

"Touching," Carmichael said, watching father and daughter with a sneer. Then, looking around, he added, "Okay, now where's the van?"

Something was hideously awry. Summer had just realized it, and from the grim set to Steve's face he recognized it too.

They were standing in the very spot where, four nights before, they had left the van.

But the van was gone.

CHAPTER **THIRTY-NINE**

Summer had to look around a second time to make sure. Here was the half-football field–size, rectangular-shaped space, here were the seen-better-days boats and the four corrugated metal walls and the sloping roof and the ground covered with gravel. The single lightbulb hanging by its cord from the ceiling dangled in the same place, though at the moment it was not switched on.

The van was not here.

Summer cast a sidelong glance at Steve, who now stood with Corey wrapped around his waist a mere two feet away. Steve glanced at her, and their gazes met in a sort of mutual horrified inquiry.

As she absorbed the import of that look, Summer was forced to give up a notion that had taken quick, promising hold of her imagination: This was not part of Plan B.

The van was really missing, and Steve did not know where it was.

Yikes!

"Where's the van, Calhoun?" Carmichael sounded impatient.

"It's here—somewhere."

"What do you mean, somewhere?"

"You didn't think I was just going to give it to you, did you? You let my little girl go, and we'll talk about where to find the van."

Oh, brave bluff! Summer gritted her teeth and tried to school her facial expression not to give the game away. Steve knew as well as she did that this was the right building. There was no possibility of mistake. They were standing in the precise spot where the van had been!

"Why you . . . !" Carmichael reached for Corey, grabbing her arm. Corey screamed and clung to Steve like a burr. With a vicious curse Steve kicked out at Carmichael.

And then a pistol butt descended with a resounding thunk on the back of Steve's head. Clark smiled viciously down at the man he had just hit as Carmichael yanked Corey toward him.

Horrified, Summer watched to the tune of Corey's screams as Steve sank to his knees.

She was dreadfully afraid that what she was witnessing was the beginning of the end—her end. Steve's end. Corey's end. Their end.

Without warning, the light came on overhead.

"Everybody freeze!"

The shout, from somewhere above them, was accompanied by a flurry of movement. Head snapping up, Summer saw half a dozen men, some in police uniforms and some not, poised on the raised decks of a nearby cabin cruiser, with rifles and pistols and God knew what other kinds of guns pointing at their little group on the ground.

At the same time, a stampede of pounding feet caused Summer to glance around. Police officers, dozens of them, rushed them, surrounding them in a tight circle.

"Hands up! Get 'em up!"

"Throw down your weapons! Right now! Throw 'em on the ground!"

"FBI!"

"DEA!"

"Police!"

"You're under arrest!"

Carmichael and company looked wildly around. Finding themselves surrounded and outgunned by about twenty to one, they slowly, reluctantly, one at a time—dropped their guns.

It was over, just as quick as that. Summer hoped. She still wasn't positive if their putative rescuers were the good guys or just more of the bad.

Until she saw that her white-haired ex-father-in-law was one of the half-dozen men supervising proceedings from the deck of the trailered cabin cruiser. She couldn't account for his presence *here* —when she'd sneaked the call to him from outside the grocery store she had told him to come to Harmon Brothers' funeral home with the rest of the gang—but boy, was she glad to see him.

"Hi, Sammy," she called weakly. He grinned and gave her a wave. All around her handcuffs were being snapped on the bad guys' wrists and they were being led away. Limp with relief, unable to believe the nightmare was really, truly over, she dropped to her knees beside Steve, smiling at Corey, who was crouched on her dad's other side, her arms wrapped tightly around Steve's shoulders. The tears hadn't yet had time to dry on the girl's cheeks.

"Plan B?" Summer asked Steve.

"You might say that," Steve said. His cheek rested briefly on Corey's brown hair.

"You scared me to death."

"I scared myself."

"Were you really scared, Daddy?" Corey had been listening to this exchange wide-eyed. The three of them made a compact little island in the sea of lawmen bustling all around.

"Absolutely. Especially when I thought they had you." Steve smiled at her tenderly.

"But you saved me." She hugged him. "I've missed you, Daddy. Are you going to go away again?"

"No." Steve shook his head. "Not ever again. I promise, Corey."

"Then maybe you can talk Mom into letting me start dating. She says I'm too young."

"Good God," Steve said faintly, rolling his eyes toward Summer, who had to repress a grin. Being plunged back into the deep end of fatherhood—to a blossoming teenage daughter yet—was an adventure for which he didn't seem quite prepared.

Fortunately for Steve, his daughter chose just then to take a good look at him for the first time. "What happened to your face? Did they—beat you up?"

"It looks a lot worse than it feels," he reassured her without really answering. "Corey, this is Summer. Summer saved *me*."

Corey had been casting covert glances at Summer that were both curious and, Summer thought, not entirely favorable. Now she looked at Summer with frank astonishment.

"You saved my dad? How?"

Caught by surprise, Summer looked at Steve for inspiration. Steve grinned at her.

"Her dog peed on the bad guy's foot at a crucial moment," he said with a lurking grin.

"Oh, Daddy!" Corey clearly did not believe that, but before the conversation could proceed any further the three of them were suddenly no longer alone.

"We found this in the Lincoln. One of the prisoners said it belonged to you." A heavyset man in a gray business suit held a squirming Muffy out to Steve in a way that told Summer the little dog had done something to make herself less than popular. She had seen that look on men's faces more times than she could count.

"Yo, Les," Steve greeted him. "Good to see you, man."

"Good to see you, too. Is this yours?"

"She's mine, but I can't take her," Summer said. "My hands . . ." Then inspiration struck. "Corey, would you hold Muffy until they get me out of these cuffs?"

"Oh, yes!" Corey was clearly rapturous at the idea as she

reached out to take Muffy. Holding the little dog carefully, Corey sank cross-legged on the ground with Muffy on her lap.

"She's beautiful," Corey breathed, stroking Muffy's ears. Muffy licked Corey's chin. The girl practically melted with bliss right there in front of their eyes.

"She's been wanting a dog for years. Her mother doesn't like them in the house," Steve said under his breath to Summer.

"I'd watch that animal if I were you," the man said to Corey. "She, uh, wet on my shoe."

"She really did?" Corey's eyes lit up with pleasure. "Dad, you weren't lying? Summer and her dog really did save you?"

"Yep, they really did." Steve smiled as he watched his daughter crooning over Muffy. Then he glanced up at the man who still stood over them.

"Not that I'm not glad as hell to see you, but what are you guys doing *here*? You were supposed to be waiting for us at a funeral home in Murfreesboro."

"Hey, we have our methods."

"Before you tell me all about it, you think you could do something about these handcuffs?"

"Oh, sorry. That's really what I came in for. We got the key off Clark. Can you believe that asshole? He tried to talk me into letting him go. 'Cause he's just got two years till retirement and he doesn't want to lose his pension, he said. I told him, Buddy, where you're going you won't have any use for a pension." He bent to unlock Steve's handcuffs as he spoke.

"He and Carmichael killed two cops up on Clingmans Dome. And a reporter. And they also killed the two women you found in her"—here Steve nodded at Summer—"house."

"Yeah, I know. We got it all on tape."

"On *tape*?"

"The reporter—Todd, I think his name was—was calling in the story to his paper when he got shot. His editor heard the whole thing, and promptly called the police. The lucky thing was, Clark and Carmichael took Todd's cellular phone with them and they never turned it off. It was on the whole time; we just recovered it from their car, and it was still on. There were some officers listening to every word that was said in that car until it got out of range. And Todd's editor recorded every word. What we've got on those two amounts to a confession on tape."

With an air of triumph, Les straightened, lifting a jangly pair of handcuffs into the air. Steve, freed at last, brought his arms forward and shook his hands. He wrapped an arm around Corey, who smiled at him with an air of sweet abstraction before turning her attention back to Muffy, who was on her back in the girl's lap waving her paws in the air and wearing a blissful expression.

"So that's how you found us—through that poor man's telephone," Summer said in surprise, then glanced at Steve. "I wondered why you told Carmichael and Clark where the van was so easily—and so clearly. Did you know that phone was on?"

"I hoped." Steve grinned at her suddenly. "No, I prayed."

"Plan B," Summer said, smiling at him with her heart in her eyes. It was good to know her hero had had some heroics up his sleeve after all.

"Then there was Plan C, and Plan D . . . well, I'll tell you about them later," Steve concluded as a uniformed police officer came into the warehouse. He made a beeline for Les.

"What is it, Grogan?" Les greeted him.

"We just got word that there's a guy from some security company out front. Our guys won't let him in the warehouse complex and he says there's been an unauthorized entry and he needs to check it out."

"I guess he's right. We're it," Les said. "Hell, tell him we're police."

"We told him that, and he says that we're not the unauthorized entry if we used the correct code to get in, which our guys say we did. We got it from the property owners. But apparently there's some sort of security system in place so that if the wrong code gets punched in at the front gate three times in a row, this security company is alerted. The guy says that happened about twenty minutes ago, and he needs to search the premises. He's pretty agitated."

"Tell him to get un-agitated or we'll run him in." Les sounded impatient with the whole subject. Summer glanced at Steve, eyes widening. That was why he had "forgotten" the code! He'd been deliberately trying to summon the security guard!

"Plan C?" she asked under her breath.

He grinned at her. "Hey, I was grabbing at straws. It could have worked. It could have not worked. Just like the phone. I was looking out the window and I saw Clark pick it up—and I didn't see him turn it off. There was a chance in a million that that phone was still on—but still it was a chance, and any chance is better than none. I remembered the code thing from when I used to come here. It was a chance, too."

"I'll deal with it," Les said irritably to Grogan, and headed off with Grogan following just as another, younger man in a suit broke away from a huddle of men in suits and walked across to join them.

"Hey, what about me?" Summer, returned to the present in a hurry, called after Les indignantly. Her arms and shoulders were tingling in jealous response to Steve's new freedom of movement.

"Oh, sorry." Les glanced over his shoulder, looking a bit shamefaced, then retraced his steps, crouching behind her to unlock her handcuffs. "I'm Les Carter, by the way."

"He's the head of the Organized Crime and Intelligence Unit for the Tennessee State Police," said the newcomer to Summer as he shook hands with Steve, who—though his movements were a trifle wobbly—had by this time managed to get to his feet. "And I'm Larry Kendrick, of the Bureau of Narcotics Clandestine Intelligence Network. DEA," he translated, seeing Summer's blank look. "We'll want to ask you some questions later, Miss McAfee."

The handcuffs came off at last, and Les stood up behind Summer. She wiggled her fingers, trying not to wince at the pins and needles that shot up her arms as she moved them slowly forward.

"We'll need a statement from you, too, Miss McAfee," Les said.

"Hell, it's Mrs. Rosencrans, she's my daughter-in-law, and you two bullies are going to leave her alone till the morning, if I have to put her in protective custody. Got it?" Sammy, fat brown cigar sticking out of one side of his mouth, came up and fixed the other two men with a stern look. Summer was so glad to see her portly, white-haired ex-father-in-law that she scrambled to her feet just for him. If Lem had been anything like his father, their marriage would have lasted fifty years.

"About that security guard . . ." Grogan said under his breath to Les Carter.

"I'm coming, I'm coming," Les said irritably, and, waving a hand at the group, left, with Grogan trailing in his wake.

"I'm your *ex*-daughter-in-law, Sammy," Summer reminded him. "Lem and I have been divorced six years. He's remarried."

"Once family, always family," Sammy said cheerfully, and shook hands with Steve. "Hello, Calhoun."

"Hello, Chief Rosencrans."

"You almost got my daughter-in-law killed."

"I know, and I'm sorry about that."

"I don't want it to happen again."

"Not if I can help it, sir."

"Good. Summer, your mama is at the Holiday Inn in Murfrees-boro. You'd better give her a call when you get done here. She is in a right tizzy over you."

"She flew in from California?" Summer barely repressed a groan. She loved her mother dearly, but just at the moment she did not feel up to giving her a play-by-play description of everything that had happened. And then there was Steve— Casting her dirty, disreputable beloved a sideways glance, Summer wondered what her mother would make of Steve. In a perfect world, he would have at least had time to get over his black eyes before he met her mother.

"Both your sisters are here, too." Sammy sounded as gloomy as Summer felt. Summer could imagine the hell the three McAfee women had put him through in the last few days. "God in heaven, they're hot about you being put on the wanted list. I told 'em there wasn't anything I could do about it, but they've been all over me like flies on honey."

"I gather that's taken care of?" Steve asked.

"All cleared up. You don't have to worry about being arrested."

"Sam, can you come over here a minute?" Les Carter called from near the door. With a muttered "excuse me" Sammy was off.

"Do you know anything about Elaine?" Steve muttered to Larry

Kendrick, keeping a wary eye on Corey as he spoke. Corey sat cross-legged near Steve's feet, playing with Muffy and seeming not to pay a bit of attention to the adult conversations that swirled above her head. But if she was like most children, Summer reflected, she was missing not a word of anything that was said.

"Nothing yet. We got that guy who was in the hospital with the burned face—Charlie Gladwell—to tell us where they took her. We'll have her safe before they know anything's gone down, don't worry."

"For Corey's sake . . ." Steve cast a glance down at his daughter and looked up at Kendrick again.

"We'll get your kid's mother out of this in one piece," Larry Kendrick said reassuringly. "I appreciate you calling me in on this, you know. It could be big, very big. By the way, where's the van?"

"Where's the van? You mean none of you guys have it? I thought sure you moved it before we got here."

"The van wasn't here when we got here. Come on, Steve, don't play games with me. You know where it is."

"I don't. I swear. It was here." The two exchanged measuring looks. "On Saturday night, or, rather, Sunday morning when we left it, it was here. Ask Summer, if you don't believe me."

Summer nodded agreement.

"Somebody else must have grabbed it." Kendrick made an urgent beckoning gesture to one of the other men in suits. He didn't bother introducing the man who came up but whispered furiously in his ear. The man nodded and walked quickly away.

"When you called me today and sent me over here to stand guard over this van, you *really* thought the thing was here?" Kendrick asked Steve. "It wasn't some sort of trick to get us in place to catch the bad guys and save your ass?"

"You called him today and told him the van was here?" Summer glanced at Steve, surprised. "When?"

"At the grocery store, when I was calling everybody else. You went to the ladies' room, remember? I decided that I better let somebody know where the van was just in case I didn't make it out alive from our little rendezvous with destiny. I didn't want to worry you with that possibility, so I waited till you were out of the way to make the call. The whole way up here in the back of that Lincoln, I was hoping Kendrick and his crew might still be hanging around. When I saw the van was missing, I thought they'd taken it and gone."

"Plan D?" Summer cocked a fond eyebrow at him. She would have been a little miffed that he hadn't confided in her if she hadn't called Sammy and alerted him to the funeral home scheme while Steve was in the rest room. Clearly neither she nor her beloved believed in leaving much to chance.

Steve grinned. "Yeah."

"*We* didn't take the van," Kendrick said grimly. "If you know where it is, now's the time to tell me, Steve."

"Jesus, Larry, do you think I'm playing some kind of game? The van was here. Now I don't have a clue where it is."

"Okay. Okay." Kendrick held up a calming hand. "It's important we find it, that's all."

"Daddy, there's Uncle Mitch," Corey said suddenly, interrupting.

Following her gaze, Summer watched as a tall, lean, extraordinarily handsome man walked with slow purpose toward them. When she could tear her eyes away from goggling at his blond, blue-eyed splendor, she glanced at Steve. Steve was suddenly narrow-eyed and grim-jawed as he watched his erstwhile best friend approach. Summer wondered if he expected some kind of verbal or physical assault.

Knowing what lay between the two men, Summer felt Steve's tension as if it were her own.

CHAPTER FORTY

Mitch walked up to them and, to Summer's surprise, held out his hand to Steve. "Glad you made it," he said quietly. He nodded at Larry Kendrick. "Hello, Kendrick."

"Thanks. I'm glad I did, too," Steve answered, clasping Mitch's hand briefly before releasing it. For a moment, Summer wondered if, knowing men, that was all that was going to be said by these two with so much history between them, but then Mitch smiled at Steve. It was a beautiful smile, Summer had to admit. A beautiful smile on the face of a beautiful man.

"Long time no see, pal." He glanced down at Corey. "Hi, squirt."

"Hi, Uncle Mitch," Corey smiled up at him, clearly oblivious to the emotional undercurrents swirling among the adults. "I got kidnapped."

"So I heard. I was on my way to rescue you, you know."

"My dad did that." Corey glanced down at Muffy, then stood up with coltish grace. She was going to be tall, Summer decided, looking at her, and very pretty one day. "How come you don't come to see Mom and me much anymore? When Daddy first left, you used to come over all the time. Mom said you guys were dating."

The expression on Steve's face at this revelation was a study in contradictions.

"Your mom and I were just friends." Avoiding Steve's gaze, Mitch reached out to tug at Muffy's ears. "Since when did you get a dog, squirt?"

"It's Summer's." Corey nodded at Summer. "You know Mom doesn't like dogs. She says they make her sneeze, and they have fleas."

"Summer, this is Mitch Taylor. Mitch, Summer McAfee," Steve belatedly made the introductions. Summer shook hands with Mitch. His clasp was warm, firm. Having heard so much about him, Summer had formed her own image of what he should look like, but her mental picture did not do Mitch justice. Though Steve had told her that Mitch was far handsomer than he, Summer had not expected Mitch to be one of the handsomest men she had ever seen. Wavy blond hair, bright blue eyes, tanned, perfect features, a blindingly white smile. Tall. Muscular but lean. The guy was good-looking enough to be in the movies.

No wonder Steve had lost so many girls to him.

Glancing at the man who still kept firm possession of her heart, Summer surprised a wry look on his face as he watched her eyeing Mitch. She supposed she was looking dazzled. She supposed, too, that Steve had experienced this reaction to Mitch from every woman he had ever introduced his friend to in his life.

She took a step closer to Steve, so that her shoulder just brushed his hard bicep, and smiled into his eyes. She would have taken his hand if Corey had not been present, but instinct told her to go slowly around Corey: Young girls were notoriously jealous of their fathers' affections.

Steve's eyes crinkled in response, and Summer knew that for her there was no contest at all. No matter how physically breathtaking Mitch was, he could not, in her estimation, compete with the uncompromising masculinity that Steve exuded. The one man was a beautiful object to be admired; the other exuded raw sex appeal.

Mitch was a young girl's dream; Steve was a grown woman's.

Les Carter came up to them and looked at Corey.

"Your mom's out front in a patrol car. We're going to put you and her up in a hotel here in town for the night. Are you ready to go?"

"Is my mom okay?" Corey voiced the question that, from his expression, Steve hadn't quite dared to put into words.

"She's fine. Nobody hurt her. She was real worried about you, though. I think once she sees that you're okay she'll be as good as new."

"I'll walk you out," Steve said to Corey, putting his arm around his daughter's shoulders. He glanced at Summer, "Be back in a minute," he mouthed. The three of them, Steve, Corey, and Les Carter, headed outside.

"Oh, I almost forgot." Corey pulled away from Steve and ran back to Summer, Muffy cuddled against her chest. "I guess I better give you your dog back."

Summer looked into Corey's face. If she tried, she could see traces of Steve's features, softened and feminized in Corey. "Would you like to keep her for the night? She's my mother's really, not mine, and she'd probably be just as happy with you as with me."

"Oh, could I?" Corey smiled dazzlingly. "I'll take good care of her. Thanks, Summer."

And she ran back to join her father and Les Carter.

Steve sent Summer a look over Corey's head. Summer grinned at him. At least his ex-wife was a woman. Muffy wouldn't relieve herself on her foot.

"I've got to go see what I can do about locating that van. Are you sure you and Calhoun left it here?" Kendrick asked Summer.

"One hundred percent positive."

Shaking his head thoughtfully, Kendrick walked away. Summer was left alone with Mitch. Steve's Mitch. Deedee's Mitch. She had heard so much about him, knew so many intimate details about his

life, that for one of the few times in her life she found herself
tongue-tied. She could not think of one single thing to say.

Mitch solved her dilemma by speaking first. "You and Steve
have had yourselves quite an adventure," he said, smiling at her.
"Suppose we all three go grab a pizza and you all tell me all about
it?"

The very thought of a pizza made Summer salivate. She was
starving—which, she thought, was getting to be quite a usual state
with her. She had just opened her mouth to thank Mitch very
much and agree when Sammy and Les Carter rejoined them.

Sammy looked at Summer. "I had to twist their arms, but I
finally got Carter here and Kendrick to agree to let you eat and get
a good night's sleep before they start in on you."

"We've got you and Calhoun hotel rooms for the night." Les
Carter sounded less jovial than Sammy. "In the morning, we'll
want to get your statements."

"What about supper?" Summer said plaintively, as Mitch, with
a nod at the other two men, seemed to melt away. There went her
pizza, she thought, gazing after him.

"We'll provide that, too." Les Carter relaxed enough to smile at
her. "Miss McAfee, are you *sure* that this is the place where you all
left that van?"

"Yes," Summer said, growing tired of the whole topic. The
location of the van did not interest her very much at the moment.
Supper and a bed did.

"I told you, you're going to have to wait and badger her in the
morning," Sammy said firmly. "Come on, Summer, I'll treat you
and Calhoun to supper and drop you off at the hotel. We've got all
of y'all separate rooms."

Sammy's slight emphasis on *separate* was not lost on Summer,
but she hoped it went over Les Carter's head.

They met Steve coming back in on their way out, and the three
of them went out to dinner, just making it past the TV crew that
had pulled up with a screech of brakes. A young black woman
jumped out of the WTES van, and Steve dodged behind Sammy.

As Sammy said, tomorrow would be soon enough to give a
statement to the press.

At nine-thirty at night, in the small town of Cedar Lake, there wasn't a huge choice of restaurants. It was just getting full dark, and Summer was glad. She looked a mess, she knew, and Steve was positively disreputable. But she was so hungry, she didn't much care how she looked, and she had a hunch Steve felt the same way.

Steve was strangely preoccupied all through supper. They ate at Sally's Diner, which was, from the looks of it, a chain restaurant such as a Frisch's or a Jerry's that had fallen on hard times and been purchased by a local entrepreneur. At any rate, except for a pizza carry-out it was the only restaurant open in town. Seated on a carved wooden bench in front of a large plate-glass window, Summer tucked into an inch-thick charcoal-grilled sirloin steak, baked potato bursting with butter and sour cream, and salad loaded with croutons and Italian dressing, and tried not to mind that Steve spent most of the meal staring abstractedly out into the firefly-lit night beyond the window. She gave Sammy a heavily censored account of what had befallen her and Steve, leaving out pertinent details such as Steve's state of undress when they met and exactly how close they had subsequently grown. Sammy listened, puffing on his cigar and shooting occasional shrewd glances at her from under bushy white brows. She had a feeling that there was little he didn't know.

"It's a ring of rogue cops," Sammy said to Steve as the three sipped coffee after the meal. "We've identified about a dozen—six of them my boys. There are more, but we're not sure how many, or who they are. We're working on that. It's a drug network, and it's not just in this state, by the way. It stretches all across the South through Georgia and the Carolinas and Florida, and it involves politicians and businessmen as well as cops. We'll find out who they are, too. It's just a matter of doing some grunt work now. From what we've been able to piece together, a drug cartel out of Colombia provides the drugs—cocaine, mostly—and it gets to this country any which way it can: private planes, couriers bringing it through customs, illegal runs across the Mexican border, you name it. Haiti's a big jumping-off point right now. That's where the bodies in that lost van of yours were headed, by the way: Haiti.

Apparently the ring had a deal with Harmon Brothers to store drugs in their vaults and to provide them with bodies when needed. From what I've been told, it's easy to get drugs into this country. It's hard to get cash out. So, when necessary, bodies and coffins were provided by Harmon Brothers, stuffed with cash and sent home to their 'grieving relatives' in other countries. Customs never looks too hard at corpses, apparently."

"So Harmon Brothers knew what was going on." Summer cast a sideways look at Steve, who was frowning down at his coffee. She had never, in the admittedly brief but intense time she had known him, seen him so morose.

"They knew. At least, some of the higher-ups in the company knew. Exactly who was involved and how deeply, I couldn't tell you at this point. It's getting kind of murky the deeper we get into it, but we'll get it sorted out."

"I suppose you know that there are DEA and CIA fingerprints all over this thing." Steve looked up at last. "I caught on to that when I was investigating three years ago. I just never got the chance to pinpoint the details."

"Had a little interruption in your career, didn't you?" Sammy gave a sympathetic chuckle. "So what exactly did you find out?"

"Nothing too specific, at least nothing that I could take to a prosecutor and they could prove in court. But apparently the CIA made a deal with the DEA to let drug deals go down in return for intelligence information on the countries where the deals were spawned. Latin American countries, mostly."

"You mean the government is using drug dealers for spies?" Summer gasped.

Steve gave her a crooked smile. "Something like that. I don't think we'll ever get completely to the bottom of it. What we've uncovered here is just the tip of the iceberg. Some of these dudes —they call 'em 'assets' but what they are is a bunch of drug smugglers and mercenaries—are actually paid by the CIA to infiltrate these drug rings. In return for information, they're allowed to pretty much do their own thing without interference."

"There's big money in drugs," Sammy observed, with a glinting, under-the-brow glance at Steve. Then the waitress brought their check, and the talk turned to more general topics.

An hour later, Summer stepped into a tub of the hottest water she'd been able to coax from the ancient faucets of her hotel bathroom. She was ensconced for the night at the Dew Drop Inn, a fifties-era motel that offered necessities rather than luxuries. The room was small, and the bathroom was smaller, but it sported a standard double bed that was going to feel like nirvana compared to the surfaces she'd slept on lately, as well as a toilet and a bathtub with a shower. It even had mini bottles of shampoo and moisturizer and mouthwash on the chipped Formica vanity. Summer, having already washed her hair and wrapped it in a towel, felt positively blissful as she sank chin-deep into the water that was hot enough to turn her skin instantly pink.

The only fly in her ointment was that she missed Steve. But Sammy had very firmly escorted her to her own room, while Steve had been left to find his way alone to his. Watching him go, Summer had been amused to note that Steve's room was at the far end of the long, rambling, single-story motel where the accommodations had more the flavor of connecting cabins than hotel rooms.

Sammy was very protective of her, just as he had always been. She hadn't had the heart to remind him that she was thirty-six years old, no longer married to his son, and perfectly capable of deciding whether or not she wanted to sleep alone. Instead, she had regretfully watched Steve vanish into his room and kissed Sammy's cheek by way of good night.

"See you in the morning," he said gruffly as he turned away from her door. The first thing she had done was run herself a steaming-hot bath.

Then she had called her mother.

Soaping her legs, sparing a fleeting regret for the absence of a razor, Summer thought back on that conversation with her parent. It had been all she could do to dissuade her mother—and her sisters—from rushing from their hotel instantly to her side.

"I'm fine, Muffy's fine, we'll both see you tomorrow," she had concluded firmly. "And I'll tell you everything then."

She might tell them a little more than she had told Sammy, Summer decided, leaning forward to rub suds into her toes, but she wasn't going to tell them *everything*.

Some things they didn't need to know. Though, being women and her relatives, they would probably guess.

A drop of cold water splashed onto her spine.

Startled, Summer's head spun around so fast that she nearly gave herself whiplash.

CHAPTER FORTY-ONE

"Hi." Steve, still clad in the orange Nike shirt and cutoffs, was leaning against the bathroom door grinning at her. She was sitting with her back to him and her knees bent because of the small size of the tub, so not an awful lot of her person was on view, but his eyes gleamed appreciatively over as much of her as he could see.

"How did you get in here?" Summer gasped, instinctively clapping the washcloth she'd been using over her bosom. The washcloth was small, and thin, and didn't cover much, but that didn't matter. It was the thought that counted.

"Cheap lock. I used the laminated list of motel rules that I found on my bedside table to jimmy it. Next time, put the chain on." Steve straightened away from the doorjamb, and held up a brown paper bag. "I brought you a present. Toothpaste, toothbrush, a comb and a lipstick. Courtesy of the last of Renfro's money and what passes for the hotel gift shop."

"A toothbrush?" Summer reached eagerly for the bag. He grinned and drew it back out of her reach.

"Come and get it."

"Steve Calhoun, a toothbrush and toothpaste are too important to kid around about! Put that bag down on the counter and get out of this bathroom! I'll be finished in a minute."

"Okay," Steve said obligingly. Setting the bag on the counter, he withdrew, pulling the door shut behind him. Summer was too eager to get hold of the toothbrush and paste to question his apparent willingness to oblige. Giving in without an argument wasn't like Steve—but she didn't think of that.

Stark naked except for the towel wrapped around her head, and dripping wet, Summer stood in front of the sink watching herself in the mirror as she scrubbed her teeth when Steve opened the door and walked back in.

He was naked, too. Her glance absorbed the details: He was broad-shouldered, heavily muscled, liberally gifted with luxuriant black body hair in all the right places—and extremely well endowed.

"Get out of here!" Summer ordered around a mouthful of toothpaste, scandalized on principle alone. Despite the fact that he was her lover and her love, she felt suddenly, ridiculously shy. New settings came complete with new rules: she'd never been alone with him in a motel room before.

"You're not turning modest on me all of a sudden, are you?" he asked with a lopsided grin that nevertheless missed nothing of her body. "With an ass and tits like yours, you don't have any reason in the world to be shy."

"You sweet-talker, you," Summer said with bite as soon as she had rinsed out her mouth.

"It's a compliment. I swear." His eyes twinkled at her, and he awarded the ass in question an approving swat.

Then, without another word, he stepped into her tub.

"*I'm* taking a bath," Summer protested as soon as she had recovered from the smack. Was she really going to be able to make a life with a man who smacked her bottom? "What do you think *you're* doing?"

"Joining you." He was leaning back in the tub, rubbing the soap in lazy circles over his shoulders and chest and arms. The contrast between bronzed skin and white tile and suds and soap was striking. His legs were bent sharply at the knees, his wide shoulders cleared the water by a good six inches, and his head rested against the chipped tile wall rather than the rolled rim of the tub. But he looked supremely content. And very cute. Summer decided to forgive him that chauvinistic swat. Once he was hers, he could always be retrained. . . .

"Joining me?" Her voice was indignant. "I'm not in there."

"Get in." The invitation was accompanied by a seductive grin. It was amazing, Summer thought, just how sexy a man could look with two black eyes, a scabbed-over cut on one cheek, and enough assorted bruises to keep a doctor happy for days.

"There's not room."

"We'll make room." He reached out, grabbed her hand—and before Summer knew it she was being partly dragged, partly coaxed into the tub. She collapsed chest-down in a heap on his stomach, her legs caught between his and bent at the knee so that her calves climbed the tile wall.

"You're right," Steve said as if making a great discovery. "There's not room."

Sliding her to one side, he stood up with a great squelching sound. Summer had just an instant to admire his body—she really did admire his body—before he bent, stuck his shoulder in her stomach, and stood up with her.

Summer shrieked, and immediately clapped a hand over her mouth. She didn't know for sure, but she suspected the walls were thin.

Hanging over his shoulder in a fireman's carry, the towel around her head falling loose to be left behind on the floor, Summer gritted her teeth to keep from yelling and pounded his back with her fists. He paid not a bit of attention as he stepped from the tub with her and carried her into the bedroom.

"Put me down, you . . ." she growled threateningly, giving him a particularly solid whack between the shoulder blades.

"Yes, ma'am." The teasing note in his voice should have warned her.

But still she wasn't prepared as he collapsed on the bed with her. She shrieked again as she landed on her back, bouncing on the soft mattress.

This time he clapped a hand over her mouth. "Shhh! Somebody might call the police."

Oh, ha-ha. Very funny. But before she could tell him what she thought of his jokes Summer thought of something. "Steve, no! We'll get the bed soaked!"

"Do you care?"

If Summer had had a chance to think about it, the answer to that would have been no, she did not care. But she didn't have a chance to think about it, because he was sliding up her body and she was scowling at him and he was kissing her and loving her and she couldn't think about anything at all but him.

Much, much later, they headed for Steve's room to spend what was left of the night because Summer's bed had, indeed, gotten very wet. Snickering behind their hands like schoolchildren, they crept along the yellow-lighted sidewalk in front of the rooms. It must have been about midnight, but except for the moths fluttering around the small sconces outside each door not a creature stirred.

As they reached the door to his room Steve swung her around into his arms and kissed her.

"Hey," she protested playfully when she could talk again. "Haven't you had enough of that yet?"

"Nope." He kissed her again, lingeringly, smiling as he lifted his head. "I don't think I'll ever get enough of *that* as long as I live. It's one of those forever kind of things."

"Is it?" She leaned against his chest, hands curled around the straps of his muscle shirt as her lips formed a secret little smile.

"Isn't it?"

He felt very big and solid against her, and his eyes as they met her gaze were no longer dead and hopeless-looking as they had once been, but warm and bright and almost carefree. Summer looked up into that unhandsome but powerfully magnetic face and had her answer.

"Yes," she said clearly. "It is."

He grinned, kissed her, and let her go, patting the pockets of his cutoffs.

"Here it is." He fished the key out of a pocket and inserted it into the lock.

"Why not just break in?" Summer asked sardonically as he stood back to let her precede him into the room.

"And waste a perfectly good key?" He shook his head at her as he followed her inside. Summer was already groping for the light switch as he closed the door.

She caught just a glimpse, the merest hint, of a man in the shadows leaping forward before Steve was felled with a mighty blow to the back of the neck.

He collapsed without making a sound.

Summer was too shocked even to scream.

CHAPTER FORTY-TWO

It was a beautiful night. A warm breeze caressed Summer's face, swirling tendrils of hair across her cheeks. Thousands of stars twinkled down from a midnight blue velvet sky. The moon was a mere sliver, a silvery crescent that would have been right at home in a nursery rhyme. Frogs croaked in the nearby lake. The cicadas were once again in full chorus.

Summer lay on her side in the dirt, gagged and trussed like a Thanksgiving turkey, watching as Mitch dug a shallow hole to bury her and Steve in.

Steve, still out cold, lay nearby. Like her, he was bound and gagged. Though that precaution seemed almost wasteful, as it appeared likely that he would die without ever regaining consciousness.

Lying there on the cool ground, listening to the hypnotic rhythm of the shovel digging into the earth, Summer thought that Steve had the better of it. She wished she were unconscious, so that she would not have to experience this.

Not far away, the headlights of a car cut through the darkness. She lay in the construction site she had noticed each time she had passed through Cedar Lake, and the road was tantalizingly near. If only the big earth-moving machines weren't in the way. . . .

Then Summer realized something: Even if the Caterpillars weren't there, no one could see this far into the field. It was so dark that she, only a dozen feet away, could see Mitch only in silhouette. Aside from the sounds that reached her ears, she had only known he was digging when an errant moonbeam struck silver on the shovel blade.

Steve was stirring. Like her, he was bound hand and foot, and wrapped like a mummy in nylon rope for insurance. His feet moved, and his shoulders moved. Summer thought his eyes opened, because she saw a faint gleam through the darkness. But she couldn't be sure. With all her heart she longed to go to him— she tried rolling on her back. Steve was only a foot or so away.

Suddenly Mitch was there. Instinctively Summer lay very still, like a rodent in the flight path of a hawk. But it was to Steve's side Mitch went.

"You're awake." Mitch's voice was a soft murmur as he dropped down on one knee beside Steve. "Damn it, Steve, why didn't you stay away?"

Steve made a sound that was rendered unintelligible by the duct tape that bound his mouth.

"You think I want to do this? Hell, I'd rather cut off my right arm. But you've left me no choice."

Steve made another sound.

"All right, buddy, I'm gonna take the gag off for a minute. You ask me what you want to know, and I'll tell you. You deserve to know why this is happening to you. But if you yell, or even talk above a whisper, I'm going to have to kill you with this." Mitch touched the shovel that lay beside him. He bent over Steve, and removed the duct tape gag. Summer knew that was what he must have done, because she heard a low ripping sound, followed by Steve's voice, hoarse and low but unmistakably Steve's:

"When I started sleeping with Deedee, you were already having an affair with Elaine."

Mitch was silent for an instant. Then he said, "Elaine told you, didn't she? I was afraid she would, sooner or later."

"She told me tonight, I think because I was temporarily in her good graces because both she and Corey survived the day." Steve paused, then added with harsh accusation, "Is that why you killed Deedee? To get free so you could have Elaine?"

Mitch sounded surprised: "Hell, no, I wouldn't kill Deedee for Elaine. I killed her for . . . *Shit.* How'd you know?"

"Elaine told me that you used to come to the house a lot while I was at work. She told me that you came on to her a good eight months before Deedee died, and she was bored and unhappy and she did it. She told me that you asked her for the key to my office, not just on the night Deedee died but other times, too, so you could keep tabs on what I was doing. She suspected you were dirty. But she didn't care. Not until Deedee died. When Deedee turned up dead in my office, she guessed you were involved. But after that she was too scared of you to talk. What just happened with Corey made her realize that the only way she and Corey would ever be safe again was if you, and your buddies, were behind bars.

"I've been dirty for years, Steve." His tone was confessional.

"Hell, do you think I don't know that? I finally figured it out. I would have caught on sooner, except I hated to face the truth when it stared me in the face. But why, Mitch? Just tell me why."

"It was so much money," Mitch said. "They offered me so much damn money. Not to do anything, just to look the other way while they ran drugs through here. It was the easiest money I've ever made in my life. Thousands and thousands of dollars at a time, just to look the other way."

"You took the van, didn't you?"

There was a moment's silence. Then Mitch gave a little bark of laughter. "You always were a good detective. How did you figure that out?"

"Who else would have checked in the boat warehouse but you? On the phone today, just in case I didn't make it alive out of my encounter with your friends, I told Larry Kendrick that the van was in the warehouse. He got there as fast as he could. The van was already gone. Somebody—somebody who knew what was in it —had to have found it between the time I left it Sunday morning and this afternoon. Who could that have been but you? Only you and I knew about the damned boat warehouse. Where's the van, Mitch?"

"In a place where it will never be found." Mitch's voice hardened suddenly. "Just like you and your girlfriend there will never be found. They're going to pave this field tomorrow. It's going to be a parking lot for a new marina they're building down at the lake, and you're going to be buried under it."

"Why do you have to kill us? We're helpless—and you have the money. Why not just take it and run?"

"Do you think I wouldn't if I could?" Mitch asked fiercely. "But if I do that, they'll be after me. Not just the police, or even the FBI or the DEA, but the cartel. They'd find me, sooner or later. They'd hunt me to the ends of the earth. I'd never know a second's peace."

"How is killing us going to keep the cartel from coming after you?"

Mitch chuckled. "They're going to blame it on you, buddy. They're going to think you and your little girlfriend stole their fifteen million dollars and took off into the night. See, you're going to vanish without a trace. Nobody's even going to know you're dead."

Summer felt a shiver run down her spine. To be murdered was a hideous fate to contemplate, but to be murdered and have no one know it—her mother and sisters would search the world for her for the rest of their lives.

"Steve, old buddy, old pal, if there was any way I could not do this I would. But don't worry. I'm going to knock you over the head before I do it, so you won't feel a thing. It's not going to hurt." Mitch reached for the shovel.

Summer's heart leaped.

"Wait!" There was an edge of desperation to Steve's voice. "You still haven't told me why you killed Deedee."

Mitch paused and turned back to Steve. "Remember how you were investigating us, Steve? Les Carter lent you to Rosencrans and you were investigating dirty cops right and left. And you were getting mighty close, too. We were starting to feel you breathing down our necks. The cartel was getting worried. They told me to stop the investigation. To stop you. They gave me two choices: I could buy you or kill you. Hell, you were always such a damned Boy Scout, I knew you couldn't be bought. And I couldn't bring myself to kill you. We were tight, buddy, remember? With Elaine's help, I was able to keep tabs on what you were up to. I had time to come up with a solution. And then you started that thing with Deedee. It was perfect. I knew if you got caught having an affair with her in a way that made a public scandal, you'd be fired. Bye-bye investigation. So I set it up. Don't you see, man? I killed Deedee to save *you*." Mitch's voice broke. "You dumb fuck."

He bent over Steve. Summer watched, dumbfounded, as Mitch kissed Steve with unmistakable passion full on the mouth.

"I always loved you, you stupid damn Boy Scout, and you never even had a fucking clue. But now it's down to you or me. Winner take all, babe."

With that Mitch leaped to his feet and picked up the shovel, all in a single swift movement. Steve was just starting to say something, or perhaps make some sort of outcry, when the blow fell.

Summer heard that *thunk* like it was her own death sentence. As Mitch turned to her she saw the moonlight glitter on the tears that were running down his cheeks.

FORTY-THREE

"He that falls into sin is a man;
that grieves at it is a saint; that
boasteth of it, is a devil."

—Thomas Fuller

Deedee was having trouble with her atoms
again. She seemed to be growing weaker. She'd been following
Steve about like a kite on a string, but he hadn't seen her for a
while. Which was just as well. She didn't want to cause trouble for
him with his new girl.

She couldn't materialize, but she could see, and she could hear.
She heard what Mitch said to Steve, there in the dark in that
muddy field, she saw what he did and was intending to do, and
suddenly everything was crystal clear: the past and the future, too.

On the night she died, Mitch had confronted her with the evidence of her and Steve's affair, reducing her to whimpering, sobbing guilt because, after all, Mitch was the one she loved. Then he
told her he'd forgive her only *if* she'd help him teach Steve a
lesson he'd never forget.

She'd thought Mitch was jealous. The notion thrilled her. Sleeping with Steve had finally turned the tables. Now Mitch knew what
it felt like. Throughout their years together, *he* had been the ever-

elusive object of desire, not she. Now, finally, thanks to her affair with Steve, it was her turn. Mitch was obsessing over her. She should have known better. But then, the reality was almost unbelievable. How could she have guessed Mitch was obsessed, not with her, but with *Steve?* Had she been blind, not to have suspected what Mitch was? Not to have seen?

But, like Steve, she hadn't had a clue. She had been so crazy in love with Mitch that she would have agreed to anything he asked of her, and she did. First Mitch had gotten her to read a joke "suicide" statement into a video camera. Then he'd taken her to Steve's new office, rigged a nylon rope from a *plant hook,* of all the stupid things, dragged Steve's desk beneath it, and told her to get up there and put the noose around her neck so that it would look as though she was about to hang herself.

Steve was on the way up, he'd said, and they were going to give his old buddy the fright of his life.

Steve would never lay a hand on *his* wife again, Mitch told her with a glint in his eyes that made her heart beat faster. In all their years together, she'd never seen him so worked up. All because he was jealous of her and Steve. She'd been excited, unsuspecting, *stupid.* She'd kicked off her shoes, climbed up on that desk, and put the noose around her neck, just like Mitch told her. And tried not to grin at the thought of what Steve was going to say.

Then Mitch jerked the desk out from under her and left her there to choke and kick and die.

The son of a bitch. He'd murdered her in cold blood, and now he was going to kill Steve and his new girlfriend as well and it couldn't be allowed.

It wasn't going to be allowed.

This was her mission, Deedee realized: to keep Mitch from killing again.

But how?

She watched as Mitch dragged Steve's bound, inert body over to the shallow pit he had dug and rolled him inside, then carried the woman over and dumped her in after Steve. She saw Mitch cover them in a thin layer of dirt, then climb aboard a big yellow steamroller, produce a key from his pocket and start the engine.

The steamroller started to move. With a rumbling growl it headed straight down the field toward the soon-to-be grave.

What could she do?

Deedee tried, with all her might. She willed herself into the cabin of that steamroller, willed herself into the seat beside Mitch, willed herself to materialize.

The steamroller moved inexorably toward the grave, leaving a road's width of flat, hard-packed earth in its wake. It was drawing closer to its target with every passing second. Deedee thought she could detect the darker shadows of bodies lying in the shallow depression Mitch had made.

She felt the tingling. Suddenly she was *there,* sitting beside him. As if he sensed that he was no longer alone, Mitch glanced her way.

And saw her. He turned white as milk, staring. Deedee waggled her fingers at him. He screamed—and leaped from the cab of the steamroller.

He landed on his hands and knees in the soft earth. The steamroller kept moving. Deedee tried, but she couldn't turn off the key. Her fingers were as ephemeral as mist—she couldn't grip a thing.

She flew out of the cab after Mitch. *He* would have to do it. He was on his feet, looking shaken but okay. Okay, that is, until he saw her.

Mitch took one look, screamed, and ran as if she were the devil himself. Deedee flew after him, skimming the earth, fingers outstretched as she tried to grab his shirt.

He had to get back into that cab and turn off the key.

Mitch fled across the field, blubbering with terror as he scrambled up the slope toward the road with her plucking at his shoulder.

Deedee saw what was going to happen seconds before it did, but she was powerless to change a thing. Mitch darted out onto the road right into the path of an oncoming truck.

The force of the collision was unbelievable. Blue arterial blood was already trickling out of Mitch's nose and mouth before he ever hit the pavement forty feet down the road.

CHAPTER FORTY-FOUR

Summer saw Mitch jump from the cab and run, screaming, away. But she didn't have time to think about it, to ponder the whys and wherefores. Her attention was riveted on the giant gray wheel of the steamroller as it drew nearer and nearer to the depression where she and Steve lay. Fortunately, moving her head had kept it free of dirt. Mitch, anxious to be done with his task, had not buried them very efficiently. And she had brushed the dirt away from Steve's face with frantic movements of her head.

Steve was still unconscious. She kicked him, desperately, fiercely. With Mitch gone from the cab, they had a chance—but he had to wake up.

With her mouth taped, she couldn't say a word. Screams emerged from her throat only to be muffled by the suffocating gag. They were barely audible to her own ears.

The steamroller was perhaps twenty feet away.

Steve's eyes blinked open. Summer could see them gleaming at her through the darkness. She kicked him, hard, convulsing her body so that her feet came in jarring contact with his knee.

"Ow!" he said, looking at her. Summer, beckoning frantically with her head, rolled away.

Whether he realized how close they were to death she didn't know. But he followed her, both of them tumbling like rolling pins over the soft, cool earth.

The steamroller went by with scant feet to spare, and kept going until it plunged into the lake.

CHAPTER FORTY-FIVE

It was Saturday. Mitch's funeral had been held in Nashville the previous day. Steve had attended, and Summer had gone with him, holding his hand tightly throughout the service. Steve had been stoic, his face grim, his eyes shadowed. No matter what Mitch had done, or why he had done it, there were still lifelong bonds of friendship between them that neither logic nor death had entirely managed to break.

Steve, simply, was not ready to talk about Mitch, and Summer was wise enough to let it alone.

At the funeral, she had met Elaine.

Steve's ex-wife was a petite, attractive blonde, and Summer's first thought on meeting her was to wonder if Steve had married her because she reminded him of Deedee.

But that was all water over the dam, Summer told herself. Elaine didn't have Steve. Deedee didn't have Steve. *She* had Steve.

And Steve was hers. She knew that as surely as she knew the sun would come up in the morning. Sometimes, in life, one was lucky enough to meet the person that God or fate or whatever higher power was in charge of these things had fashioned to be the *yin* to one's *yang*. That had happened for her, and for Steve.

The details—marriage, children, incorporating Corey into their lives—had still to be worked out. As yet, they had had no time.

But the certainty of forever was there, for both of them. Summer knew it every night when she slept in Steve's arms, every morning when she awoke and gazed into his eyes.

They'd been staying in the Holiday Inn in Murfreesboro. Police investigation or no police investigation, Summer had a business to run.

She had returned to her house only long enough to pack her clothes. For her, the home she had loved was ruined, indelibly stained by the murders of Linda Miller and Betty Kern.

She hadn't had time to start thinking about hunting for a house or an apartment yet, either. Monday would be soon enough for that.

At the moment, Summer was with her sisters and mother having breakfast in the coffee shop of the Murfreesboro Holiday Inn. Muffy was in her mother's room upstairs enjoying what must have been her dozenth can of Kal Kan. The other three McAfee women would be returning home the next morning, and Summer knew she would miss them. But right then, she could cheerfully have done without their presence.

Their topic of conversation was Steve.

"He seems very nice, I must admit. But, Summer, as far as I can ascertain he doesn't have a job." This was her mother.

"You've only known him for a week." This was Sandra. "Don't you think you need a little longer to make up your mind?"

"If you're in love that quick, he must be awfully good in bed. Or wherever." This was Shelly, with a giggle.

"Shelly!" Both Margaret McAfee and Sandra rounded on Shelly with shocked faces. Shelly shrugged. Summer's face burned. She hadn't told them anything intimate that had passed between her and Steve—but then she hadn't needed to. They had known everything, all three of them, just by looking at her.

Families!

"We're all adult women here. And you have to admit, he is kind of sexy-looking. Of course, he's not nearly as handsome as Lem," Shelly persisted.

"Lem was a total prick," Sandra said with precision. Her mother and sisters looked at the pretty forty-year-old with surprise.

"Well, he was," Sandra defended herself. "We could all see what he was doing to Summer: He was turning her into a regular little Stepford wife."

Summer hadn't realized that her family had known. She gave Sandra a grateful smile.

"That's true," Margaret McAfee nodded. "I don't think any of us have any real objection to your young man, Summer. Although he needs a job. How is he going to support . . . ?"

"I can support myself, Mother," Summer said. "I have a business, remember?"

"But . . ."

"Good morning, ladies. Are you ready, Summer?" Steve appeared beside the table, and Summer's cheeks pinkened as she wondered just how much, if anything, he'd overheard. Oh, well, he'd have to get used to her family, just as she'd have to get used to his.

There would be plenty of time for that. They had all the time in the world.

She smiled up at him. Clad in well-pressed khakis with a brown leather belt and a tucked-in navy blue polo shirt, with tan boat shoes on his feet and a watch on his wrist, he looked like a different man from the grubby bum with whom she had shared four days on the run. He was clean-shaven, his black hair brushed back from his forehead. With his strong football player's body and his aggressively masculine face, he was a very striking-looking man. A man she could be proud of. Despite the fading twin shiners and the yellowish bruises along his jaw.

"Won't you join us for coffee, Steve?" Margaret McAfee smiled up at him. Like her daughters, she was an attractive brunette. The only difference was the passage of an additional twenty-five or so years—and the careful weekly application of a bottle of Loving Care in dark auburn to her head.

Steve shook his head. "Thanks, but I promised Corey we'd take her to pick out the puppy before lunch and she thinks before lunch is around nine a.m. She's already called me twice, to find out what's taking me so long. I appreciate your giving me the name of the kennel where you got Muffy, by the way."

"I'm just glad they were still in business and that they had puppies available," Margaret said.

"Don't think you're doing your daughter any favor by buying her a Muffy clone," Sandra warned him. "She is not my idea of a house pet."

"Muffy is a champion," Margaret, accustomed to being teased about her beloved dog by her daughters, said with dignity. "And, like all true champions, she has her idiosyncrasies. I admit that. But never think for a minute that she is not an extremely intelligent animal. Why, she even saved Summer's and Steve's lives."

Margaret's favorite part of Summer and Steve's adventure was the part where Muffy peed on the bad guy's foot.

"Yeah, and how!" Sandra and Shelly dissolved into giggles. Summer took that as her cue to rise.

"We'll see you later." She waved good-bye to her mother and sisters and walked out of the restaurant with Steve trailing behind.

Outside, in the parking lot, he caught up with her.

"I do have a job, you know," he said, entwining his fingers with hers and casting her a sideways glance.

So he *had* heard. "I don't care whether you do or not," she said with perfect truth, smiling at him.

"Actually, I have my choice of several. Chief Rosencrans says he needs a chief of detectives. Les Carter offered me my old job back. And Larry Kendrick wants me to come on board at the DEA. Actually, I think he wants to keep an eye on me in case I suddenly start flashing wads of cash." He grinned. The van had been found, submerged just beyond the ramp leading from the boat warehouse into Cedar Lake, and the bodies had been in it. But the money Mitch had stolen was still missing. A search was under way. And not just by the police, either. Word had leaked out, as word always did, that fifteen million dollars in unmarked bills was hidden somewhere in the vicinity of Cedar Lake. People were coming out of the woodwork to hunt for it. As Sammy had said, if that money was not found soon, Cedar Lake was liable to become another Sierra Madre. Treasure hunters would be pouring into the area for the next century, looking for the lost millions in cash.

"Take whichever one you like," Summer said as they reached Steve's car. It was a red Mazda 626 parked in the middle of a sea of other cars, and he had to maneuver past a badly parked green '88 Olds to open the passenger-side door for her.

"I thought I'd stay here in Murfreesboro," he said.

"Oh?" Instead of getting into the car, Summer turned to face him. Her hair was washed and blown dry to curl softly around her face, she wore just the right amount of cosmetics for a hot summer's day, and she was dressed in an airy yellow sundress and leather sandals. She was looking good and she knew it, and she basked under the appreciative glint in his eyes as they moved over her.

"Yeah. Since you have a house and a business here and all." His eyes were black and inscrutable as they focused once again on her face.

"I don't have a house here anymore. I refuse to live in that one. Come Monday, I'm going to put it on the market and start looking for another place to live. Although my mother wants me to come to Santee to live with her, and Sandra says I should move out to California, and Shelly—"

"Wants you to come to Knoxville," Steve finished for her dryly. "I'm going to be house-hunting myself come Monday. Maybe we could join forces. Two people, searching for one house."

Summer stared up at him. He was very close, with one arm draped over the top of the open car door and the other hand absentmindedly playing with her fingers.

"Are you by any chance asking me to live with you?" she asked, striving for a light tone.

He shook his head. "Nope."

"No?"

"I thought we agreed that this is a forever kind of thing."

"Yes, we did."

"Well then—I'm asking you to marry me."

Summer was dumbstruck. She hadn't expected that. "But—but," she sputtered. "We've only known each other a week."

"Sometimes that's all it takes."

Summer looked up at him, up at the lantern jaw and hard, thin lips and blade of a nose, up into dark eyes that she had once considered soulless. Now she knew better.

And she knew something else too: Steve was right.

Sometimes a week is all it takes.

"Yes," she said, and went up on her toes to lock her arms around his neck and her lips to his.

He kissed her breathless, right there in the full glare of the summer sunlight in the busy parking lot of the Murfreesboro Holiday Inn.

CHAPTER FORTY-SIX

"God gives quietness at last."

—John Greenleaf Whittier

Deedee was very weak. At any time now the summons would come, she knew—but the summons to where? To Heaven—or back to that netherworld where she had existed before?

She had completed the mission that had kept her Earthbound: She had made things right for Steve.

Soon it would be time to go. To join Mitch? If she had gleaned any inkling into the way the universe worked, he was locked in a netherworld of his own.

There were some things she needed to do before the summons came. But it was hard to make her atoms behave. Forget materializing—she didn't have the strength for that. She just wanted to get where she needed to go.

With a tremendous effort of will she concentrated on her mother's house. It took a while—the maelstrom was weak, too—but eventually she arrived.

Her mother was in the kitchen fixing a meal. Supper, she supposed, because it was growing dark outside. For a moment Deedee lovingly watched her as she cut up a chicken for frying.

Her mother's hair was iron-gray now. Her face was wrinkled. She was getting old.

Aunt Dot was in the living room, watching the news. The Ouija board was on the coffee table, temporarily forgotten.

Deedee concentrated hard. Slowly the pointer began to move, tracing aimless circles on the slick cardboard.

It took a few minutes to get Aunt Dot's attention, but once she had it it was absolute.

"Sue!" Aunt Dot's screech as she jumped to her feet would have awakened a log.

"Goodness, Dot, what is it?" Her mother came rushing in, wiping her hands on a frayed kitchen towel.

Wordlessly Aunt Dot pointed to the Ouija board. Just for good measure, Deedee induced the pointer to perform an extra-fancy swirl.

"Oh my God, it's Deedee again! Dot, sit down here! Deedee, baby, talk to me!"

She hastily pulled up a stool, Aunt Dot collapsed back on the couch, and both of them dove for the quivering pointer. Her mother's thick, chapped fingers were shaking.

"H-I-M-O-M," she began.

"Oh, God, it is Deedee," her mother moaned.

"Hush, Sue, what's she trying to say?"

"T-O-N-I-G-H-T-G-O-D-I-G-U-P-M-Y-G-R-A-V-E—"

"Go dig up her grave!" Aunt Dot shrieked.

"Hush, Dot, hush! Deedee, baby, I love you! Go on!"

"T-H-E-R-E-S-M-O-N-E-Y-T-H-E-R-E-L-O-T-S-O-F-M-O-N-E-Y—"

"Money? In your grave?" her mother whispered.

"D-O-N-T-T-E-L-L-A-N-Y-B-O-D-Y-I-T-S-F-O-R-Y-O-U-"

"What's she saying?"

"She said don't tell! Now hush!"

"M-I-T-C-H-H-I-D-I-T-T-H-E-R-E-I-T-S-F-O-R-Y-O-U-"

"Mitch hid it?"

"Hush, Dot! Deedee, you didn't kill yourself, did you? Baby, I know better. I always knew better!"

"M-I-T-C-H-K-I-L-L-E-D-M-E-"

"I knew it! I knew it!" her mother screamed. "Didn't I always tell you Mitch did it?"

"T-H-E-M-O-N-E-Y-B-E-L-O-N-G-S-T-O-N-O-O-N-E-T-A-K-E-I-T-"

"I don't care about the money! Deedee, I love you!"

"I-L-O-V-E-Y-O-U-T-O-O-M-O-M-T-A-K-E-T-H-E-M-O-N-E-Y-"

"Where are you? Are you in Heaven? Are you with God's angels, my baby?"

"Don't cry, Sue!"

"T-A-K-E-T-H-E-M-O-N-E-Y-A-G-I-F-T-F-R-O-M-M-E-T-O-Y-O-U-"

"Are you with the angels, Deedee?"

"Keep your fingers on the pointer, Sue!"

"I-M-O-K-A-Y-M-O-M-T-A-K-E-T-H-E-M-O-N-E-Y-I-L-O-V-E-"

"The pointer's slowing down!"

"Deedee, don't go!"

Deedee could feel herself weakening. By sheer strength of will, she finished: "Y-O-U."

And then she was sucked away into the deepening twilight.

This time she surfaced, not through any will of her own but because the maelstrom spit her out, on a glaringly bright stage. TV cameras crowded the wings and were mounted on platforms in the middle of the audience. The crowd, clapping from their plush seats, was a faceless, eager blob. A man walked out on that stage, shook hands with another who had just finished singing and playing the guitar. As the guitar player exited, Deedee recognized him: Jerry Wood, up-and-coming country star.

A sign in hot pink neon against the maroon velvet curtain at the back of the stage solved the riddle of where she was. It read: NASHVILLE LIVE.

Deedee realized she was about to witness Hallie Ketchum's live singing debut, before a national television audience yet. Immediately she took stock of her atoms. If only she could summon the strength she'd had before, she would help Hallie out.

Where was Hallie? In the wings somewhere, no doubt. Deedee searched but couldn't see her anywhere.

Maybe in a dressing room . . .

She found Hallie there, slumped over her dressing table, her face resting in a sea of cosmetics jars and brushes and cotton balls. Electric curlers were in her blond hair.

She was dead. Deedee knew, with a deep, abiding sense of certainty, that her soul had left her body just moments before.

Two lines of a white powder and a razor blade on the glass tabletop nearby told Deedee the story. Frightened by the prospect of singing before a live audience when she must have known she wasn't the stuff of which stars are made, Hallie had turned to drugs to bolster her courage.

Instead she had died.

Just then Deedee felt it—the invisible tug that was drawing her back in.

There was a knock on the door. "Three minutes, Miss Ketchum."

The tug was stronger. Deedee resisted, staring at the inert body. Was there nothing anyone could do?

Suddenly Deedee saw the light.

It was like nothing she had ever seen before, a beam of pure white light, radiating warmth, drawing her toward it. It shimmered down through the ceiling, healing, beatific, promising an eternity of joy.

The stairway to Heaven. She had made it.

Deedee glanced back at Hallie Ketchum's slumped body, and suddenly she understood that she was being offered a choice: Heaven or Nashville.

Deedee hesitated. She glanced at the light. It drew her like metal shavings to a magnet.

"One minute, Miss Ketchum."

As suddenly as that, Deedee knew she couldn't go. The only heaven she wanted was right here.

Honky-tonk heaven for a honky-tonk angel.

Deedee felt a surge of heat and had the unsettling sensation that her atoms dissolved.

Then, suddenly, she was inside Hallie Ketchum's body, trying it on for size, so to speak, lifting her head and staring with interest at an unfamiliar face that was now her own.

Not bad, she thought, and with fingers that were surprisingly steady began to pull the curlers from her hair.

CHAPTER FORTY-SEVEN

It was Saturday night. Hallie Ketchum was on-stage at *Nashville Live,* wowing the audience with her powerful rendition of her hit song "Agony."

Meanwhile, in a country cemetery not far away, two old women, one occasionally wiping tears from her eyes, knelt beside a grave. Clad in dark sweatsuits with black scarves tied around their heads, they used gardening trowels to turn back the sod and a few inches of dirt from one side of the grave.

Finally a trowel uncovered a small plastic garbage bag tightly bound with tape. The women looked at each other, and pulled it out of the earth.

One woman tore at it with shaking hands and looked inside.

"Dot, it's just like Deedee said! There's money in here!"

"Keep your voice down, Sue! And keep digging!"

An hour later, they had unearthed a small mountain of identical bags and were busily engaged in patting the sod back down over the grave.

"Dot, there must be millions here!" There was awe in the shaky voice.

"Shhh! Don't tell anybody!"

"Should we keep it?"

"Deedee said it was all right to. Deedee said it was for us. . . ."

The two women looked at each other and simultaneously nodded. Then they began the task of hauling their loot to the ancient Plymouth parked on the dark country lane not too far from the grave.

On another road in Nashville, Steve drove through the darkness toward the house he had once shared with his ex-wife. Things were looking up. Of course, there was the small matter of a threatened lawsuit from the kid whose '55 Chevy had ended up in a thousand pieces at the bottom of a smoky mountain gorge. Then there was the van driver, who'd been unconscious and bloody but not dead in the Harmon Brothers' parking lot, who woke up insisting that he was just an innocent bystander, not involved at all, and yelling about filing assault charges against the man who broke his nose. And there were a few cynical law enforcement types who were convinced that he was hiding the missing fifteen million in cash. Until the money was recovered, he expected to be kept under careful scrutiny.

But none of that was important. His daughter was sound asleep in the backseat, curled around her new Pekingese puppy, which fortunately was sleeping too. Beside him, head resting contentedly back against the seat, face turned away so that she could look out at the stars shining far above, sat the love of his life.

Summer must have felt the weight of his gaze on her, because she turned her head and smiled at him.

Steve was suddenly very conscious of being surrounded by the warm glow of happiness, so unaccustomed an emotion to him that it was as tangible as the heat of an electric blanket.

Unbidden, he thought of Mitch. Did I ever know you at all, old friend? he wondered. And wondered too why, of the three of them, childhood pals Steve and Deedee and Mitch, he was the only one who'd been granted the gift of continued life.

Then he glanced again at the two people who meant all the world to him, felt the weight of happiness in the car, and had his answer.

He could almost hear Mitch saying it: Winner take all, babe.